Heku

Book 1 of the Heku Series

T.M. Nielsen

Find us at

www.hekuseries.com

For information about special discounts for bulk orders or to schedule book signings in Northern Utah, please e-mail us at:

info@hekuseries.com

Copyright © 2010

Manufactured in the United States of America

ISBN 978-1-4537-6031-4

Table of Contents

Meeting	1
Keith	13
Ulrich	30
The House	63
Control	85
Fight	97
Island Coven	109
Choices	144
Trust	167
Beginning	194
Bonding	209
Recovery	229
Coming Out	249
Alone	263
Returning	286
Training	302
Potential	322

Meeting

"Ms. Russo?" he asked, looking down at the woman in the house. He had spoken to her by phone but hadn't met her yet.

Emily looked up, trying not to gasp as she saw that the men stood almost two feet taller than her and had broad shoulders that threatened to bulge out of the dark green western-style shirt "Jerry, was it?"

"Yes, ma'am."

"Please, call me Emily… and you're a little early, so why don't you wait in the barn, and I'll be out in a bit," she told him, and shut the door when he and his friend headed out toward the rustic barn.

Emily quickly ran a brush through her hair and pulled on her riding gloves before heading out. She glanced once around the house for Sam, the overseer, but he was still out plowing. Her attackers were all tall and muscular, and she couldn't help but wonder if these two were also going to attack her. She took a deep breath and headed out to the barn. They needed this sale if they were going to buy feed.

"Sorry about that," she said, and skirted around the two men as she went to the stalls. "Can you ride a horse?"

Both of them glanced at her nervously. Her scent blew by them with the breeze, and they fought to control their natural instincts as the mere smell made their throats burn with thirst.

"Yes, ma'am, I can," Jerry said, watching her closely. The man standing next to him was scanning the barn with an odd look on his face, and his hands slowly curled into tight fists.

"Great, then you and I will head out," Emily said, and started putting a saddle on a beautiful Arabian mare.

Jerry looked at her carefully. His keen senses focused on her while his guard studied the barn, trying to determine why the lingering scent of his own kind would be there. Her long red hair and fierce green eyes gave away her Irish heritage. She was a small woman, petite, but exquisitely beautiful. His eyes picked up the fading trace of a bruise on her cheek, something that would already be invisible to the human eye.

Emily led the horse out to him, "Will your friend be okay here in the barn for a while?"

Jerry smiled. "Yes, he'll be fine."

Emily swiftly hoisted herself, bareback, onto a painted mare. He noticed how natural and graceful she was on the horse, something that only came when you've been raised on one. He mounted the Arabian and turned the horse toward her.

"Let's go, then," Emily said, and frowned slightly at his friend who was glancing around the barn as if looking for something.

Jerry kicked his horse softly and followed Emily out of the barn toward the pasture. A Border collie and a Blue Healer fell in behind her and began to nip playfully at each other. After only a few minutes, he saw the large herd of Angus cattle they were heading toward. Emily was a few yards ahead of him, so he studied her again. In the heat, she pulled her hair back off of her neck briefly. He caught a glimpse that made him frown, and his heart pounded in his chest.

Her voice brought him out of his intense concentration. "You're not from here. I'm guessing Texas?"

Jerry nodded. "Yes, we're from Texas."

"What brings you up to Montana for cows then?"

"I come for the best," he said, and grinned when she blushed slightly. "Might I ask you a personal question?"

Emily glanced back at him as they neared the cattle. "Depends on what the question is."

"Are you a donor?" he asked, unsure if he should even ask. Her appealing scent lingered on his tongue even out where the breeze took her smell away from him. It was stronger and more desirable than anything he had caught in his thousands of years of existence.

Emily frowned slightly. "Like an organ donor?"

"Never mind," he said. Her question answered his. His body tensed as she nervously put her hand against her neck, and he noticed her breath catch. "These are exactly as specified. We'll take fifty of them."

"We can gather them. You said you only wanted one bull?" Emily asked, glancing back at him. He noticed her eyes were no longer warm and inviting but had become guarded and unsure.

"Yes. You said he has papers?"

She nodded and turned back for the barn. "Yes, we'll have them ready tomorrow if you can get them."

"Will Saturday be okay?" he asked. He needed to buy some time to address some of his concerns about this young woman.

"Saturday's fine. My husband's gone for a few days, but will be back by then."

They went the rest of the way in silence. He watched her closely as they rode back toward the ranch house. As they drew closer, Jerry saw his guard standing outside of the barn beside a smaller, Hispanic man who had an angry look on his face.

"Sam, what's wrong?" Emily asked when they approached him.

"You okay, Ms. Em?" he asked her, glaring at Jerry.

"I'm fine... Jerry is going to buy 50 head of cattle," she told him, and slid off of the mare.

Sam nodded. "I'll hep dem. You git inside outta da heat."

Emily nodded and glanced nervously at Jerry before handing the reins over to Sam. She turned and ran into the house, and he heard the door lock. Jerry got down from the horse and tied it to a post outside of the barn before turning to the older man.

"We'll be back on Saturday to get the cattle," Jerry said, eyeing Sam suspiciously. His guard stood perfectly still, giving no indication that there was a problem.

"Your kind isn't welcome here," Sam said scathingly. "You come get the cattle and then leave. Don't let me catch you back."

"My kind?" Jerry asked, and took a step toward Sam.

Sam stood his ground. "Yes, your kind. Go away, and on Saturday, deal with Keith only. Stay away from Emily."

Not sure what to make of this entire visit, Jerry nodded and climbed into the pickup's driver seat while his guard glanced again at the barn and then crawled into the passenger's seat. They were soon driving away from the small Montana ranch as Sam watched them with his arms crossed.

"I suspect we need to talk to the Council," Jerry said, pulling a cell phone from his pocket.

"We do," the guard agreed, watching the ranch disappear in the mirror.

***

Jerry and his guard were ushered into the room by an equally tall and muscular man who wore a stark white shirt, black pants, and a flowing green cape. The room was large and had dirt floors. At the far end stood a platform where thirteen others looked down at them. They walked up and bowed to the three in the center.

"What brings you to the Council?" the woman asked, pulling the hood of her green robe down away from her face.

Jerry stepped forward. "We have some concerns about a mortal woman we met yesterday, and we feel she may need your help."

"What kind of concerns would make you think that the Council needs to intervene on behalf of a mortal?"

"Our first impression is that she may be a descendant of the Winchesters."

The woman frowned. "What makes you say that?"

"Her scent, it's sweeter and more enticing than anything I've ever come across."

"Is that all?" another man asked. He was seated beside the woman and lowered his hood when he spoke.

"At first, my guard and I found the scent of many heku in her barn. She and I headed out on horseback, and I noticed scars along her neck, brutal, vicious scars, and a lot of them," Jerry said, frowning. "I asked if she was a donor, and she became guarded and her hand covered her neck. She didn't know what I meant by donor."

"As if she was attacked by a heku?" one of the men asked. He was the largest member of the Council, and he lowered his hood, revealing pitch-black hair and dark ominous eyes.

"As if attacked by many."

"Did you discover the source of the heku scent in the barn?"

The guard stepped forward. "Yes, Chief Enforcer. While they were away, I found a place in the loft that a heku has been sleeping, from the smell of it, for quite some time. I also found a coal shed full of ashes that all smell of the heku."

"Ashes?" the woman asked, shocked.

The guard nodded. "Yes, ashes."

"I don't believe this woman to be a Winchester," the largest man said. "However, if she is plagued with attacks, then I may need to get involved."

"That's all we ask, Chief Enforcer. We know the overseer of the property, Sam, is aware of the heku. He warned us that our kind was not welcome, and when we return, we are only to deal with the woman's husband," Jerry explained.

"When are you set to return?"

"This Saturday."

"Very well, I will see what I can find," he said, and leaned back in his chair.

Jerry and his guard bowed and walked out of the council chambers.

***

The Chief Enforcer arrived in the small town of Cascade, Montana late that night and quickly found the ranch outside of town. He parked on the road and ran up to the house, scanning the area for any signs of a threat. He was sure this would turn out to be nothing, but it was his job to stop his kind, the heku, from feeding on unwilling mortals.

He found the front door unlocked and stepped inside. His senses were suddenly assaulted with a scent that broke through thousands of years of carefully controlled thirst, and he crouched slightly, a hiss escaping his ancient lips. It was only seconds before he regained full control and chastised himself for the brief lack of restraint. It was his job to protect mortals from uncontrolled heku, yet he, himself, just came close to breaking the most fundamental rule of his kind, to only feed from willing donors.

He inhaled deeply, acclimating himself to the delectable scent that filled the entire house. He could smell the water and feel the mugginess and knew she was in the bath tub. Her scent would be stronger as the water heated her body, and he couldn't risk even a momentary lapse.

Again inhaling deeply, his mind swirled at the aroma, and he stood in the doorway of the bathroom. He glanced inside and saw Emily, lying in the tub, entirely engrossed in a book. She didn't see him, didn't notice the strange man standing there. He marveled at her beauty. Her long red hair was tucked into a clip on her head, and her delicate shoulders were barely visible above the bubbles from the bath. She had an extremely beautiful face, and he moved back into the room as his breath caught in his chest. He suddenly felt something he'd never felt before. He felt the need to protect her.

Scanning the bedroom, he looked at the scattered items, a laptop opened to an Internet sale of a magnificent Arabian stallion, an iPod, a book, and a small bag. He glanced through her things and noticed no ring, no jewelry, and no makeup.

He smiled broadly as he saw a 9mm tucked away in her bag. He saw no cause for alarm, no reason for the strong protective feeling to be valid. The feeling was unnatural. The heku normally felt nothing for a mortal. Mortals were nourishment, nothing more. Mortals possessed a natural aversion to them as a means of self-preservation, and their species rarely mixed. He calmed his mind and stepped back around to the door.

"Hello," he said softly.

Emily jumped at his voice, unceremoniously dropping her book into the frothy water. She grabbed a towel and scrambled to her feet, managing not to show too much skin on her way up, then looked at him, her eyes wide. Her mind was telling her to scream, but her mouth was too dry and no noise came out.

He raised an eyebrow when he sensed her fear and realized it was oddly satisfying.

"It's okay, child. I'm not here to hurt you," he said softly, and put his hands toward her, palms out.

"Get out!" she managed to whisper.

He locked her eyes with his and concentrated. It was easy for him to control mortals with a glance, something that often proved to be useful. He was shocked when her green eyes broke his gaze, and she moved into the corner of the bathroom to get farther away from him.

"Curious," he said, watching her.

"Not again, please," she begged as her hand clutched tightly to the towel.

"Again?" he asked. Frowning slightly, he turned and walked into her room.

She saw him leave and quickly slammed the door shut, locking it behind him. The simple human gesture made him smile. No lock could keep him out if he wanted to enter. Her words enraged him, and he felt his temper rising. He fought to regain control and was soon standing calmly, waiting for her.

She emerged a short time later in a long yellow bathrobe. She peered around the door first, and then walked into the empty bedroom. The room was small and decorated with ugly bold flowers in greens and grays. She checked the closet, under the bed, and under the desk, but no one was there.

Emily quickly picked up her phone and shifted nervously as she dialed and waited for an answer.

"Keith! There's one here!" she said, nervously looking around the room.

He listened to her from in the bathroom, glad that he was able to move faster than her slow mortal mind could comprehend.

"No, here in the house, just now."

She frowned. "No, not this time. I think he may be gone."

"Yes, I know." She nodded.

"Okay, I will."

"No, I'm still alone, Keith. You need to trust me. I don't..." Her eyes fell to the floor.

"Sure, okay." She hung up the phone and tears filled her eyes.

She looked again around the room and dressed quickly. He watched her change, his eyes following the length of her toned body. He grinned at her frailty, though. Heku women were strong and built more solidly than mortal women.

"I'm sorry I startled you," he said, lowering his voice, hoping to lessen the impact as he appeared by her door.

She screamed and grabbed the 9mm out of her bag, then pointed it at him with shaking hands.

He took a step toward her. "Don't be alarmed... and you can't hurt me with a gun."

Her hands shook worse as she leveled the gun at his head.

He locked her gaze again. "Emily, lower the gun."

She hesitated, her knuckles turning pink again as she released her grip ever so slightly. Her inner voice yelled at her to shoot and not to let go of the only weapon she had. She blinked suddenly, and her grip tightened again. He growled in frustration. No one had ever so easily been able to break away from his eyes.

"Emily, lower it before you get hurt," he demanded angrily, and took a step toward her.

She hesitated and then dropped her hand but kept the gun close just in case.

"There, now we can be civilized… come… sit by me," he said, and sat on the bed, patting the spot beside him.

Emily stayed where she was, frozen.

He smiled at her, careful not to show his teeth. "Okay then, I'll begin. My name is Chevalier, and of course, I already know your name."

She watched him carefully.

"You said something earlier on the phone… *'Keith, there's one here.'* Does that mean you've met my kind before?" He watched as her body tensed.

She nodded slightly.

"Does that mean you are a donor?" He saw a brief look of confusion in her eyes before she moved toward the door a step.

"Leaving?" he asked her, slightly amused.

She froze.

"I'll take that as a no on the donor, then. Perhaps you'll tell me when you've seen my kind before, that it has become somewhat commonplace."

Chevalier waited for an answer, but it didn't come.

"Emily, breathe," he reminded her.

She hadn't realized she was holding her breath until he said something.

"You aren't making it very easy to talk, please sit down." His voice was stern, and he locked her gaze again.

She felt her willpower fading as she looked into his black eyes. His face was striking, yet kind, and she wanted to trust him. She felt that she could. Her mind flashed images of others of his kind, though, and her encounters with them had all been terrifying and brutally violent. Against what her mind was saying, she suddenly found herself seated beside him.

Chevalier smiled. "There, much better, child."

"Are you here to drink my blood?" she asked timidly, and scooted a few inches farther away from him.

"Not unless you want me to." He watched her reaction and she frowned slightly. "I take it you've never been asked before?"

Emily shook her head. This news displeased him immensely. It was against the rules of the heku to take without permission, and this woman was terrified by who knows how many attacks on her. He understood the attacks. Her blood smelled sweeter than any other, but he still couldn't imagine taking without her consent.

"You are interesting to me, Emily." He watched as she tensed, and before she could see him move, he had the gun out of her hand and placed it on the bedside table.

"Me?" She was surprised that anyone could find her interesting.

"Yes, you. I'm intrigued by you." He narrowed his eyes as he watched her. Again he was struck by the need to protect her. He wanted to reach out and take her into his arms and disappear with her to somewhere no one could find. The image flashed like a movie before his eyes, and when it cleared, she was watching him.

"I should go," she said, standing up.

"Oh? Where will you go?" he whispered as his insides turned at how frail she was, how delicate her build. She couldn't protect herself, and he felt as if it was his job to do so.

Emily slipped her boots on and headed for the door.

"You're going to leave, child?" he asked, trying to distract her.

She turned and looked over at him. "I'm not a child."

"I am sorry. No offense intended."

Emily sighed, "Listen, I appreciate what you are trying to do, but I'm leaving. I've dealt with enough of your kind to know I'd rather spend the night at a hotel than here with you."

"Ouch." His voice was joking, but her words caused his heart to ache. "When have you met more of my kind?"

"When haven't I? I've been tormented by you my entire life." She pulled on a leather jacket, and he watched as she pulled her long red hair out and buckled the front.

"I do wish you would stay. I promise to behave." Though his voice didn't show it, he was beginning to panic. He envisioned all of the things that could hurt her, and he fought to conceal a growl that erupted from deep within him.

"Sure, why don't I wait around while you sweet talk me up and then attack me anyway?" She headed out the door after grabbing her gun.

Keith

Chevalier appeared in the barn as the Dodge pickup spun out and pulled away from the ranch quickly. He instantly picked up the smell of numerous heku and frowned. Jerry was right. The smell was disturbing and out of the ordinary. He soon found the mentioned coal shed and reached down to touch the ashes, then brought some to his nose and smelled them before dropping them back onto the floor.

He went back into the barn and looked up toward the loft. He climbed the ladder quickly, and his eyes narrowed as he caught the fresh scent of a wild heku, one of his own kind that had turned themselves over completely to their instincts, leaving all signs of humanity behind them. He ran back to his car and called the Council to fill them in on what he'd seen so far. They instructed him to try to get more information, so he sat back to wait for morning. Emily's husband returned early in the morning, but he continued to wait for her.

Chevalier saw her truck return to the ranch shortly after dawn, and he got out of his car, almost immediately appearing in the barn's loft. He sat on a cot and watched out the small window that overlooked the house.

She pulled the truck up in front of the ranch house and jumped out, smiling widely as she ran to the front steps. Seated there was an elderly man with an archaic Stetson perched crookedly on his head. He was slumped over slightly in a wheelchair.

Emily bent down. "I'm back, Dad."

His eyes stared far off, empty, and unfocused. He didn't move as she pulled a blanket from beside him and wrapped it around his shoulders. She kissed him lightly on the cheek and then stood to greet another man who was walking toward her.

"Hiya, Sam."

"Ms. Em, good to have ya back." He stopped just short of the steps and smiled up at her. The man looked to be almost the same age as Emily's Dad. He was short and stout with overalls and a dusty hat that made him blend into the scene. He took his hat off and fidgeted with it.

"Sam, what's wrong?"

"Der's a spook up on the lower 20. I tell Mr. Keith, but he say it jus' a coyote, but, ma'am, I ain't never seen a coyote that done hid like dis did. Almos' cause a stampede."

"I'll go check it out. Get Patra ready," she told him, crouching back down by her dad.

"Duty calls," she said, and kissed his cheek again lightly.

Sam almost ran toward the barn, seemingly afraid to turn around and face the house.

Emily turned to the house, squared her shoulders, and walked in, shutting the door behind her softly.

He hit with no warning. He grabbed her left wrist and twisted her arm behind her back, then shoved her hard against the door, sending the door handle painfully into her ribs. "I called you last night. You didn't answer," Keith hissed, his face just inches from her. "Who were you with?"

Through the pain, she managed to gasp, "Stop it."

Keith twisted her wrist harder and slammed his body into hers again, smiling when she screamed out in pain. "Tell me."

"I couldn't sleep. I went to do some work at the office. I swear," she said, unable to move. The pain made her breathing shallow and strained.

He thought about it for a moment and then released her, a grin spreading across his face. "Well why didn't you say so? Good to see you!"

She took a step away from him as he reached out and pushed her hard to the floor. As she pulled herself back up, he sat at the table and began to eat.

Leaning against the door, she caught her breath and then turned and went into the bedroom. She threw on a warm flannel shirt, grabbed her leather gloves and cowboy hat, and tried to make a break for the front door, rubbing her wrist absentmindedly.

"Where you going?" he asked, pouring clear liquid from a flask into his Coke. Keith was older than Emily, and his face showed the hardened skin of someone who worked outdoors. He was of average height, but was well built and sported a dark farmer's tan.

"I'm taking Patra out," she said, and reached for the door handle, hoping that was the last of it.

Keith laughed ostentatiously. "I've been alone for four days… mostly." His grin got wider. "I don't see you staying to take care of me."

She didn't reply as she left and made her way to the barn. Waiting for her was the beautiful painted mare, who shook her head swiftly when she saw Emily approach. Emily grabbed Patra's large head and pressed her forehead and nose into the soft velvet of the horse's muzzle. After a few seconds, she jumped onto the mare's back and headed her out of the barn.

Emily waved to Sam, who was taking her father back inside the house as a cold rain began to drizzle. She clicked her tongue twice, and Patra began to walk slowly south. She had a long Remington lying across her lap with the Blue Healer and a Border collie following behind her.

She was just enjoying her freedom. The dogs were loping along, exploring, as Patra broke into a gallop. The wind tugged at her long red ponytail, and she shut her eyes to savor the feel of the wind and the smell of the hay. As she approached the south twenty, she slowed the horse to a walk and dismounted to open the gate.

Her body froze as the hairs on the back of her neck stood up.

Someone was watching.

"Who's there?" she asked in as calm a voice as she could muster.

The dogs were crouched on their bellies, and Patra was snorting and shying. She took the horse by her bridle and attempted to calm her. The feeling passed as suddenly as it had begun, and she climbed back onto the mare.

She led Patra to the trees and scanned the forest for any movement, but she didn't see anything, then slowly made her way to a large clearing and lifted her rifle, using the scope to more closely look around. Things were quiet, only a gopher was visible, and there were no signs of a coyote.

Emily rode for the rest of the afternoon, not seeing nor feeling anything else out of the ordinary, just enjoying the feel of the powerful animal between her legs, moving to her command. The slightest pressure from a knee or heel was all she needed. The dogs bounced and played, chasing jackrabbits and flushing birds.

She neared the ranch house as the sun was about to set, and she felt her heart rise in her throat. She knew what she had to do tonight, and she felt the dread rising. She'd had four days of peace and quiet, and she realized that now was the time to pay for that solitude.

Emily took her time unhooking the saddle and putting it back on the stand. She brushed Patra carefully and enjoyed the quietness of the barn.

Just as she was locking the mare's stall door, Keith's arms wrapped tightly around her waist. "Welcome back, Emi."

She pulled away from him and headed back to the ranch house.

"Your dad's asleep. We have the night to ourselves," Keith said, placing his hand on the small of her back.

Emily nodded. "Let me get a hot shower and a bite to eat, and I'll be ready."

Keith swept her off her feet and carried her quickly into the house. "You know I like the scent of a woman."

Emily winced as he threw her down on the bed.

***

She crawled out of the bed when Keith began to snore. The hot water from the shower felt amazing, and she took longer than usual to finish up. Throwing on a robe, Emily went to the refrigerator and opened it. She scanned inside but didn't find anything interesting to eat. Grabbing a piece of cheese, she shut the door and turned around.

"Hello, again," Chevalier said to her from the dark shadows of the kitchen.

Emily gasped and covered her mouth with her hand to stop from screaming.

"Surely, you can find something better to eat than that," he said, stepping out of the shadow toward her.

"You can't be here!" Emily whispered, and glanced toward the bedroom door.

"I can be anywhere I want," he told her, raising his eyebrows and grinning.

Emily ran to him and put her hands against his chest, trying to push him out the door. "Please get out."

The feel of her hands on his chest sent a shiver through his body and made his mind whirl. He steadied himself as she pushed against him as hard as she could. He didn't budge.

"Get out," she whispered again. Emily looked at the bedroom door in a panic as the snoring stopped.

She felt a rush of air and found herself in the barn, and she staggered from the change. Chevalier gently steadied her with his hand.

Emily looked around as Patra whinnied loudly at the sudden intrusion.

She peeked out the door of the barn toward the house. Chevalier stood, watching her.

"You can't be here, please go," she said, still watching the house with one hand perched on the barn door.

"Let me see, child," Chevalier said. He reached out and took her hand, examining her wrist.

She tried to pull her hand away from him, but he didn't release it.

"Let go," she demanded.

His eyes grew darker as he gently touched her swollen wrist and bruised hand, and she pulled harder against his hand.

"Interesting," he said, letting go of her wrist.

"What are you doing here?"

"I'm interested in how you know my kind. I'd like to talk," he said, sitting down on a chair-shaped stack of hay.

"I can't. You're just going to cause me trouble," she said as she instinctively felt her sore ribs where the door handle had hit her earlier.

"Yes, I see that. I can take care of him easily enough," he said, and smiled, hoping she would take him up on his offer.

"No!" she shouted, and her eyes were afraid. "Just leave, please."

Chevalier held his hand up and inhaled, his eyes suddenly scanning the barn.

"What?" She looked around.

"Hush, child," he whispered. He stood and sniffed the air again. Finding a trail up into the loft of the barn, he climbed the ladder as Emily watched him with curiosity.

She sighed as he disappeared into the loft, then looked around and wrapped her robe tighter around herself. The barn was cold from the recent rain. Emily went and held Patra, using the warmth from the horse to help keep away the chills.

Chevalier could smell the foul beast from below, the stench of one of his own kind that let themselves be overcome by their desires, no control, no caring. He breathed in the disgusting odor and moved closer. He wasn't far into the loft before he saw the hay quivering slightly.

"Get out, wild one," he hissed, and the shivering bump in the hay became still.

He heard a low growl.

Chevalier crouched, his hands balling into fists. "Now, or I will kill you in there."

The feral heku emerged. He was stooped low and covered only with a torn loincloth. He was dirty and had gashes across his skin. His hair was matted on top of his head, and his teeth were chipped and black.

"This is my farm, leave!" he hissed at Chevalier.

"You have no rights to this place." Chevalier stood tall and looked at the vile heku.

"Mine, mine, mine," the heku chanted. "The man is mine."

"How long have you fed on the man here?"

"Mine, mine for 50 years." The chanting was getting on Chevalier's nerves.

"With his permission?"

"Mine… mine… mine… always."

"Tell me," Chevalier growled, moving closer to the other.

"I don't need his permission. He is mine!" the wild heku said, and took a step away as he noticed Chevalier's intense eyes.

"That's enough of a confession for me. As Chief Enforcer, I hereby banish you," Chevalier growled.

"Nooooo! No banishment for me," he begged.

Chevalier pulled a small dagger from his pocket, poked his finger, and let a drop of blood fall. The growls and begging from the wild heku turned to screams that pierced the night. He could hear the horses kicking in their stalls and the cows running away from the sound. The wild one turned to ash before him, and Chevalier fell to his knees. Such magic took a lot from the Enforcer, and he steadied himself against the hay.

He listened intently and barely picked up the sound of Emily disappearing into the house. He sighed and sat down on the hay, out of breath. As Chief Enforcer of his heku faction, he was able to perform magic that others couldn't, but at considerable risk to himself. He shut his eyes and meditated, listening to the sound of the wind through the barn roof. When he felt strong enough, he stood up and scraped the ashes from the loft floor into a small leather bag and cinched it tightly.

***

Chevalier sat in his place on the Council, the 13 highest-ranking heku of his faction. He watched over the proceedings, knowing his turn was coming. As much as he wanted to concentrate on the trial at hand, he found it difficult with Emily alone on the ranch. Part of why the Council was addressing him, he figured. Storm, one of the highest ranking heku in Chevalier's coven, sat in the audience and watched him eagerly.

"Chief Enforcer, it is your turn to take the stand," the only female on the Council said. She was Selest, one of the three Elders of the Equites.

Chevalier stood and took his place, facing the Council.

"Chief Enforcer, we were told you encountered a situation that you found may need our further attention," Selest said to him, and then sat down.

"Yes, Elder, I have. I followed up on the report from Jerry and found a young mortal woman who seems to have been plagued by our kind for most of her life. I even found a wild one hiding in her barn that has been feeding on her father," he explained.

"Is the father a willing donor?"

"No, the father is in no shape to make any decisions. From what I have seen, he's no longer able to speak and seems to be unaware of his surroundings." There was a hiss through the Council.

"This wild one was feeding on a mortal invalid?" the tallest Elder asked.

"Yes, for 50 years he's been on the ranch and has been feeding on the father for quite some time, Elder Leonid." Chevalier's voice was disappointed.

"And did you banish this wild one?"

He nodded. "I did."

"Then your job there is finished?" the third Elder, Maleth, asked.

"I want to continue to study the woman. There's something strange about her. Her blood doesn't smell like others… it's sweeter, and with all of the attacks in her past, I am afraid her enticing scent may cause further attacks." He kept his immense desire to protect her to himself.

"It's abhorrent what has happened to this mortal child. We envision a life where mortals no longer fear us, and attacks such as these undermine our progress," Leonid said.

Chevalier nodded.

"We give you full powers for this matter, Chief Enforcer, and we trust you will use them wisely… we give you carte blanche." A gasp was heard around the entire room, and Chevalier nodded. He knew that the Elders were keeping something from him. He'd never heard of anyone being granted such powers.

He held out the bag of ash. "What is to be done with the wild one?"

Selest stood and motioned for the large heku in the corner to come forward. "Derrick will take him and bury his ashes. We'll see how a thousand years of banishment will cure his appetite."

Chevalier handed the bag over to Derrick and then left. Storm followed him out of the room.

As Chevalier walked down the hallway, deep in thought, Storm touched his arm softly.

"Please... don't be mad, but when you left suddenly for Montana, I did some research."

He stopped and looked at her. "Of what type?"

She sighed and handed him a large folder before speaking, "I know you've heard the story of the Winchesters. We all have. I wanted to go over the file though, just as a precaution. Back in the early 16th century, there were mass heku hunts and slayings. I'm sure you remember them. The commoners actually thought they were hunting the infamous vampire. In Europe, the hunts were being led by the Winchester family. That one family is credited with killing over 100,000 heku. The head of the Winchester family, Miles Winchester, had four daughters, the youngest of whom was named Elizabeth."

Chevalier wondered where this was going.

"The reason the Winchesters were so intent on killing the heku was because their family was known to our kind as being a 'dulcris cruor,' or Sweet Blood, a trait handed down in the female line. Their blood called to any immortal around them, and they were haunted by violent attacks. Elizabeth, however, fell in love with one of her attackers and left the Winchester family to be with him. That union produced four daughters. These daughters were not only part of the dulcris cruor family, they also had some of the innate traits of the heku father, who was head of his coven. You can see how this made them especially powerful."

"These women were powerful enough to kill a heku with a single glance, yet the heku followed them, stalking them in the shadows, and eventually they would risk their own lives for just one taste of the Winchester blood. The Winchester women were sought after by the most powerful covens in the world, offered riches and wealth. If a coven should have one of the Winchester family in their midst, said coven would be unstoppable, one that would become a type of royalty in our world."

"In the late 1800s, the females from the Winchester line made a pact to no longer further their line, and to stop the torment of the immortal. The dulcris cruor caused extreme attraction to the family by both immortals and animals. The attacks became so brutal that their pact was made to stop the harassment. One sister, and only one, made a mistake and broke the pact after falling in love with a man leaving for the new world.

"She has only one direct line, a line that ends with a sole female heir…"

"Do the Elders know any of this?" he asked, his mind spinning.

"I don't know, and there's no way to be sure if it's even relevant. It's all I could find when I was searching through our Montana coven listing." She hesitated and then walked away.

***

Storm's words rang through his head as he sat in his First class seat, headed back for Great Falls. The folder she handed him was on his lap, and his fingers tapped it lightly. He couldn't hold off any longer. Opening the file, he was suddenly faced with the photo of a remarkably beautiful woman. She was standing alongside an Arabian stallion. The photo was in black and white, indicative of the year that was imprinted on the back side: 1959.

There was but a single notation, written in longhand on a piece of parchment inside of the folder.

> *Last Known Member of the Winchester Line*
>
> *Name: Elizabeth Ann Barnett (maiden) (deceased)*
>
> *Location: America (no further, though strong ties in Montana and North Dakota)*
>
> *Married: Confirmed*
>
> *Husband's Name: Unknown*
>
> *Children: 1 son (deceased), 1 daughter (name unknown)*
>
> *Source: Father Emarcus Belaery (Head of Drakni Coven), deceased*
>
> *Note: No indication she knows of her abilities, further study required.*

***

Chevalier sat on his bed in the hotel in tiny Cascade, Montana, and thought about the powers he was granted. The rules they, as heku, were to follow, were to protect their secret from the mortals, but also to protect the mortals themselves. He wondered how much the Elders already knew of what Storm had told him. As far as he knew, no one had ever been granted the ability to break the rules of conduct that their kind held in such high regard.

He thumbed once more through the small file on Elizabeth Ann and sat up suddenly when his eyes caught something he hadn't seen before. Standing behind the woman and her horse was a man who looked alarmingly like Sam, a Sam of the same age as he currently was. This man could have been Sam's father, but the image wasn't similar. It was exact. Hiding the file deep inside the locked safe, he headed out to his car. He had a photographic memory, and this was Sam down to the last wrinkle and the small mole he had on the right of his neck.

He was also confused by his growing feelings for Emily. Never in his thousands of years had he felt like this for a mortal. It was abnormal for his kind.

Chevalier was out in his car in less than a second and pulled it onto the country road that led directly to Emily's ranch.

He grabbed his phone and dialed. Storm answered on the first ring. "In your research, did you come across any type of protector for the Winchester family? Maybe even a long-standing ally?"

He could hear as she ruffled through papers before answering. "No, nothing like that, sir."

Chevalier sighed.

"There is one other thing I found, something you need to be very careful of. The dulcris cruor, as I've said, is appealing to all immortals, but apparently its call to the heku is so strong that the feeder is unable to stop once they begin. Unable as in... until the blood is gone. Each taste gets more and more appealing until finally the will to stop is no longer present." Storm rattled the information off quickly.

Chevalier clicked his phone shut and sped up. He could see the ranch ahead of him. The Dodge pickup was parked in front of it. He drove past it and parked in an abandoned farmhouse not more than a mile away. He could traverse the distance quickly without anyone noticing.

It was dusk when he reached the farmhouse. Lights were on in the house, but also in the barn, and he heard voices.

"Is it broken?" Emily asked, and her voice sounded strained.

"I don't tink so. Jis hold still," Sam replied. He sounded like he was concentrating, "Remine me ta teach you how t'punch."

"It's a little late for that, don't you think?" She sounded slightly amused, but then she groaned. "Stop that. That hurts!"

Chevalier appeared in the loft and watched them from above. Emily was sitting on a bale of hay with her hand outstretched to Sam. He was winding it tightly with an elastic bandage.

"Ya should go to da hospital, Ms. Em," he said to her matter-of-factly.

"That's all I need, Sam. I just assaulted him. You want me to land in jail?" she asked, and smiled weakly.

Sam motioned toward the house. "He's not lef yet."

"He's not going to leave either. He told me that... I just don't want to go back in there now that he's been drinking." Emily winced as Sam continued to bandage her hand.

"You stay in Sam's bunkhouse, den."

"It's okay, Sam. I'll stay here in the barn. There's a make shift bed in the loft."

There was a long silence while Sam thought it out and finally agreed. He took a hard look at the house, glanced back at Emily, and then walked to the bunkhouse.

Emily stood up from the hay and looked at the long ladder leading up to the loft. She sighed and started up it one-handed. At the top rung, she inhaled sharply and brought her hand to her face. A deep splinter had embedded into her palm, and a trickle of blood spilled onto the ladder.

Chevalier meant to wait for her quietly in the loft, but the smell of blood assaulted his senses, and all he wanted was to taste just a little of it. He had a vision of grabbing her and holding her pinned as he tasted the hot blood from her neck. He began to salivate, and his head throbbed with hunger. He could feel his muscles contract, ready to attack.

He stopped suddenly. The moment only lasted a fraction of a second, but he recoiled slightly at how far it had gone. He turned to see if Emily had seen him, and he knew immediately.

She stared up at him, still standing on the ladder. "I thought I told you to go away."

Chevalier breathed deeply of her heady musk and shut his eyes to force his instincts back under his control. He opened them slowly and looked down at her as a drop of blood slid precariously down her wrist.

"That you did." He moved to her quickly and took her hands, pulling her off of the ladder and up to face him.

Too fast for Emily to fight back, he had her pinned to his body, and his sharp canines dug easily into the flesh on her neck. She gasped and pushed at him, trying to make him stop. The euphoria began to sweep over her, and her eyes shut as she quit fighting.

He pulled away from her, relishing in the taste of her blood as it quenched the thirst and wet the back of his burning throat. He met her gaze and was shocked that the euphoric feeling had lasted only a few seconds. She was now staring up at him with her piercing green eyes, and her anger shone brightly in them.

Emily reached out and slapped him, then began to head down the ladder.

"Just like the others…," she grumbled as she ran to the house.

Chevalier barely made it to the door of the bunkhouse when it opened and Sam looked at him.

"You shouldn't have done that," Sam said plainly, and then the pain hit.

Chevalier's body was wracked with fire. Every fiber of his being felt as if it had suddenly exploded in flames. He was knocked to his knees, and his mind screamed with more pain than he'd ever felt. He was only partially aware as Sam pulled him inside the bunkhouse and shut the door. What seemed like an eternity later, the pain started to subside, and Chevalier could see Sam standing beside him with a broom.

"What... happened...?" he was able to ask with much effort.

"Hrm," Sam grunted, his eyebrows rising. "She must have gotten distracted. There's no ashes to clean up this time." He put the broom away.

Chevalier's head swam, and he drifted into unconsciousness. He found his body unable to move. The weight of it was improbable. Through the darkness, he could clearly hear everything going on at the small ranch.

The cock of a shotgun.

The barn door opening.

Heavy footsteps returning to the house. "I don't see anyone in there, Emi. Was it another one of them?" Keith asked with disgust.

"Yes, I've seen him a few times, but this is the first he's attacked. He seemed different though, at least at first. He wasn't begging me to join some stupid coven or jumping from the shadows to bite me."

"How do you attract these weirdoes?" he asked her.

Emily's voice sounded worried. "Maybe Sam got him?"

"That old man? What's he going to do, hit the guy with a bridle?" Keith was obviously having fun.

"It's not funny, Keith. Go check on Sam."

Keith sighed and walked out the door of the house just as Sam opened the bunkhouse door and stepped out.

"Evening, Sam," Keith said cordially.

"Hello, Mr. Keith."

"Seen anyone around tonight? Any ashes?"

"No, sir, no ashes. Mayhap he run?"

"Hasn't stopped her from killing them before. If you do find ashes, just keep up the story that I killed them."

"Yes, sir, I un'rstand."

Sam returned to the bunkhouse as Keith went back into the house.

Sam looked down at Chevalier as he opened his eyes slowly. "You broke the code."

Chevalier stood and shook his head clear of the pain. "Who the hell do you think I am?"

Sam blinked. "What do you mean?"

He was able to pull himself up to his tallest height. "I am Chief Enforcer of the Equites, and as such, we take this as an assault on the Council. I am no longer bound by the laws of my kind. I suggest you tell your mistress that so much as a burning in my little finger... and I'll kill her."

Sam glared. "Touch her over my dead body."

Chevalier looked at him. "I have business with her. If she wants to continue to breathe, I suggest she find time to meet with me."

Sam blinked and Chevalier was gone.

Ulrich

Chevalier's phone rang softly as he lie in bed thinking about what had transpired. He hesitated, then answered, "Yes, Storm?"

She sounded nervous, very uncharacteristic for her. "Sir, are you in trouble?"

"No, why?" He sounded tired and still strained from the pain earlier.

"I had a phone call from one of the Old Ones." She paused to see if he responded, but then continued. "It's Lord Ulrich von Weiskgaard, from the Valle. He wants to meet with you immediately."

Chevalier frowned slightly. He was one of the Old Ones, so why did she seem so nervous? "About?"

"He won't say, sir, but he did mention that the meeting need not include any of the rest of the Council."

He thought that sounded odd, but agreed. "Very well, where shall we meet?"

"Lord Ulrich is in Great Falls."

He shook his head, wondering what could be up now. "Okay, tell him to meet me in the conference room at my hotel in one hour."

"Yes, sir..." She hesitated, and then hung up.

Chevalier tried to clear his head, but his thoughts kept turning back to Emily. She had unknowingly tried to kill him that night, yet he still felt the urge to protect her. He noticed, frustratingly, that even as his thoughts were trying to focus on the upcoming meeting, they still held her image closely as if trying to bring her to him. The very thought of her brought his instincts forward and he longed for another taste of her blood.

The concierge booked the room for him easily. It was always amazing what a simple $100 bill would do to a mortal. He sat at the head of the table and watched the clock, anxious to get this meeting over with so he could get back on track at the ranch.

The doors opened and in walked Lord Ulrich. He was obviously one of the Old Ones, and as he looked at Chevalier, his eyes were scrutinizing. He wore the black suit and conspicuous black cape that had long been abandoned in the new world. Behind him were six well-dressed heku, obviously the top ranks of his coven.

He stood at the table and one of them removed his cape and pushed a chair up for him. As he sat down, they formed a semicircle of protection around him. Last to walk in was Sam. He was still dressed in denim overalls and looked quite out of place with the others in the room. He shut the door behind him and sat down at Ulrich's right.

Chevalier eyed Sam suspiciously.

"I am Lord Ulrich von Weiskgaard, head of the Debalih Coven. I know who you are… so now I ask a simple question… What are you doing with Emily Russo?"

Chevalier narrowed his eyes. "Seven of you, how remarkable. So tell me, how long have you known of the existence of this killer here in the middle of North America?"

Ulrich's eyes widened. "How dare you address me so!"

Chevalier grinned mirthlessly. "I dare much. I was burned at the stake with the Templar. I enjoyed a Bloodbath in Jerusalem. I have been around much longer than any of your whelps in attendance here. I daresay that the insolence, if there is such, lies on the part of old world covens that've apparently hidden a violation of the pact into some place where they believed that they could hide it indefinitely."

Ulrich glared at him.

Chevalier sat at the conference table and propped his feet up. "Nonetheless, we must take this opportunity to deal with the issue."

One of the young heku slapped Chevalier's boots off the table. "You will not address Lord Ulrich in that manner!"

Chevalier stood up, his hands in fists. "I will address him in any way I see fit."

Ulrich smiled with a gleam in his eyes. Chevalier tried to remember where he had seen those eyes.

Ulrich motioned to his coven, and they left without a word, except Sam, who stayed in his chair. "Enough with the frivolities. I come seeking answers, so I'll ask you again, what do you want with Emily Russo?"

"What I'm doing is of no concern to you. It's Equites business," Chevalier said bluntly.

"It has everything to do with me. I assure you."

"What you did makes you no better than Keith!" Sam yelled, standing up.

"I am nothing like Keith!" Chevalier yelled, pounding his fist on the table and splintering it. "Drinking Emily's blood without permission was necessary. Keith finds it fun to beat on someone who relies on him."

"Sam, let us be," Ulrich said calmly. Sam turned into a small cat, jumped off the chair, and ran out the door. "My familiar can be very protective of her."

"Apparently"

"I know that you are part of the Council, and I also know the Elders have been after Elizabeth Winchester's family for years. I've been able to keep them safe, it seems, until now. What do you want?

What can I give that will get you to turn around and leave Emily alone?"

Chevalier noted the sorrowed expression on Ulrich's face and thought carefully before speaking. "I don't want anything from you. I'm not here to destroy her."

"Then what do you want?" His eyes narrowed as he grew angry.

"I still don't think it's any of your concern."

"It is my concern when my family is involved," Ulrich said, clenching his jaw.

The eyes, they were familiar. They were Emily's eyes. The truth hit Chevalier. Ulrich was the heku with whom Elizabeth Winchester had fallen in love.

Ulrich sat back in the chair. He seemed exhausted. "I've watched over my family for hundreds of years, and during that time, the heku blood was almost bred out of the line. I was so close to having my descendants fully mortal, no longer sought by the Councils as murderers."

Chevalier waited, trying to wrap his mind around what he was hearing.

"Emily's mother had almost no power at all, and then he found her. Elizabeth Ann married Allen Flynn and had a son. Elizabeth's father was Irish, and she had his temper, but had yet to display anything beyond that. None of the powers are held by the males in the family, so I couldn't tell if the hundreds of years of torment had come to an end. For one brief period of time, I sent Sam on an errand away from the Flynn family, and another heku found her." He paused and pain crept into his voice. "He had the power to clear the mind. Elizabeth Ann didn't even know what was happening."

"Then Emily was born." Everything was becoming clear to Chevalier.

Ulrich nodded. "I wasn't sure if the baby was Allen's or not. I also wasn't sure if another heku could bring back the powers that I bestowed, unknowingly, upon the family. The heku kept visiting Elizabeth Ann, and one night, he lost control. Her blood had become like a drug to him."

Ulrich's voice softened. "He killed her, and when he still wasn't satiated, he also killed her son, desperately seeking more of the dulcris cruor. Emily was only two years old, and when he approached her, smelling the scent of the sweet blood on her, she turned him to ash in less than a second. It was then that I knew that it had all started over. She was even more powerful than my own daughters."

Chevalier's muscles tightened as he realized how quickly the factions would have Emily killed if they knew what he knew. He suddenly felt like taking her far away from them, hiding her, protecting her.

"She can't know what she can do." Ulrich's voice strengthened.

"Why?" Chevalier asked. It didn't make sense.

"If she makes the same decision her ancestors did, not to carry on the family line, then my Elizabeth will die out, nothing left of her or us… I watch over her and make sure she's safe, with the help of Sam."

"Safe? You call living with Keith safe?" Chevalier growled at him.

"Keith was a fortunate accident. I don't meddle in the mortal affairs of my granddaughters... I only step in when the immortal interfere."

"Fortunate accident?" Chevalier asked, confused.

"Yes fortunate. He's weak minded and takes credit for the missing that Emily has turned to ash. She finds protection being with him, and with that protection comes some comfort. As long as Keith takes credit for getting rid of, shall we say, admirers, then she won't know that she has killed."

"How many?" Chevalier asked.

Ulrich looked into his eyes. "I don't trust you enough to divulge any more. I just tell you I will not stand by while my bloodline is polluted by yet another heku."

"I... what??" He fumed when he realized what Ulrich was implying.

"Stay away from her."

"I have no intention of being a father any time soon." The word 'polluted' had touched a nerve.

Ulrich studied his face. "You have no desires for her at all?"

Chevalier's face was steady as he lied. "None at all." His thoughts echoed in his head, *"Like no other."*

"She's of the dulcris cruor. The more of her blood you feed on, the more you'll want her, and trust me, you will end up killing her. Let her be. Let her live her mortal life and start again breeding out the

heku. She's a caring girl. If she finds out how many she's killed..."
His eyes watched Chevalier. His piercing gaze was so much like
Emily's.

Chevalier stood. "Enough, I do what I want, and I'll not sit here
and be told what I can and cannot do."

Ulrich mirrored his movement and stood. "If you go to the Elders,
then believe me, I will know and Emily will disappear. I've done it
before, and I will do it again." With one swift movement, he swept
out of the room and disappeared into the daylight, leaving Chevalier
alone with his thoughts.

Chevalier's mind was miles away when he arrived at the ranch.
The sight of the ambulance sitting quietly in front of the house brought
him back from his thoughts. He quickly appeared in the loft of the
barn, at the small window that overlooked the front of the ranch house.

It was obvious what was wrong when the paramedics wheeled out
the gurney, the sheet entirely covering its occupant. Emily ran out of
the house toward it, but Keith stopped her, gently grabbing her arm.
Sam was standing at the bunkhouse door watching.

The ambulance left with no lights, no sirens, just a quiet exit.
Emily turned to Keith, and he wrapped his arms around her. The sobs
stopped as her body went limp. Keith reached down and picked her
up, cradling her in his arms lovingly. He went back into the house and
shut the door.

Chevalier was hit with a sudden yearning to go into the house and
take her from him, to cradle her in his arms and gaze into her eyes. If
he could just lock her gaze, he could lessen the pain. He noted briefly

how silent the ranch was. The horses, the cattle, everything seemed quiet and still in the brisk morning air.

The following days passed quickly. Chevalier studied the house from the loft, watching as people came and went bringing flowers and food. Each guest came with open arms and left with red eyes.

"*He must have been loved,*" Chevalier thought to himself.

During the days that followed Allen's death, there was no sign of Emily.

The fourth night was cold. The wind was howling, and the moon was almost full. Chevalier was again sitting in the loft watching the house. He was moments from knocking on the door to make sure things were alright, when the door suddenly opened with a loud bang. Emily ran from the house toward the barn. All she wore was jeans and a t-shirt. She hadn't even bothered putting on shoes.

"Emily, don't do this!" Keith yelled, following her out of the house.

The doors to the barn swung open and Emily appeared. She was bareback on a sleek black Thoroughbred stallion. She kicked the horse, and he immediately launched into a fast gallop.

Keith stopped and watched her leave, then sighed and went back into the house.

Chevalier only had a moment to think. With his keen senses, he was able to pick up everything that was happening in less than a second. Emily was riding too fast, and the moon wasn't bright enough for the stallion to be sure of his surroundings. She could barely hang on, not having bothered putting on even a bridle. She was out in the freezing cold and there was a hint of the smell of alcohol on the wind.

His movements were a blur as he left the barn and ran after her, keeping close to the trees. Even with his speed, he had a hard time keeping pace with the horse. Emily ignored the gates and pulled the stallion into a jump. Chevalier made himself move faster. He had to catch up with her and stop the horse before...

It happened too quickly for even Chevalier to help. Emily pulled the horse into a hurdle over a gate and when he landed, the stallion's feet hit the ground improperly. Emily hit the ground first, and the massive Thoroughbred rolled over her and then scrambled to his feet. Chevalier stopped suddenly and watched. Emily was unmoving on the cold hard ground.

He approached slowly. The stallion stomped at him and moved back a few steps. As he got closer, he noticed that Emily was not only breathing, she was crying.

He knelt down beside her. "Are you hurt?" he asked as the rain started.

She looked up at him with tear-filled eyes. "I found you."

Her breathing was labored.

The rain began to turn to sleet. He reached down and picked her up, cradling her as he'd been longing to do for days. He carried her swiftly into the trees where it was dry. "You were looking for me?"

"Yes," she said softly. "I need you to help me."

How could he be holding a killer? She looked fragile and pale in the dark night. He found it hard to imagine how quickly she could kill him.

"Anything," was all he could say. He was acutely aware that he would do almost anything for her, still not understanding why.

Emily turned her face into his neck and pulled her collar away from hers with a shaking hand. Her warm breath was on his neck as she spoke. "Kill me, please."

He looked down at her exposed neck, and the vein throbbed invitingly. What he saw also shocked and angered him. Beside the delicate vein were scars. Marks left by greedy and uncaring heku, heku who had long since turned to ash.

***

The doctor Storm sent was also a donor, so she was able to serve two purposes. Emily was still unconscious. The concussion wasn't as serious as it could have been. Four broken ribs and a broken collarbone along with scrapes and bruises over most of her body, was the final tally from the horse falling on her. Chevalier was feeling better with the fresh blood in his system, and his mind was clear to think. The doctor had given Emily a hefty dose of morphine to kill the pain and assured Chevalier that she would be asleep for hours.

He watched her as she slept. Her delicate features were more pronounced with her pale complexion, a sign of the concussion. Her breathing was still labored, which worried Chevalier, but the doctor had assured him it was just due to the broken ribs, which were now tightly bound to try to prevent further damage. He wanted to reach out and touch her face, to feel the warmth of her skin beneath his fingers, but he was afraid it would wake her.

He glanced briefly at the morning paper, which was still sitting on the floor under the hotel room door. Chevalier grabbed it, staring at the front page. Just below the bold writing "**Local Cascade Woman Missing**" was a picture of Emily, smiling brightly beside her painted mare. The article misrepresented the information. It stated that she was out riding in the afternoon but hadn't returned, and that her horse was found dead late that night by searchers. Chevalier frowned. If Emily found out he had killed the stallion, she wouldn't be happy. His anger had gotten the best of him when her injuries became apparent, and out in the storm, it was easy to catch and kill the skittish horse.

He tucked the newspaper into his bag and pulled out the small silver cell phone. He wasn't sure yet who he was going to call or what he would tell them when he did. He was harboring a woman that the entire state was looking for, an innocent killer. Chevalier hoped that Storm was right in trusting the doctor. By now, she had surely figured out that the woman in his hotel was the missing one from the papers.

The decision was easy for him, the decision on how to handle Emily and her abilities. It went against everything Ulrich told him, but Chevalier didn't feel any desire to follow those instructions. He had in his possession a weapon that was greater than any he'd seen, and with an impending war, her talents would be immeasurable. First, though, he had to tell her about them and then had to teach her how to control them. He couldn't take her back to his coven and have them be in danger.

His house in the cold mountains of Colorado would work perfectly. It was only accessible by snowcat year-round, so it was isolated and safe. There, he would be able to try to teach Emily how to control what she didn't yet know she could do. He also noted, solemnly, that it would keep her out of the protection of Ulrich's eye. It wasn't past his notice that it also put him in grave danger. He could vividly remember the intense burning pain she had once inflicted upon him, but he didn't have a choice. He needed her in the coming war, but he also didn't think he could live without being near her.

Emily stirred in her sleep, her fists clenching slightly. "Please," she asked softly.

Chevalier froze. He wasn't sure if she was waking or merely talking in a dream. He watched her as her eyes fluttered beneath her eyelids, her breathing coming faster and her soft brow furrowed briefly. Whatever she was dreaming wasn't pleasant. He smiled to himself, again amazed at the simple human frailties that plagued such a natural killer.

He stood up quietly, walked over to the bed, and reached down, gently touching her soft cheek. Almost immediately, her hands relaxed and her features returned to the quietness of sleep.

Chevalier turned to walk back to the chair when he heard her speak again, one single word, so soft he couldn't be positive that she even said it.

"Chevalier"

He turned to look at her, but nothing had changed. Shaking his head slightly, he sat down and picked up the cell phone, still contemplating who to call and what to say. He knew the Council would want an update soon and thought it would be better to do it by phone than have them send representatives to talk to him. He stepped into the adjacent room and shut the door to make his call, still trying not to wake up Emily.

It was a few minutes before he could be connected to an Elder. Even in his world, red tape surrounded everything, and the need for secrecy made it worse.

"Chevalier, do you have news for us?" The voice sounded eager.

"Not a lot yet," he said, lying smoothly. "The girl is interesting and may be of use to us, but I'm not sure she has the powers of the Winchester family. It'll take more time to be sure."

"We aren't sure you have much more time, but do what you think is right. We trust you."

"I will. I'll call when I know something." The click of the phone ended the conversation before he let something slip or let the extreme urgency enter into his voice.

He opened the phone again and dialed. This time, it rang only once before someone answered.

"Yes, sir?" Storm sounded pleased to hear from him.

"I'm leaving here. Don't call me. If I need anything, I'll call you."

There was a brief silence, and he could tell she was debating whether or not to ask more questions. "Are you bringing her here?"

"No, and if I'm lucky, no one will know where I've gone."

"You can tell me, sir. What if there's trouble?"

"I can't risk the Elders finding my location. I trust you, but I don't trust them."

She began to ask another question, but he ended the call when static on the line alerted him that she might not have been the only person listening.

Chevalier went back into the room and began packing his things. He looked at the medication left by the doctor, noting he had five more doses of morphine and syringes to administer it. She had also left hand-written instructions on how to care for each of Emily's injuries.

***

As soon as it was dark, Chevalier loaded his things into the back of a black Bugatti Veyron and lowered the passenger seat as far back as it would go. He went inside and checked to make sure he'd left nothing, then watched Emily for a moment before he gently pulled her arm out from under the covers. He couldn't have her waking up during the trip down to Colorado. After cleaning a small area of her upper arm with alcohol, he pulled the cap off of the needle and carefully injected one full dose of morphine.

He put the cap back on the needle, deciding to dispose of it outside where no one would find it. A small trickle of blood escaped the puncture wound. Chevalier breathed deeply, and the pleasing aroma made his mind whirl. He touched one finger to the drop of blood and brought it hungrily to his mouth.

Once he regained complete control, he reached down tenderly and picked Emily up, gathering the blankets around her. He normally refused to use his full speed when in a public place, but he couldn't risk her being spotted. It was only a fraction of a second before he was setting her down gently in the car. The morphine was working. She didn't even move as he buckled her in and deftly slipped into the driver's seat.

He let the car idle for a few minutes as his mind did the math. It was around 830 miles to the small town closest to his home in Colorado, and his car topped out at 250 mph. That seemed dangerously fast to anyone else, but with the fast reflexes inherent to heku, it was perfectly safe. Accounting for weather and other obstacles, he figured he could be in the snowcat in just over four hours. Once he loaded up the snowcat with supplies, it was another two hours to get to his house. That last dose of morphine should keep Emily comfortable and unaware for the entire ride.

She stirred only once during the trip, when the soft drizzle that started around midnight turned into a violent hailstorm. It was in Buford, Colorado, where he stopped to grab supplies. The tiny town consisted of one small store and a cabin. He paid a local teenager to go into the store with a list of supplies while he waited with Emily. The boy glanced at the sleeping girl once, but Chevalier brought his finger to his lips, indicating that she was sleeping.

After leaving Buford, it was only a few miles to the turnoff. The tiny dirt road was partially hidden by thick evergreens and large aspen trees. From here, it was slow going. The road was neglected, and its winding path was riddled with local wildlife. Slowly, the terrain turned from dark green to white as the year-round snow began. Up ahead, he caught sight of the curved outline of the private garage. He went through two locked gates before drawing up to it and opening the large door, then he pulled the Bugatti inside and shut the door behind him.

The snowcat was already partially stocked with supplies and extra fuel. Speed wasn't a problem here. No one was around the area for miles. He quickly passed the supplies from the car into the snowcat and made a make shift bed out of the backseat. Emily gasped slightly as Chevalier picked her up, but she settled down comfortably onto the bed. It was still dark, which was how he preferred to travel.

The lights from the snowcat lit up the stark white snow as he moved slowly out into it. He drove the snowcat a lot slower than he preferred, trying not to jostle Emily around and cause her to wake up. The two-hour trek up the mountain went smoothly, and the time allowed him to consider all of the options for teaching Emily about her ability. The trick was how to teach her without her turning it on him. He suddenly worried what would happen to her if he were to die, leaving her alone in the treacherous high country.

It wasn't until he was almost to the house when he saw it. It was securely hidden by dense trees and overgrowth. The windows were black and lifeless as he pulled the snowcat into the garage and shut the door behind him, surrounding them in complete darkness. He stepped out into the garage. Its stinging cold didn't bother him, but he shut the door quickly to keep Emily out of it.

The wall panel lit up when he touched it, bringing the generators to life, fully charged by the solar panels. He adjusted the temperature in the house up to 75 degrees and with a short code, the fireplaces all came alive, blazing with warmth. He went back to the snowcat and picked Emily up, holding his breath. She was starting to stir a bit. Chevalier entered the spacious house and headed for the nearest bedroom, where the bed was very near the fireplace. Laying her down gently, he covered her with a heavy down quilt, then went to work getting the supplies out of the snowcat and putting them away in the house.

***

A snowstorm raged outside of the sizable house, and the wind howled through the White River National Forest as Chevalier sat in an ancient rocking chair and watched Emily sleep. He suspected it wouldn't be long until she woke fully. She'd opened her eyes several times, but they were unfocused and soon closed again. His plans were made, well laid out for his protection, but he hoped they would produce fast results. The unending faction war wouldn't wait for him.

With a gasp, Emily sat up in the unfamiliar room. Her hand suddenly grasped her side as the broken ribs screamed at the movement. Chevalier was sitting by her side in an instant, slowly lowering her back onto the bed.

"It's okay, Emily. Lay down," he assured her, gently positioning her so her head was propped up a bit, making it easier to look around.

"Where am I?" she asked, her eyes taking in the large bedroom.

"You're safe. You are in my home." He stayed on the bed, a hand firmly on her shoulder, so she wouldn't hurt herself trying to get up.

Her piercing green eyes looked deep into his and narrowed slightly. "How long have I been here?"

"Four days. What's the last thing you remember?" He was hoping it would save some time if she remembered some of the night they left the ranch.

She thought for a moment and a sudden realization showed on her face. She nodded. "I was on Coal, and I was looking for you."

He smiled. "You found me."

She frowned as the memories came back to her. "He fell. Coal did... I... I don't remember anything after that."

"Coal fell on you. That's why you are hurting. You have a broken collarbone, several broken ribs, and a concussion."

"How is Coal?" she asked suddenly, worry showing in her eyes.

Lying always came easily for him, but he didn't want to lie to her. "He wasn't hurt in the fall. He stood right back up and then I brought you here."

"Where is here?"

"That's something I will tell you later. For now, you only need to know you're safe. I won't let anything happen to you."

She cocked her head slightly to the side and listened. "We're alone?"

Chevalier simply nodded.

She studied his face. "Am I a hostage?"

"No," he said, and smiled broadly. "You may leave when you want to... and are well enough to travel."

"Does Keith know where I am?"

"No"

"Does anyone?"

He sighed. "No."

"I have to get back. I have to watch after the ranch and…" She paused, her mind taking it all in. "Keith is going to kill me."

Chevalier shook his head. "You can't travel yet, plus… there's a severe snowstorm out there. We won't be going anywhere. You must be hungry."

Emily nodded.

"I'll get you something. Behave and stay in bed." He stood up carefully and was out of the room before she could even see him move.

As soon as he was gone, she braced her ribs with her hand and swung her legs out of bed. She was tangled briefly in a long white nightgown, but was able to free her feet after some effort. She wondered how she had gotten into the gown and where it had come from. It was long sleeved and billowy, similar to one she'd seen in a museum.

Once she was sure she was steady, she stood up, gasping softly as her ribs protested against the movement. Her left arm seemed weak, and when she moved it, a sharp pain raced down her shoulder. She braced herself against the headboard as her head swam dangerously close to unconsciousness, and black started to encroach on her vision. After a few moments it cleared, and she took a cautious step away from the bed.

With sore, stiff muscles, she made her way to the large window. Her hand touched the soft lace curtains and pushed them aside. The view was breathtaking. Her bedroom was on the second floor, and the window looked down over the side of a mountain where the trees were barely visible beneath the deep snow. Emily wasn't sure how far she could actually see on a clear day. The falling snow made it hard to see more than half a dozen yards or so.

She jumped as his hands slid around her waist. "What part of stay in bed did you not understand?" he asked softly.

Her eyes were locked on the window. "It's so beautiful out there."

"Hmm, well I prefer what's inside," he said, smiling slightly.

She felt heat rise to her face. She always hated when she blushed, but had no control over it. Chevalier led her away from the window with his hands still tight against her waist, in case she started to fall. He picked her up effortlessly and laid her back in bed. She inhaled deeply. The food smelled wonderful, and she realized she was starving.

The room was silent as she ate. The food burned her mouth, but her hunger won out. The taste was exquisite, like nothing she'd tasted before. It had been so long since she'd eaten that she filled up quickly.

"Aren't you going to eat?" she asked, noticing him watching her.

"No," he said, amused.

She put the fork down on the dainty silver tray and turned to look at him fully. "You're a vampire."

"Okay"

"Aren't you afraid of Keith finding you?"

Again, his voice sounded amused. "No."

Her lips thinned. "He has a way of finding vampires and killing them."

"Yes, I know, but child, I am not a vampire."

"Am I here so you can kill me?"

"No"

"Are you going to tell me why I'm here?"

"Eventually"

She wrinkled her nose. "Are you always so cryptic? Hey, if you aren't a vampire, what are you?"

Chevalier had been waiting for this. "I am a heku."

"A what?"

"A heku. My kind was here long before your ancestors were mere specks on the ground. We've watched civilization grow and have tried to stay out of the way. Mythical creatures of the night, the vampires, werewolves, ziang shi, zombies… they were all designed to explain our presence, but we are none of those." It wasn't nearly the entire story, but was enough for now.

He removed the tray and she lay back against the soft down pillows, her sore muscles complaining.

"It's my turn," he said, pulling the rocking chair closer to the bed.

"For what?" She tensed.

He braced himself, and for a brief moment wondered if her reaction was any indication that the burning pain would begin. "For questions, I have some for you."

She relaxed some, and in return, so did he.

He started his well thought out plan, which began simply as getting to know as much about her family as he could. "I want to know about your mother."

"My mother?"

"Yes"

She looked up at him, confused. "She's dead."

"Yes, I know, but what do you know about her?" He smiled warmly, making sure his sharp teeth didn't show.

"Well, she died when I was two. She was in a car wreck."

That answered one of his questions, about how truthful Sam and her dad had been to her. This would complicate some of his plans. He would have to start further back in her history if he was to make her understand her abilities.

"And your brother?"

She frowned. "I don't have a brother. I'm an only child."

"So sorry, my mistake. Do go on."

"She wasn't very old when she met my dad. He inherited the ranch from his father. All I really know about her was that she had a way with animals and that she was very beautiful."

Chevalier nodded. He had no doubts about that. "I see. What about Sam? Do you know much about him?"

"Sam… what's not to say about Sam? He's taken care of the ranch and my dad for as long as I can remember. Dad once said that Sam's dad worked for my Grandpa."

He leaned closer to her as she continued, her eyes suddenly faraway.

"He's always been a friend. I remember when I was six, and a strange man followed me home from school. Dad was out with the cattle, so it was just Sam when I got home. I was so afraid." She shuddered slightly. "He held me like his own daughter while I calmed down and then left me with hot chocolate and instructions to stay put. When he got back, the man was gone."

"Strange man?"

She nodded. "Yes."

"Did a lot of strangers follow you home?"

Again, she nodded. "Dad said I had a magnetic personality." Her face was suddenly serious. "He warned me to stay away from them, but there always seemed to be someone there, in the shadows. Sam helped them stay away somehow. He is like a grandpa to me."

"Did anyone ever tell you anything about the strangers?"

She looked over at him. "How could they know anything about them? They were just strangers."

He shrugged. "Just asking."

"Dad once mentioned that Mom had the same problem. I guess everyone does if it comes down to it." She looked back up at the ceiling.

Chevalier wondered if he could ever convince her how wrong she was. He noticed how she winced a bit, her breath catching.

"Enough for tonight. It's time for some pain meds, it seems." He stood up and grabbed the syringes from the bedside table. When he turned back, Emily was watching him, her eyes a mixture of pain and fear.

Suddenly, her face dissolved into a relaxed gaze and her eyes became unfocused and glassy.

Thinking quickly, he yelled, "Emily, stop!"

She jumped slightly, her eyes coming back into focus and staring at him. The look of fear had returned. "Don't come near me with those."

He fought to control his breathing, aware that he had been only seconds from the burning pain. "It's morphine, for the pain."

She shook her head. "No."

He hesitated, afraid to move near her. "Are you saying that you aren't hurting?"

Emily set her jaw. "No shots."

"Are you hurting or not?"

She flung the covers back and threw her legs off the bed, grasping her side and groaning when the world began to spin. She was barely aware that he was at her side. The slight pinching in her arm let her know she had lost. She'd had the pain medication. Emily began to protest but felt herself fall back into unconsciousness. She fought to surface, but soon, the morphine took over.

He laid her back in the bed and covered her with the blankets, his hands shaking. He flashed to the front room with his hands against the windowsill. Chevalier's entire body was shaking, realizing how close he had come to becoming a pile of ash. He thought of how suddenly it happened, her fear turning to nothingness. None of her attackers had a chance. He was sure they ran as soon as they were done with her, too far away to stop what was inevitable.

Once his nerves calmed and his hands were steady, he stood up and gazed out the window. The snowstorm had added at least 24 inches of new snow. He couldn't leave that day if he wanted to, even the snowcat would have problems on that night. Sighing heavily, he returned to Emily's room and sat in the rocking chair. He watched her sleep, again marveling at her intense beauty. With the patience that centuries granted him, he waited, going over the plans once more in his head.

* * *

Emily opened her eyes slowly. She still felt groggy from the morphine. She looked around the room and noticed she was alone. Light was shining from the window, and she wondered how long she'd been out this time.

She sat up as quietly as she could, took the remaining syringes out of the drawer, and had them well hidden before Chevalier appeared in the doorway with another tray of food.

He smiled. "How are you feeling?"

She turned and glared at him. "Drugged, thank you very much."

Chevalier found this amusing. "Well, do you want to eat before you begin yelling at me for it?"

"How do I know you aren't poisoning the food?" Studying his face, she frowned.

Chevalier chuckled, "Child, if I wanted you dead, you wouldn't be here right now."

She grimaced at the title 'child' and then sat down slowly into a chair by the frozen window. "Fine."

He set the tray down on the small table and looked out the window. "The snow is letting up."

Emily ignored him as she ate, her mind going over her possible options. After she finished, she looked up at him. "You have no right to keep me drugged."

He raised an eyebrow. "Who is going to stop me? Besides, it's not like I'm being mean. You need pain medication to recover."

"I'm feeling fine."

He smiled. "Mmhmm. I need you in perfect shape soon, and I'll do what I need to, to get you there."

"What for?"

"In due time." He walked over and stoked the fire.

She stood up while his back was turned and fought to keep from groaning. The pain seemed a little better, but turning incorrectly caused extreme pain. "Where are my clothes?"

"Are you going somewhere?" It infuriated her that his tone was light and still amused.

"Yes, I'm leaving."

Chevalier stood up and turned to look at her. The light from the large window behind her illuminated the white nightgown and showed the silhouette of her body underneath it. He composed himself before answering. "No, you aren't."

Emily put her hands on her hips. "You said I could leave when I wanted."

"No, I said when you wanted and when you could handle the trip."

"I can now."

"No, you can't. Why don't you lie back down before you fall?" He noticed the color was draining from her face.

Emily didn't answer. The darkness was invading her vision again, and her head began to throb. She took a deep breath and steadied herself against the chair until it had passed. When she was sure she wouldn't faint, she turned her hauntingly beautiful green eyes to him. "I'm not going to fall."

Chevalier shrugged and went over to the nightstand. He opened the drawer and began to reach for a syringe when he noticed they were missing.

"Where are they?" he asked, knowing she wasn't going to tell him.

"Gone"

"Damnit, Emily, where are they?" The anger in his voice made her take a step back, putting the wall to her back.

"Gone," she said again, a little more timidly.

In an instant, Chevalier was at her, his hands on the wall at her shoulders, pinning her. She jerked her head away, her hands rising defensively to cover her face. The gesture infuriated him, not with her, but with the reason she did it.

He took her wrists gently in his hands and pinned them at her sides. Chevalier placed his cheek against hers. Breathing in her scent, he flicked her earlobe lightly with his tongue and was pleased that she shivered. "I will never hit you," he whispered into her ear.

He pulled his head back to look directly into her eyes. He locked her gaze and concentrated. It was only a few moments before her breathing matched his. His eyes boring deeper into hers, he whispered, "Where is the morphine, Emily?"

He could see the conflict in her face and could tell she was struggling to unlock his gaze, to regain control. Softer, he asked again, "Emily, where is the morphine?"

He was amazed at her restraint. Mortals normally became his to control with just a single glance, yet she took immense concentration.

Her voice was soft, his acute ears barely picking up her words. "In the bottom of the dresser."

He responded by gently brushing his lips across hers. Emily pressed her body slightly against his, arching her neck up toward him. He couldn't control it any more. He pressed his lips against hers and felt the warmth of her touch. He let his instincts forward, the aching he had in his body for her coming out.

Chevalier let go of her hands, moving one to the small of her back and one to her neck. He pulled her in closer to him. She didn't hesitate, and her body fit closely into his. His lips pried hers open. The smell and taste of her breath sent spasms deep within him. Emily bit his bottom lip gently.

Suddenly, she tensed. Her entire body became rigid, and she placed her hands on his chest, trying to push him away from her. She breathed heavily. "Please, I can't."

The instinct within him demanded that he take her, and he refused to move as his mind fought within itself. She pushed harder against him, her arm and ribs screaming in pain.

"Chevalier, don't," she begged.

He took a deep breath and stepped back, caging the beast that had nearly taken over. As his breathing slowed, he trusted himself to look at her. She was still close enough that he could smell the blood pumping quickly through her veins. Emily was watching him, her face a mixture of embarrassment and confusion and her eyes began to water.

Chevalier moved to her, pulling her into an embrace with her face pressed against his chest. He caressed her cheek with his finger and pressed his lips softly against the top of her head. "I'm sorry. I shouldn't have done that." He could feel her wet tears against his skin.

"Please lay down," he encouraged. "I'll behave. I promise."

She nodded against his chest and pulled away from him, refusing to meet his eyes. When she laid down, she admitted to herself that the bed felt nice. The pain in her side lessened as she rested against the soft pillows.

Chevalier pulled up a chair, realizing that she still wouldn't look at him. Her eyes were shut, but her body was not yet relaxed. "Let's continue."

Emily looked up at him suddenly.

He smiled. "The questions… I didn't finish."

She nodded.

"Tell me about Keith," he began.

She frowned and shook her head slightly. "What about him?"

"Start at the beginning… how you met."

She watched as her hand absentmindedly traced the pattern on the bedspread and shrugged. "He worked for my dad, as a field hand. I was only 14 when he started, but I think I had a crush on him from day one. When I was 17, he finally talked Dad into letting us date." She paused, her eyes becoming thoughtful. "I don't think Dad ever trusted him. I never quite understood why. Then a few months later, we got married."

Chevalier couldn't help but comment. "I can understand why Allen didn't trust him."

Emily looked over at him. "Keith can be a handful, yes, but all in all, he's a good guy and he's good for me."

"What makes you say that?"

She shrugged. "How else could I handle the attacks? He takes care of them for me and all I have to do in return is put up with his temper. He also helps me run the ranch. I'm not sure I could do that on my own."

"Would you stay with Keith if he no longer protected you from them?"

Her eyes showed a hint of fear. "I can't leave him."

"Fair enough." He fully planned on dealing with that later on. "What about your job, what do you do?"

"I'm imagining by now I'm fired."

"Okay, what did you do?"

"I code."

His eyebrows rose, but before he could respond, she continued.

"I write programs for the government. No one else knows what I do, or shall I say, what I was doing for them."

He noted some skepticism in her voice. "I'm not interested in what you do for the government."

"What are you interested in then?"

"Again, child, we will get into that later."

"Stop calling me child. I'm not a child. I'm 23." Her jaw set, and Chevalier fought to stop from chuckling.

"I am sorry, please continue."

"That's it… I write programs for the government. I prefer my time on the ranch, obviously, but it helps pay the bills."

"If you could guess, how many times in your life have you been attacked by heku?"

"Including just now?" she snapped.

"Ouch… no, not counting just now."

"I don't really know, several times a year I guess. Sometimes it's worse than others. At times, they come in droves, all begging me to join some stupid coven." She thought for a moment and then turned toward him, wincing slightly at the ache in her side. "Is that what you want? You want me to join your coven?"

"No ch… dear… I don't believe my coven could handle you," he said with a chuckle.

"Hmm, I'm not sure if I find that offensive or not."

"No offense implied," he assured her.

"Chevalier, I need to go back to the ranch." Her eyes were pleading.

He shook his head. "Not yet."

"Keith must be worried sick. He and Sam can't handle the ranch without me. It's my ranch."

"I'm sure Keith and Sam are doing fine."

"You can't be sure of that! For all I know, they abandoned my animals and left them to fend for themselves."

He sighed. "Would you feel better if I made a call and had them checked on?"

"No, I would feel better if you would let me go."

"Not yet." The tone of his voice indicated that that part of the discussion was over. "I will make some calls in the morning. For now, it's time for you to get some rest."

"No pain meds," she told him sternly.

"Emily, I've told you, the doctor said you need all of the doses so you can heal and get some rest."

"I won't let you."

Her stubbornness never ceased to catch him off guard. "You know there's nothing you can do about it. Things would be easier if you would just sit still and take it."

"Please"

Her soft voice made Chevalier hesitate a bit.

"Emily, think of it this way. Each day you are getting stronger. Will you take the morphine willingly if I promise that when you wake up you can take a hot shower and get dressed? I'll even show you around the house."

Her breathing started to pick up, matching her racing heartbeat. "No, please don't."

Panic filled the air.

Chevalier made a split-second decision just to get it over with. Emily barely had time to fight back, and when it was over, she quickly fell into the darkness.

He headed out to the snowcat. He had to find something to quench this thirst, to help keep the beast at bay. He noted the time and only had about eight hours to get into the tiny town of Meeker, find a donor, willing or not, and get back before she started to stir again. He watched the dark house as the snowcat made its way into the night. His heart sank at the thought of leaving Emily alone, but he didn't see as though he had a choice.

The House

The voices were all around her in the dark forest. She couldn't make out what the whispers were saying, but they were growing louder as she ran, desperate to get away from them. Chevalier was ahead of her in the clearing, but she couldn't reach him. He beckoned to her with his hand. She could see his mouth moving, but he was too far away to hear what he was saying.

They were getting closer, closing in on her from all directions. She could finally make out what they were chanting, and the words brought a new horror to the dark. It wasn't her they wanted. It was Chevalier. She had to get to him, to warn him, but her feet were moving in slow motion.

She screamed for him, if he would just run…

"Emily," he said, sitting on the side of her bed.

She looked up at him, her breathing rapid. The realization that it was a dream wasn't sudden. It came through the fog of her mind.

"Emily, what's wrong?" he asked. His words hurried and concerned.

She couldn't answer him, couldn't pull her mind clear of the medicated slowness.

Chevalier reached down and pulled her into a cradle on his lap, then held her close as she shivered. "Tell me what's wrong."

She buried her head into his chest, trying to block out the voices from the dream.

He sighed heavily. "Was it a nightmare?"

She nodded, refusing to pull her face away from the comfort of his chest.

He gently ran his fingers through her hair. "It's okay. It's over now."

He held her for longer than he expected she would let him. At one point, he was able to shut his eyes and focus on her, her scent, her breathing, and her heartbeat. The sounds were comforting to him somehow. At long last, she sat up and looked around the room.

She smiled sheepishly. "Are you still going to let me take a shower?"

"Of course, my dear," he assured her. He helped her to her feet. The pain seemed to be markedly improved this morning, and she didn't turn pale or begin to black out.

"I have the bathroom ready for you. Anything you need should be in the cupboard, but if you are missing anything, just yell, and I will get it."

She nodded and followed him to the bathroom. The bathroom was larger than her bedroom on the ranch. Its soft peach colors were in contrast to the man beside her, who always wore black. The room was warm and well lit, comfortable. There was a large jetted garden tub in the center of the granite tile floor and a double shower in the corner. She watched as he walked out and shut the door. As she locked the door behind him, she thought she heard him chuckle.

He was still laughing to himself as he neared his study. He stepped inside and shut the door, glad that he had soundproofed that one room. The small silver cell phone was in his hand in an instant and moments later she answered.

"Warwick Consolidation," Storm answered.

Chevalier grinned. He always thought it was funny when she used the façade for his business number. "Storm, it's me."

"Oh, sir!" She sounded relieved. "I'm so glad you called. Everyone's trying to get a hold of you. There are news crews just off the island…"

He cut her off. "News crews?"

He could hear her sigh. "Yes, it's all been a big mess. Lord Ulrich tried for a few days to contact you when Emily went missing. When he couldn't get through to you, he had Sam point the finger at you for her disappearance. That led them here."

A low growl escaped him. "You can tell Ulrich that I will call him when I feel like it and not before. What have the news crews said?"

"Nothing out of the ordinary. No one here will talk to them, and they haven't found anything bad about the company," she assured him.

"Thank you, Storm. I'm very pleased to see everything was handled perfectly."

Her voice lightened with his compliment. "Are you coming back soon?"

"I'm not sure. Things are progressing slowly here, but I hope to move things along faster, as soon as she's healed."

"Sir, are you falling for her?" The concern in her voice was touching.

"No, Storm, this is all business." He hoped she couldn't hear the tension in his voice.

"I'm worried about you. She's dangerous."

"I do keep that in mind, I assure you."

The long pause was awkward. "I know you do, sir."

"I need a favor."

"Anything, sir."

"I need to get a check on the Russo ranch. See if Sam and Keith are keeping up with things. If they are falling behind, I want their bills anonymously paid and send over help, someone who knows about animals and offers to work for room and board."

She knew better than to question him again. "Yes, sir. I think Kyle used to work on a farm. I'll send him over."

"Make sure he watches out for Sam. Sam is Ulrich's familiar."

"Yes, sir, I'll make sure he knows."

"I'll call and check in on things later."

"Are you sure we can't send someone else to help you?" It was obvious she was offering.

"No, stay there. I need you on guard, Storm. I can trust you more than the others and right now, trust is what we need." He shut the phone and listened. The sound of the shower had just turned off.

He left his office and moved silently into the bedroom. When she emerged from the bathroom, he was sitting on the bed waiting for her.

"Feel better?" he asked again, appreciating her beauty.

"Much, thank you." She was toweling her hair dry and sat gently in the chair by the fire. "Thank you for the clothes too, though I've never been big on dresses."

He grinned. He knew that when he'd purchased the light-blue cotton dress. "I took the liberty of buying you a wardrobe for while you are here."

She looked over at him. "All dresses?"

He laughed. "No, not all dresses."

She quickly braided her hair and stood up, her muscles still sore. "You also promised me a tour of the house."

"That I did," he said, standing and taking her hand in his. He felt her start to pull away, but held her hand tighter.

They walked through the house slowly. He watched her out of the corner of his eye, the way the feminine dress brushed against the contours of her body as she walked. She asked lots of questions and insisted on seeing inside all 45 bedrooms and antechambers. She seemed frustrated when he wouldn't show her the inside of his office but marveled at the vast library with its tall columns of books.

They stopped in the kitchen for lunch, and he watched her again as she made herself a sandwich. She caught him watching her, and she blushed before turning away to finish.

"This seems like quite a large home for one person," she noted, sitting down with her plate.

"It's been full before. It's not always just me." Emily noticed that when he spoke to her, his voice was like silk, calm and soothing.

He could see her thinking through that. "Your coven?"

He nodded.

"And do you often bring hostages here?" She didn't look up as she ate.

Chevalier grinned. "I've told you, you aren't a hostage."

She simply shrugged.

He frowned slightly. "What was your nightmare about?"

Her body tensed slightly, but she didn't answer.

"It's okay, I guess it's really none of my business. It's just that you were screaming my name."

The blush rose again to her cheeks, and Chevalier found he liked that. "I don't remember it now."

He knew she was lying, but decided not to force it.

After eating, she cleaned up quickly, and they began to return to her room. She stopped to look at a large mirror, though he noticed that she avoided her reflection. It was the antique frame she was looking at, "How old is this?"

"Early 17th century."

"There's something odd about it, like it's not fit properly." Her fingers traced the edge of the mirror.

He took her hand and pulled her away from the mirror, realizing that at times she was too observant for her own good. "It's just an old mirror. Do you realize that you never look at yourself in the mirror?"

"I hadn't noticed."

He had a sudden idea and pulled her to face him. He looked down at her, his eyes locking hers. "You are very beautiful."

She blushed and looked down at the floor, trying to pull away from him.

Some of her actions began to make sense. "You should be told that, and often. I would imagine Keith knows it, even if he doesn't say it."

"Keith sees me for what I am." She again tried to pull away as her eyes fixed on the floor, and a bright blush flushed her cheeks.

"Oh? And what is that exactly?"

"Please let me go," she asked softly.

"No, I want to know what he's told you… what he's said about you."

Her body tensed, yet she didn't speak or look up. Her free arm wrapped around her, as if to hide. She suddenly felt very self-conscious in the light dress.

"I need to lay down," she told him. He knew it was a lie, but granted her the out.

Chevalier guided her through the corridors silently, a tense air around them. He purposely took the long way around, hoping to confuse the location of the mirror. She seemed relieved to be in the familiar room again, the fire blazing warmth into it.

Emily slipped into the bathroom to put on her nightgown, and when she came back out, Chevalier was gone. She watched the snow swirling outside of the window and eventually fell asleep.

***

Chevalier sat in his study, hours upon hours he thought about the fragile killer he currently housed. Maybe Ulrich was right. Maybe she wasn't strong enough to know what she was capable of doing. He guessed, though, that many hadn't given her a chance to show her inner strength. He knew it was time for harsh realization, for her to know what she could do and had done in the past. His inner turmoil was raging. Somewhere amid debating between running away with her to a remote island or throwing her into the middle of an extremely dangerous heku battle, he walked quietly into her room and watched her sleep.

How could anyone not find her astonishingly beautiful? He thought, looking down at how her long lashes framed her eyes, how her lips were soft and almost pouty. Delicate wisps of her red hair had escaped the braid and were lying lightly against her face. He suddenly understood how someone could miss that, how someone could convince her that she was anything less than exquisitely beautiful.

Control

It wasn't enough for Keith to physically control her. He had to also be emotionally controlling. She was obviously still terrified of him, afraid to get close to anyone else for fear of retribution. He found it hard to blame Emily for allowing that to happen. It seemed as if his own kind drove her to find protection from anyone who would give it. There was hope. He would soon tell her that she could easily defend herself. Maybe then, the strong hold that Keith had over her would break.

Then, she would face any mortal's worst fear, to be thrown into the very center of a violent heku war that could last centuries, longer than she had as a mortal. He had a pang of guilt for what his true purpose was, training a new weapon. He was fooling himself if he didn't see the bond forming between them, though. The training wouldn't all be fighting and tactics. He enjoyed being with her and especially the time they were alone together.

For now, he had a task to do before she woke up. He stole away as quietly as he could and shut the door behind him, locking it from the outside. He couldn't have her out wandering the mansion while he was occupied. He smoothly navigated the labyrinthine corridors and stopped at the mirror Emily had inspected. He placed his hands on it and pushed hard, sliding it back along hidden tracks, then disappeared behind it, and the mirror moved back into place.

Chevalier took the steps down 3 at a time until his feet landed in the pitch-dark room. The dirt floor and musty smell were familiar to him. He didn't need lights for this, in fact, it would be easier if the darkness were around him, a more natural setting. He grabbed the small drawstring bag from the table and opened it, dumping a pile of ash onto it.

He then drew an intricate dagger from his pocket and pricked his finger, allowing a single drop of blood to fall onto the ash. Instantly, he assumed a defensive posture, ready to attack at the slightest sign of a problem. The ash quivered and began to form.

A hiss escaped his lips as the form took shape into a tall heku. He appeared slender and young, afraid of his surroundings, obviously not entirely aware of what happened to him.

"Where am I?" he growled. Turning toward Chevalier, he matched his crouched posture.

"You will address me as sir, or you will return to ash," Chevalier demanded through clenched teeth.

"I will not address you as sir until I know who you are and what your intentions are." His voice was high-pitched and ground on Chevalier's nerves.

With a sudden movement, Chevalier was perched at his back, his hands around the man's neck. "So you say you are ready to return to dust?"

The man's eyes filled with terror. He suddenly understood that he was in the presence of one of the Old Ones. "There was a misunderstanding, sir. I am but a humble servant to you."

Chevalier grinned, his teeth ominous as he returned to his place and faced the new heku. "You attacked a young woman…"

"Yes, sir, the red head. She smelled so delicious." Chevalier could sense the heku re-tasting Emily's blood.

The growl came from deep within his chest, "Who gave you permission to break one of the rules?"

The young heku stammered, "N... N... No one did. I just couldn't stop. She, she was standing so close to me. The breeze caught her hair, and the aroma filled the air."

Chevalier had him. "What is your name?"

"Steven"

"When were you turned?"

"1958... sir."

"Ahhh, a young one. Well, you are going to help me, Steven." Chevalier pointed at a cage in the corner of the room. "Do step in."

Steven knew he couldn't fight back, couldn't resist the strength of one of the Old Ones. He stepped into the cage and immediately sat on the cot. "Are you going to turn me in to the Elders?"

"No, but I do think you'll later wish I had." Chevalier locked the cage's door. He remembered when he had the cage installed, the technology and craftsmanship that went into a cage strong enough to hold a heku indefinitely had just barely been found.

"What exactly will I be helping you with?" he asked timidly.

"You'll see, and I expect full compliance. You do what I say, when I say it. You will not so much as breathe without an order from me, is that understood?" Chevalier watched his reaction and was pleased at the compliance.

"Yes, sir."

"Then I'm off. Please do try to be quiet. No one can hear you scream from down here anyway... well... no one but me," he chuckled, and ascended the stairs, leaving the young heku alone in the dark.

He heard the loud knocks from halfway across the house and hurried his steps, sure she would be furious with him, something he didn't find all together unpleasant. As he drew closer, he could hear her yelling, "Open this door immediately, Chevalier! You said I wasn't a hostage!"

He unlocked the door and she fell forward, as if she'd been pushing on it. He caught her gently and righted her to standing. He knew it was coming, but failed to react out of compassion for her feelings. Her right hand slapped hard against his face. While it didn't cause him any pain, he still brought his hand up to cradle his cheek, hoping it would help her feel as if she had accomplished something.

"You will never lock me anywhere again, is that understood?" She was furious. Her eyes burned with rage.

Chevalier fought back a smile as she issued almost the exact same warning he just used on the young heku downstairs. "I understand, and I do apologize, but I won't agree to those terms."

His words infuriated her, and her eyes darted across his face. "What?"

"I do what is best for you... and if I feel it would not behoove you to walk aimlessly around my home, then I will do what I see fit, even if it involves locking you in a room." The matter-of-fact way he stated it made her blush return, and her eyes began to fill with tears.

"Please, Emily, don't cry."

"I'm not crying. I'm mad!" she screamed, and wiped a rogue tear off of her cheek.

"Just calm down, you'll be happy. I came to tell you why we are here."

Even with her anger, the curiosity calmed her. "You are?"

"Yes, come sit down, we'll talk." He motioned her back into the room.

He pulled two chairs to the fireplace and grabbed a blanket from a high shelf in the closet. She sat down and curled up with the blanket, her hands around her knees, watching him. "Go ahead."

He watched her face, not quite sure exactly how to start this. "Heku have plagued you your entire life."

"Yes I know, seems they still do." The anger in her voice was evident.

"Please, Emily, it's very important that you stay calm and not get angry."

"Too late, keep going."

He sighed, "When you ran to tell Keith or Sam that you were attacked, what do you remember happening immediately after you told them?"

"I'm not sure what you're getting at," she said, and sounded like she was genuinely trying to understand.

"You were mad?"

"Of course."

"Did you faint? Lose track of time? Black out for a moment?"

She frowned. "No, why are you asking me that?"

He braced himself, ready to stop her the instant her face showed signs of distress. "What if I told you that Sam and Keith have never killed a heku before? What if I told you... they aren't even remotely capable of doing so?"

"Then I'd ask you where they all went. It's not like they all just decided to take a hike."

He answered calmly and slowly, "It was you, Emily."

"What was me?" She pursed her lips into a thin line.

"That got rid of the heku. You did it. It wasn't Sam, and it wasn't Keith." He leaned toward her a bit.

She smiled a crooked, unsure smile. "I thought you'd be serious."

"I am serious, and it's very important that you understand and believe me." He tried to lock her gaze, but she turned to watch the fire.

"I'm not strong enough to kill them," she whispered.

"I think you are stronger than you even know."

"Keith kills them." She was trying to persuade herself.

"You do it, Emily. It's a natural, built-in self-defense mechanism passed down through the women in your family."

"You're fast. You're strong… I can't fight that. I'm lucky if I can open my own pop bottle." She was smiling now. Chevalier noticed it wasn't going as smoothly as he'd hoped. She was in denial.

"When you get mad… no, furious… with a heku that has tasted your blood, you are able to reduce them to ash in a matter of seconds. Take it from me, it's fast and extremely painful."

"I tried to do this to you?"

"Yes"

"Then why aren't you dead?" She raised her eyebrows.

"You were… interrupted."

She turned to face him fully. "Chevalier, this is stupid. I don't know why you are saying this, but it's insane, and it's a waste of my time."

"What do you want me to do to prove it to you? You have no idea how important it is for you to learn how to control this. There's a coal shed full of ashes that proves how important it is that you learn to control it."

Something in her posture changed. "Coal shed?"

He leaned closer to her. "Sam and Keith dumped all of the ashes into the coal shed, ashes from heku that you killed. There were…" His words trailed off.

Emily sat rigid in the chair. Her eyes darted quickly back and forth on the floor in front of her. He could tell by her expression that she was remembering events, a lot of them. He decided to let the memories run their course, hopefully bringing proof of what he was trying to tell her.

"Get out," she whispered, still watching the floor.

"Emily"

"I said to get out."

He watched her for a moment, and indecision crept into him. He hated to leave her, just as she was about to realize her abilities made her a murderer. He could lessen the pain if she would let him, yet he understood her need to be alone, to suffer with her thoughts without an audience.

Chevalier reached out and touched her hand lightly. "Emily."

She jerked her hand away, as if stung. "Don't touch me. Just get out."

He nodded slightly and left the room, too fast for her to see him move. He shut the door softly behind him and sat across the hallway from the door, watching it. A few minutes after he sat down, he heard the light click of the door lock. This action was no longer amusing to him.

Darkness fell on the house, and he heard no sounds coming from inside the room. He left the hallway long enough to make a plate of food. Chevalier knocked softly on the door. "Emily, please eat. I'll put it outside of your door, and I'll leave."

He sat back down in the chair to watch her door, knowing he'd have time to disappear if she decided to open it, but he knew she wouldn't.

Time passed slowly as nightfall ended, and the house was again flooded with daylight. There was still no sound from Emily. Chevalier wondered if he should go check on her. He'd never let a simple lock on a door keep him out of anywhere, yet there was an implied desire for privacy when they were used. He decided to wait it out. If he'd not heard from her by twilight, he would be forced to break her secure isolation.

He made a fresh plate of food, watching as the sun set behind the Rocky Mountains. It was time to intervene.

"Emily, I'm coming in." He waited to see if she would respond. When he heard nothing from inside, he pushed against the door, easily breaking it free of the door jam. The sound of cracking wood echoed through the silent house.

He froze as he surveyed the room. It looked empty. He walked quickly toward the bathroom door but finally saw her as he moved past the bed. She was in the corner of the room on the floor, curled up into a ball. Her arms were wrapped tightly around her knees, and her face was buried between her arms. Chevalier watched her. She was so still that he had to move closer to even see her breathe.

He crouched down beside her. "Emily?"

She didn't respond.

He reached out and touched her softly on the arm. She gasped slightly and pulled her cold arm away from him.

He softened his voice, "Emily?"

She inhaled deeply and when she spoke, her voice was strained and tense, "What do you want?"

"To help." It was all he could think of to say.

"It sounds to me like you should stay away from me," she said with disgust.

"I'm safe with you."

She risked a glance over at him. Her eyes were red and swollen. "How do you figure?"

He half-smiled. "You only attack those who have recently drank your blood, I think… although that's only a theory."

She turned her face back into her arms. "Why me?"

Chevalier touched her foot and noticed that it was ice cold. He figured she'd sat under the window all night, far from the warmth of the fire. "Come sit by the fire, and I'll tell you."

She didn't move. "Tell me here."

"You are freezing, and you've got to be hurting. I don't want to pick you up and move you, but I will if you don't get up." His voice was still silky, smooth and calming.

"Don't touch me," she hissed at him.

"Fine." He stood up to grab a blanket and then wrapped it around her. "We'll sit here."

For the next hour, Chevalier went over the Winchester family, the heku slayings, and the story of her history up until her Mother. He wasn't ready to tell Emily about how her mother died or how she was the product of a vile heku attack on her. He could tell by the tensing in her muscles that she was taking the story as truth and hating herself more and more for it.

He sighed, "Tell me what you're thinking, please."

Emily didn't move.

Chevalier leaned back against the wall to wait. He was amazed at her resolve. He knew it was hard for mortals to stay still for too long, yet she wasn't moving at all. His mind played against several options. He could forcibly move her closer to the fire. He could leave and let her be, or he could sit and wait it out. By dawn, he felt his age-old patience waning. Watching her all night, unmoving, was painful for him.

"Enough, Emily, I'm moving you," he said, then stood and picked her up from the floor before she could protest. She was tense and silent as he carried her to the bed. When he sat her down, she curled up on her side away from him. He covered her with the down blanket and went over to stoke the fire.

"I know what you're thinking," he said, and turned to look at her as her face disappeared into the pillow. "You aren't an evil killer."

Her body shook under the covers.

"There are rules you know, heku rules. These rules govern our actions and are punishable by death." He watched, but when she had no reaction he continued, "One of the rules, the one I consider most important, is in reference to not feeding without approval. It's a fierce yet intimate betrayal to do so. Having never given approval to a heku, it is then within your right to fight back. It's not your fault if your fighting back is lethal."

She flinched at his words.

"I wanted to stress to you though… technically, you didn't kill any of them. Becoming ash isn't an end to a heku's life. It's merely a temporary stasis away from the normal."

She sat upright and looked at him. "They aren't dead?"

He forced a soft smile. "Technically, no."

"Technically?"

"Some consider us dead already, though I find that insulting. What you do to them is force them into a state of consciousness that transcends the body. It's good for them, lets them think about what they've done, and maybe allows them to re-evaluate the course they've chosen."

"Technically…"

"What you did was self-defense, period. I personally think they were asking for it."

"You included?"

He grimaced at her words. "That was… well… unfortunate, and I apologize. You have such sweet blood…" He inhaled deeply. The very memory of the taste made the thirst fight to surface. "It's hard to resist."

Her hand covered her neck instinctively. "You haven't told me why this is so important to you. Why the secluded location… the secrecy, why am I even here?"

He chose his words carefully. "I want to help you control it."

She sounded weak, "Can it be controlled?"

"I don't know," he told her honestly.

"You're in danger around me. Why are you doing it?"

In an instant, he was sitting on the bed at her side. "Because I care about you."

"Do you care enough about me to take me back to the ranch and leave?" She turned toward him hopefully.

"I'm not going to abandon you. I'm not going to let the attacks continue. Eventually, someone may notice and decide you are a risk."

"Someone?" She was sitting up now, focused on his words.

"You do understand that you pose certain risks to the heku community as a whole. Some may not take that lightly. If I can show you how to control it, you will no longer be a threat." He locked her gaze, trying to calm the situation.

"And if I can't control it?" she asked before looking away.

"We'll handle that when we come to it."

"How are you going to help me then? What if I turn on you?" She shied away from him.

He smiled. "I won't feed from you, Emily, and then I won't pose a risk. However, you are right. We need someone for you to focus your attention on."

She stiffened. "We aren't alone in this house then are we?"

He shook his head. "No, we no longer are."

"Who is it?"

He watched her closely for a reaction. "I brought him back. It's something a few of us can do. He's one that you... well..."

"One that I... ashed?"

He nodded, trying not to smile at her terminology.

"I'm hoping that your blood is still running through him. It would give you the opportunity to train your abilities without him having to re-feed."

She frowned. "I don't even know where to start."

"I think we start by introducing you."

She gave him a crooked half-smile. "You make it sound like a date."

"Promise me you'll wait here. Don't go wandering off. I'll go and get him."

"Now!?" She started to get out of bed.

"It's okay... I can control him. You won't be in any danger." He gently wrapped his arm around her waist, keeping her from leaving. "Sit, please."

Her fists clenched.

"Promise me you'll wait here."

She nodded, the tendons in her neck standing out. She looked around the room after he disappeared, and things seemed surreal. Her mind was awhirl with images of her attackers. She found it hard to breathe, and her heart threatened to stop in her chest. She jumped when she heard them behind her. It had been too fast, and she had expected to have some time alone.

"Steven, this is Emily."

Emily turned slowly to face them. Chevalier was in a defensive crouch. He placed himself between Emily and Steven and was watching Steven carefully, his back to her.

Steven reeled. He recognized the girl and inhaled deeply, salivating at her aroma. He crouched down slightly, his eyes focused on her neck.

The deep growl from Chevalier stopped him, and he stood up straight again, his eyes still watching her intently.

"It's nice to meet you, Emily," he said politely, but his tone was tense and strained. He licked his lips slowly.

She swallowed hard and took a step back.

"Here's what we're going to do," Chevalier said, still watching Steven. "Focus on him, Emily. See if you can find the anger you once had for him."

She looked over at Steven, but her eyes averted his. She began to sweat slightly, fear building up inside of her.

"Emily, breathe," Chevalier reminded her.

She didn't realize she'd been holding her breath. Steadying herself on the bedside table, she looked up at Steven again. She studied his face, his harsh eyes, and the look of hunger on his face.

Chevalier's muscles tightened, and he sprang just as Steven jumped at Emily. Steven's teeth were bared, and a growl erupted from his chest. The blur of their fighting was intermingled with gasps and the crack of bones. Emily ran to the bathroom and locked the door, cowering in the corner. Chevalier wrapped his arms around the young heku's chest and restrained him. With one quick movement, he grabbed Steven's head and wrenched it around, breaking his neck. The injured heku fell to the ground, and his body quickly began to heal, but it gave Chevalier a moment to regain control.

Chevalier looked down at him, enraged by the attack. "You have no idea who you are dealing with, and I won't tell this to you again... never even think about touching her!"

Steven managed to sit up, his neck still at an odd angle. "She smells so good."

Steven inhaled deeply, savoring the aroma of the room.

Chevalier's foot connected with his jaw, shattering it and dropping him back to the floor. "Do it again. I dare you."

"How do you do it?" he asked, his jaw healing quickly. "How can you be around her with the smell of her blood so near to you?"

Chevalier knelt beside him. "Control, boy... something you better have soon."

Steven's eyes grew wider. He clutched his chest and screamed an inhumane, guttural scream. His body writhed in agony on the floor as he fought to stop the torment. Chevalier ran full force into the bathroom door, sending it into splinters on the floor. Emily was curled up in the corner. Her eyes were glazed over and unmoving. He reached out and touched her face.

"Emily, enough." His tone was forceful.

She jumped at his voice, her eyes coming to rest on his. She was shivering. Fear had taken over her body.

The screams from the bedroom stopped suddenly.

He whispered softly, "It's okay, Em... everything's fine."

"It was so quiet... I thought... he..."

"Emily"

"I thought he'd killed you," she said, her eyes filling with tears.

Chevalier smiled. "Not a chance. You did well, child. I'm very proud of you."

She looked up at him, confused.

"Stay here. I'll go take care of Steven." He stood up, but didn't walk away when he felt her hand close around his ankle.

"Please don't go."

"I won't be long. It's okay. He'll be too out of it to resist me." He gently pulled away from her grasp.

Emily watched the door, waiting for Steven to come for her. Her head began to throb with the tension. It was taking too long. A noise in the adjacent bedroom made her heart skip a beat, and she readied herself for an attack. When Chevalier stepped through the doorway, she buried her face in her hands and fought back the tears.

He sat down on the floor beside her and watched her for a moment. "You did very well."

"I didn't do anything but hide in here." Her words were mumbled beneath her hands.

He smiled. "No, Emily. You fought back... you did just what we were waiting for."

She risked a glance up at him. "I didn't do anything."

He sighed, wondering how she could control something she has no memory of doing.

Control

Things progressed slowly. Emily didn't seem to be able to control any of her abilities and hadn't been able to use it on Steven since the first day. Hours turned into days and those blurred into weeks. Chevalier called a halt to it all, ordering a day of rest for everyone. The tension in the house had grown immeasurable, and tempers were beginning to flare.

It irritated Chevalier how much Steven longed for Emily's blood, how he looked at her and wanted to touch her. It wasn't long before Steven began to repress the feelings, hiding them from the Old One and Emily. It wasn't helping things that Chevalier hadn't quenched his thirst in almost four weeks. He found himself watching Emily's neck closely, his throat burning with every throb.

Chevalier had ulterior motives for calling a day off. He needed to head back down to civilization to calm his thirst. With Steven locked in his cage and Emily lounging in the library, he took his leave and flashed to the snowcat. Watching the home disappear into the trees, he had a sudden pang of guilt. For the first time, he thought he may be fighting a losing battle, putting both Steven and Emily through unnecessary torment.

He knew Ulrich would have heku searching for them all over the world. It wouldn't be long before one of them located this home. He could take care of a handful of them at a time, but eventually, Ulrich would come and bring his minions with him. He would take Emily away. Chevalier had no doubt that after that, he wouldn't ever see her again, no matter how hard he tried and how much he searched.

He pulled his car into the small town buried deep in the mountain and counted himself lucky. A suburban full of California tourists were wandering around, taking pictures and looking around the ground for colorful rocks. One older woman wandered away from the rest. She was headed directly for the nearby group of trees with her camera dangling around her wrist. Chevalier waited for her and satiated himself within just a few minutes. He gazed into her eyes and whispered a story about mosquitoes and bees. She headed back to her group, grasping her wrist, unsure of what just happened to her.

He'd been gone for just over four hours when he pulled the snowcat back into the mansion's garage. He listened to the quietness of the house but couldn't hear any footsteps and thought that she was still immersed in the book, curled up on the over-stuffed couch in the library. He could hear Steven in the dirt room, calling out, complaining about his thirst.

Chevalier stepped into the library, but it was empty. He inhaled deeply, but her scent was faint in the room. She'd been gone for some time. The nearer he got to the bedroom, the stronger her aroma became. It seemed to be oddly more potent than usual, as if intensified. The cause became clear as he approached the room and could feel the mugginess in the air and hear the jets from the tub.

He hesitated for a moment. Part of him desired to turn away and give her privacy. Another part of him longed to see her and to move closer to the scent of her blood. The latter won and he stepped quietly into the bathroom.

Emily was lying in the jetted tub. Bubbles cascaded over the side, smelling of fresh strawberries. Her eyes were closed, and her breathing was deep and rhythmic. She had fallen asleep. A book lie open on the side of the tub, and he glanced at it quickly. She was reading Anna Karenina. He saw the irony and smiled.

As he sat quietly on the edge of the tub, he remembered the similarities from the first time he'd seen her. He watched her, the bubbles moving gently with the jets, leaving small windows into the water. First, a fleeting glimpse of her milky thighs, then a flash of her soft breasts, rising and falling with her breath. He was hypnotized with the images, the all too brief look he caught before the bubbles shrouded it. His eyes lingered long after the offending bubbles obscured his view of the tight contours of her lower abdomen.

His trance broke as she jerked awake. "Chevalier!" she gasped, grabbing a towel from beside the tub and pulling it into the water.

He smiled as the blush rose quickly to her cheeks. "Yes?"

She had to fight the towel to cover herself. The jets made it almost impossible to keep the towel where she wanted it. "Get out!"

He stood and watched her struggle. "Why should I, when the view's much better in here?"

That left her speechless and she stood, deciding the towel would cover more of her if she were out from the jets. She carefully kept the towel pressed to the front of her, but grimaced when she noticed his eyes travel up her firm thighs to her exposed waist, following up her delicate curves to her neck and came to rest on her eyes. Her face burned with embarrassment, the blush deepening.

"You really shouldn't sneak up on people," she said, trying to figure out how to get out of the deep tub without exposing more.

Chevalier grinned, enjoying her predicament. "It wasn't hard. You were asleep."

"Turn around. I need to get out."

"No"

"What?" She began to fidget.

"I said no." His grin widened.

"Wh... what... why not?"

He moved closer to her. "Why don't I join you in there?" He began to unbutton his shirt, exposing his chiseled chest.

"No!" she yelled, placing one hand against his chest to push him away from her. The feel of her hands on him sent a shock through his body. She briefly let her hand linger on his chest, but then sharply drew it back.

Before she could protest again, he had his pants off and was stepping into the bubbly water. She caught a quick glance of his perfect form and turned her eyes away, embarrassed.

"What are you doing?" she asked him hurriedly, still avoiding looking at him.

"I told you. I'm taking a bath." He reached out and ran his hand gently down her leg, enjoying the goose bumps that rose at his touch. "Sit down."

"I... um... I think I'm done actually. Wh... why don't you just en... enjoy yourself, and I'll well leave you erm... alone." She stared at the wall, using all of her power not to look down at his flawless body.

"Suit yourself," he said as his fingertips lightly tracing an invisible line up her hip. Her skin was soft beneath his touch.

Emily clutched the towel tighter to her as her entire body tensed. A panicked sound escaped her lips, fear taking over, "Please," she whispered. "Don't look at me." In an instant, she was out of the tub and ran through the door, slamming it behind her.

Chevalier sighed and picked up the book, reading aloud the first line he saw. "*He could not be mistaken. There were no other eyes like those in the world. There was only one creature in the world who could concentrate for him all the brightness and meaning of life.*"

He smiled, relaxed into the jets, and shut his eyes.

***

The room was empty when he emerged, fully dressed and ready to face the consequences of his actions. Some things, he reasoned, were worth it. He couldn't help but grin as he followed her scent into the hallway.

She wasn't hard to find. The hot water intensified the sweet aroma only she possessed. He stood in the doorway of the kitchen, watching as she searched the cupboards for something. She seemed to have spotted what she wanted, high up on the top shelf, and before Chevalier could understand what she was doing, she hoisted herself onto the high counter and was on her tiptoes, reaching for the elusive item.

She let out a small scream and fell backwards as he touched her waist to steady her. His quick reflexes caught her mid-fall, and he cradled her close to his body.

"Don't do that!" she yelled, hitting him on the chest.

"I'll stop doing that, when you stop trying to kill yourself." He hesitated and then placed her gently on the floor.

She moved away from him, a small bottle in her hand. She added the contents to a boiling pot on the stove and turned the burner down before turning to him. "It's not safe to sneak up on people, Chev."

He ran through her words in his head. No one had ever called him Chev. "Hmm, well, would you like me to put bells on?"

"That would be helpful, yes." She turned back to the boiling pot and began to stir.

He moved closer to her and pressed his body against her back. Chevalier gently pulled her hair away from her face before wrapping his arms around her waist. "What are you making?"

She didn't answer but leaned her head back against his shoulder. He looked down at her and noticed her eyes were shut. She was still warm from the bath, and her scent filled his senses as he pressed his lips against her hair.

This time he was ready for it when she tensed, and he didn't release her. She raised her head and grabbed the spoon, stirring again.

"Why do you do that?" he asked.

"Do what?"

"Pull away from me. It's quite aggravating." He spoke into her ear softly.

"I don't know what you mean." He let go of her as she turned to find a bowl.

"Of course you don't," he mused.

Emily filled the bowl with steamy stew and sat at the counter to eat. He watched her and noticed she blushed more as time went on as she obviously was aware of his gaze.

"Why do you do that?" she asked, not looking up.

"Do what?"

"Watch me." This time she raised her piercing green gaze at him accusingly.

He grinned. "I like what I see."

She frowned and continued to eat in silence. Once the kitchen was clean, she headed out to the spacious living room where white couches were positioned in front of massive windows that overlooked the majestic Rocky Mountains. She sat in the middle of the couch, pulled a blanket over her, and stared out the window, drawing her knees up to her chest.

Chevalier stood behind the couch. "I'll not stop."

"Stop what?" Her eyes didn't move from the snow-covered trees.

"Watching you and appreciating what I see."

She sighed, "Maybe if you watch long enough, you'll find something else."

"I doubt it."

"Maybe if you watch long enough, you'll see the truth," she whispered, soft enough he had to strain to hear.

He moved to her side and took her hand in spite of her protests. They sat in silence, watching as the sun crept behind the Rockies and disappeared, leaving the snow to glimmer in the moonlight. She fell asleep shortly after dusk, so he picked her up carefully and cradled her in his arms, knowing she wouldn't let him do that if she were awake. He wanted to reach into her mind and remove the doubt, the self-loathing, anything planted there to control her. He concentrated on the rhythmic sound of her breathing, to stop the anger that encompassed him whenever he saw what Keith had done to her.

A sudden thought occurred to him. As vile as it seemed, he wondered if that was the key to her abilities. Maybe he was wrong, maybe it wasn't heku blood that allowed her to turn heku to ash, maybe all she needed was motive. If her greatest fear was intimacy, maybe that's what he needed, forced intimacy. His conscience screamed at him. It was wrong and abhorrent, but the possibilities were endless.

He swiftly laid her down on the bed and covered her with the down quilt and then headed down to get Steven. The darkness was again comforting to him. Steven glared out at him from the small cage. Chevalier would normally reprimand him for such behavior, but tonight, he needed Steven to concentrate on only one thing.

He opened the door. "Get out. I have something for you to do."

Steven stepped cautiously out of the cage and dropped to his knees before Chevalier. "What is it, master?"

Chevalier fought back the disgust for what he was doing. He struggled to remember it was ultimately for her own good. "Tonight... tonight I let you touch Emily."

Steven's eyes brightened. "Thank you, master, thank you."

Chevalier glared down at his young slave. "You will do exactly as I say, nothing more, nothing less. There will be no improvising and no, I repeat no… biting."

Steven's face fell. "No biting?"

"None"

"Then, sir, what will I do?"

Again Chevalier repressed the feelings of revulsion he felt for his actions. He took a deep breath and began, "Your goal is to… get close to her. Try to kiss her, even if she fights, caress her skin, and…" He paused, he couldn't say it.

"And what, sir? Am I to try to…" He hesitated, remembering how protective Chevalier was of this girl.

"Yes"

Steven seemed unsure, his brow furrowed. "Anything you say, sir." He remained on his knees.

"You will stop when I say though, no hesitation," he hissed through his teeth.

Chevalier rocked back on his heels. The fierce personal loathing wasn't entirely concealed behind his mask of control. "Do it now." He shut his eyes against the image of what was coming.

Steven stood up and headed to the door, too fast, too excited, and it infuriated him. If tonight didn't work, Chevalier decided to rid himself of this loathsome creature by his own hand. He followed behind Steven.

They both stopped outside of her door. Her breathing was deep and relaxed. She was still asleep. Steven glanced once at Chevalier, who nodded, and then he stepped inside. He watched her for a moment as his tongue ran around his lips at the prospect of what he was going to do to this frail, beautiful creature.

His eyes were on Chevalier in the doorway as he carefully knelt beside the bed and slipped his hand beneath the covers. Chevalier fought to control the beast aching to tear the young heku's limbs from his body.

Emily stirred a bit as the foreign hand gently reached her side and began to find its way higher. Steven's eyes left Chevalier and looked down at Emily's peaceful face as his hand caressed her breast. It had been years since he'd last felt the softness of a woman.

Her eyes opened in a panic, and she thrust forward to sit up, but Steven's other hand was against her neck, restraining her to the bed. His hand began to creep down her chest, circling her navel lightly and slipping down past her panty line.

Her face filled with intense rage, fury beyond what Chevalier thought her capable of. With eyes focused securely on Steven, he jerked back suddenly and fell to the ground, writhing in immeasurable pain. His screams permeated the entire house as she scooted to look over the edge of the bed at him. As her eyes met his, the screams grew in intensity until there was nothing but silence. She breathed quickly and knelt on the bed, staring down at the pile of ash on the floor.

Chevalier seemingly appeared instantaneously beside the pile of ash with a large smile on his face. "You did it, Emily!"

Her eyes were wide. "He was… he…"

Chevalier nodded. "Yes."

She turned an icy glare at him "You knew??"

"I wouldn't have let him get far. I promise… I needed you to feel true anger." His voice was soft.

"You let him do that?" she snapped at him.

"I was in full control."

She glared at him and pulled the covers over to cover herself.

"Forgive me, Emily. I promise you, he wouldn't have gotten any further." His eyes were soft and caring.

Her face was a mixture of horror and relief. "I felt that…"

He looked over at her. "Can you do it again?"

"Are you offering?" She was so pleased with herself that teasing came naturally.

He grabbed her off the bed and pulled her into a tight hug. "We can go now, Emily. We can go back."

She wrapped her arms tightly around him. "I get to go back to the ranch!"

He pulled her back so he could look into her eyes. "Not the ranch, my home, my coven."

The ecstatic expression on her face disappeared. "What do you mean your coven?"

He set her down and looked at her. "My world is where you belong."

"No, I belong on the ranch." She set her jaw and watched him.

"It's not safe to..."

She cut him off, "I can apparently protect myself. Isn't that what this entire thing has been about? Controlling the ability to ash one of you?"

He nodded but shrugged. "Yes… mainly, but you can't live in your world. Things get too dangerous. You belong in my world, with my people."

"That's it then, isn't it? Just another ploy to get me into a coven. You are just like the others."

"It's not like that, Em."

"It's not? Then have you not been planning on me joining your adoring minions since the start? You didn't want me to ash your followers… that wouldn't look good, so first you had to teach me to control it." The angrier she became, the faster she spoke.

"I care about you. I want you with me."

"Oh right, me and how many others, Chev? Tell me how many of your followers you've wooed into bed."

He cringed at how clearly she saw some things. "You are different."

"Yes I am. I can kill you. That pretty much makes me different. I won't go and watch you flaunt me around your coven. I won't go and watch you as thousands of female heku hang on your every word, swooning over you." She mimicked a love-struck teenager, "Ooooh, Chevalier, how big and strong you are. What sharp teeth you have."

His eyes grew darker. "Watch what you say, Emily."

"I won't watch what I say. You've had this coming for a long time!" She squared her shoulders off to him, showing no fear.

"My coven is my family. We protect one another and watch out for one another. There's no way you could understand the complex nature of it," he said as his eyes narrowed.

"That sounds amazingly similar to the Manson Family. Do mass orgies entertain your days, or do you prefer to fuck each individually?" she asked as he took a step toward her, his fight for control losing out to his temper. "Is that what you were doing? Trying to get me into bed for some initiation?"

"Emily," he hissed her name.

"Don't Emily me! What makes you more mad, the fact that I know what's going on, or the fact that you didn't get me into bed before you lost your shot?"

The control was over. He slammed into her, pinning her against the wall with his hand on her throat, and her feet no longer touched the floor. "You will watch your tongue around me and show nothing but respect for my coven, do you understand me?" His voice had changed, it was hoarse and guttural.

She grasped at his hand around her throat, clawing with her nails, trying to loosen his grip.

Sudden awareness hit him like the weight of a thousand bricks. He removed his hand from her neck and she dropped to the floor on her knees, gasping for breath. He was out the door in an instant, locking it securely from the outside. She heard a large crash as he threw a heavy object against the wall and screamed in anger.

After a few minutes, Emily pulled herself up from the floor and stumbled to the bathroom. She peered into the mirror, studying her neck. There were bruises forming, outlines of his fingers. She turned around and sank onto the floor. Sobs escaped her as her body shook.

Fight

Just before dawn, she heard the front door unlock, but she didn't move from her position on the bathroom floor. She could see Chevalier in the bedroom, frantically throwing things from the dresser into a bag. She found herself wanting to inflict some pain on him. She figured just a slight burn wouldn't hurt. The ability comforted her as she watched him race around the bedroom.

When Chevalier appeared in the doorway of the bathroom, his eyes were soft and gentle, "We're leaving." He threw some clothes onto the counter and shut the door behind him.

Emily dressed quickly, not bothering to complain about the pink summer dress he'd thrown in for her. She ran a brush through her hair, ignoring the way it pulled painfully when it encountered a knot. She left her hair down and stepped out into the bedroom, where Chevalier was sitting on the bed.

"I was mistaken," he whispered. "You don't belong in my world. Ability or no, my world isn't safe for you."

She didn't know what to say, so she stood still, watching him. He looked up at her finally and cringed at the purplish bruises that stood out from her white skin. He stood up. "How badly are you hurt?"

Her hand covered her throat, but she didn't speak. Her eyes were locked on his.

"I broke my promise to you, something I will have to live with for eternity, so I won't break another. As promised... you are free to return to your ranch. The weather is good, and you are completely healed." He grabbed her bag as if to prove he wasn't going to fight it.

She slipped on the soft moccasins that were warming by the fire and opened the closet. It was bare except for the wool lined parka. After zipping it, she followed Chevalier out of the mansion she'd grown accustomed to and took her place in the snowcat.

The snowcat seemed to move hopelessly slow as they sat in silence, ignoring the beauty that surrounded them. Chevalier couldn't look at Emily. The reminder of his lost temper stood out too vividly, and Emily couldn't look at him, afraid he'd see through her and know that a new fear had arisen. The fear she would never see him again.

The Bugatti sped quickly toward Montana, the scenery flying by. Only an hour into the drive, Chevalier couldn't take the silence anymore. "I am sorry, Emily, that this didn't work out."

Her voice cracked, "I don't want to be just another underling to you."

He glanced over at her. "Is that what the problem is? You don't want to be a subordinate?"

She shrugged. "Some of it."

She couldn't tell him that she'd begun to crave his attention, to relish in the solidarity of just the two of them that the mansion enabled. She couldn't tell him of the jealousy she felt when she thought of members of his coven being close to him. She envisioned being lost in the crowd, just another face to him.

He watched as her mind struggled to come to terms with losing him. "Please, I need to know what you are thinking, to explain the look on your face."

She shook her head.

Chevalier sighed. He could guess at the problem that stemmed from low self-worth. How could he convey how much she meant to him? He'd never felt this way about anyone, not even the eldest of his coven, for which he'd pledged his life.

"I was right about one thing. My world isn't good enough for you. Your innocence, your selflessness, it's all foreign to us, and I'm not sure how long you could last, surrounded by the immortal." He wanted to tell her that there was another option, the option to run away together, but he was afraid of the rejection she was bound to give after what he'd done.

Her voice was timid, "Why do you... well... any coven, want me so badly? My entire life has been full of heku trying to coerce me into a coven and for what? Am I just a plaything? A toy that can kill enemies?"

Her words stung, "It's not like that with me."

"What happens to me when I'm surrounded by heku? Their strength, their beauty, immortality? What happens to me, the ugly and weak human?" She was watching the mountains fade behind them.

"You are far from ugly and what do you mean what happens? Do you think I would just push you aside and forget you exist once you joined me?"

Her silent answer was deafening to him, and he pulled over and stopped the car. Gently, he took her chin in his hand and turned her to face him. "Emily, you could never be one of my many subordinates. Can't you see that? You are much... much more. You mean more to me than they do. You are more beautiful to me than any them. They are my family. I am ultimately responsible for their safety, and they mine... but you... you cannot imagine how important you are to me."

"You mean to your coven." She tried to turn her face, but his steel grip held her.

"No... to me." The intensity of his eyes was intimidating, and she dropped her gaze away from him.

"I... am... afraid."

"Of what? Tell me so I can help," he urged.

"I'm afraid of everything. I'm afraid of losing you when we return. I'm afraid of dissolving into the coven, never able to be myself again. I'm afraid of causing tension in your ranks. You of all people know how tempting my blood is, yet you encourage me to move into a house full of heku. I'm afraid of crowds and people and..." Her words were abruptly cut off by his lips.

The kiss was brief, and when he broke it off, she leaned toward him, eager to feel his touch again.

"Emily," he said, looking into her eyes. "You won't lose yourself. You would always be of utmost importance to me. You don't have to be constantly surrounded by heku. You could have your own home in the city if you want."

She cut him off. "City?"

He nodded as what she was thinking dawned on him. "Yes, city. My coven works similar to a city, each family unit in their own home, each individual is important in their own right. We don't all share one home. We don't all spend every waking hour together. As for attacks..." He straightened up. "I am Chief Enforcer. They wouldn't dare cross me. Of course, if you choose to get your own home, I would understand, but you are always welcome to stay with me."

She thought about that as he pulled back into traffic and sped off at an abnormal rate of speed.

"How many are there?" she asked, unsure if she was being too nosey.

He seemed proud. "There are just over a 1,200 in my coven."

"That many... you mentioned family units..."

"Yes, much like a family."

"Who is in yours?" Her tone revealed underlying questions, but he couldn't figure out where this was going.

"I'm not sure what you mean... the entire coven is my family."

She nodded. "How many share your home then?"

Chevalier couldn't help but grin. "Are you trying to find out if I have a harem?"

She didn't answer.

"None, I live alone. In my line of work, I need privacy." He didn't want to delve deeper into his life than was necessary.

She turned onto her side and watched out the window. She wasn't sure if he had noticed the way he spoke in uneven circles. One breath saying she could live with him, in another saying he had to live alone, for privacy. None of this was an option though. She had a ranch to run, a life outside of the mythical world of heku. She was now able to handle the attacks herself, so there was no reason to move, no reason to torment herself or risk falling in love with a heku. Any more in love with a heku, her mind corrected.

"Once you leave the ranch, will I see you again?" Her voice broke the tense silence.

Chevalier thought for a moment. "Perhaps."

She turned to look at him, his face hard and expressionless. "What if I don't want you to disappear?"

"You have to choose, Emily. You can't live in both worlds... you have to make a choice."

"Why?"

"It's complicated. Our worlds don't intertwine smoothly. If you choose to join my world, then everything else would vanish. Any hold the mortal world had on you would be null and void. The same holds true if you choose to stay in Montana. My world would simply cease to exist for you... except for the heku attacks. That's inevitable."

The rest of the ride was silent as she mulled over the two possibilities. She came out of a daze when Chevalier pulled his car in front of the ranch house. Her heart skipped a beat as she looked around the ranch. Everything seemed just as she had left it. The cattle were all eating and Patra was out in the corral. Sam poked his head out of the bunkhouse, his face shocked. Another man, a younger blond man, came out after Sam and looked at the sleek car. He didn't seem as surprised as Sam was.

Emily turned to look at Chevalier. "I don't have a choice. The ranch is my responsibility, and I can't leave it. As much as I want to be..." She paused to choose her words carefully, "As much as I want to be near you, I have obligations here."

His face was unreadable as he stared straight ahead and nodded slightly. She opened the door and stepped out, shutting it behind her. Sam ran at her and hugged her tightly. She stayed in his embrace and watched the car speed away.

Chevalier knew that Ulrich would arrive soon, and he wouldn't see her again. He wasn't good for her. He'd proven that, maybe her life would be better with Ulrich.

Sam took Emily around the ranch and showed her how things were going. He introduced her to the new field hand, Kyle. They both talked about feed prices and pasture plans, the number of cattle, and calves coming. Emily wasn't paying attention. She didn't notice that Coal was missing. She didn't hear how well Keith had done taking care of things and how hard they had looked for her. She watched the road, trying to see if he would come back.

Emily finally made it into the house. The inside looked severely neglected. There was a sink full of dishes, and trash and dirty clothing was piled in the corners. She went to work immediately cleaning up. It kept her mind off watching for Chevalier and wondering when Keith would get back. The house was hot, not warm and comfortable like the Colorado mansion had been. The smell in the house was awful, so she opened up a window, which only let in more hot air.

"Emily?" Keith yelled from the front door.

She smiled at the sound of excitement in his voice and pulled off the thick rubber gloves. "In the kitchen, Keith."

She ran to meet him, and he met her with a tight embrace. "Emily."

His smell was off. He was dirty and musky, very much unlike her companion for the last few months. She looked up into his eyes and stepped back. He was mad. He took one step toward her. "Where have you been?"

"It's a long story, Keith, but I'm okay. I'm back," she tried to assure him

He was too fast and suddenly backhanded her to the ground. She strained to get up, but she was knocked back down by a swift kick to her side as his cowboy boot connected with the recently healed ribs. She could taste blood in her mouth.

"Did you have fun on your little vacation?" He ended his question with yet another kick into her back.

"Keith, please," was all she could manage. It was hard to take a breath.

"You're just a little dirty slut aren't you? Is that what you've been doing? Whoring around in the city?" He grabbed her arm and violently dragged her to her feet.

Keith noticed the bruising around her neck. "Oh… I see someone else tried to teach you some manners too… you love that, don't you?"

She tried to pull away from him. Her mind was swirling, and her dress became soaked with the stream of blood coming from her mouth. He used her arm and slammed her into the wall, and she could hear the violent thudding of her heartbeat in her head as it connected with the plaster, denting it. The world began to turn dark as she fought to stay conscious.

"Guess we'll have to start over and teach you who is boss around here, bitch," Keith said, dragging her into the bedroom. He threw her down on the bed, and as she scrambled to get away, he swiftly pulled down his pants and dropped onto the bed. He pulled her back toward him, hiking her skirt up and tearing her panties painfully away from her body.

"You'll like this, you dirty slut. See if you can remember who gets the respect around this place."

Keith craned her legs apart and moved toward her quickly. She braced for the violence that was coming, but it didn't. Moments passed before she dared to open her eyes and noticed Keith was gone. She didn't wait to find out what happened to change his mind, but pulled her dress down and opened the window above the bed, then jumped out of it head-first into the garden.

Emily fell hard against the ground. Her head was still pounding and the taste of blood in her mouth was making her stomach turn. There was a loud crash inside of the house as something heavy landed against the China cabinet. Still confused, she got to her feet, steadied herself, and ran to the front of the house where she stopped and stared. Parked in front of the old ranch house was the black Bugatti.

Before she could move, she was swept off of her feet and carried at an inhumane speed into the barn. She barely had time to register that it was the new field hand, Kyle, that was carrying her. He sat her down softly on a pile of straw and began to press a rag against her forehead to stop the bleeding. The pressure against her head caused the blackness to come again, and this time, she couldn't fight it off, so she surrendered to it.

As Emily began to become aware, she could hear voices coming from the darkness.

"Over my dead body, Sam."

"*What was Chevalier doing to Sam*?" she wondered.

"You have no right to her! She belongs to Lord Ulrich." Sam's words seemed different, not the long drawl she was used to from him.

"She does not belong to anyone."

"Then you take that up with him. For now, I'm taking her away." Sam seemed angry.

Things began to swim into view as strong arms lifted her up to sitting and a cool glass was at her lips. "Drink."

The voice was unfamiliar, but she did as she was told. The cold water felt good against her battered mouth and washed away the taste of blood. As soon as she finished, she was carefully lowered down onto the bed.

"No, Sam, it was her choice. She chose to stay here." There was a slightly pained tone in his voice.

"It's no longer her choice. I was given orders and as soon as dark comes, I'm taking her away." She wanted to talk, wanted to ask Sam where he was taking her.

A familiar growl erupted and she knew Chevalier was mad. "Again, over my dead body, familiar. You touch her, and you're liable to lose an arm."

Familiar? Her mind was trying to answer them, to ask questions, but the sounds never escaped her lips.

"Any harm to me or to her will be dealt with by my master." Was Sam threatening Chevalier?

A cold compress was placed against her cheek. She winced slightly, and then relaxed as the ice did its job and helped the pain. Emily felt someone sit beside her on the bed, but she couldn't force her eyes to focus enough to figure out who it was.

"There are two of us, Sam. You can't stop me from taking her, and once you get back, you can tell Ulrich that he's going to have to come and get her."

"Ulrich?" she managed to say in a whisper.

"Shhhh, child." The strange voice was soft and reassuring.

As soon as he spoke to her, the shouting stopped. Silence filled the house, and Emily wondered if the arguing had been a dream. She heard footsteps come into the room, and her eyes adjusted. It was Chevalier and Sam, both glaring at each other. The man sitting by her on the bed was Kyle. He smiled down at her when her eyes met his.

Chevalier turned away from Sam and sat by her on the bed, opposite Kyle. "Emily, are you okay? Are you still hurting?"

She shook her head, but the world began to spin again.

Sam began to approach the bed, but Kyle hissed at him, and he took a step back. Emily paid more attention to Kyle and suddenly noticed that he had the same elongated canines that Chevalier had. Somehow, that didn't surprise her. What did surprise her, was that he hadn't attacked her, hadn't tried to feed.

"Keith?" Her words were muffled by her swollen lips.

"He's taken care of," was all Chevalier would say.

"He killed Keith, Emily. He's dangerous," Sam spat at them.

Chevalier stood up faster than her mind could register and pushed Sam out of the room. She heard the door slam as they left the house.

Left alone with Kyle, she covered her throat with her hand and looked up at him. "Please don't bite me."

She was shocked when he laughed. "You are safe with me, child."

Kyle glanced out the window, and then back down to Emily. "Do you need anything? There is some ibuprofen in the cupboard, or another drink… or food perhaps?"

He seemed so polite, so caring. She wanted to thank him, but it hurt to talk. She nodded and then panicked when he quickly left the room. She had just started to sit up when he returned with two pills and a glass of water in his hand. He helped her slowly to sit up and take the medicine, and then returned the ice pack to her cheek when she laid back down.

Without warning, Kyle picked her up, cradling her in his arms. He stepped out into the fresh air, and she noticed the sun was setting. It was almost dark.

He opened the door to the black car and laid her down carefully in the seat, reclining it. "I'll get her some things to take with you," he told someone.

"Make it fast. I don't know how long it will take Ulrich to get here." It was Chevalier he was talking to.

"Sam?" she managed to say.

Chevalier buckled her into the seat. "He left. We have to get out of here, Em. I'll explain later."

She didn't have the strength to question him, to demand to know what happened to Sam. All she could focus on was that Keith was dead at the hand of her heku.

Kyle returned with a bag and tossed it behind the seat.

"Stay here, Kyle. I need you to handle damage control. Don't tell Ulrich anything more than my phone number. I'll have more instructions once I get her back to the coven and get her settled. Can you take care of the ranch on your own?"

"Yes, sir, if I can use my speed and strength unhindered, it won't be a problem," Kyle assured him.

"Use discretion, but do what you can to keep on top of things."

"And... Keith?" Kyle asked, disgust in his voice.

"Bury him deeply. If anyone asks, tell them he ran off after someone he met in a bar." Chevalier thought briefly. "Just say he got tired of waiting for Emily and left." More was said but his voice was too low for Emily to make out the words.

"Will do, sir. Are you really taking her to the coven?" He sounded surprised.

Chevalier nodded. "It's hard to explain, but yes."

"Okay," Kyle said slowly.

"And Kyle... thank you. I owe you a lot for this." Kyle and Chevalier shook hands, and then Chevalier was in his seat pulling the sleek car onto the highway.

Island Coven

Emily drifted in and out of sleep all through the night. When dawn came, she opened her eyes and looked at Chevalier. He seemed relaxed and content. She cleared her throat before speaking. "Déjà vu, huh?"

He smiled over at her. "Why yes… it is oddly familiar."

"Did you really kill Keith?" She already knew the answer.

He sighed, "Yes."

"I'm sorry he made you do that."

"I'm not. I've wanted to do that for months," he said matter-of-factly. He didn't seem upset at all by the thought of killing someone. "Kyle called me back when he heard the shouting and smelled blood."

Chevalier's jaw tightened. He was still angry.

"Your life would be so much simpler if you'd have kept going," Emily told him, pulling her seat back into the upright position.

"He was going to kill you."

She whispered, "I've never seen him that mad before."

"He didn't deserve to share this planet with you. I just wish it hadn't come down to…" He quit talking, his jaw flexing again in anger.

She reached out to touch his arm and ran her fingers along the hard muscles and veins. "Thank you."

He raised an eyebrow. "You aren't mad?"

She shook her head and was silent, her mind deep in thought for the next hour.

"Who is Ulrich?"

Chevalier considered not answering for a moment, but then decided against it. "Do you remember the story I told you about Elizabeth Winchester marrying a heku? The one that started all of this?"

"Yes"

"Ulrich is the one."

She sat up straighter. "And what's his claim to me?"

Chevalier glanced at her.

"I heard you talking to Sam."

He sighed, "He's been watching over his family. He thinks I may corrupt you."

"Corrupt me?" She made a face.

He decided not to go into further detail.

"Where is your Coven anyway?" she asked, looking out toward the flat plains.

"I can't say. It's safer not to speak of the location."

"Why is that? No one's in the car but us."

"It's just safer. Take my word for it."

"End of subject, gotcha."

He smiled.

"Kyle packed some sandwiches. Are you hungry?" He reached behind the seat and pulled out a small cooler.

She dug around and pulled out a sandwich and a cold drink, then winced while eating. It felt like Keith knocked some teeth loose. After eating, she curled up in the seat and watched Chevalier.

"Can I help you with something?" he asked, grinning when he noticed her watching him.

"Kyle seems very nice," she said, watching his reaction.

"Yes, he is."

"Does he know about me?"

"No"

"Then why didn't he try to bite me?"

"I told him not to. I gave him precise instructions to take care of you but never to feed. I told you, Emily, my coven won't defy me," he said, gritting his teeth.

"You trust them enough to be outnumbered by them a thousand to 1?"

"Implicitly." He glanced over at her. "It's going to be okay, Emily. Don't worry about it. I'll always make sure you are protected."

"I can't go home, can I?" She knew the answer but wanted him to say it.

"No"

She was silent beside him.

"There were two choices. You could either come with me, or stay there and be taken by Ulrich. I asked Kyle to sell off your ranch," he said quietly.

Emily looked away when her eyes filled with tears. "That was my Dad's ranch."

"I'm sorry. It's too dangerous now."

"Why was Kyle so surprised that you were taking me to your coven?"

"It's complicated," Chevalier said, tightening his grip on the steering wheel. "Heku don't normally want to spend time with a mortal. We feed, and we leave. It's that simple."

"But with me?"

"With you, it's different. I don't know why, but I'm drawn to you. It may take some time for the coven to get used to a mortal being around longer than a few hours."

Emily turned to face the window. Eventually, she drifted off into a sleep full of nightmares.

***

The sound of lapping water woke Emily up. The blinding light shone in her eyes as she struggled to see through it. The car was silent, but she still felt as if she were moving. Undoing the seat belt, she opened the car door and stepped out onto damp wooden planks. They were on a ferry, no land in sight. She looked around. The Bugatti was the only car on the large ferry, and she couldn't see any people.

There were voices on the wind, but she couldn't make them out, so she made her way to the back of the ferry and saw a recess in the deck that led to stairs. As she descended, the voices became quiet. She emerged into a small room with a table in the center. Chevalier was seated there, a warm smile on his face.

There were two others with him, a beautiful woman with dark hair and a stunning face, and an older man who looked away quickly when Emily met his eyes.

"I'm sorry," she whispered. "Am I interrupting something?"

Chevalier stood up and motioned for her to come closer. "No, we were just visiting. Emily, this is Storm and Walen... please come and sit."

Emily sat in the chair on his right as Storm watched her closely and Walen avoided looking at her. She hadn't looked in a mirror but could only imagine what she looked like with the bruised neck and face.

"These are the highest ranking officers in my coven. They met us, so we could go over some details of your arrival," he explained.

Emily looked over at Storm and was shocked by her beauty. From what Emily could understand of their conversation, things were pretty normal. Word had gotten out that Chevalier would be back soon, and everyone was excited. Kyle had let Storm know that she was coming too, and preparations were made for her arrival. Talk turned to politics within the city walls, and the words they used were strange and confusing.

Emily suddenly felt terribly uncomfortable. "I'll leave you be then and go back up top." She stood up and walked up the stairs quickly, feeling the eyes boring into her back.

She shivered as the cool ocean wind brushed past her. The breeze had gotten stronger since she went down, and the dark clouds began to look ominous above her. She went back to the car and sat inside, leaving the door open for fresh air. She could still hear the voices but was thankful she couldn't make out the words. Emily found her bag behind the seat in the car and dug around inside until she found her book. Propping her bare feet on the dash of the car, she settled down to read.

The sound of engines startled her. She jumped slightly and then heard the chuckle beside her.

"Good book?" Chevalier asked, smiling.

Emily watched the small boats surround the ferry, tossing ropes to attach themselves to the hull. She looked over at Chevalier nervously.

He grinned. "It's okay. They are going to tow us in. We're almost there."

She looked out the windshield and noticed a large island coming swiftly toward them. A tall cement wall surrounded the island, blocking her view from anything on it, and a pier jutted out from the beach, lined with armed guards and fierce looking dogs. The dogs stiffened, their hackles rising as the ferry drew nearer. Emily sat back against her chair.

"It's okay. They won't hurt you while you are in the car." His eyes were now protective, no longer amused.

"While I'm in the car?"

"They protect the pier, only heku can get by them."

"And the cement fence?"

He watched her reaction. "Well guarded."

Emily felt like she was heading to a prison, a place where she would be watched and carefully monitored, a place which she would never be able to leave. She started to panic, her breathing picking up rapidly.

"Emily, calm down." Chevalier touched her arm softly.

She opened the door, jumped out, and ran as Chevalier called from behind her. She had to get off the ferry, had to get away from the fortress. She could swim well, there had to be land close by. As she neared the back edge of the ferry, strong hands wrapped around her waist, pulling her toward the center.

"Where are you going?" Chevalier asked softly into her ear.

"Away, let me go," she demanded, but his hold on her strengthened.

"You can't jump off the ferry, Emily."

Her heart was pounding loudly in her ears, her breathing coming faster as she struggled against his hands.

"Stop it, you're going to get hurt… I'm not going to let you drowned."

Her nails were digging at his hands, trying to pry them off of her. She had to get away from him. No matter how hard she tried, his fingers wouldn't move. They held tight and steady. She screamed, hoping the Captain would hear her and come save her from the prison they were nearing. He said it was a city, not a fortress, guarded by dogs and armed guards.

"Let me go, Chev, right now! I have to get back." She'd given up trying to move his hands and was squirming to get out of his grasp. He turned her quickly so she was facing him, and he locked her eyes.

He concentrated on her, and just as he thought he might be able to control the situation, her eyes shot to the side, and she brought up one knee, hitting him hard in the groin. His grip didn't lessen, but he wasn't able to lock her gaze again.

"What's wrong? Tell me."

Anger flowed through her words, "You said it was a city. You didn't tell me it was a prison, Chev, a place to keep mortals out and what? Also keep them in? Are we going to play the hostage game again?"

He sighed, "It's not a prison. You can come and go as you wish. Once I get orders out to the coven, no one will harm you, and no one will hold you hostage. I wouldn't do that."

She glared at him. "Then let me go."

"Not tonight, it's late and a storm is coming. Give it a try, Em. I'm breaking a lot of rules bringing you here, but you'll see. You will be like royalty to them. Give them time to show you how much you mean to us. Give me time to show you how much you mean to me."

His distraction worked. Before he was done speaking, the ferry came to a stop and was tied to long posts on the pier. Storm was off the ferry first, barking orders at the armed guards in a language Emily didn't understand. Most stared straight ahead, while others peered at her from under their hats.

"Now get in the car before the storm hits." He was leading her back to the waiting Bugatti. She crawled in and fastened her seat belt. It was too late. She couldn't get away. Her heart sank as Chevalier drove down the pier and into the fortress.

Once inside, things looked better, she had to admit. The island was lush and green and full of wildlife. Birds of all colors flew around, and small squirrels played in the trees. There were beautiful houses lined with flowers and exotic bushes. Each home was well spaced from the next, giving off an air of privacy. Many people came to their doors and waved as they drove past. Most of them stopped and stared curiously when they noticed her sitting beside him.

The winding road led up a small hill that was free of any buildings, and they drove onto a large mesa. Centered, was a mansion with tall granite pillars and rows of intricately designed windows. High turrets reached up from the four corners, and she could see armed guards in them.

A small bridge emerged, and as they crossed it, she looked down to see a swift stream full of orange and white Koi. The house sat back away from the rest of the city, but as they drew closer, she noticed the armed guards again. Four of them were standing outside large black double doors. Emily looked nervously at Chevalier.

"This is my home, welcome," he said, smiling.

The closer they got, the bigger the mansion appeared. At first she thought it was about the same size as his home in Colorado, but it wasn't, it was much larger. Storm was already at the door, though Emily couldn't imagine how she'd beat them there. She was standing calmly between the four guards and watching their approach.

As Chevalier pulled the car up to the front door, a stout man ran out and opened his door for him. Emily jumped as another man appeared at her door, out of nowhere, and opened it, bowing to her. He put out one gloved hand to help her out of the car. She looked at his hand, unsure she wanted to trust him enough for the help, but in the end decided she had no choice, she was gravely outnumbered.

The guards each saluted Chevalier as he walked past, though he was ignoring them and was focused on something Storm was saying. Emily followed behind them, already feeling left out and afraid. One hulking maid looked up at her and growled, her teeth coming into view. Storm looked at her, and she instantly shrank back and out of sight. Emily was watching where the girl disappeared and ran right into Chevalier. He chuckled and took her hand.

She turned to look into the house and couldn't help but gasp. The front room was massive and two stark white columns of stairs led up to a second floor. The stairs were lined with golden handrails and covered in soft green carpet. There were doors lining the large room, but none of them were open, so she couldn't tell what was in them. Chevalier led the way up the closest staircase and Storm followed.

"This is Anna," Chevalier said, and a stunningly beautiful heku appeared at her side and smiled warmly. Anna had long blonde hair, and she was tall and muscular. "She will get you anything you need and will be at your beck and call. Don't hesitate to call on her if you want to find something or need to go somewhere."

It already felt like she was being abandoned by him. He seemed to have felt that and strengthened his grasp on her hand. "I'll be around, of course, but she is here to help you."

He led the way down a long hallway that had only two doors in it. The left door, he pointed out, was his room, and the right was hers. The door opened suddenly, and they walked inside. The antechamber they stepped into was larger than her room in Colorado and was done up in black and red. Victorian era couches and chairs were placed around the fireplace which was being stoked by yet another heku. Double doors opened up from the antechamber into the bedroom.

Emily froze in the door, unable to take in the vastness of this one room. A large bed draped with black netting was front and center in the room. Four large wardrobes made of dark cherry wood were across from it, and a chandelier hung from the ceiling, its crystal décor throwing intricate rainbows beneath it. While checking out the room, she peeked through the black French doors and noticed a bathroom similar to the one in Colorado. The floor was dark blue granite, and the jetted tub was larger than the other and also dark blue. Eight showerheads lined the four walls of the double shower, and the glass door was etched with a dolphin.

When she turned around, they had been joined by a few other people, but Storm was gone. Chevalier was talking to an older man and motioned Emily over to him. "Em, this is Gordon. He'll be your chef. Just tell him what you want, and he'll make it for you. I've told your maid, Helen, to stay out of here unless given permission to enter. No one is to be in here with you without your prior permission."

He smiled, knowing this was all foreign to her. "That should give you some privacy. They are anxious to have you here and to serve you. I'm sure they would be able to make a pain out of themselves if you let them... ah, Margaret."

Chevalier turned to a tall, bulky woman who waddled when she entered the room. "Emily, this is Margaret. She is your tailor. Again, anything you want, and she will make it for you. You still have most of the clothes that you left Colorado with, but I'm sure you'll need more."

Margaret was staring oddly at Emily's dress, and when Emily glanced down, she gasped. She had forgotten it was covered in dry, caked blood.

"I'll get to work right away. I'm thinking black is your color, dear?" Margaret seemed warm and sincere.

"She's not a heku, Margaret. Keep the colors light and the clothing comfortable." He smiled at Emily.

"Yes, sir," Margaret said, wobbling off as fast as she could go.

"Chevalier," Emily said, looking at the crowded room.

With one glance from Chevalier, the entire room emptied out in an instant. The door shut behind them.

"Yes?" he asked, moving closer to her.

"I don't need all of this. It's too much," she protested.

"Let them treat you like you deserve. It's good for them, and they are looking forward to it." He moved another step closer, close enough to embrace her.

She felt his protective arms and relaxed a bit, still unsure about what she'd gotten herself into. "I don't want this, Chev. You said you lived alone, peace and quiet you know?"

"Oh I do live alone. These heku don't live here. They are my servants. You won't hear a thing. I prefer the quiet myself." He expected the protests.

"Do they know... know anything about me?" she asked, almost afraid of the answer.

"They know what I've told Storm to tell them, enough to keep them from harming you, but that's it. They don't know anything about your past or your abilities."

She nodded and pulled away from him, again glancing around the room.

"I have a meeting. I hope you understand. Why don't you get cleaned up and changed and then have a look around the castle? You may go anywhere except my office." He grinned, remembering how that had made her mad before.

"You're leaving?" Panic filled her voice, but his use of the term 'castle' didn't escape her notice.

"Just for a little while. You are safe here, and Anna is here in case you need anything." He kissed her forehead lightly.

"What if I need you?" she asked, and grabbed his arm, hoping to go with him.

He pulled away gently. "Anna can find me anywhere."

Chevalier smiled softly and left the room, shutting the heavy doors behind him. The silence was almost painful, and her body shook with terror. Here she was, alone, in the middle of a city full of heku that could kill her before she even knew anything was wrong. The one person she trusted had left her in the care of more of the heku. A night alone with Keith wasn't looking too bad now. It seemed safer than her current location.

She noticed her bag sitting on an ancient chest at the foot of the bed, so she quickly opened it and pulled out a clean change of clothing. The French doors leading in to the bathroom didn't seem secure. There was no way to lock them. Walking across the sizable bedroom, she locked the double doors and went back to the bathroom.

The shower felt good. It calmed her aching muscles, and she was able to wash the blood from her face and hair. She kept glancing out into the bathroom though. She felt like eyes were on her, and the glass door to the shower wasn't helping. She wondered if she could get a lockable door.

Jeans and a t-shirt, her favorite clothing, made her feel much better and a lot less conspicuous. She'd always hated shoes, so opted to go barefoot and went out into the antechamber. Anna was standing in the corner waiting for her with a welcoming smile.

"What would you like to do, Lady Emily?"

Emily winced at the title. "Just Emily, please."

Anna's face dropped nervously and then returned to a smile. "Anything you wish. Where would you like to go?"

"The kitchen? I'd like to find something to eat please." She reached to open the door, but it opened before she could touch it. A heku stood at the door and bowed when he saw her.

"I can call Gordon. What would you like to eat?" Anna was at her side.

"I'd rather just make it myself, if that's alright."

Anna bowed. "As you wish, child."

Emily followed her through the castle. She felt silly calling it a castle, though, like there were kings and queens and fairy princesses running around in today's society. She watched everything around her as they made their way to the kitchen, and she noticed that any time they encountered a heku, the heku bowed and disappeared. Everything was immaculately clean and beautifully decorated. She supposed Chevalier would have it no other way.

Anna opened the door to the kitchen and quickly whispered something to whoever was inside. When Emily entered the kitchen, it was empty, so she looked around. There were 14 stoves, and the ceiling was lined with pots and pans of all sorts and sizes. There were three doors, one lead to the pantry, one to the walk-in refrigerator, and one to the walk-in freezer.

Emily stopped and turned to Anna. "I thought heku didn't eat."

"We don't, dear," Anna responded politely.

"Then why the kitchen and the food?"

"For you, child," Anna explained, smiling again.

Emily grimaced. She hated that everyone was calling her child. She went to work making her dinner. She was starving and all of the travel was wearing on her, and she was ready for a good meal and bed. Anna was quiet as Emily went to work cutting up vegetables for a salad while the steak and large potato broiled. Filling her plate, she looked around for a place to eat and saw Anna standing at a door, waiting for her.

She stepped out into a vast dining room with a large table that ran along the middle. The candles on the table were lit, and the lights were turned low. She sat at the end of the table and began to eat as Anna disappeared behind her. She counted 82 plates at the table and felt odd the entire time she was eating, alone at a table large enough for most of the residents of Cascade.

Anna reappeared just as Emily was done eating. She stood up from the table and went to grab her plate, but it had vanished. Her eyes were wide when she turned questioningly to Anna.

Anna smiled proudly. "You won't lift a finger here to clean. It's all done for you."

Emily sighed. This would be harder than she thought. "What time is it?"

Without looking at a watch or clock, Anna responded, "It's almost 10pm, child."

Emily winced at the name and politely asked Anna to return to her bedroom. She was feeling exceptionally tired by the time they reached the long hallway with the two doors. She watched Chevalier's door closely as they walked toward her own door, but it didn't open. Anna opened the door to the antechamber and stepped inside. The fire was dying down, and the room was warm and pleasant.

Emily turned to Anna. "That's all, thanks Anna. I'm just going to bed."

"Yes, child. I will wait here for you in case you need anything."

Emily frowned. "You don't have to wait here. You'll get bored."

"No, I'm never bored. Call me if you need me," Anna said, and walked over to wait in the corner.

Emily walked through the double doors and locked them behind her. It was childish, she knew, to lock the doors against heku, but it felt better than not doing it.

As she got closer to her bed, she noticed it had been turned down, and a soft silken pink nightgown was lying on top of it. She scanned the room, making sure no one was in there before undressing and pulling on the nightgown. She hadn't noticed before, but there were floor-to-ceiling curtains lining one side of the bedroom. Emily went up to them and pushed the heavy velvet curtains back, revealing a large balcony that overlooked the fields beside the castle.

She tried the door and found it unlocked, so she stepped out into the cold night air. The storm had passed, and the island was eerily quiet. Her eyes were just scanning the horizon, looking for any sign of life when she jerked as arms wound around her waist.

His voice was amused. "Sorry, Em. It's just me."

"Don't do that!" she reminded him, calming her breathing.

She turned around and pulled away from his grip, blushing deeply as she noticed him admiring her in the silk. Instinctively, she wrapped her arms around her torso, covering herself.

"I hear you don't like your chef. Would you like another?" He was concerned.

"No, I can cook for myself."

"Oh I have no doubt about that, but why not let poor Gordon do it for you?"

She suddenly felt like a child that was about to get scolded.

He started to wonder if pampering Emily was going to be harder than he first thought. "I'll tell you what, let them do it for you. Let them do their jobs for a week… and then we'll compromise, deal?"

She nodded.

"Now come inside before you catch pneumonia." He took her hand and pulled her back into the dark room, shutting the door behind them.

He suddenly swept her off her feet, cradling her in his arms. His skilled lips met hers and pressed passionately against them. The kiss, the way he held her, it all seemed too intimate, and she tensed, her hands pushing against him. He didn't stop as his tongue traced the outline of her lips and forced them apart. He growled slightly as his tongue explored her mouth. She gave up and stopped resisting. Her hand wound through his black hair, balling into a fist.

She couldn't remember the walk to the bed, but she was suddenly being laid down on it. His body pressed into hers as he lay on top of her, his kiss becoming stronger. Her body curved up into his, and she could feel his hands gently brush against the outside of her breast. She could feel his chest pressing against hers as her breathing came faster. Her inner being was yelling at her to stop, to let him keep the desire he had for her. She knew that if he were to get his way, things would change, and he would know the kind of person she was.

He hissed her name into her ear as she pushed him off of her. He rolled to her side and took her hand in his, running his tongue gently along the inside of her wrist as she shivered.

"Chevalier, no…," she said, but his lips pressed against hers again, stopping what she was going to say. He ran his hand from her waist down along her hip and squeezed her outer thigh. She felt incredible to his touch, and he craved more. His lips again explored her soft mouth, tasting her sweet breath.

His mouth left hers and traveled down her neck, pausing at the vein, exploring its throb with his tongue. He kissed down her neck to the top of the nightgown and brought a hand up to lower it. She gasped and took his hand away, moving away from him. The bed was large enough to move to the edge and be far enough away from him he couldn't reach.

He looked up at her, desire burning in his eyes. "What's wrong?"

"I've told you, I can't." She shied away from his eyes.

"Keith's gone, you're no longer tied to him. You're free." He scooted closer to her and reached out. His hand landed on her waist, and he pulled her closer to him.

"Please…" She looked up at him, pleading.

He sighed, "Fine, for now, but I wish you would tell me why." He pulled her close to him and embraced her, burying his face in her soft red hair.

"Not with you, Chev, ever," she said plainly. "If that's why I'm here, why I'm getting my every wish granted, then you might as well send me back to the mainland."

He grinned. "It's not why you are here."

"Then why am I here?" she asked, and propped herself up on her elbow.

"We'll talk later. For now, it's late, and you should get some sleep." He was off the bed in an instant, but walked slowly, mortally, out of the room.

***

The voices drew closer. The woods surrounding her were dark and closing in around her. She was running as fast as she could through the tangled roots and branches, running to save him. She knew he was here, lost in the black trees, but she couldn't find him, her frantic searching becoming more hectic as the voices called to him. She had to find him... she had to find him before they did.

"Emily?" Chevalier woke her, gently touching her arm.

She sat up and looked at him. Her breathing was rapid, and she'd broken out in a light sweat. The room was dark. It was still late at night, but his face shown in the dark like an angel. She buried her face into his chest, finding comfort in his arms wrapping tightly around her.

"It was just a dream." He shushed her like you would a toddler, but she didn't shrink from it.

She felt herself falling back to sleep. The images from the dream seemed far away when he was beside her. She fell asleep in his arms and didn't dream.

Small beams of light streamed into the room and fell on the dark bed. Emily was still cuddled in Chevalier's arms. Her fists were clenched tightly to his shirt. She relaxed her grip as she began to wake up, for a moment forgetting where she was. The memories from the past 24 hours came creeping back into her mind, and she pulled closer to him.

"Good morning," he whispered to her.

She nodded, not wanting to move. The bed was extremely comfortable, and she was warm under the down blanket.

Chevalier smiled. "If you plan on staying in bed all day, then we should have some food brought in."

She sighed softly, "What time is it?"

"It's almost one."

"In the afternoon?" She sat upright and looked around the room. He reached around her and pulled her back down.

"Yes"

"Why didn't you wake me up?" she asked, and watched his face.

"Did you have somewhere to be?" He was grinning again.

She shrugged and snuggled deeper into his arms.

"Did you have plans today?" she asked, not sure she really wanted to know.

He kissed the top of her head softly. "Yes."

She squeezed her arms tighter around him. "You're leaving again?"

"No, you and I have some more training to do."

"Ugh, why?" She didn't even want to think about the weeks they had spent with Steven.

He smiled. "You can't become more adept at what you can do, without practice."

She frowned and looked up at him. "You brought Steven?"

"No, I left him back on your ranch with the rest of the ashes. It'll be good for him." His tone was light and amused again.

Emily scooted away from him and propped herself up on one elbow. "Then who am I going to be practicing on?"

His face showed indecision as he considered what exactly to tell her. "There were some problems while I was away, and I need to deal with them. I thought you could practice while I did it."

Her breath caught. "You want me to ash them? Are you kidding me?"

He took her hand into his. "Em, you have to practice. You can't do so on anyone but a heku. Why not on ones that are about to go into stasis anyway, for crimes against the coven?"

"No, I won't do it, Chev! I won't be a monster around here, people afraid to so much as look at me." She got out of bed and headed for the wardrobe. "Oh there goes our punisher! Don't tick her off, or she'll turn you into ash."

Chevalier grimaced, and then appeared in front of her. "No one will know, Em. I wouldn't do that to you."

"No," she yelled and stopped in front of him, meeting his gaze.

"You need to practice, to learn more control."

"Not like that."

"Then how?" He raised an eyebrow.

"Don't make me do this," she pleaded.

A low growl erupted from him, "I won't force you to do anything." He was able to calm himself some. "How do you propose to hone your skills?"

She shrugged and walked around him, opening up the wardrobe. It was full of pastel colors and flowing fabrics. She rifled through them and noticed they were all delicate, feminine dresses. "Great."

Chevalier watched with some amusement as she went through the other wardrobes, finding slight variations from the first. She stormed back to her suitcase and removed the jeans and t-shirt, then disappeared through the French doors into the bathroom.

Chevalier sat to wait for her on one of the velvet covered chairs. He sighed when his phone rang. "Yes?"

"There's a problem, sir. Ulrich is going to the Elders," Storm said, sounding concerned.

Chevalier frowned. "To do what? The Elders will…" He paused and lowered his voice, "The Elders would kill her if they knew how many of us she's turned to ash, so he can't tell them about her. What exactly is he going to complain to them about?"

"He's going for a type of custody battle, sir. He is claiming that you have taken his granddaughter from him. He's also planning on saying it was more of a kidnapping. I know what he wants to do. He wants the Elders to bring Emily in to them so they can ask her themselves."

Chevalier hissed.

"Sir," Storm continued. "I know you already know this, but if she leaves this island and comes anywhere near the Elders, it would give Ulrich the chance to take her back."

"I know, Storm," he growled at her. "Tell the Elders I'm contesting his claim, and I'll be there in the morning."

"Yes, sir, we'll have everything ready."

Chevalier shut his cell phone and slammed it down on the table, shattering it into several pieces. His eyes burned with rage.

After a few minutes, he was able to regain control. He had to tell Emily he was leaving again, this time for longer, and he could only imagine how she was going to take it. She emerged from the bathroom, still sulking, but she froze when she saw him.

"What's wrong?" She stayed back away from him.

"I have to go away for a few days." He stood up but noticed that she took a step back.

"I'll come with you."

"You can't. I need you to stay here."

Her eyes narrowed. "Is this about me?"

"No, Emily, it's just something I have to do. You'll be safe here, and I'll be back before you know it." He tried to reassure her with a smile.

"Is Storm going?"

"Yes"

"Well, of course she is. It won't matter. I'm leaving today anyway." She headed over and zipped her suitcase shut.

"Emily," he said, his shoulders slumped. "Please don't do this. Just stay until I get back."

"Why should I, Chevalier? This has all been a misunderstanding, and if I get back now, I can let Kyle go and get back to the ranch where I belong." She was watching the floor.

"It's already gone. The ranch has been sold."

She looked up at him suddenly, angry that the tears were coming so easily in front of him. She fought to keep the tears out of her eyes but wasn't having any luck. "It's gone?"

Chevalier nodded.

She turned away from him as the tears started flowing more easily.

He silently moved up to her and wrapped his arms around her waist. "Emily…"

She jerked out from his grasp, still not turning around.

"Emily, just stay here, I beg you. When I get back, we'll figure things out." He granted her wish not to be touched.

She mumbled something quietly under her breath, but he caught it, "If you come back."

"Just a few days... I'll be back. I promise. Why don't you enjoy yourself? Go out and look around the city. It's safe for you now."

She shrugged and halfway nodded.

Chevalier took one step toward her and then reconsidered and left her alone in the large room.

As soon as the doors shut, she grabbed a nearby vase and threw it against the doors, shattering it in a violent crash. The sound made her feel a little better, but she quickly realized she was alone yet again.

Emily sat on the bed and looked around. She started to feel uneasy and bored in the room, so she sighed and headed out the doors, determined to look around on her own.

Anna met her gaze as she left the bedroom. "Yes, Lady Emily?"

She ignored the title. "You get a day off, Anna."

"Pardon me?" Anna asked politely.

"A day off... no following me around? Go home... visit family..."

Anna looked at Emily, confused.

"It's a hint, Anna. I'm exploring alone today." Emily cursed under her breath as she reached for the door, and it opened before she reached it. The heku outside her door bowed to her again.

"And stop bowing!" she screamed at him.

She could feel Anna and the door heku watching her as she left the hallway. Emily looked both directions and decided that left looked interesting. The entire place seemed abandoned. She couldn't see a single living thing, but she knew they were there, hiding from her for some reason. Maybe it was Chevalier's idea of privacy, but for her, it was just creepy.

Some of the doors were locked, but most opened up into rooms that were breathtakingly beautiful, yet smaller than the one she was in currently. She found a library. It was as large as the city library in Great Falls, but the books were all older and didn't fall into any organization as far as she could tell. She accidentally ran into the kitchen again, and not feeling hungry, she just shut the door.

It had been hours she'd spent going through the castle, opening doors, and exploring old rooms full of antiques and art. As she rounded a dark corner, she screamed, and then laughed at herself when she recognized the suit of armor in the shadows. She studied the armor for a moment, and as she reached out to touch it, a hiss sounded from the shadows nearby. She drew her hand back and turned to the noise, but couldn't see anyone there.

She screamed again as a voice sounded behind her. "Emily?"

Emily spun, ready to attack, but calmed instantly, "Kyle!"

He grinned at her. "I have something for you. Please allow me to show you." He motioned down an adjacent hallway.

She followed him through the confusing hallways. "Kyle? Is it... well is it all gone?"

He nodded to her.

"How did you sell it so quickly?"

"The city bought it as soon as they heard it was for sale."

"Great, they'll turn my ranch into a strip-mall."

Another large door opened with invisible hands, and they stepped out into the bright sunlight of day. Kyle immediately pulled on sun glasses and began to walk across a lush yard toward outbuildings. Emily had to almost run to keep pace with him. As they came closer to the building, she noticed it was a barn, and her hopes began to grow.

"Do you have animals here?" she asked, getting excited.

"Not many, but we are getting more soon." Kyle opened the large door and let Emily inside.

Emily froze, and her entire body suddenly erupted with emotion. "Patra!"

She ran to the mare and wrapped her arms around the horse's neck. Patra responded by picking at Emily's red hair with her mouth. Emily pressed her face into the horse's powerful neck and let the tears go. When she regained some composure, she turned to Kyle, who was standing silently by the door, trying not to watch them.

Kyle barely had time to react as she ran and threw her arms around him. "Thank you, Kyle, thank you." The tears were streaming again.

Kyle stood still as his eyes darted around to make sure no one was watching. He wasn't sure how Chevalier would take the situation. They had all been issued strong orders not to touch Emily.

His shirt became wet with tears. He gently pulled her off of him and moved a step back. "Just a gift, Lady Emily. I thought you might enjoy a taste of home. I put some personal items in the barn's storage shed also."

Kyle's eyes were understanding and deep with wisdom. Emily could tell that he was exceedingly old. His eyes told a story of things known only to those with a long history.

"Let me get you a saddle," Kyle said, heading toward a side room in the barn.

"No thanks, Kyle, I have this." With one quick jump, she was on Patra, leaning over and hugging the horse again.

"Very well, is there anything else you require? Shall I ride with you?" He hesitated. It seemed innocent enough, and he worried about sending her out alone, but it was well known that the girl belonged to the Chief Enforcer.

"Oh please, come with me!" She sounded truly excited.

Kyle nodded and proceeded to saddle a beautiful buckskin mare. Only a few minutes had passed before he was on the horse, looking graceful and comfortable. "Shall we?" he asked, heading out the barn door.

The ride was just what she needed. The mesa was large enough to break into a full gallop, and she enjoyed the feel of the wind through her hair. The freshness of the air was exquisite, and she instantly felt better. Kyle kept up with her easily, never speaking, and letting her lead the way. Emily brought the horses to the tree line and then set out along the edge of a small forest.

Kyle saw him an instant before Patra reacted. He yelled at the strange heku, but it was too late. The horse was startled. Patra reared up to paw at the stranger, whinnying loudly. The sudden change sent Emily off the back of the mare, and she landed with a thud on the ground. In less than a second, Kyle was off his horse and had the intruding heku by the neck, a fierce growl erupting from deep within him, and the young heku was terrified.

Emily sat up slowly. It all happened so quickly, that she wasn't sure what was going on. Her head throbbed where she'd hit the ground, and when she touched it, her hand became wet with blood. She covered the gaping wound with her hand and stood up, steadying her feet underneath her.

"Kyle, don't, it's okay," she said, seeing the seething way that Kyle was watching the new heku.

Kyle stiffened and smelled the air, then spun toward Emily. His hand was still wrapped tightly around the other heku's neck.

Emily recoiled back a step. Kyle's eyes were fierce. "Get back to the barn," he ordered.

"Let him go, please." She could tell by the look on the strange heku's face that he was on the brink of death.

Emily met the new heku's eyes and saw something that made her fear him. He was watching her, his breathing was fast, and his lips were drawn back into a grimace. Suddenly, he was fighting to get to her. Kyle's hands were the only thing restraining him.

"Now!" Kyle yelled at her.

She was on Patra quickly and kicked her hard into a gallop, racing for the barn, too afraid to look back. Once in the safety of the barn, she dismounted and tied Patra to a post. She could hear a sharp inhale from the shadows around her, and she ran, without thinking, trying to make it back to the house.

The house full of heku.

She froze halfway between the barn and the house, suddenly unsure of where to go. She could feel the blood running down her neck and back.

Emily spun. The house was closest, the barn opposite it. To her left was an empty field, and to her right was a steep drop to the houses below. She couldn't see anyone, couldn't hear anyone. Her senses heightened with fear.

Someone touched the back of her head, and she turned on them. It was Anna.

"Come, child," she said as she pressed a towel hard against the flow of blood from Emily's head.

Emily couldn't move. She watched the heku's face to see if she was going to attack.

Anna just smiled warmly, but her teeth stood out sharply. "Please, come inside where I can look closer."

Emily took a step away from her.

"It's okay, child. You can trust me. I won't hurt you... please... Kyle has the other. He can't get to you now." Anna was holding a towel drenched in blood, but it didn't seem to bother her.

Emily took one tentative step forward.

Anna smiled again and motioned for the door. "Come, you need to get that looked at."

Emily realized that if Anna wanted to hurt her, she could do it outside. She didn't feel she had an option other than to head inside with her.

Anna pressed the towel back to Emily's head as they walked through the castle. They headed to the third floor, one Emily hadn't been on, and she looked at Anna cautiously.

"There are some medical supplies up here, a precaution necessitated by your arrival," Anna explained.

Anna led Emily into a small room that looked similar to a doctor's office. She sat on a chair as Anna pulled back the blood matted red hair and hissed slightly, "He's not going to be happy about this," Anna said, mainly to herself.

Emily winced as Anna poured a stinging liquid into the cut, but it subsided and the pain numbed.

She could tell that Anna was trying to suture the cut. "Do you know what you're doing?"

"Yes, I do," Anna said, her voice light and comforting.

It was over in a few minutes and Anna was handing Emily a white pill, "Take this."

Emily hesitated and looked up at Anna.

"It's for the pain."

She shook her head. "I don't take pain medications."

Anna frowned. "He won't like it if you are in pain."

"He," Emily stressed, "will have to live with it."

A flash of concern crossed Anna's bright face before the smile returned. "As you wish. Let me take you back to your room. You might want to lie down."

Anna was shaking. Emily caught it only briefly but hopped down and followed Anna back to her room. She stepped inside, shut the doors, and looked around at the emptiness.

How had she gone from complete bliss to fearing for her life in an instant? Was this how her stay here was going to be? Chevalier assured her that no one would attack her, yet he was out of the way for a day, and it happened.

The sharp knock on the doors shocked her. She stared at them, unsure if she should open them or not.

"It's me, Kyle," the soft voice said from behind the door.

Emily relaxed. "Come in, please."

She was glad to see him, happy to see him calm and relaxed. Emily smiled brightly when he stepped in and shut the doors. She was finally not alone. She was with someone she could trust.

"I came to apologize," he said, wringing his hands.

"No... Kyle, that wasn't your fault!" She was afraid he was going to apologize and then leave again. She took a step toward him.

He looked unsure and continued, "It was... I should have been closer to you. I could have stopped him before your horse reacted."

Emily shook her head. "I don't blame you, Kyle. Did you..." she said, and then paused. "Where is he?"

Kyle watched her for a moment. "I left him for the Chief Enforcer to deal with."

Emily's eyes grew wide. "What will Chev do to him?"

Kyle shook his head. "I don't know. It's not up to me."

Kyle bowed slightly and turned to leave.

"Stay, please," she said, and took a step toward him.

He turned toward her slowly. "You wish for me to stay?"

A blush rose to her cheeks. "Yes."

He thought about it for a moment and then nodded.

She smiled. "Tomorrow, can we try again… take the horses out?"

Kyle smiled warmly at her. "Anything you wish."

Emily frowned. "It's not an order, Kyle. If you don't want to go, then say so, and I'll go by myself."

"No, it's not that. Yes, I do want to go." He walked over to a plush chair and sat down.

She stood for a moment and remembered the blood in her hair. "Let me take a quick shower. You won't leave though, right?"

"I will not."

"Okay… I won't be long." She grabbed clean clothes and headed for the bathroom.

"Shall I get you something to eat?"

"I am kinda hungry." She paused at the French doors and turned around.

"I will have Gordon make you something. What would you like?" He moved so quickly that Emily's eyes couldn't see him. To her, he just suddenly appeared at the double doors.

"Something simple, tell him to surprise me." She disappeared into the bathroom.

Kyle opened the doors and spoke to Anna, then returned to the now empty room. He walked the perimeter of the room, his senses reaching out for anything abnormal. As he passed the doors to the balcony, he stopped to lock them, and continued to survey the room. He paused for a moment outside of the French doors and briefly glanced over them.

He was startled to see her in the shower, the glass doors hiding nothing from his keen eyes. He marveled at her tone body, the soft whiteness of her skin, and the perfect curves she hid beneath unflattering clothing. He inhaled deeply, salivating at the aroma of her blood and picturing the throbbing vein of her neck in his mind. Kyle jerked suddenly, aware of what he was doing, and then proceeded to ascertain if her room was secure. He cursed himself. That brief lapse in judgment could cost him his life. Chevalier made it abundantly clear that Emily belonged to him and was to be left alone, yet here he was, walking around her bedroom while she stood naked just a few yards from him.

"Much better," she said, stepping out of the bathroom. She was brushing softly through her hair, making sure she didn't brush near the stitches.

"Your meal should be here soon." He felt like keeping formality would save him from further distractions.

Emily nodded and sat down next to him. Kyle stood up nervously and began to stoke the fire.

"May I ask you a question?" Emily asked.

Kyle nodded, still focused on the fire.

"What exactly were Chev's orders? I mean... what did he tell everyone about me?" She waited for him to turn, but he sat where he was, facing away from her.

"I'm not sure he meant for you to hear them." His tone was even and controlled.

"I'm sure he didn't... but I still want to know."

"Then, my dear, you should take that up with him."

Emily nodded. "Why is everyone so afraid of him? What has he done to deserve so much compliance?"

She could see that Kyle was smiling. "He is Chief Enforcer, which is enough."

"Enforcing what exactly?"

"The laws and rules of the faction."

"And what does he do if they aren't obeyed?" She leaned toward him, anxious for an answer.

Kyle turned and looked at her. "You are full of questions, aren't you? Again, something you should take up with him."

Emily wrinkled her nose. "Faithful to the last drop. Have you ever defied him?"

Kyle's mind quickly replayed the image in the shower. "No."

"Hrm… dedicated."

Kyle stood up and headed for the door.

"Please don't leave," she said, and stood up.

"I'm simply answering the door. Your meal is here," he told her, opening the double doors.

Emily hadn't heard the knock. It was frustrating how much better they could hear than she could.

Kyle returned with a tray and set it on the table by Emily's chair. The smell of the food drifted up to her, and she realized she was very hungry and the food smelled delicious. She looked down and gasped at the size of the hamburger and the mound of cheese covered fries beside it.

"Wow, Gordon must think he's feeding an army," she commented, stealing a French fry and savoring the taste.

"Are they to your liking?" Kyle sat down again.

"Oh… very much, these are amazing." She picked up the hamburger and took a bite, chewing slowly. Suddenly, she felt awkward eating in front of him. She grabbed the plate and held it out for him.

Kyle chuckled. "No, thank you."

Emily shrugged and set the plate back down. "What do you all eat anyway? I'd think with a thousand of you here it would be hard to keep the blood supply going."

He frowned slightly. It wasn't natural for her to speak of such things. "We have our ways."

"Not going to tell me, are you?" She grabbed another fry.

Kyle smiled. "No, I am not."

Her mood became more serious. "Did anyone come looking for Keith?" She took another bite of the steaming hot hamburger.

"Yes." He grimaced when he remembered what Keith had done to her, and his hands balled into fists.

"Who?"

"Cassi," he said, and watched for a reaction. When she frowned, he felt bad for telling her.

Emily looked over toward the curtained window and then back to Kyle. "What time is it?"

"8:40 pm"

"How do you do that?"

"Do what?"

"Tell the time without a clock." She was curious as she'd seen no clocks or watches in the entire building.

Kyle cocked his head to the side curiously. "I just… know the time."

Emily raised her eyebrows. "How?"

Kyle smiled. "It's a natural ability. If you would like, I can get a clock in here for you."

Her mouth was full of fries, so she just nodded vehemently.

She pulled her knees up into the chair and wrapped her arms around them as she watched the fire.

"I should be going now," Kyle said, and stood up.

"No!" The sound in her voice made him jump.

"Is there a problem? Something I should know about? Is someone bothering you?" Kyle surveyed the room again. It hadn't dawned on him that with her human senses, he would be well aware of an intruder before she would.

Emily stood up. "No, please, don't leave me alone."

Kyle frowned. "It's not proper for me to stay."

"You mean... Chev would be mad if you stayed all night?" She guessed.

He didn't answer.

"Please, Kyle, I can't be alone." Her eyes were pleading.

He sighed and looked toward the door. "I can ask Anna to stay in here."

"I don't want Anna. I want you... I don't know her, and I don't like how she calls me child." Emily set her jaw, and her eyes narrowed.

Kyle laughed softly, "Alright, I will stay."

She grinned. "If Chev gives you a hard time, tell him to come talk to me."

Emily yawned despite herself and headed for the large bed. She noticed how Kyle had returned to his seat by the fire. She guessed that in bed, she wouldn't even be able to see him. Standing behind the bed's curtain, she slipped off her jeans and crawled into bed in her t-shirt and pulled the cool sheets up around her.

"Good night, Kyle," she called out, and all she heard in return was a soft laugh.

***

The dream was different this time. She was still running, but it was along the beach. She could hear footsteps behind her, coming closer. They were running. The voices echoed off the rocks around her, calling out to her in patronizing tones. It was Keith. He was coming for her, his cold, dead hands just inches from her neck.

"No!" she screamed, hoping someone, anyone could hear.

"What are you screaming for, slut? You owe me... you owe me my life, and I'm going to take it out of you." Keith was slurring his words like he'd been drinking.

She pushed herself harder to try to get ahead of him.

"You wait till he fucks you, Em. You wait until he sees what a slut you are, the dirty whoring slut." His hand touched her hair briefly. "I kept you around because I felt sorry for you, you know that? No one will want you, Emily, no one!"

His hands touched her arm...

"No!" Emily screamed, clawing at the cold hands on her arm.

"Emily," Kyle said softly. "It's okay."

Her eyes adjusted to the dark quickly, and she saw Kyle's face. He was afraid and touching her arm softly. It was Kyle that had touched her, not Keith.

Kyle sat on the edge of the bed and gasped when she fell into him, pressing her face against his chest to block out the images of Keith in the dream.

He hesitated and then wrapped his arms around her lightly. "It was just a dream. Keith isn't back."

"How did you..."

"You were talking in your sleep. I apologize for listening, but it's hard to block it out when you are screaming." He sounded truly sorry and she'd heard that before, it must be true.

She grabbed onto his shirt, her hands shaking. "Are you positive? What if he's a heku now? He'll come back and kill me."

"He's not one of us. I can promise you that." Kyle fought back a chuckle.

Emily nodded and lay back on the bed, pulling the covers tight around her. Kyle stood up to return to his chair. "Wait, Kyle, sit with me."

The look on Chevalier's face as he demanded they stay away from her flashed into his mind. Chevalier also told them to give her whatever she wanted. He saw both sides and decided he would rather face Emily's wrath, than the Chief Enforcer. He looked down to tell her no and noticed her pleading eyes and how her whole body shook with fear.

He lowered his shoulders and sat down on the edge of the bed, as far from her as he could get. It wasn't long before she was asleep again.

Choices

"It does give me a right! She is my blood, my family." Ulrich slammed his fist down on the granite table.

"That gives you the right to nothing! She's an adult woman, who chose to stay with me." Chevalier's eyes blazed with fury.

"I have the inherent right to protect my offspring. Does the Council deny that right?" He looked up at the Elders.

"We do not deny that you have some rights, as far as family is concerned, but our decision has not yet been made. Now I suggest you both sit down and keep your tempers under control. To think this is all over a mortal!" The only female Elder, Selest, looked down at them from the platform. She glanced to the two men on her left, and they nodded, astonished that two heku were fighting over a mortal.

"I will ask this one more time… Lord Ulrich, what do you benefit from having Emily Russo live with your coven?" The smaller of the male Elders asked.

"I benefit by having complete protection of one of my offspring," he stated plainly.

"Do you, therefore, deny that Emily Russo is a direct descendant of the Winchester family and thereby capable of powers beyond both mortal and heku?"

Ulrich glanced quickly at Chevalier and glared. "I do deny that. She has shown no powers beyond any mortal. The abilities mentioned died out a long time ago."

"Are those your findings also, Chief Enforcer?" Selest asked, and looked down at him.

"It's inconclusive at this time, which is why I want to keep her in my care, where she can live safely, and I can learn whatever talents she may have." Chevalier avoided looking at Ulrich, afraid their secret may be given away with a glance.

"She is my granddaughter! If she has any abilities, it should be I that find them. I can teach her how to control them. I can teach her how to use them," Ulrich said, pleading. He knew that as an enemy, the Elders would not see his view.

"She doesn't want to live with you." Chevalier raised his voice, and the Elders motioned for both of them to sit again.

"I won't tell you again, both of you will stay calm in this court room!" Elder Leonid said, and both complied immediately.

The entire room was suddenly quiet. No sound at all could be heard as the Elders debated silently. After almost an hour, Elder Selest stood up.

"It is our decision to allow Chevalier to continue to monitor the situation and report back to this Council, and we, in return, will keep Ulrich informed." She sat down when she was finished talking.

Chevalier sighed and turned to Ulrich, his eyes burning with fury. Without addressing them further, Chevalier quickly left the court room, anxious to avoid a confrontation.

***

The ferry couldn't move fast enough for Chevalier. He worried about how long the court session had lasted. He told her that he would be gone only a few days, but he had been gone for a week. He knew he could trust his coven, but lingering doubts about a select family of newly turned heku made him nervous and anxious to get home. He also felt incomplete without her. He could picture her eyes, the vivid green that flared when she was mad. He missed the blush in her cheeks and the way she felt in his arms. He tapped his dashboard lightly with his fingers. Any sign of patience had worn off.

Storm sat quietly beside him, unsure how to handle his sudden impatience. As soon as they arrived at the pier, she stepped out of the car and went to talk to the guards. Chevalier put his car into gear and sped through the city toward the castle. It was late. He knew she would be asleep, but he just wanted to see her.

As he stepped out of the car, he noticed the guards shift nervously. He frowned slightly and studied their faces. They were like stone statues. He narrowed his eyes and walked into the castle. The air inside seemed tense at his arrival. Things were too quiet. Not one servant was in sight, there was no hint of whispers, and even the sound of everyday cleaning was absent.

Chevalier surveyed the entryway and saw nothing amiss, and no sign that anything was wrong. He quickly ascended the stairs and stepped into Emily's antechamber. Anna was in the corner standing perfectly still, not even meeting his eyes.

"Anna?" he questioned.

"Yes, sir?" Anna replied, and he wondered at the tone of her voice.

He studied her every movement. The muscles in her neck were tense and strained. "How is she?" He didn't know why, but he felt almost afraid of her answer.

"Fine, sir."

His brow furrowed. "That's it? Fine?"

Anna nodded.

The scent caught Chevalier's attention. The scent from her bedroom was wrong. His eyes raged. "Who is in there with her?"

Anna froze.

He stormed into the room, one of the doors splintering as it hit the stone walls. His eyes focused in on the bed. He could see Emily under the covers, but his attention was on the lone figure sitting at the foot of her bed, looking at him as he entered the room. The form stood up quickly and stepped back toward the wall.

"Sir," Kyle whispered. Chevalier was inches from him in less than a second, staring down at him.

His voice was low and furious, "What do you think you're doing?"

"Sir, it's not what you…" Kyle's voice was cut off by Chevalier's hand wrapped tightly around his neck.

Kyle flew through the air, landing with a violent crash against the stone wall. The impact cracked the rough stones and sent shatters of broken rock and sand against the floor. Kyle flipped onto his feet and faced Chevalier, keeping his face calm and non-aggressive. "Please, sir. It's not what you think."

Chevalier turned to the bed to face Emily. The thunderous crash should have woken her, but she didn't move, didn't stir. Her smell was off. The sweet aroma was masked somewhat by a harsh chemical. He turned back to Kyle, who was still at the wall, his hands palms out toward Chevalier.

"Sir, let me explain, please." Kyle was standing tall, his shoulders squared and ready for attack, though his posture wasn't crouched as if to defend.

Chevalier instantly materialized several feet in front of him. "Start talking… and it better be good." His eyes narrowed, and his hands balled into tight fists.

Kyle whispered instinctively, "She hasn't slept since you left, sir. There was an attack the first day, and she was having nightmares…" He paused as the furious look in Chevalier's eyes grew more intense.

"Attack?" he hissed.

"Yes, sir, the first day we were out riding and a young one was hiding in the trees."

Chevalier grabbed a nearby chair and threw it through the plated window to the balcony, ripping the large curtains down with the force. "Who?"

Kyle winced slightly, "It was Ethan, sir. She fell when the horse bucked, but we handled it. Ethan is waiting for you, and Anna was able to stop the bleeding." He stopped talking when Chevalier inhaled sharply.

He took a step toward Kyle. "Continue."

"That night she started having nightmares, screaming through the night. She begged me to stay, sir. I promise you. She begged me." Kyle waited for the fury, but Chevalier wasn't moving, yet his body was shaking with rage.

Kyle continued, "Last evening, I finally talked her into taking a sleeping pill. She had dark circles under her eyes, and she'd quit eating. Henry studied up and found that it was the lack of sleep. It took hours to convince her to take it, but she finally did. Nothing else happened, sir. I swear to you."

Chevalier's eyes narrowed again. "You couldn't sit in a chair? How dare you sit on her bed."

"That was her too, sir. The first night I was on the chair when the nightmare began. She said she felt safer, the closer I was... I would never have done anything. I swear my allegiance to you." Kyle lowered his eyes, showing submission.

"Get out." Chevalier's whisper was riddled with power, and Kyle bowed once and ran out of the room as a blur.

Once the room was empty except for he and Emily, he went to her and sat gently on the side of the bed, touching her cheek softly. He didn't like the way she smelled and was uncomfortable with how still she slept.

Chevalier inhaled her scent deeply, his mind searching for anything wrong. He caught the hint of dried blood, but the sharp stab of medicine covered the sweet smell.

"I'll be back," he whispered, bending down to press his lips gently against her forehead.

He appeared out in the antechamber. The doors hung limply from their hinges. Anna stiffened in the corner.

He gritted his teeth, "Dried blood?"

Anna nodded. "Yes, sir. She hit her head when the horse bucked her off. I stitched her wound. It is healing."

"Nightmares?" His body was tense.

"Yes, Chief Enforcer, every night, she screams." Anna's eyes were fearful.

"What does she scream?" He watched her face for any indication that she was lying to him.

She cleared her throat, feeling his intense gaze on her. "It varies, sir, some nights she screams about someone named Keith. Mostly... it's for you." She dropped her eyes.

Chevalier sighed and his voice softened, "What has she been doing during my absence?"

Anna relaxed slightly. "She won't let me shadow her, sir. I tried. I really have... but she orders me to stay behind."

He laughed slightly. He had no doubts that Emily had done just that. "But you still know..."

Anna nodded. "Yes, sir."

"What then?"

"She mostly spends her day out on her horse, sir. She rides along the trees and down to the beach."

"You let her out alone in the city?" He winced.

"No, sir!" Anna stressed. "We wouldn't do that, not after the first attack."

"Then who was with her?"

Anna braced for his fury. "Kyle, sir."

He took a step toward her. "Kyle and who else? Or was Kyle with her every day?"

Anna simply nodded, her voice catching in her throat. "It was her request, sir," she whispered.

"Oh?"

"Sir." She decided to take the punishment and tell him everything. "The nightmares, they kept her up. She finally refused to sleep and a few days ago, she stopped even eating. Any noise and she jumps. She turns pale if she catches sight of anyone other than Kyle and I. Emily said that Kyle kept the fear away. She trusted him to keep her safe while you were away, and we decided, together, to honor those wishes."

Anna was able to relax when Chevalier stood up out of the angry crouch. "Fix this room," he said, and in the blink of an eye he was leaving the room with Emily cradled in his arms.

***

"Good morning," Chevalier whispered as Emily began to stir. He'd been watching her sleep for the past 14 hours, wondering how much sleeping medication the immortals had given her.

Her eyes flashed open and she curled up against his chest. "You're back!"

Chevalier held her tightly and then put his fingers under her chin, bringing her face up toward his. "How are you?"

He had the chance to study her face. She still had dark circles under her eyes, the pallor making them darker. Her eyes were sunken and tired.

"I'm fine." She smiled up at him.

"Gordon is bringing you some breakfast, dear."

"Just coffee please. I'm not hungry."

"Nevertheless, you will eat." He tried to sound commanding but had a hard time being stern as those flowing green eyes peered up at him.

Emily lay back on the bed and stretched a bit. This bed was harder than the one she was used to and her back was aching. She looked around and frowned. "Where am I?"

"I moved you to my room. I'm having some work done on yours." He decided to keep his violent tendencies to himself.

She yawned into her hand and returned to studying his room. This gave him the chance to study her further. He was a little shocked to see the delicate fabric and low cut of the soft pink flowing nightgown that revealed a hint of her soft breasts. He would have to thank Margaret for that later. He gently ran his finger along the low neckline and cursed when he heard Gordon coming with her breakfast.

"Come in," he said, irritated.

Gordon entered with a large silver tray, and the smell of bacon and eggs filled the room. He placed it on the bedside table and lifted the cover, smiling. "Finally, the chance to make something other than coffee." His grin fell when he saw Chevalier's expression, and he hurried out of the room with a bow.

Emily sat up and turned to the tray to make up a cup of coffee. Chevalier noticed, appraisingly, the low cut back of her nightgown. It perfectly showed the smooth skin on her back, her pale complexion, and the perfect curve of her fragile spine. He gently ran his fingers up her spine and grinned as she shivered. She turned back to the bed and sat up. The steaming cup of coffee was cradled in her hands.

He reached out and took the cup away from her protesting fingers. "Food Emily, not coffee... food."

"Coffee first," she said, reaching out for it.

He moved it farther from her, out of her reach. "I think you've had enough caffeine. Eat... please... for me."

Emily reached over and grabbed a piece of bacon and sat back against the headboard to eat.

"I'm so sorry. I honestly had planned on being gone only a few days and then to hear that..." He paused to calm his voice, "That you were attacked in my absence."

She tensed. It was still fresh in her mind. She grabbed another piece of bacon, not wanting to talk about it.

"I lied to you again, and I suppose saying I'm sorry isn't good enough. I promised my coven would keep you safe in my absence." His eyes dropped to the bed.

She gently touched his cheek. "You can't protect me from everything, Chev. Kyle was there with me. Nothing happened."

He looked into her eyes. "That's not how I heard it."

She reached back and touched the back of her head. "That? That's nothing. Patra doesn't take nicely to heku apparently, though she is getting used to Kyle."

"Patra is here?" he asked, shocked.

Emily smiled brightly. Her face suddenly lit up. "Yes, Kyle brought her here for me."

Chevalier nodded. He had to give Kyle credit. He was taking care of her as he had ordered. "Eat more."

She glanced over at the plate and then back to Chevalier. "Where did you go?"

He sighed. She might as well know. "To court, with Ulrich."

She gasped, "Over me?!"

Chevalier nodded. "It's okay though, they have granted me more time with you."

Her eyes darted around the room. "But someday they may change their minds? Someday, I may be forced to live with him?"

He didn't answer.

"I won't do it... no one can make me." She set her jaw. He didn't want her to be upset so he kept his thoughts to himself. He knew that if the time came, she wouldn't have a choice.

"Don't worry about it now, Em. If the time ever comes... If the time ever comes, we'll handle it then, okay?" He realized she was done eating and handed her coffee to her.

She sipped it, letting it burn her tongue.

"Ash anyone while I was away?" He grinned at her, trying to lighten the mood.

Emily couldn't help but laugh, "No."

"I had some clothes brought in to you. Get dressed, I have something I need to do, and I want you to come."

She looked at him expectantly. "We're leaving the island?"

He grinned. "No, we aren't even leaving the castle."

She sighed, slightly disappointed, and got up to get dressed. She noticed, irritated, that his bathroom had locking doors.

She looked around the large bathroom. It was empty except for a vanity mirror, a shower, and a pile of clothes folded neatly on the counter. To her horror, the walls were lined with mirrors. She slipped out of her nightgown and quickly into her clothes. Her eyes fixed on the floor. She was glad they were jeans. She didn't like all of the dresses that Margaret kept bringing her.

As Emily turned to leave, she caught a glimpse of herself in one of the mirrors and sighed. She hadn't noticed that her jeans had diamond cut-outs down the length of the legs from her hips to her ankles. While not a t-shirt, at least the pale blue shirt wasn't revealing. She would have to throw the jeans away when she got a new pair. It took her only a few minutes to throw her hair into a French braid and head back out to Chevalier.

He grinned at her, and his eyes fell almost immediately to the small glimpse of her smooth white thighs and toned calves that her jeans provided. She blushed and laid her nightgown down on the foot of the bed. Emily glanced around the room and saw that her breakfast tray was gone, and the bed was made.

"Are you ready to go?" Chevalier asked, laughing at her blush and taking her hand in his. He was pleased when she didn't pull away from his touch.

Emily nodded and let him lead her out of the room. Before she could see what was going on in her room, the door shut, as if by itself. She had the feeling they were hiding something.

"Where is Kyle?" she asked as they descended the stairs.

"He is back at his post." Chevalier knew that Kyle would be doing his best to stay off of his radar.

The rest of the walk was in silence. It seemed to Emily like they should have gotten to the ground floor already, and the narrow stone walkway seemed to be spiraling downward. She hadn't seen windows for a while, and the way was no longer lit, so she couldn't see anything. Chevalier was guiding her. Her eyes didn't adjust, either, and she was getting frustrated, not liking being without one of her key senses. Finally, a light shone in a rectangle ahead, they were nearing a door.

The door opened just as they got to it, and she saw that a brightly lit room was on the other side. The room was circular with a platform at one end. Four chairs were high on the platform behind large oak desks. The rest of the room was full of rows and rows of chairs facing the other four. Emily recognized this as a type of court room, and she started to panic, holding tighter to Chevalier's arm.

There was only one other person in the room, the door guard who held an ominous looking sword in his hands. Emily found that odd. Why a sword instead of a gun? Chevalier led them up to the platform and sat in one of the center chairs, motioning for her to sit at his left. As soon as she sat down, Storm appeared and sat in the chair on his right. Over the next few minutes, others piled into the room, taking the chairs on the lower level and all seemed to be watching her closely. She began to panic.

Kyle walked in, looking nervous, and sat in the chair beside Emily. She was comforted to see him. "What is this?" she whispered to him.

It didn't escape Chevalier's notice that she asked Kyle the question instead of him, and his insides tightened.

Kyle knew his place and didn't answer, staring straight ahead. Emily just sighed and returned her eyes to scan the room.

When everyone was seated and quiet, Storm stood up.

"Bring him in," she demanded, and the guard by the door left quickly, returning within only a second, dragging the young heku into the room, the strange heku that had scared Patra and tried to attack her. Emily's entire body tensed. She was ready to run from the room, but when she started to stand, Chevalier's hand shot out and touched her leg.

"Don't do this, please," she whispered to Chevalier. He didn't respond. He was watching the young heku with loathing. Her breathing picked up. She couldn't imagine what was going to happen to him.

"Please." She tried again.

Chevalier silenced her with an icy glare.

Storm faced Ethan, who was sitting in an old chair on the bottom level. "Charges have been brought against you, charges of the gravest nature. Your age doesn't protect you from disobeying the direct orders of the Chief Enforcer. Do you understand these charges?"

"Yes," Ethan said softly, and his eyes were directed at Emily. She could feel the rumble from beside her, both Chevalier and Kyle were growling.

"How old are you, Ethan? For the record," Storm asked, holding a clipboard.

"213 years," he said, licking his lips.

"Mind yourself!" Storm barked at Ethan, and he recoiled under her words, looking back at her. "Did you, or did you not, receive the direct order that the girl wasn't to be harmed, that she belongs directly to the Chief Enforcer?"

Emily frowned and grimaced at the word 'belongs'.

"Yessss," he hissed again, his eyes falling on Emily. "But she is so sweet, so tender. I can't resist her." He leaned a little closer to the front of the room and inhaled.

"No!" Emily screamed, just as Chevalier appeared at Ethan's back. His hands wrapped tightly around the young heku's head. Before Emily could shut her eyes, Ethan's head was off and sent flying into the wall of the court room.

Emily stood. All eyes were on Chevalier as he quickly dismembered Ethan. She was able to run from the room, unnoticed. She fought her way up the impossibly dark hallway, winding farther and farther up, feeling her way along the wall. There were no sounds behind her, yet she ran, tripping on loose stones and imperfections in the floor. As the hallway became lighter, she recognized her surroundings and ran out the back door in the kitchen, headed straight for the barn.

Patra was waiting just inside, saddled and ready for her daily ride. Emily deftly hoisted herself up onto the mare and was in a full gallop before even clearing the barn doors. She headed the opposite way she normally did, going straight for the beach. Once the sound of the ocean was near and Patra's hooves hit sand, she slowed the horse and held tightly to the saddle's horn, trying to calm her breathing.

She slid off the horse and nuzzled her face into the horse's warm neck, and then broke down into heart-wrenching sobs. The sight of Ethan's head slamming into the stone wall was horrifying. She'd seen Chevalier mad, but never that enraged. She kept reminding herself that it was her fault. Because of her, this creature had died. Emily sunk down onto the sand at the foot of her horse. She could hear the ocean clearly but couldn't see it because of the tall cement wall. She shut her eyes and focused on the rhythmic pounding of the waves against the rocks. The monotonous sound cleared her mind of the headless heku.

Patra nibbled at Emily's hair and brought her out of the trance. She stood up and noticed it was starting to get dark. The cold wind blowing off the ocean sent a chill down through her. She ran her fingers through the mare's mane, her mind wondering where to go and what to do. This world of Chevalier's seemed more dangerous now. She didn't feel safe in it and didn't feel like she even remotely belonged. The sound of footsteps approaching made her body stiffen and her breath caught.

She peered around Patra's neck and saw a tall man approaching. His dark face was hidden in the dying light. The mare whinnied loudly and stomped her foot at him as he got closer. Emily stood, frozen to the horse's side, unable to move. She could feel Patra's muscles tighten. She was about to run. Emily grabbed the bridle to steady the horse as the sound of the approaching steps stopped. There was no sound but the waves against the beach.

Emily stood motionless against the horse for a few minutes, not sure if the stranger had gone or was standing just on the other side of Patra. Her heart beat violently in her chest as he spoke, his voice soft.

"Emily?" he asked her.

She didn't move, didn't breathe.

"I won't hurt you, child," he reassured her. "I came to show you the way back."

She swallowed hard, her mouth dry with fear. "I know the way… back."

Emily screamed briefly as something sounded from the saddle behind her, and she ducked down away from it.

"Calm, child, it's just a coat." The stranger's voice was farther away now.

Emily managed to turn slightly and see the coat lying over the saddle. She peered around Patra and saw the stranger standing 20 feet away, watching her. Her skin broke out into goose bumps as the wind picked up. She looked up and saw dark clouds covering the rising moon.

"You must be cold," the stranger said from where he stood, not moving closer.

"I'm fine," she managed to say finally, and slipped back around behind the mare. "You take the coat if you are cold."

The soft laughter filled the wind, and she fought against feeling comforted by its warmth and sincerity.

"If you won't wear the coat, at least go back to the castle, they are very worried about you."

Emily leaned her head against Patra, unsure what to do.

Finally, the heku spoke again, "Do you wish me to leave?"

She nodded, knowing that he couldn't see her, but she wasn't able to speak.

"Very well," he said sadly, then suddenly he was gone.

The darkness was full now. Any light from the moon was blocked by the black clouds. Emily sat down again on the sand and wrapped her arms around her knees for warmth. The coat sat invitingly above her on the saddle, and her mind began to wander.

How many people would die because she was there? How many would be in danger because of her raw emotions and the ability to disintegrate a heku at will? How could she survive in a world where beings were torn apart for breaking the order of one man? It all seemed fierce and primal. The laws and regulations she was accustomed to seemed irrelevant here. From what she had seen, the heku followed Chevalier. No one doubted his methods or his orders and no one disobeyed, completely out of fear.

Her mind wandered to Ulrich, the unseen heku that watched over her. Was his coven similar? Did he have this much control over his people? Could he harm her as she felt Chevalier was capable of doing? Did he have the temper and the ability to rip another person's head from their body? She winced as the image again came into her mind.

Her mind returned to the beach as it began to rain. The cold drops almost immediately soaked her hair and clothing. Emily clutched her knees tighter to her and watched as the vapors from her breath became visible in the frigid air. She began to shiver uncontrollably but still refused to put on the coat. It seemed like a symbol of restraint, a symbol that she'd given up and agreed to embrace this sadistic lifestyle.

Patra's skin twitched. She was visibly irritated about being out in the cold rain, but Emily still didn't move, didn't know where to go. The waves grew fierce and were now slapping hard against the cement wall. She imagined that the beach on the other side had disappeared with the tide. Emily could feel the cold drops sliding down her face and back, her body shaking more violently than before.

The crashing of the waves masked the approaching footsteps, and she didn't realize that she wasn't alone until they were standing in front of her. She tried to look up at them, but she was too tired. Her teeth chattered, and her body shook with cold.

Chevalier crouched down, his hands slowly reaching for her, palms out. "Emily, you need to get inside." His voice was soft and concerned, but her mind raced back to the court room.

"N.. N… No," was all she could manage. She felt the coat being slipped over her back, and she wiggled it off.

"You are going to freeze to death out here." This time it was Kyle's voice from behind her, and she realized that he must have been the one that draped the coat over her shoulders. She heard the sound of someone settling into Patra's saddle.

"Kyle is going to take Patra back to the barn. It's too cold out here for her," Chevalier told her as she felt the comforting presence of the mare leave.

Chevalier sat down facing her. "I don't want to force you, Em, but I will if you don't get up soon."

"You killed him," she whispered.

He sighed, "Yes."

"It's not right to just kill someone," she said through chattering teeth.

"Emily, it's important when dealing with a thousand natural predators that everyone obeys the rules. I set the rules... and if they aren't obeyed, then I deal with it." He watched her eyes, his voice soft and smooth.

She began to shiver harder. "H h h how l long bef fore you k k kill m m me?"

Chevalier frowned. "I'm not going to kill you. Remember, you aren't one of my charges."

"S s so, h h how w w will you d d deal with m m me if I b break a r rule?" Her lips were turning a vibrant blue.

"You don't have rules, Emily. You aren't in my coven, and you are too important for me to punish you for breaking a rule. I am Chief Enforcer of the faction. I am not your Chief Enforcer." He stood up and touched her arm. "Get up."

"O o o or wh wh what?" She glared up at him.

"Or I'll pick you up." He was getting frustrated with her.

She'd never known this kind of cold, the cold that seeped deep into her inner core. Her skin was no longer cold. It was numb, which wasn't all together unpleasant. She was finding it hard to concentrate now, and her hands and feet ached painfully. She buried her head, putting her forehead against her knees that were still tightly wrapped by her arms, though she couldn't feel them any longer.

"Emily?" he asked softly, bending down closer to her.

She shivered violently and didn't answer.

With one swift movement, Chevalier picked her up and grimaced at the icy cold of her body. She continued to shiver but didn't protest as he carried her back to the warmth of the castle.

He headed into her room. The repairs were made, and Anna had a hot bath waiting. He set her down gently on the tile, but she couldn't feel her feet, and she sank down onto the floor. She set to work unbuttoning her shirt, but her fingers were stiff and frozen. Chevalier sighed and reached down, pulling her shirt over her head.

"N n n no," she began to protest.

"Hush up, no more protests. This time I'm not kidding," he warned.

Emily's clothes were wet and clung tightly to her frozen body. Chevalier gave up and simply ripped them off of her. He growled slightly as he picked up her naked body. It was colder than it should be, and he was worried that she might get sick. He sat her down slowly into the warm jetted tub, ignoring how wet his shirt got, then he stood back and motioned for Anna to leave.

Emily's violent shiver became worse, and she couldn't manage to say the words to make him leave. The chattering sound of her teeth filled the bathroom, but she couldn't seem to stop that either. The warm jets sent painful stabs through her body as the blood returned to her limbs. She couldn't help but moan slightly as the stabbing tingles crept up her arms and legs.

Once the shivering stopped and she'd sunk down into the warmth, Chevalier moved to sit by the side of the tub. He was too angry to appreciate her body beneath the water, too angry to notice she didn't complain that he was there.

"Was that entirely necessary?" he asked, more demanding than caring.

She answered softly, "I have nowhere to go."

He frowned. "Why do you need to go anywhere?"

Emily curled up into her protective ball, knees pulled tight against her chest with her arms wrapped around them. She looked down at the water, and a tear dripped down her cheek.

Chevalier reached into the water and rubbed her back softly, "All of this because of Ethan?"

She shook her head. "No."

"What is it then? Tell me."

"You'll get mad," Emily whispered.

"I'm more likely to get mad if you don't tell me what the hell is going on." He reached to her chin and pulled her face toward him and looked deeply into her tear filled eyes.

Emily avoided his gaze. She knew she didn't have the strength to fight him right now.

"Emily...," he hissed at her, and her heart skipped a beat.

She pulled her face out of his hands and looked down at the water again. "I'm afraid."

"To tell me?"

"No..." She paused and ran her hand along the surface of the water. "Of you."

"I'm a heku, Em. You should have been afraid of me from the start." His voice lightened.

"You killed him," she repeated.

"Yes I did, and I'm sure he won't be the last." He frowned again as her body tensed at his words.

"How many people die before you realize I'm not worth it?" She watched the ripples in the water.

"Damnit, Emily." He hit the edge of the tub with his fist, cracking the porcelain. "You're lucky no one else judges your self-worth by your eschewed views."

"No one should die for me, Chev. My life isn't any more important than anyone else's."

"Ethan didn't die because he tried to..." Even the thought made him angry. "Attack you. He died for disobeying my rules."

Chevalier grabbed her face more forcefully than he originally intended, and pulled her to face him. "You aren't expected to follow the same rules. I told you, you aren't a subordinate to me. If they can't obey the rules I've set forth, they know the consequences long before they are allowed to join this coven. You are right, you have nowhere to go. However, you belong here with me, so that's not a problem."

Her eyes were wide and shocked.

"Now get out, get dressed, and come out to eat. Gordon just brought your dinner." He stood up and walked out of the bathroom.

Emily wasn't sure if he was mad or how mad he was, so she decided to do what he asked. The only clothing in the bathroom was the silk pink nightgown that she had complained to Margaret was too low cut. Without wanting to cause problems, she slipped into it, ran a brush through her matted hair, and then decided to leave it down.

The fire in the bedroom was roaring, and the warmth from it felt good. She was warm from the bath, but her muscles still ached from the cold. Chevalier was sitting by the fire with a silver tray on the table between him and the other chair. As she sat down, he picked up the silver cover and motioned for her to begin.

She wasn't feeling very hungry but again decided not to cross him, and began picking at the steak and potato.

"Kyle tells me you've been having nightmares about Keith?" He watched as the firelight danced across her skin, still pink from the bath.

Emily nodded and took another bite.

"Tell me about it."

She froze. She couldn't tell him what Keith was saying in the dream. He still had views that she was good. On the other hand, she couldn't make him madder. She felt like her life was on the edge as it was.

"I don't remember," was the answer she decided to give.

His eyes narrowed. "I'm not accustomed to being lied to."

She looked up at him, her eyes daring. "Fine then, yes I do remember them, but no, I won't tell you what he's saying."

Chevalier shrugged. "Fine, but I will tell you something… Keith was a liar and a manipulator. If you believe a single thing he ever said to you, then you are a fool."

Her glance turned to a glare. "And you don't know what you are talking about. Keith knew me for nine years before you came along. I am pretty sure he had a good idea about me."

"An idea that I plan to disprove." He leaned closer to her. His eyes suddenly amused.

Emily brought her knees up to her chest.

"Stop it," he ordered.

She looked up at him with wide eyes. "What?"

"Stop pulling yourself into a ball!" His fists were clenched.

She thought for a moment and then wrapped her arms around her knees, watching him. "I thought I wasn't a subordinate."

"You aren't, but you are in my care and when you wrap yourself into your protective little ball, it shows how insecure you are, and I won't have it. I won't have you hiding your body from me. I won't have you pretending no one looks at you, and no one values you. I'm tired of watching you beat yourself up over it." He quickly moved over to her, picked her up gently in his arms, and pressed his lips to hers.

Emily didn't hesitate and wrapped her arms tightly around his neck, winding her fingers through his hair. His lips were soft and sent warm shivers up her spine. She felt herself being laid down on the bed, then his heavy body pressed against hers. As his tongue pried her lips open and began to explore her mouth, her body tensed, the panic setting in. She tried to move out from under him, pushing against his chest with her hands, but he didn't move.

She turned her face away from him. "Stop, Chev."

His voice trembled with anger, "Not tonight, Em. You aren't pushing me away tonight."

"Please, let me go," she protested as he ran his soft tongue up the length of her neck and began kissing along her jaw line. She shivered and inhaled sharply, submitting to him.

Trust

"You've done it now, slut. Now he'll know how dirty you are." Keith smiled at her, and his eyes were empty and rotting. He took a step toward her, and she turned and ran naked through the trees.

"Run all you want. You can't run from your whoring life. You can't run from him knowing the truth about you," Keith called as he ran after her.

"Did he say he loved you? I think not. Do you know why? Because he feels pity for you! Who else would take you if he won't? I'll tell you... no one, Emily. No one wants you because you are ugly and worthless." His voice echoed through the trees.

She screamed as his cold, dead hands clamped against her arm.

"Shhhhh, Em, it's okay." Chevalier was pressed against her side with one arm draped over her. She could feel his body against hers, and she remembered.

Emily tensed under his arm and began to pull away when she realized she wasn't dressed, and the pounding in her head was growing worse after the dream.

"No you don't... you aren't leaving," Chevalier told her, and his arm held her to the bed.

"I need to go," she said, again trying to get up.

Chevalier kissed her shoulder lightly. "Go where?"

"Please... let me up." She pried at his hand.

"Tell me where, and if I think it's a good enough reason, then I'll let you go." He moved his hand to wrap it around her.

Emily pulled the blanket up higher to cover herself, but Chevalier grabbed it and lowered it again.

"Stop it," he said lightly.

"I'm cold." She tried again, but he held the covers tightly.

"No, you aren't. You are hiding." He kissed a line from her shoulder up her neck. "Now go back to sleep, and this time… ignore what Keith is telling you."

"But..."

"You talk in your sleep." He could feel the warmth from her blush, and he smiled.

She rolled onto her side away from him and glanced at the clock Kyle put in for her. It was almost 3am. She decided to stay awake and watch for 7am, but soon, her eyes began to feel heavy, and she was comfortable with Chevalier pressed against her back with his arms around her.

***

"Good Morning," he whispered, kissing the tip of her nose.

She glanced at him. He was on top of the covers and fully dressed, smiling down at her. She could feel the blush rising to her cheeks, and she pulled the covers tighter around her.

Chevalier chuckled, "Gordon is almost here with your breakfast."

Her eyes widened. "No! He can't come in here."

"Why not?"

"Chevalier, stop him, please. Don't let him in here!" The panic in her voice stopped his laugh, and he got up to talk to Gordon in the antechamber. Emily took the opportunity to run for the bathroom, taking the bed sheets with her as a cover.

Chevalier entered the bathroom just as Emily was pulling on a robe and cinching it tightly around her waist.

"What was that about?" he asked, watching her.

"What was what?" She turned to look at him.

Chevalier just looked at her, waiting for an answer.

She sighed, "How many of your coven have you slept with, Chev?"

The question shocked him, but he held his face steady, "I don't see how that is relevant."

"Oh… it's quite relevant."

"How so?"

"Is it safe to assume the answer is a large number?" She walked past him and out into the bedroom.

Chevalier followed her, not sure where this was going. "I wouldn't say large, per se."

"That's it then… I don't want to be added to that number based on one lapse in judgment." She sat down and picked at the eggs on her plate.

He grinned. "Is that what it was… a lapse in judgment?"

"Yes." She pulled the robe down over her legs.

"I see, so… so you fear that Gordon will count you in with my many… shall we say… exploits?" He was enjoying this, and it infuriated her.

"Exactly"

"Then do you care if I am counted along with your exploits?" He sat in the chair across from her casually.

She didn't answer, the blush rising quickly to her cheeks.

His eyes narrowed, and then he started to laugh, "My God, Emily. How many men have you been with?"

She pushed the plate away, no longer hungry. "It's none of your business."

"Oh do tell. You were quite good at it, so I can only guess at the high number." He laughed harder as her blush grew darker.

The humiliation was too much, and Emily briefly considered jumping off the balcony. He noticed her gaze and stopped laughing, studying the look on her face and the darkening blush. She walked over and began going through the closest wardrobe.

Chevalier wondered at her sudden silence and the body language showing she was extremely uncomfortable. His mind shifted to the conversation they had about Keith. She met Keith when she was 14, and then it struck him.

"Oh," was all he could manage to say.

After a long, awkward silence, he moved to her side as she rifled through the wardrobe. "I'm sorry, Em. I wasn't thinking... I guess I didn't realize it'd only been..."

"Don't... just don't say it... we shouldn't be talking about this." She grabbed what she had her hand on and disappeared into the bathroom.

Chevalier decided to leave her alone. She seemed to need some time to adjust to what happened, and he was all too eager to make use of his private office. It was only a few seconds before he unlocked his office door and went to step in but saw Storm running at him.

"Wait!" she called to him.

"Yes, Storm?" He hated how his voice sounded irritated with her.

She paused for a moment and then continued, "You promised a follow up with the Wilson case, sir. He's no longer waiting patiently."

"Not today, Storm." She looked hurt but walked away from him.

He walked into the solitude his office provided and heard the door lock shut behind him. Ignoring the piles of papers and stacks of books, he sat in the large mahogany chair and buried his face in his hands.

"What was he doing?" he wondered.

How had he come so far as to seduce a child? He let his feelings take over, and that was never safe, not when he'd spent his entire life gaining control of his most intrinsic emotions. He delved deeper into his mind and body, trying to figure out what it was with Emily that he couldn't live without, why she brought out such strong desires. He shuddered to think it could be love. He, the Chief Enforcer, didn't love. He commanded. He punished. He took, but he didn't love.

The image of Kyle sitting on her bed during the night brought the sudden rage back, and he fought the urge to break something. She brought out his protective tendencies, which always led to violent ideations. There was so much to protect her from, not the least of which, herself, her dead husband, and now the disobedient in his own coven. Ulrich was also on his mind, his warning for Chevalier to stay away from her, and his promise to make her disappear. Chevalier thought also about his promise to Ulrich that he wasn't interested in Emily, another broken promise surrounding her. She seemed to be collecting them from him.

He sighed and shut his eyes, deep in meditation.

***

Emily waited to see if Chevalier would come back soon, but after a few hours, she knew that Keith was right. She let it get too far, and now he wanted nothing to do with her. What she needed was something to occupy her mind, something that would let her think. She needed to decide where to go now that Chevalier would want her to leave. She didn't want to go to Ulrich. She didn't know him, and Chevalier didn't trust him.

She walked out of the bedroom, pausing to tell Anna that she wasn't needed again today, and then set about going through the castle. She didn't find anything interesting, just more bedrooms, some servant's quarters, and a large ballroom with wooden floors and long green drapes covering the walls. One door she went to open was heavy. She could budge it just a little, no more than an inch. It was dark inside and sounded like a large room.

Emily set her feet firmly and put both hands on the door, pushing as hard as she could. She groaned with the strain, but again, all she could manage was about an inch. She stopped when she heard a chuckle from behind her, and she spun around.

She smiled. "Kyle!"

"Having problems?" He walked past her and easily opened the door.

She shrugged and walked into the room, then her mouth fell open. The room was uncommonly large and housed an empty pool. She began to walk around it and could hear Kyle walking behind her.

"Why is it empty?" She stopped to look at him.

Kyle laughed, "We're heku. We don't swim for fun."

"Then why do you even have a pool?" She narrowed her eyes at him.

"Well, that's tough. Okay so..." He was hesitating.

"Sooooo... what?" She prompted.

He sighed, "This used to be a ceremonial room. A donor stepped into it by accident and... well... he can't be in the ceremonial room. So we moved the ceremonial room, but we had to do something with this one, and to keep up human appearances, we put in a pool."

Emily laughed, "That's pretty pathetic, but okay... no one swims?"

"Never," he said, looking around the large empty room.

"Hmm, that's too bad." She stepped down into an empty hot tub and sat down on one of the benches that lined the outside.

Kyle followed her down and sat across from her, his eyes amused.

Emily glanced around the massive room to make sure no one was around, and then turned back to Kyle. "May I ask you something?"

"Depends..." he said, watching her. He was drawn to her green eyes.

She smiled slightly. "If I wanted to... can I leave?"

He raised his eyebrows, "Yes, I'll open the door for you."

She sighed, "Not here, here… the island."

"You are leaving us?" He tried to hide the shock in his voice but failed.

Emily shrugged. "If I do, will anyone try to stop me? I mean those armed guards with the dogs on the pier?"

"Well," Kyle began, "I'm sure that Chevalier would try to stop you, and I would try to talk you out of leaving, but you aren't a prisoner here. The guards on the pier keep people out, not people in."

She fought back the tears. "I don't think Chev would care much if I left."

Kyle moved closer to her. "Did you two get into a fight?"

Emily couldn't help but smile weakly. "You could say that."

"I've seen the way he looks at you. I don't think he would like it if you leave."

"Don't be so sure, Kyle." She shrugged.

Kyle tried to read her face, tried to figure out what the problem was, so he could help. "If you are right, then I would still ask you to stay."

"That's sweet, but I don't think he would even want me on this island. It's only a matter of time before he gets back and asks me to leave. I just need to figure out where to go, now that my ranch is gone." One stray tear betrayed her and escaped her eye.

Kyle reached up and gently wiped the tear way. "No family or friends?"

She shook her head. "Dad and… well Keith, were the only family I had, and I didn't have time for friends."

"I won't let you go homeless, Emily. I have a few places you could stay. I even have one in Europe if you want to get far away." He sounded sad.

Emily looked up at him. "You do? You would let me stay there until I got a job and got back on my feet?"

Kyle nodded silently.

She relaxed a bit. "Thank you. That's… that's so nice of you."

Kyle stood up and offered his hand to help her do the same, "Let's go riding. It's nice out, and I won't let you leave today."

Emily nodded and followed him out of the pool room and into the barn where their horses waited, already saddled. Emily grabbed Patra's large head in her hands and kissed her nose. "It's okay, Patra. I'll take you with me when I go."

Kyle watched as Emily slid easily onto the painted mare, and they set out along the tree line, walking the horses slowly.

"Do you want to talk about it?" Kyle asked after some time in silence.

Emily shook her head and looked away from him.

"If you decide you need someone to talk to…"

She nodded and shut her eyes, feeling the warmth of the sun on her face.

"Hey, I thought heku couldn't be out in the sun," she said finally, looking over at Kyle.

"Not can't… we just don't prefer it… it's obnoxiously bright." He smiled, adjusting his sunglasses.

"Garlic?" she asked.

"We don't eat."

"What if I threw it at you?"

Kyle laughed, "Then I'd probably throw it back."

"Holy water?"

He raised an eyebrow, clearly having fun. "Are you trying to kill me off?"

Emily smiled despite herself and shrugged, "Doesn't matter I guess. I'm not Catholic."

The rest of the afternoon they spent riding the mesa, for a while running along the beach. When the sun started to set, and the weather cooled off, Kyle insisted they return to the barn.

Emily slid off of Patra and unhooked the straps, then turned around to lay her gloves on a nearby stand, and when she turned back around, the saddle and saddle blanket were already gone. She noticed Kyle's horse was also bareback now.

"I can do that," she said, picking up the brush.

"Do what?" Kyle was leaning against a stall watching her.

"I can take off a saddle you know. I'm not a wimp." She began to brush Patra down.

"Never said you were... we have people for that though, and they are quite efficient." Kyle mimicked her and grabbed a brush. "Course... I don't see how you can lift a saddle when you can't open a door."

Kyle laughed when the brush flew out of Emily's hand and hit him softly in the back. Emily grabbed a bucket of water and started washing down Patra, who clearly enjoyed the attention. The barn was warm, and washing down the horse was making it warmer, so Emily slipped off her polo, leaving on only a light camisole. Kyle quickly glanced at her but turned away when he again realized how beautiful she was.

"So... now that it's too late for you to leave tonight, what do you want to do?" he asked, still brushing the buckskin mare.

"Hmmm... I don't suppose there's a TV in this place?" She led Patra into a nearby stall and went over to the large barrel of oats and struggled to lift the lid.

"I'm sure I could find one, yes." He watched her out of the corner of his eye, trying not to be too obvious.

She finally managed to get the lid off and dumped a large bucket into Patra's stall. "Any DVDs?"

Kyle laughed, "Some."

Kissing Patra again, Emily left her in the stall and shut the door. "What's so funny?"

"You are, dear… you know you can be quite amusing?" He turned to lead his horse into a stall.

Kyle gasped when the cold water from the wash bucket was suddenly thrown at his back, drenching him. He shut the stall door and turned slowly, a grin on his face. Emily caught one look at his face and turned away, running toward the house. It wasn't a fair chase. She hadn't made it to the door of the barn before he was standing in her way, facing her and laughing.

"You shouldn't have done that," he said, taking a step toward her.

Emily planted her feet and set her jaw, "I'm not afraid of you."

Before she even realized what was happening, Kyle had her across his shoulder and was running in a blur across the yard toward a freshwater stream that led into the ocean.

"You wouldn't!" she yelled when she figured out his plan.

"Oh?" he said, gently sitting her down in the deep cold water.

Emily gasped and stood up, now entirely soaked. Kyle's heart fluttered. The thin white camisole was now sheer, and he could clearly see the shapely contours of her breasts as she climbed out of the water, unaware he was watching.

"That is freezing!" she yelled, shivering. She slapped him on the arm as she walked past, headed for the house.

Kyle appeared at her side with the shirt she'd left in the barn. She slipped it on, now cold, and he was able to breathe again. He chastised himself. It was things like this that could get him in trouble with the Chief Enforcer.

"She is mine." Kyle could hear Chevalier's voice in his head.

"Come on, let's see if we can find a TV," he said, opening the door for her and checking quickly to see if anyone had seen them. His clothes were dry now. The cold wind coming off of the ocean had dried them quickly.

Kyle led her up the long staircase and past a few hallways, stopping at a set of white double doors. He used his key to unlock the doors and open them for her. Emily stepped into the room and smiled. The room was all white, and one end held a massive flat-screen TV that was mounted to the wall. The floors were lined with giant beanbags, overstuffed pillows, rows of carefully folded blankets, and soft rugs. One entire wall was dedicated to shelves full of DVDs.

"You've been holding out on me!" she said, and walked over to look at the movies.

Kyle sat down on a beanbag and watched her. It was fairly safe here. He would hear if anyone approached. She started thumbing through the movies as he watched her. He marveled at the way her back moved, the curve of her waist, and how her hair hung down softly, barely brushing her outstretched arms.

He blinked and turned to the TV, then glanced back at her when she began to laugh. "Find something?"

Emily turned around and held out a movie, still laughing, "You have *Interview with a Vampire!*"

Her laughing was exquisite and Kyle smiled. "I hadn't noticed."

"Let's watch it," she said, walking over to the DVD player.

Kyle was startled when she joined him on the beanbag and pulled up a blanket, laying it across their legs. Emily leaned forward as the movie started.

Part of the way through the first hour of the movie, Kyle began to get irritated. The heku were portrayed completely wrong, and their vulnerabilities were insulting. He was sure that Emily would see the problem and choose another movie, but when he glanced at her, she was thoroughly engrossed.

He watched her face. It was more entertaining than the movie. She was feeling the emotions of the characters and didn't noticed him watching her. He was shocked when she even cried when one of the simulated vampires died. He was amazed at the intense emotion she could put out for a façade.

Kyle grinned. At times he forgot how utterly human she was. She glanced at him and then back to the movie, blushing.

***

The next three days were spent the same, as Kyle tried to keep Emily entertained so she wouldn't leave the island. They rode the horses in the morning, spent afternoons doing various things, and then each evening was spent in the white movie room, watching whatever it was that Emily picked.

The fourth day was different, though. Emily wasn't as playful or talkative as before. She opted to walk with Patra, as opposed to riding, and Kyle began to get worried. They hadn't mentioned Chevalier, though Kyle knew exactly where he was. Emily assumed he'd left the castle, and Kyle didn't have the heart to tell her he was there, just in meditation in his office. He didn't know the kind of fight they had but was sure that Chevalier wouldn't want her to leave in his absence.

The movie that night was a romance, but Emily was asleep before the relationship even began to evolve. Kyle carried her back to her room and put her to bed, taking his place at the foot of her bed as normal.

***

The hard knocking on his door broke his concentration and irritated him. "Enter!" Chevalier bellowed at them.

Anna came in quickly, her head low and bowed. "Sir?"

"What, Anna?"

"Sir, please, I am worried about Lady Emily." Anna continued to stare at the floor, feeling awkward being in Chevalier's study.

He stood up and took a step toward her. "What's wrong?"

"A fever, sir. Kyle summoned me a few hours ago."

Chevalier glared as he realized Kyle was spending time with Emily again, and then he swept out of the room, followed quickly by Anna. The door shut and locked behind them on its own. It only took him a few seconds to appear in Emily's antechamber, and he knocked lightly.

"I said go away!" Emily called from the other side of the doors.

Chevalier looked at Anna and smiled. "It's okay, Anna. I'll take a look."

Ignoring her call to go away, Chevalier stepped inside the room and shut the heavy door behind him. He looked around the room and saw Emily sitting in a chair by the fire. She didn't look over at him. He walked over and sat down in the other chair.

"Sooo." He paused, hoping she would begin, but he continued when she didn't, "How are you feeling?"

Emily's insides reeled. She hadn't expected Chevalier to come back, and she figured he was just feeling guilty about abandoning her. It wouldn't be long before he left again, returning only when she'd gone.

"Fine," she snapped at him.

"Anna seems to think you are sick."

"Anna is delusional."

Chevalier chuckled, "That she is. However, she is still worried."

Emily coughed into her arm and turned back to the fire.

"Hmm," he said, watching her more intently now. He frowned at the flush in her face. It wasn't like the blush that lingered on her cheeks when she was embarrassed.

Chevalier stood up and put his hand on her forehead, which she promptly slapped away. He got enough of a chance though to ascertain that she was feverish.

"Okay, Emily, no more playing," he said, picking her up.

"Put me down, Chevalier. I'm not in the mood." She kicked, trying to get away but was soon on the bed. "Gah, you're as bad as Kyle."

Emily scrambled to get out of bed, but Chevalier held her down, "I'm not kidding, Emily. You stay put." His voice was stern.

"You aren't my father, Chev." She glared at him, but he refused to release his hold.

He reached out and felt her forehead again. She felt hot and sweaty, and her color was off. "You are getting sick."

"I'm fine."

"Anna," Chevalier called.

"Yes, sir?" Instantly, she appeared at his side, her eyes on Emily.

"Find a doctor. Talk to Storm and make sure it is a discreet one."

"Yes, sir," she said, running off.

Emily looked up at Chevalier, and her snide remark was forgotten when she saw the worry in his eyes.

Chevalier sat at her side for the few hours it took to locate a doctor to come within the island walls. Chevalier watched as Emily fell asleep, her breathing labored and raspy. He started to become angry with Storm. It was taking too long to locate someone to come and help.

Just as Chevalier was about to whisk Emily away to the mainland, the doctor arrived with apologies about the time. The ferry had some engine trouble. The doctor was about to introduce himself when his eyes fell on Emily, and his brow furrowed.

He dug around in his bag and pulled out a stethoscope, and placed it against her chest, inhaling sharply.

"It's pneumonia," he mumbled, pulling out a thermometer and scanning it across her forehead. "104.2, we should get her to a hospital, but as the ferry is no longer running, I'll do what I can."

Chevalier didn't like the sounds of that. "Do more than you can," he demanded.

The doctor rifled through his bag and pulled out a syringe, which he filled from a small vial. He pulled the blankets down and hiked her nightgown up, then turned as he heard Chevalier hiss.

"This has to go into her thigh… that's all," he said, watching to make sure he wasn't about to get attacked. He'd been oddly curious about this island since he was a child, and though he knew the risks of coming out here, he jumped at the chance to see inside the gray walls.

"What is it?" Chevalier's voice held authority and anger.

"Antibiotics, she can't take a pill, so it has to be an injection," he explained, and then paused to wait for more questions. When none came, he gave her the shot and covered the small puncture wound with a bandage.

The doctor stood back and watched Emily strain to breathe, the muscles in her throat standing out. Her chest heaved heavily as her body struggled to get oxygen. It hadn't escaped Chevalier that Emily didn't open her eyes when the doctor gave her the medicine.

Chevalier didn't move for hours. He sat, watching her, willing her to continue to breathe. Her fragile body stayed incredibly warm, and she stopped responding at all to commands. Kyle joined them but kept a safe distance, choosing to watch from the corner of the room. Anna sat beside her also, holding her hand.

The doctor came in every few hours to check on Emily. He wasn't pleased with the outcome. The antibiotics hadn't started to work yet, but he promised them that they would soon. He left the room when he wasn't needed because Chevalier's accusing stares made him uncomfortably aware of his volatile surroundings.

Emily's fever broke the following night, but her body fought to continue to breathe. The strain began to show on the faces of all in the room. Anna changed the wet cloth on Emily's forehead often, but there was nothing else to do but watch her. The doctor was concerned about the lack of fluids in her body, but the pneumonia had progressed, and he was afraid to move her. Storm gathered a crew and they went back to the mainland, returning with I.V. supplies and oxygen. Emily seemed to breathe easier with the extra oxygen, and the doctor felt better once the I.V. began to replenish the fluid in her body.

The time watching over Emily gave Chevalier the opportunity to think about what was happening with him, and as much as he hated to consider it, he conceded that he might actually love her. His heart ached watching her suffer, and if there was someone to kill for it, he would. He realized that no one could know his true feelings for Emily. They could be construed as a weakness, and then all he fought for would be lost. He had control on his side, control of himself and his coven.

The next morning, the doctor came back into the room to check on Emily. He was always amazed at the three heku that sat vigil over her bed, and at how much they cared about this young woman. None of them moved as he placed the stethoscope on her chest and then smiled when she moved slightly with the cold. It was the first he had seen her respond in over two days.

"She sounds better today," he told them, and noticed the look of adoration on the heku's faces. He scanned her forehead again and showed the results to Chevalier, 101.1. No one spoke, so he gave her another dose of antibiotics and left the room.

That evening, Chevalier called for the doctor. Emily's body was no longer straining to breathe. Her back was no longer arching, and the muscles in her neck had relaxed. She seemed peaceful, and had it not been for the rasping, he wouldn't have even believed she was still breathing.

The doctor rushed in and immediately placed a stethoscope against her chest, but he smiled. "She's okay. It's okay. Her body just doesn't have to fight quite so hard to breathe."

Chevalier smiled softly at Emily, and again, the doctor was taken aback by the care the immortals were giving this one mortal. It was comforting knowing that the mythological evil beasts could care. "As soon as she wakes up, I'll need to go back."

The doctor waited. He'd been slightly suspicious whether he would make it back, or if he would become a permanent resident of this city of the immortal.

Chevalier nodded. "That should be fine. Just leave us what we need to care for her."

In her sleep, Emily reached up and tore off the oxygen cannula. Chevalier quickly replaced it just to have it torn off again.

"Leave it alone," he said softly.

"No," she answered. Her voice was so quiet it was hard to hear.

He couldn't help but grin. The soft sound of her voice was encouraging. He'd spent the last few days thinking he may actually lose her, and he wasn't sure if his heart could beat without her.

He replaced the cannula, yet again, and this time she didn't move. A few hours later, the harsh cough began, and her labored breathing returned, though not as fiercely as before. Again, they called for the doctor.

He couldn't help but smile at the panicked look on their faces as he heard the rough cough. "It's fine. That's what we want... coughing is good. Coughing irritates the airway, though, so it's going to make it hard to breathe."

"This is good?" Anna questioned, watching Emily cough violently.

"Yes, it is," the doctor tried to reassure them.

Storm made the arrangements to send the doctor home the following day and to pay him immensely for his help. Chevalier was surprised to learn that the doctor offered to come back if the need arose. It was always good to have resources on the outside.

Once Emily fell back to sleep and there was a break in the coughing, Chevalier appeared in the corner with Kyle.

"You have some explaining to do, and it better be good." Kyle could feel the intense rage emanating from Chevalier.

"Sir?" he asked, not sure how much Chevalier knew.

"It seems that in my absence, you spent a lot of time... too much time, with Emily. Explain yourself," Chevalier hissed, and took a step closer to Kyle as his hands clenched into tight fists.

Kyle's mind pulled out the excuse he had formulated. "She was going to leave, sir. I simply tried to keep her here."

It worked, and Chevalier's anger ebbed slightly. "This required you to spend the entire four days with her?"

"I was afraid that the second she was alone, she would leave." Kyle crouched defensively, "She was convinced you wanted her to."

Chevalier's anger immediately left him as Kyle's words sank in. "She thought I wanted her to leave?"

"Yes"

Chevalier studied Kyle's face and he hissed, "How close did you get to her?"

Kyle didn't ease up from his defensive posture, "Chevalier, I wouldn't…"

Chevalier stopped him with a growl, "Are you falling for her?"

"No!" Self-preservation kept Kyle from confessing the truth.

"She is mine," he said through gritted teeth.

"I know, sir." Kyle tried to relax to show his respect for the Chief Enforcer. He had to hide his true feelings, feelings that would get him killed.

"Then leave." The command was whispered, but the expectation to obey was strong. Kyle instantly disappeared from the room.

Chevalier walked back to the bed just as Anna was replacing the cool cloth on Emily's forehead. She pretended that she hadn't seen what just transpired, and she didn't comment. She liked Kyle, and what she had seen of him lately could be detrimental to him.

Emily's hand shot out and wrapped around the tubing coming from her arm. Chevalier was quick enough that she didn't have time to remove her I.V. He brought her hand to his lips and kissed it lightly. "No, Em, leave it alone."

He could be himself around Anna. Her life depended on her ability to keep what she saw to herself. Anna re-taped the I.V. down, not watching Chevalier.

"Take it out, please," Emily whispered, her eyes still shut.

Chevalier bent down and brushed his lips softly against hers, then whispered into her ear, "Leave it, Love."

He heard Anna gasp slightly, and he sat up. Emily's eyes were open, and she was looking at him.

"Emily?" he whispered, touching her cheek lightly.

Her eyes moved from him, over to Anna, and then returned, but she didn't speak. She reached her hand up and pulled the oxygen off of her face. Chevalier grinned and returned it. "Leave that alone."

Chevalier and Anna watched as her eyes suddenly slid shut again.

Emily slept most of the night, with interruptions from coughing fits. Only once did her breathing turn raspy for a while, but it was quiet again within a few hours. The light of dawn came through the cracks in the heavy curtains, and she opened her eyes.

"Chev?" Her voice was cracked and soft.

He looked down at her and kissed her forehead softly. "Yes?"

She tried to clear her throat but ended up starting a coughing fit instead. Chevalier pulled her gently into a sitting position to help it pass, and then laid her back down.

"Shhh, don't talk," he encouraged her as Anna left to get a fresh cool rag.

Emily's pale complexion brought out the vibrancy in her green eyes, but her lips were dry and cracked.

"You came back," she said softly, watching his reaction.

"Of course I did.   I know what you're thinking, and you're wrong. We'll discuss this later though."   He adjusted her pillows.

Her eyes scanned the room. "Where is Kyle?"

He pulled her up to sitting again as she began to cough uncontrollably. By the time it stopped, she was exhausted and fell back to sleep when he laid her down.

Chevalier watched her sleep. He gently ran his fingers across her collar bone. It protruded from her tight skin, and he worried about how thin and pale she'd become. Her arms were finally cool, so he pulled the blanket up around her and waited.

The next morning, he was finally alone with her. The cool rags were no longer necessary without the fever, so he told Anna to take the day off to go feed. She was looking haggard. Chevalier pulled the heavy curtains back and let the morning sun into the room. When he turned back to the bed, Emily was watching him.

He smiled. "How are you feeling?"

"Perfect," she whispered, watching him closely.

Chevalier sat down on the bed beside her and took her hand, but she pulled it away weakly.

"You don't have to do that," she whispered, unable to draw up the strength for more.

He took her hand again, and this time, he didn't let her pull it away. "No one is forcing me."

She reached up with her other hand and pulled off the oxygen.

Chevalier sighed and tried to put it back on, but her hand was in the way.

"No," she said softly.

"Em, you need it. Put it back on." He tried again, but she blocked him with her hand.

She glared at him, "You put it on."

He gently moved her hand and put it back to her face. "I don't need it. You do."

She coughed forcefully and then settled back down on the pillow. "You don't have to stay here. I don't need a pity friend."

Chevalier waited while he got his anger under control. "No one's making me, and I don't pity you."

"It's okay, Chev, as soon as I'm better, I'll leave." She turned her face away from him and shut her eyes.

He growled softly, "I don't want you to leave..." He glanced around the room once then bent down and whispered into her ear, "I love you too much to for you to leave."

Her mouth fell open and she turned back to him, her eyes searching for signs of humor or sarcasm, but she found none.

"Don't look at me like that. You knew it all along." His face was stern, but then he smiled.

She turned away from him again as the tears welled up in her eyes. She shut them to hide the evidence but soon fell asleep.

A soft voice woke her up, and she watched as Gordon delivered a shiny, silver tray to the bedside table. He smiled when he saw her look at him, bowed, and then disappeared. Chevalier pulled the dome off the top and set it down before turning to look at her.

Chevalier smiled. "Dr. Edwards said you need to start eating again. I had Gordon bring some soup. I hope you like chicken noodle, or is that too... prosaic?"

Emily shook her head. "I'm not really hungry."

She sat up coughing.

"Well, he also mentioned if you'll eat, we can remove the I.V." Chevalier grinned, playing off her weaknesses.

She reached over and quickly yanked out the I.V., wincing at the sting. Chevalier hadn't been watching her at the time, so he was a fraction of second too slow to stop it. "Damnit, Em, you're a horrible patient."

She yanked off her nasal cannula to toss it onto the floor, but Chevalier caught it before it hit. "Nope, put that back on."

Emily swung her legs over the side of the bed and scooted to stand up, but his hands on her shoulders forced her back onto the bed.

"Stop it, Chev." She coughed and then tried again.

"Will you please stay down?" His voice was a cross between amusement and frustration.

"No, I'm well enough to leave now." Her body betrayed her with a violent coughing fit.

Chevalier wrapped his arms around her waist, frowning as he felt her ribs sticking out against her skin. "Lay down."

Emily didn't lie down, but she did stay seated. When she'd tried to stand, she discovered that her legs weren't strong enough to carry her yet.

"Fine, we'll sit," Chevalier said, releasing his hold on her. He grabbed the bowl of soup and offered it to her.

Emily stared at it.

"Eat… for me," he said.

She sighed and took the bowl. The soup felt wonderful against her parched lips and throat, and the warmth of it spread through her body. She hadn't realized she was getting cold.

Once she finished, she returned the bowl to the intricately decorated silver tray and turned to face Chevalier on the bed, sitting cross-legged.

"So now…" he began, facing her in a similar fashion, "let's talk about you leaving, shall we?"

Emily nodded.

"Might I ask why?" he asked, looking closely at her. He noticed again how thin she'd become and how she was almost as pale as he was.

She stared down at her hands. "I know what you must think about me now. It's only fair to give you an easy out." Coughing stopped her from saying more.

Chevalier's eyes narrowed. "So you know what I think about you, do you?"

Emily nodded.

"I'm guessing it's along the lines of… hmmm… let's use the immortal words of Keith '*You're just a little dirty slut aren't you? Whoring around in the city?*" He paused. "Is that close?"

Emily winced and nodded, still staring at the pattern on the quilt.

"Let me see if I can continue then… useless?" He watched her.

Emily nodded.

"Worthless?"

Another nod.

"Insignificant and repulsive?"

She didn't react. She was concentrating on the flowered pattern of the quilt to keep from crying.

"So does that mean that you count Keith and me in the same category?" he growled.

The words shocked her and she looked up at him with wide eyes, "No."

He moved closer to her and touched her cheek lightly. "Then stop comparing us and stop letting his words cloud the way I feel about you. It's insulting."

Her eyes met his and he saw the hesitation there, the brief glimpse that she for once doubted what her ex-husband said. Chevalier took the opportunity of weakness and concentrated on her eyes, willing her to submit to his trance. Her body relaxed, and her breathing matched his own.

"Emily… I love you, and you need to trust me. I love everything about you." His words flowed toward her like music. She was unable to pull away from their mesmerizing qualities. "You are worth it."

Chevalier pulled back away from her, broke the gaze, and waited while his words sunk in. As the trance broke, she couldn't remember what had transpired but suddenly felt relaxed and comfortable.

She glanced over at the tray and picked up a piece of a quartered sandwich. A blush rose to her cheeks as she realized Chevalier was watching her with a smile.

"Come in, Anna," he called, though she'd heard no knock.

Anna hurried in and set a glass of orange juice down on the table, then suddenly disappeared again.

Emily frowned toward the door.

"You don't like Anna, do you?" he guessed.

"She treats me like a 2-year-old," she said, and then continued to eat.

"Dear, to her, you are very young."

"It doesn't matter. I'm still an adult."

"That's fine. I'll replace her for you."

"Let Kyle do it." Emily didn't notice the way Chevalier's body tensed. She reached for the ice-cold orange juice.

"Kyle?" he asked, calming his voice.

"Yes, he doesn't treat me like a toddler, and we have a lot in common." Chevalier was glad her attention was elsewhere as he fought to regain control of his anger.

"Kyle isn't right for the job."

Finally, she looked over at him. "Yes, he is... he's my friend."

Chevalier relaxed as she used the term friend. "I still don't like it. You need a woman around."

"I do not!" She looked at him with an icy glare. "You act like I miss my Mommy! You're about as bad as she is. Kyle does what you told me Anna should. He shows me around, helps me find things, and keeps me safe."

"Still..." Her coughing cut him off, and he continued once she'd calmed down, "Still, Kyle has things to do elsewhere."

"Fine, I don't need anyone then. Let Anna go, but don't replace her." She looked at him, proud she'd solved the problem.

"I can't leave you alone, Em." He wasn't getting through to her.

"That's odd. You already did," she said, and then saw him wince. She decided to try to reason with him. "Listen, Chev. Kyle is a good friend. I'm comfortable around him, and I don't have to pretend. He knows how to lighten up around me. Everyone here is so wound up tight because they are afraid of you. It gets a little nerve wracking. You know he can protect me. He already has."

He knew he couldn't fight her. "Okay, if that's what you really want."

"It is." She coughed hard and then turned back to him.

"But... he stays out in the antechamber while you sleep."

"I don't like to be alone at night." She lowered her eyes again, a little embarrassed.

Chevalier moved closer and kissed her forehead. "Who says you will be alone?"

He laughed when the blush returned to her cheeks.

He grinned. "Enough already, finish eating and lay down."

With not quite half of the food gone, she laid back onto the bed and cuddled down. Sitting up for so long had really made her tired, and it was only a few minutes before she fell asleep.

A dream jerked her awake, and she looked around the dark room, suddenly feeling cold and alone.

"Chev?" she called into the darkness, but it was Kyle's voice that responded.

"He stepped out, Em. Are you okay?" He stayed a few feet back from her bed.

"I'm okay, just a nightmare." She patted edge of the bed beside her.

Kyle didn't move at all toward her. He used to sit beside her while she slept, but she understood how Chevalier had probably put an immediate stop to that.

Kyle smiled at her. "You got me demoted."

She gasped, "I did? How?"

"From the head of my own guard unit… to babysitter." His voice was light and amused.

"Ugh, babysitter…" She lay back on the bed and rolled away from him. He chuckled and returned to the chair by the fire.

Beginning

The feel of hands grabbing her out of bed forced a short scream, but a hand quickly covered her mouth.

"Quiet, Emily." It was Kyle, and he was already running with her in his arms, down an unlit stairway.

The frantic way he moved scared her. She thought back briefly to the past two weeks she'd spent mostly in bed and couldn't wrap her mind around what the problem was. Her coughing had stopped a few days ago, and she'd even managed to go out onto the balcony for a while the previous evening.

In the darkness, there were hurried voices, and she realized they weren't alone.

"We don't know yet. Just get her down there," a female voice said, inhumanly fast.

"Which direction?" Kyle hissed at the other woman.

"East, they have to come through the city to get here," she answered.

Emily was too frightened to speak, too afraid to ask the questions that were on her mind. Her eyes furiously tried to adjust to the darkness but failed.

The descent ended, and they were all running through what felt like a damp tunnel. She realized that at the speed the heku ran, they had to be hundreds of feet below the ground now, and the panic swelled further.

Kyle finally put her down and gently led her to a chair, where she sat and curled up, wrapping her arms tightly around her legs. Someone put a blanket over her shoulders, and she shivered at how cold it was.

"Do we dare?" a strange man said.

"We should be okay down here," the woman replied.

"No," Kyle hissed, and nothing else was said about it.

"What's going on?" Emily finally managed to ask, and she could feel eyes on her, though she was unable to see anything in the blackness.

She felt someone sit beside her and take her hand. It was Kyle. "Don't worry, Emily, okay? Things are under control."

"Then tell me! I'm already worrying."

He sighed, "The Island is under attack."

"What? By who?" she gasped.

"Other...," he paused, "heku."

"Another coven is attacking?"

"Not exactly."

"Is it Ulrich?" Her mind was trying to wrap around it.

"No"

Emily just shook her head. "Then who is it? Who would want to attack?"

"Our world is as riddled with wars and hatred as yours. Chevalier has made a lot of enemies in his years, and grudges aren't easily forgotten. We are okay, though. This coven is ready to fight." She could feel him sit up taller.

Emily stood up. "Then I should fight with them."

Kyle's smile seeped into his voice, "They fight with teeth, Em. You can't fight against that as a mortal."

"I can too! I'm stronger than you think." She tried to find her way to the door in the dark, but all she could feel were the wet, cold stone walls.

Cool hands took her arm and led her back to the chair. "Nevertheless, we have orders to stay down here with you."

"Oh great, just what I bet you all wanted to do while your city is under attack, protect the human," she yelled at them, and was infuriated when the three heku with her chuckled.

"Please, Kyle, I can help. You have to trust me." She noticed things had gotten quiet as Kyle placed his hand over her mouth.

Emily heard whispers in the darkness, too low to make out, but the stress was intense. A light blazed suddenly, and in an instant, she was able to take in the full picture. They were sitting in a cave with a bed and chairs set up in the corner. A stone door led out to a rock hallway that disappeared in the darkness.

The three heku were crouched low defensively and watched the door as they stood between her and whatever was coming. Within a few moments, she heard the fast footfalls of a group of people coming down the stairs. She hoped they were from this coven, but the stance of the other three cast doubts.

Five heku emerged and immediately met the crouch. They were all men, dressed in red, and were unlike the heku she knew. One had deep scars across his face, and his body was full of skeleton tattoos. The others were snarling with their teeth exposed menacingly. Four of the five enemy heku had matching red tattoos on their faces. Emily sat, frozen in place, as the three heku took a step backwards toward her, their hands curved into claws.

The tallest of the heku hissed toward her, "She comes with us, alive."

The fight began in a blur, and Emily couldn't tell who was who in the mass of movement. There were snarls and curses, and the violent sounds of tearing and breaking. The bed splintered as someone was thrown into it but was immediately snatched away by unseen hands. She recoiled when the head of one of the enemy heku was thrown against the wall behind her and missed her by only a few inches.

She could feel it. She could feel the anger swelling up inside of her, and she fought to control it. There were now seven heku in this room, and she wanted three of them alive, but she didn't have that much control. The growls and howls of pain continued as the female member of the coven fell unconscious to the ground. Emily's eyes watched her with horror when she didn't move. The blurs didn't slow down. She couldn't tell who was winning or who was losing, and she felt as if she was losing control. Something deep within her was fighting to get out, fighting to surface.

"Nooo!" she screamed as the terror peaked, and then all grew quiet. Kyle looked at her, his eyes wide. The other male heku spun to face her, and she noticed the large gash down the side of his body. She couldn't see the other four enemy heku.

The look of shock on Kyle's face lessened as he realized who she was. He'd heard the stories, knew of the rumors, but now he knew it was true. He'd been protecting one of the Winchesters.

Emily's body began to shake as she realized how close she'd come to being taken by the enemy heku. Kyle and the other man looked tired and fatigued. She understood by the look in their eyes that they had been losing.

"Shut that door," Kyle barked at the other man, who immediately sprang into action. They began to throw the remains of the first heku to die into a pile, and she noticed how both of them carefully avoided going anywhere near the ash on the floor.

"I'm sorry, Kyle," Emily said with tears welling into her eyes.

He looked at her differently. She was no longer the weak, delicate human to which he had grown close. She was now a deadly weapon, a heku killer, with the power to kill in less than a second. There was no defense against her, and no way to avoid her. She noticed the change in his eyes, the way he stared at her from across the room as if afraid to come to her, and she buried her face in her hands.

Kyle frowned as she hid her face, and he realized that, though a powerful weapon, she wasn't an unfeeling killer. She was still his beautiful and fragile mortal. He walked slowly to her and sat at her side, wrapping his arms around her. She buried her face in his chest, thankful for the touch.

The door opened noiselessly, and Chevalier stepped through. His eyes enraged at the sight of Kyle with his arms wrapped around Emily. He was more infuriated when Kyle didn't let go as he stared at them, and then he saw it. The ash on the floor of the protective cave, the unconscious member of his own coven, and the dismembered body of an enemy, and he growled.

Emily's eyes were still hidden in Kyle's chest, so she wasn't aware of how quickly Chevalier killed the heku from his own coven and added the parts to the pile in the corner. He looked at Kyle and glared.

"I'm not going to tell anyone, Chevalier," he said, trying to save his own life.

"Let go of her," Chevalier demanded.

Kyle released his hold on Emily, and she was in Chevalier's arms in a second, cradled against his chiseled chest, and her body shook cruelly. "I'm so sorry, Chev. I couldn't help it."

"It's okay, Em. It's okay." He stroked her hair lightly, his eyes still glaring at Kyle.

"Chief Enforcer," Kyle whispered.

"One word…," he hissed at Kyle.

"Never." Kyle's eyes met his straight on. He wasn't lying. "I've promised my life to protect her."

"Go help clean up. There are still a few Encala running around the city."

Kyle nodded and disappeared up the steps.

Chevalier sat Emily down on the chair and knelt to face her. "You did very well. I'm proud of you. Are you okay? Did they hurt you?" He glanced over her, looking for any sign of an injury.

She shook her head and stared at the ashes. "I didn't mean to."

"It's alright." He kissed her forehead. "You know if they had gotten to you, they would have killed you. You defended yourself, nothing more."

She nodded. "What is going on?"

Chevalier sat beside her on the long couch and sighed. He'd hoped it wouldn't come to this, this soon. "There are three main factions among the immortals. The three have been warring since long before your ancestors were figuring out how to make fire."

She watched his eyes.

"The Encala, they are the most troublesome of the factions. They like to start war over insignificant things and also like to think they are much stronger than we are. They were the ones here today and found themselves gravely outnumbered and out strengthened."

He watched her for a moment, and then continued when she didn't speak. "There's also the Valle faction. They are more peaceful than both mine and the Encala, but they won't stand by for long if they feel threatened. My faction, the Equites, is the largest and strongest of the three. We've all lived peacefully for almost a hundred and fifty years, but lately, we've been receiving word that the Encala are getting restless. They tried to enlist the Valle to join forces and exterminate all of the Equites."

Chevalier touched her hand softly, "The Valle were offended by this and sent word that a war was starting."

"So you knew this was coming?" She looked at him shocked.

"I only knew it was a possibility."

"You should have told me," she said angrily.

"I know. I realize that now. I was hoping it wouldn't come down to these petty attacks, and we could avoid a war." He reached down and brushed his lips softly to hers.

"But it's over now," she said, pulling away from him.

He shook his head.

"Can't the Elders help? Put a stop to this?" she asked.

"No, the Elders... my Elders, are Equites. They are the ruling body for my faction only, and each faction has their own set."

Emily pulled her knees up to her chest. "Why did they attack?"

"A coven of the Encala up in Greenland was attacked, and the entire coven was wiped out, all 130 of them." His eyes grew sad. "They blamed us for the attacks."

"Did you?"

"No, we don't attack unprovoked." The question irritated him a bit.

The room grew silent. All she could hear was the dripping of water against the wall. Finally, Chevalier stood up and reached out to take Emily's hand. "Let's go. The last of the Encala are gone."

"What about them?" She glanced quickly at the ash and bodies.

"I'll send someone for them. It's okay. They won't know you did it. I will take the blame." He started up the dark stairs.

"Will you get into trouble?" She hesitated.

"No, I was defending the coven." He led her back up the stairs. It seemed to take forever with her slow mortal feet, but eventually, they came out into a hidden room in the castle. The wall moved easily for Chevalier, and he pushed into the adjacent room. Emily was shocked to see it was her bedroom.

"I didn't know that was there!" she said, stepping into the familiar room.

Chevalier smiled. "It wouldn't be a secret room if we advertised it."

Emily looked around, horrified. The furniture had been thrown around the room, and the heavy curtains were torn to shreds. Her clothes were scattered and the walls had large, uneven gashes in them and scorch marks.

Chevalier stood behind her and wrapped his arms around her waist. "I owe Kyle a great debt. It was fast thinking to take you down as soon as he did. A few minutes later and…" He shuddered.

Her eyes were taking in the damage. "They were after me?"

Chevalier nodded. "Yes, any mortal involved enough in a coven to stay permanently is a prime target. They don't know why you are here. They only know that you must have something the coven would protect."

"Was it Ulrich?" she whispered, her eyes catching the shattered glass on the floor.

"No, Ulrich's coven is in the Valle." He pressed his lips against the back of her head.

"How many died today?" she asked, her words catching in her throat.

Chevalier sighed, "I don't know yet. We were able to kill all of them. There were maybe only 600 of them. Do you know, had it not been for this war, you and I would have never met?"

She turned in his arms and looked up at his face. "How do you figure?"

He smiled. "Jerry's coven was looking for more cattle. They received a tip in an e-mail that your Angus cows were the best. He followed that tip, found you, and set up the meeting. When he met you, he knew immediately that something was different about you. Later, we found that the Encala were the ones that tipped him off. We suspect they were trying to set him up. Had he fed from you, I would have been forced to destroy him. He is a high-ranking officer in of one of the largest Equites covens."

"Did they know I'm a… what I can do?" She was studying his face.

"I don't think so. I think they only knew that you have an amazing smell." He ran his nose along her neck, inhaling.

Emily was too distracted to respond. Her mind was buzzing with everything that she had seen and heard, and she still couldn't shake the feeling that she murdered, again.

Chevalier sensed the tension in her body. "It's okay, no one's coming to get you. I promise. Besides, I'm pretty sure no one would want to cross Kyle. He's become quite enamored with you."

"Stop, Chev." Emily smiled, a blush rising to her cheeks. "He's a friend."

"Let's get out of here and let them fix up this room, shall we?" he asked, looking at the remnants of the once beautiful room.

Emily nodded and then remembered that she was in her nightgown. "After I get dressed."

She walked over and pulled open the wardrobes, one at a time. Her things had been ripped and torn and scattered across the room. She wrinkled her nose and turned around to face Chevalier, who was laughing softly.

"Margaret?" he called, and the plump heku waddled into the room happily.

Margaret gasped as she saw the fragments of clothes thrown across the room.

"Margaret... we'd like to get out. Can you whip something up for her please?" Chevalier was watching Emily.

Her face lit up, and she shuffled quickly out the door. Emily felt exposed as she stood in the cold room wearing only the revealing pink satin nightgown. She walked over, brushed some bits of furniture off the bed, and wrapped the blanket around her before sitting down. It was only a short time before Margaret returned and handed some clothes to Emily, then disappeared.

She walked into the bathroom, cringing as she felt the soft fabric in her fingers. It was obvious that Margaret had taken liberties to improve Emily's style away from jeans and t-shirts. She searched through the fabric for any sign of a bra, and then froze when she couldn't find one. The blush crept back into her cheeks.

First, she slipped on the dark-blue top. It was a halter top, cropped short, exposing her midriff, and the top button was inconveniently missing. Emily sighed, and having no choice, she pulled on the pants, which were just as bad. The dark blue pants were cut low across her hips and fell smoothly down to her ankles. She hesitated and then turned to look in the mirror, vowing to get Margaret fired for this nightmarish ensemble.

"Are you coming out?" Chevalier asked, amused.

"Yeah, when she brings me the rest of this outfit," Emily called out to him, and she heard him chuckle.

"It can't be that bad. Margaret is very good at what she does." He was toying with her now. She could tell his voice was closer.

When Emily stepped out from the French doors, Chevalier gasped, his keen vision instantly taking her in. His eyes fell to the muscles in her tight abdomen and the way the pants were perched low on her delicate hips, accentuating her small waist. He grinned as he noticed the missing top button. She blushed deeper than he'd seen her.

"Remind me to give Margaret a raise," he said, moving closer to her. His hands ached to touch her soft skin.

"No, you are supposed to fire her for this," Emily said, and her body shivered at his light touch.

"Mmhmmm," he mumbled as his lips pressed against hers. The feel of her bare skin against his arms felt amazing to him.

His arms tightened around her waist as he pulled her up closer to him, her feet dangling inches from the floor. His lips pried her mouth open, and he began to explore her with his tongue. Emily's fingers were wound through his hair, and she tightened her fists as her body began to warm and respond to his touch. The pain ignited Chevalier, and he spun and dropped both of them down onto the bed.

A knock on the double doors infuriated him, and he growled at the door, "Go away!"

Storm's voice sounded, "Sir, the Elders are requesting an immediate report on the attack."

He sighed and kissed the side of her neck. "Don't move until I get back."

Chevalier stood up angrily and took a few steps toward the door. He turned to glance at her quickly and groaned. She was lying on the bed on her back with her hands clasped together above her head, causing the curve of her supple breasts to peek out from under her shirt. She realized it and dropped her hands quickly, blushing.

"Not an inch…," he said, leaving quickly.

Storm glanced at him quickly as he shut the doors behind him. "Are you okay, sir?"

She hadn't seen him like this. He was furious and she actually feared wrongly for the girl.

"Where do they want to do this?" he hissed at her.

"There's a conference call waiting. I can send them into your office," she said hurriedly.

Chevalier opened his office door and slammed it hard against the frame. The phone on his desk was already ringing. He took a deep breath and answered it.

"Chevalier here."

"Chevalier, we waited for you to give us a report. It's been too long since the end of this skirmish," Elder Selest hissed.

"I was..." He paused and couldn't help but grin. "Occupied."

"Very well, begin." The voice was monotone and businesslike.

"It was the Encala, no surprise." He glanced at some papers Storm had handed him. "There were 587 of them, all taken care of."

"Good, they again overestimated their strength," the female Elder said. "What were your casualties?"

He looked at the number on the sheet he held and added one, the one he killed to keep Emily's secret. "My coven lost 138."

There was a sharp intake of breath from the phone. "We're sorry, Chevalier, for your losses. We are meeting with the Encala and Valle Elders tonight. This attack was uncalled for."

"What of the girl?" a voice from the phone asked.

He frowned. "Her powers are very weak, no use to us probably. She knows too much now and one of my coven has grown attached to her, so she has decided to stay."

He heard three simultaneous sighs from the phone. "Very well. It's your coven. We will continue to search for more of the Winchester family. We're starting to think the line died out."

Chevalier grinned. It was exactly what he wanted them to think. "Good luck with that."

He pressed the button to disconnect the call and hurried back up to Emily's bedroom, then growled, irritated, when he stepped in and the room was full of members of his coven, repairing the damage from the Encala.

"Where is she?" he demanded of the closest heku.

The woman turned and bowed to him. "I believe she went to the kitchen, sir."

"Gah!" He stormed out of the room and headed into the kitchen. He took notice of the damages done to his home and began to count himself lucky that Emily hadn't been killed. He still had to find out how the Encala found the secret passageway down to the protective cave room, though.

He heard Emily's laugh from outside the doors to the kitchen and couldn't help but smile. He stepped in and the two young chefs immediately bowed to him. Chevalier was disappointed to see that Emily had managed to find a sweater.

"I thought I told you not to move," he said, sitting down beside her.

"It's hard to stay still when your room is invaded by repairers," she told him.

Chevalier glanced at the still bowing young heku. "As you were."

They immediately began preparing a meal.

Emily slapped him lightly on the shoulder. "You should be nicer to them."

He frowned. "Who?"

One of the young heku hurriedly shook his head at Emily.

"Oh... yes... well... good job," he said to the chefs, who froze for a moment and then started working again.

"Very smooth, Chev." She hoped the sarcasm wasn't wasted on him.

The two chefs looked at each other, unsure they actually heard someone call the Chief Enforcer, 'Chev'.

"What's the plan for today?" he asked her.

She shrugged. "Breakfast first, and then I haven't decided... I may see if Kyle wants to take the horses out."

She didn't see the pained expression that drifted briefly across his face. "I see… well Kyle may not be available today."

"Why is that?" Emily asked, and then thanked the heku who handed her a plate of hot pancakes.

"There's still some security to go over. We also think there might be an informant among us. He'll try to ascertain who that might be." He was watching her eat.

She looked over at him. "What will you do to them if you find one?"

Chevalier smiled. "Let's say you and I go riding today."

She nodded, knowing he was avoiding her question.

After breakfast, they walked together out to the barn. The horses weren't ready for the ride today. All hands were busy cleaning up from the small battle. Emily put a bridle on Patra and led her out into the barn as Chevalier fit a saddle to the buckskin mare.

She effortlessly slid onto Patra, bareback, and waited for Chevalier to mount up.

Emily clicked her tongue, and Patra began to walk forward. It was warm out this afternoon, so she slipped off her sweater, aware that she was again being watched. She led the way to the tree-line, and then followed the curve of trees out to the beach. They kept the pace slow. She wasn't sure she could handle a gallop, because she was still recovering from the double pneumonia. Chevalier didn't care how fast they moved. He spent most of his time watching her.

"You miss your ranch, don't you?" he asked as they set out along the beach.

She nodded.

"Would you like me to get you some livestock here?" He suddenly realized how easily that could be done.

Emily turned and looked at him. "Really?"

He nodded and smiled.

"With no servants... all mine?" she questioned.

"If that's what you want, then yes."

Excitement glowed in her eyes. "That would be wonderful! I can only wander the castle so many times before I'd go insane."

"Then consider it done. As soon as the cleanup is finished, I'll get someone right on that." He was pleased at how well she was taking his small gift to her.

Chevalier got a mischievous glimmer in his eye, and just as Emily was about to question him, he blurred and appeared on Patra behind her. He quickly spun her to face him and positioned her legs over his. "There... I like this better."

"I don't think this is an American Equestrian approved riding position though," she explained, and then laughed.

"Mmhmmm," he mumbled as he began kissing along her neck.

Bonding

Emily waited, crouched behind a stone pillar in the field beside the castle. She was hunkered down, patiently holding the small gun firmly in her hand, and her breathing was steady. There was a sheen of sweat on her forehead as she peeked around the corner and drew back quickly. Looking down, she noticed her tennis shoe was untied. She set the gun down beside her, tied it, and then picked the gun back up.

It was almost time, time to defend herself again. The cows around her ignored her as she waited, her legs beginning to strain. She checked her gun again. It was fully loaded.

She heard footsteps coming toward her from the barn. She held her breath, afraid it might give her away, and she got ready to aim and fire.

"Emily?" Kyle called to her.

She kept still.

Kyle sighed, and she could hear him. He was almost close enough to launch her attack. After taking a deep breath, she rounded the corner, took aim, and fired, shooting long streams of water directly into his face. He was caught off guard, so she took that opportunity to run.

"That's it!" he shouted, and followed after her.

She ran as fast as she could but heard him gaining. She took a blind aim behind her and shot again, not sure if she'd hit him. Mid-stride, her feet disappeared out from under her as Kyle picked her up and threw her across his shoulder.

"You cheated!" she yelled at him.

"I did not cheat. I ran... Someone who attacks someone else should take their abilities into consideration."

"Ha-ha, now put me down." She was laughing.

"No." He began to run faster, and she could feel the wind blowing past her.

"No!" she screamed, sure of what he was doing.

Kyle didn't answer.

"Stop or I'll tell Chev!"

She heard him chuckle, and the sound of waves came closer.

"Kyle, no! It's cold!" He didn't slow, and she saw the sand turn to wooden planks.

"Good afternoon, sir," said one of the guards, hiding a laugh.

"Good afternoon, Travis."

"Stop!" she shouted. "Travis, help me!"

The guard laughed, "No can do, Lady Emily."

She felt herself fall off of the pier the three feet down to the icy cold ocean. She surfaced, the cold water knocking the breath out of her, then swam up to the beach and stepped out, soaking wet and shivering.

"Some guard you are," she teased Travis.

He smiled and chuckled, his teeth glistening in the sun.

She spun and looked at the pier, but Kyle was gone.

"Wimp!" she shouted after him, and she thought she heard laughing on the wind. She tossed her water gun to Travis, and he glanced at her questioningly.

"If he comes back, shoot him," she said, starting off for the castle.

The guards at the front of the castle grinned at her and opened the door. She stepped in, her clothes dripping water all over the floor. A towel flew out at her from the dark shadows and landed at her feet.

"Thank you," she mumbled, and headed to her room to change.

As she walked up the stairs, she saw Chevalier standing at the top, watching her with a grin. "Long day?"

"Kyle tossed me into the ocean!" She knew tattling wouldn't do any good.

"I see... and before I behead him... who started it?" he chuckled.

She began to dry her hair as she passed him. "Heku... always sticking together."

Chevalier walked behind her, laughing, "You know, it's not fair for you to ambush him. He can smell you from 200 yards away, less if you are upwind of him."

"I was downwind. I made sure of it, and I did get off a few good shots." She grinned and walked into the antechamber. Kyle was standing in the corner smiling. "But he cheats."

Kyle cleared his throat.

Chevalier raised an eyebrow at him and smiled. "We all cheat. It's our nature."

Emily disappeared into the bedroom and headed right for the wardrobe. Chevalier looked again at Kyle and shook his head.

"One hot chocolate coming up," Kyle said.

Chevalier nodded and walked into the room, shutting the door behind him.

"I don't think Kyle knew what he was getting himself in to when he took up this position," he said, sitting down on a chair by the fireplace, though there hadn't been the need for a fire in months.

"Oh... he knew." She disappeared into the bathroom.

"Which reminds me, I heard a congratulation is in order," he called into the bathroom.

Emily walked out in dry jeans and a t-shirt. "Hrm... not planned exactly."

She took the hot cocoa from Gordon and thanked him, and then sat down in a chair by Chevalier and sipped at the warming drink.

"Well, Kelly does apologize." Chevalier was trying not to laugh. He wasn't sure why he found it funny.

"He shouldn't have let your monster out while Patra was in heat," she grumbled. "I'm not saying this place doesn't need more horses, but we could have at least gotten her a paint stud instead of that grouchy Arabian you ride around." She frowned. Chevalier's horse was ornery and temperamental.

"Well, maybe he found her mouth wateringly appealing."

Emily blushed and sipped on the hot cocoa.

"So what brought on the sudden attack on Kyle?" He was still working on being casual about their relationship, but at times, found it hard. He couldn't help but find it irritating when the two of them were together so much, and they had begun to have inside jokes that he didn't understand.

"He made fun of Patra for being pregnant." She glared at him, and he took the sign to drop the laughter at her mare's expense.

"You don't find it the least bit funny?" He grinned and looked at her eyes. "I've been thinking…"

"Yeah?" She was watching him because he seemed nervous, which was extremely uncharacteristic of him.

Chevalier smiled broadly, "Marry me."

Emily sighed, "Be serious, Chev."

"What if I am?" He moved to kneel in front of her and took her hand. "Please… consider it."

"What about our secrecy? You know… mean ol'Enforcer can't be caught loving a mere mortal." She raised an eyebrow and smiled down at him.

"We'll get married in secret... just us and one other... it will finally make you mine." He smiled, knowing how much she hated to be claimed that way, but he loved to see the way she blushed when she heard it.

"Ugh... Chev... we don't need to get married. I've done that, remember? White wedding, hundreds in attendance, the stress, the panic, the pressure. You see how well that one worked out." She was still sipping at the hot cocoa.

"Not a human wedding, Emily. It's amazing how hard it is to find any type of preacher from any flavor of mortal religion that will marry a mortal to an immortal. It goes against the ethics of every theological professional in the world." He was still smiling. She was getting uncomfortable, and he found human emotions fascinating.

"Well then, what are you suggesting?" Her curiosity peaked.

"An immortal bonding... sealing us together, forever, as mates."

She frowned. "Doesn't that sound romantic?"

Chevalier leaned his head back and laughed.

"Well it doesn't! Mates... we might as well be friends with benefits or..." Her words were cut off by his lips.

He leaned back and stared into her vivid eyes. "Please, Emily. I want you to officially be with me forever."

She sighed, "What exactly does it entail?"

He grimaced a bit. This was the part he was afraid to tell her. "Well... normally... it's a small ceremony with just one other witness present."

She could tell he was leaving something out. "And?"

"Well to finalize it... there's an... well an exchange."

Her eyes narrowed. "An exchange of what?"

"The ceremony is for immortals."

"Don't you see one tiny problem with that?" Emily set her empty cocoa cup on the table.

"It can be done with a mortal too, Em. It's just different for them."

"How? You're trying not to tell me something, and that's making me nervous." She studied his eyes and the nervous twitch of his lips.

"It's an exchange of ..." he sighed, "blood."

Emily was horrified. "Ew! No way!"

He loved the way her nose wrinkled when she said that, how something so intensely pleasant to him, could be so repulsive to her.

"Well, I knew you would feel that way, so I figured we could improvise and use the mortal replacement for blood... wine." He watched her for a reaction.

"For both of us?" She could feel the panic rise to her throat.

"I'm an immortal, Emily." He thought that part of the ceremony would be obvious.

She spoke in a whisper, her hand on her throat, "You're going to bite me?"

"It won't hurt. If done right, you might actually enjoy it." He smiled and noticed her eyes turned to his teeth.

"I don't...." She couldn't even speak clearly.

Chevalier leaned up and brushed his lips across hers. "Trust me."

Her eyes filled with tears. "I don't know."

He frowned. "Do you not want to marry me, then?"

"That's not the problem." Her voice was higher and nervous. "I'm starting to think a big white wedding would be better than this."

He laughed. "Stop worrying about it. We'll do it tonight, and then you won't have time to worry."

"What!?" She stood and backed away from him.

Chevalier stood up and met her gaze. "Calm down, Emily."

Her breathing slowed, and her shoulders relaxed.

"Calm... this isn't scary. This isn't vicious. This will bind us forever."

Emily nodded at him slowly.

She broke his gaze and gasped. He hated when her stubbornness broke the gaze, and he immediately lost the ability to do it again for a while.

"Don't do that!" she said, walking toward the door.

"Where are you going?" he asked.

"To talk to Kyle."

He knew she would tell him. Chevalier figured Kyle would be the one to do the ceremony, as he's the only other heku Emily trusted. There was another motive for having Kyle there though. He wanted Kyle to see the bonding ceremony and to show him how much Emily truly belonged to him.

Kyle moved to her quickly when she walked through the doors. He could sense that she was extremely upset, and she motioned for him to follow her before he could ask what the problem was. He followed her silently outside, through the barn, and to the new corral that housed the herd of cattle. She stood in the middle of the small herd and began to cry.

"What happened?" he asked, touching her shoulder softly.

Her voice was soft, and she choked out the words through sobs, "He wants to marry me."

Kyle smiled and tried not to chuckle. "That's it? He wants to marry you, and you're this upset?"

She nodded.

"He'll be lucky to find someone to do the ceremony, but..." He froze and looked at the pained expression on her face. "He wants an immortal bonding, doesn't he?"

She nodded again.

Kyle growled, "How dare he suggest that to you!"

Not knowing what else to do, he grabbed her and pressed her to his chest. He could feel her tears wet his shirt. "Do you want me to talk to him? Try to talk some sense into him?"

She shook her head. She didn't want Chevalier mad at Kyle. She feared enough for Kyle's life because of Chevalier's temper.

"When?" he asked her softly, running his fingers through her hair.

"Tonight," she finally managed to say.

Before she could react, Kyle's lips were pressed firmly against hers with his hands wrapped around her waist. She tried to pull away, but he moved one hand to the back of her neck to hold her in place.

Kyle's body stiffened, and he quickly moved a few steps back from her. His eyes were fearful. "I'm so sorry, Em. I shouldn't have done that."

She watched him, her eyes wide.

"I... I...." Then he was gone.

Emily stood in the pasture. The cattle were grazing absentmindedly around her. The air suddenly felt too hot, and she sunk to her knees. She looked around at how normal everything seemed, as if nature itself didn't understand the thoughts in her mind and the feeling in her body. Emily found she couldn't even cry. Her tears had dried in her as her body reacted to the shock.

She could still feel Kyle's lips pressed against hers, soft and gentle, different from Chevalier's strong, passionate kiss. Emily suddenly realized that she would have to do as Chevalier asked, and it would have to be tonight. She couldn't risk losing Kyle as a friend over this, and the pain of drawing it out would be too much. Minutes passed before she found the strength to stand up and head back into the castle to tell Chevalier.

***

Chevalier and Emily stood facing each other. The rock outcropping fell steeply behind them to a majestic waterfall. When Kyle disappeared, Chevalier found another heku to take his place, an older man named Morgan. He smiled to both of them as he wrapped a thin black ribbon around their wrists, binding them tightly together.

She was shocked when he spoke, and the language was foreign to her. His words drifted softly around the clearing, as if he were singing. Chevalier watched her and smiled at the nervous look in her eyes. Morgan continued to speak quickly, and his foreign words blurred as Emily watched Chevalier and fought the urge to run.

Emily's breath caught in her throat as Morgan handed her a glass flute filled with a scarlet colored wine. She looked at Chevalier, who nodded and smiled at her. She took a long drink and handed the glass to Morgan. Before she even turned back to Chevalier, he was pressed against her, and she fought to get away from him, but his hands held her tightly and his lips were at her neck. Adrenaline surged through her body. Every natural instinct she had fought against his hands.

"Relax, Em," he whispered, just before his teeth sank deep into the flesh of her neck.

He groaned as the pleasing taste tickled the back of his throat and soothed his senses. He gripped her tighter and felt her body go limp against his. The beast rose quickly to the surface, and he drank more fervently. With great effort, he was able to pull away from her and tighten his grip. She was weak in his arms. He gently slipped the diamond ring onto her finger and kissed it softly.

Chevalier picked her up when her legs gave out completely, and he smiled at Morgan, who nervously continued. Emily laid her head against his shoulder. She found it hard to concentrate. She was so relaxed that all she wanted to do was sleep, and the soft incantation Morgan was saying helped only to soothe her. Emily drifted off to sleep in his arms.

"Emily?" His soft voice brought her out of her relaxed state, and she realized she was lying down. "Drink this."

She felt a cold cup touch her lips, and she drank deeply. The cold juice seemed to help wake her up.

"Good girl," Chevalier said, and kissed her forehead lightly as he pulled the glass away.

She looked up at him. "What happened?"

Chevalier smiled. "It's all over... you did perfectly."

"I feel strange," she said, her words seemed slow and slurred.

"That'll pass."

Emily sat up, and her head swam. The world began to spin around her as Chevalier laid her back against the bed. "Just stay down for a bit. I promise it will pass soon."

"Why do I feel like this?" she mumbled, hoping he understood her.

"Well... that'd be my fault. I had some problems stopping, and you lost a little too much blood. I apologize. Then there's my blood in your system. That doesn't help." He winced away from her.

"Wine," was all she could manage to say.

"Mostly, yes."

"Wine," she said again, and fell back to sleep.

"How dare you!" Kyle yelled, growling.

"It's none of your concern, boy." Chevalier's voice was enraged.

"It is my business... how dare you lie to her, and then feed from her like she's one of your donors. It's disgusting how you treat her."

Emily tried to yell back, to stop them from fighting, but no words came out of her mouth.

"You will not speak to me like this unless you want to find yourself without a head," Chevalier hissed.

"I'll take my chances. She can't speak for herself. It'd be worth dying knowing that I didn't mistreat someone I care about."

Chevalier's growl deepened, "If she didn't care so much about you, I would kill you where you stand for such insolence. She knew what she was doing."

"Oh really? She knew you put drops of your blood into her wine then? Because it sounded to me like she thought it was pure," Kyle shouted.

He can't talk to Chevalier like that, Emily thought. She feared for Kyle's life. Why didn't he stop? Why didn't he let her fight for herself? She wasn't worth Kyle dying for.

"It was necessary, and you know it."

"By deception?"

Emily could feel the hatred in the room, and could feel the rage building, but she couldn't move, couldn't respond to stop it.

There was a loud rush of wind and a choking sound. "You've gone too far, boy," Chevalier barked, but there was no response.

She tried to scream, to make them stop, but only a mere groan escaped her lips.

She heard a loud thud and felt someone sit beside her on the bed. She could feel her surroundings coming back, her senses turning back on as she dug her way out of unconsciousness.

"Emily?" Chevalier's voice was suddenly soft.

"Don't kill him," she mumbled, her mouth still working sluggishly.

"I didn't kill him, though he deserved it," he spat the words out angrily.

She felt strong arms under her shoulders, lifting her up, so she was sitting, then the cold glass was pressed against her lips. "Drink again," he said.

She took a long drink. It felt amazingly good. Her eyes focused on the bedroom, and she scanned it for Kyle, but he couldn't be seen.

Chevalier laid her back down and smiled at her. "Feeling better?"

She was able to manage an icy glare. "Why did you do that?" Her words were coming clearer.

He sighed, "I knew you wouldn't drink it otherwise… it was easier."

"I trusted you," she said, her eyes accusing. He averted her gaze.

"I'm sorry."

Emily turned her face away from him. "Go away."

She felt him leave and heard the doors shut.

As her mind cleared, she suddenly had an abhorrent thought, what if… "Kyle?" she called out weakly, knowing he could still hear her from the other room, but he didn't respond.

"Kyle?" she tried louder, but there was still no answer.

The door opened and a strange heku appeared, a tall, muscular heku who looked to be no older than 18 or 19 years old. "Did you need something, Lady Emily?"

She frowned. "I need Kyle."

The boy stayed in the doorway. "Kyle is unavailable. Is there something I can get for you?"

"Where is he?" She tried to sit up but only managed to prop herself onto her elbow.

"I wasn't informed." He was too polite, too young, and she instantly didn't like him. "I asked for a tray to be brought up. The Chief Enforcer said you weren't feeling well, and I thought food might be appropriate."

"Go away," she grumbled at him.

It irritated her how he bowed before leaving. She got out of bed and held onto the headboard while she felt if her legs were steady. Chevalier was right about one thing. She was getting stronger quickly. Emily had made up her mind. She could no longer trust Chevalier, and that hurt deeper than any of Keith's beatings. She fought back the tears as she threw some clothes into a bag.

The annoying heku looked at her as she stepped out of the bedroom, and he began to cross the antechamber to her. She held up a hand, and he stopped. "You stay here."

"M'Lady, I must insist…"

She turned on him. Her glare made him wince, and he returned to his place.

The hallways were empty as far as she could tell, so she made her way out of the castle and headed down the road to the pier. Some of the coven came out to greet her and shied away when she turned on them. They had never seen such an aggressive look on her face. She stepped onto the pier, and Travis turned to smile at her, but like the others, he fell back when she turned on him.

The tone of his voice was professional, "The ferry leaves in 5 minutes, Lady Emily. May I summon a taxi for your arrival?"

She spun toward him and took a step in his direction. Her piercing green eyes locked on his, and he recoiled slightly. "You'd love that, wouldn't you? Then you could ask the taxi driver where he dropped me off… very nice."

"I… I… I just thought you may… need a ride." He was shocked. Emily always treated him kindly, and this new part of her was chilling.

Emily stepped onto the ferry without responding and moved to the back, sitting on the planks to wait out the long trip to the mainland.

***

Chevalier followed her scent to the pier and growled at how it was faded. It had been a while since she'd been there. His decision to leave her alone for a few hours apparently backfired. He'd already punished the young heku in her antechamber for allowing her to leave alone. He understood she'd demanded him to stay, but his decision to choose to follow a mortal over his own had been detrimental. The four guards on the pier stiffened as he approached.

"How long ago did she leave?" He scowled at Travis.

"It's been four hours since the ferry left. It arrived safely a few minutes ago." He stood at attention.

The hiss from behind him made his heart skip a beat. "Where is she going?"

Travis swallowed hard. "She wouldn't say, sir."

"Get that ferry back here... now," he bellowed at them, and saw Travis nod.

It was a long four hours as the ferry came back to the island. The entire time, Chevalier's mind went over possibilities of where she would go, while his eyes glared at Travis' back. He tried to find some breach of protocol, some way to punish him, but there had been none.

He stepped onto the ferry, and the Captain immediately set off, seeing the look on Chevalier's face. He didn't wish to cross the Chief Enforcer today. Chevalier appeared behind the Captain, and the hairs on the back of his neck stood up.

"Where did she go?" he hissed at the Captain.

"She got into a taxi, sir." He stared ahead, afraid to look at him.

"And?" He knew the old heku was more observant than that.

"It was a Chester Taxi, cab number 3811," he continued.

Chevalier walked back to the end of the ferry and watched for the land to appear. As he regained control of his emotions, he caught Emily's scent and that of another, one that sent anger back to the forefront of his mind. Kyle was with her.

The hours passed slowly, and the ferry's Captain was relieved that Chevalier stayed out on the ferry, and when land became visible, he finally relaxed.

Chevalier waited for his cell phone to find a signal and then dialed information. They connected him quickly to the Chester Taxi dispatch. "I require a taxi to the Franklin Ferry Pier."

"Right away, sir. I have someone just around the corner." Her voice was irritatingly sweet.

"I prefer cab 3811 and will pay extra for their service." He fought to keep his voice calm.

"Yes, sir, they are about 25 minutes away, and they have been dispatched to your location. Is there anything else I can do for you?" she asked.

He answered by shutting his cell phone. Chevalier paced the small cement block by the pier and waited for the cab, then slid into the taxi when it arrived.

"Where can I take you?" he asked.

"You gave a ride to a man and woman earlier, from this same spot... take me to their location." His voice was hollow.

"I haven't picked up a couple here since a few days ago," he said, watching Chevalier from his rear-view mirror.

"Who was your last fair from here then?" He sounded confused.

"Just a lady, but she was alone." The cabbie started to fidget.

"Then take me to her."

The man turned in his seat. "Look, mister. She was awfully pretty, and alone, and I don't want no trouble."

Chevalier smiled. "No trouble at all. She's my wife."

"I don't know." The cab driver watched his passenger carefully.

Chevalier was getting irritated, so he met the gaze of the cab driver. "Take me to her."

The cab driver turned and sped off down the street, not saying another word. He pulled the taxi up to a large park and pulled over, then gasped when Chevalier threw a $100 bill over to him and stepped out. He'd never gotten a $70 tip before, and he drove away, pleased with himself.

Chevalier inhaled deeply and again picked up the scent of Emily and Kyle. Emily's trail wasn't as fresh as Kyle's, and he realized that Kyle was tailing Emily, and she probably didn't know it. As much as he hated it, he felt better that she wasn't alone. He looked around the small fishing village and scanned for any sign of her. Walking past the large sign that read 'Welcome to Jonesport America', he turned north, following their path.

He began to run when he heard the sound of a struggle and Emily's scream in the evening air. The smell of blood infuriated him as he searched for them. The entire area smelled like them, and he'd lost the newest trail. The sounds suddenly stopped, and when he heard Emily scream Kyle's name in a panic, he quickly headed for them.

As Chevalier rounded the corner, he stopped. Emily was on the ground cradling Kyle's head, and he wasn't moving. She had blood dripping from her forehead, and she was crying. As Chevalier approached them, Emily screamed briefly when she saw him, then stopped when she saw his face.

"Chevalier! Help him," she yelled, looking back down to Kyle.

He knelt down beside Kyle and winced as he saw the deep gashes on his skin, characteristic of heku bites. Chevalier glanced up and saw three heku torn into pieces that were strewn around the alleyway.

"What happened?" he whispered as he ascertained the extent of Kyle's injuries.

Emily shook her head, her eyes full of terror. "I didn't know he was behind me. They attacked out of nowhere, and he just appeared. I couldn't..." She paused, replaying the last few minutes in her mind. "I couldn't ash them. I couldn't and I tried. He fought them off. He was so mad. They were biting him and trying to pull him apart."

She shivered.

Chevalier picked Kyle up in a fireman's hold. "He'll be okay in a few days. We need to get him back to the island."

He started walking back toward the park and turned when Emily didn't follow him. She was still kneeling on the cement, staring at the bodies of the heku.

"Emily, come on," he urged softly.

She shook her head.

"Let's discuss this later. Come back with me. You aren't safe here." He took one step toward her, knowing he couldn't carry both of them.

"I can't go back, Chevalier." The resolve of her words stung him.

"Please..." He watched her.

She shook her head again. "I can't trust you anymore."

"It's not safe for you here, not since...," he sighed, hesitating to bring it up. "Not while my blood is in your veins. It makes you a stronger target."

She frowned. "I'd rather face them than know that you lied to me." Her face showed the pain and anguish she felt.

"For Kyle then, Em, come back until he's better." He knew that was cold, but he had to get her back to the safety of the island.

She hesitated and looked over at the bodies of the heku, then slowly followed Chevalier to the park.

The taxi driver watched them curiously but didn't question why the man and woman had an unconscious third with them. He figured that he wasn't paid enough to ask questions.

The four hour ferry ride was painful for both of them. Chevalier laid Kyle down on a bed in the cabin and sat, watching him. It was twice now that Kyle had saved Emily, and Chevalier owed him his life. As he sat patiently, the words Kyle yelled at him that morning made sense. He'd been too rash to get his way, and he now realized what a grave error he made in lying to Emily. He was too used to getting his way. No one dared to defy him, but Kyle had. He'd taken his duty to protect Emily to new levels.

Emily stayed up on the ferry in the cold night air, ignoring the way the freezing wind bit painfully at her exposed skin.

***

She sat in the stark white bedroom. The hard bed was abandoned in the corner, and Emily watched out the window with her legs drawn tightly to her chest. There was no warmth in this room, no touch of life, and it's exactly what she wanted.

Emily ignored the knock on the door, then sighed when it opened anyway.

"Emily?" Chevalier said, sitting down on the edge of the bed.

"How is he?"

"He's going to be okay... that many bites take longer to recover from though." His voice was soft and she picked up a hint of regret, "I'm more worried about you."

"I'm fine." She was fine, in fact, at least physically. She only had a small cut on her forehead.

"I wasn't honest with you about the bonding ceremony, and I'm sorry. I was trying to make it easier on you."

"Yeah, how'd that work for you?" she snapped.

He just shook his head. "What we didn't know... myself included, is that when it was over, we were bonded more strongly than I ever imagined. I can feel your hatred toward me and pain at what happened with Kyle. You shouldn't have to feel such things."

"What do you mean you can feel it?" She was still watching out the window.

"I don't know, exactly. I haven't before heard of a mortal and an immortal going through the bonding together, maybe it's normal. It's like every part of me is in tune with every part of you. I can feel your emotions. I can more clearly smell the blood from the cut on your head. It's amazing to be able to be that close to you." His voice was soft.

"We'll see how strongly that tie is when I'm in California," she mumbled.

"California?"

"Yeah, the place in the U.S. that's farthest from this island," she said wryly.

"Please, Emily. I can feel how you aren't joking."

She spun on him, and the anger in her eyes shocked him. "You don't lie to people you love. You don't deceive those you care about. You are so wound up in getting everything you want that you would step on anyone to get it. I can't... no, I won't, live with that."

"It wasn't like that," he sighed as she turned back to the window. "I was honestly trying to make it easier for you. I knew you couldn't drink blood. It's not in your nature, so I made it easier for you."

She huffed.

"How can I make this up to you? What can I do to get you to stay?" He was on his knees beside her.

"I don't know if I can ever trust you again," she said, her voice was starting to crack.

"I wish I could make you see how insignificant that one lie was. I know how repulsive that was to you, but in my world, it's beautiful to share of each other. The feeling that I'm tied to you so deeply is incredible, and I'm intoxicated by its power."

Recovery

Chevalier sat in his study with his eyes closed. He was concentrating on Emily and could feel how she went from alone and confused to almost exhilarated. He tried to concentrate, tried to focus to find the source of the change, but he wasn't quite able to get it. He suspected that over time, the bond would become stronger, and he may be able to tell her thoughts or to see through her eyes. Now, though, he relished in the feeling of completeness and of belonging that engulfed her. It was too much. He had to know what she was doing that had filled her so completely with joy.

He wasn't surprised to find the small guestroom to be empty, but he was able to track her out to the barn. He stood against the barn door and watched her work. He was surprised that that small body could work as she did and was fascinated by how doing so made her feel. Chevalier smiled as she took a pitchfork full of hay and tossed it onto the ground in front of some of the cattle. She slipped off the cowboy hat she wore and ran her sleeved arm along her brow. He didn't like how the cowboy hat shaded her eyes. He preferred when he could see them.

Chevalier quietly slipped back into the shadows of the barn when Emily glanced in his direction. Her human senses weren't too far off. The feeling that she was being watched was correct, but when she couldn't see anyone, she turned back to work.

Emily was enjoying being out with her cattle again. She was able to release her mind and focus on them. She liked how her muscles strained beneath the heavy hay and looked forward to the soreness it would bring the next day. She was doing more than normal. Somehow, the pain caused her mind to forget the deception. She groaned slightly under the weight of the hay on the pitchfork but was still able to push herself to throw it.

With the cattle fed, she headed into the barn and began mucking out Patra's stall. She kept turning around. The feeling of being watched was stronger in here. She dripped with sweat as she cleaned the stall meticulously and then re-filled it with clean straw. Once there was clean water and fresh oats, she went out to the cow pasture to get Patra, who was munching lazily on hay.

Patra saw Emily coming and stepped away from her.

"Come on, Patra. It's time to go back inside," Emily said, walking casually up to the horse.

Patra reared slightly and took a step back.

Emily frowned. "What's wrong girl?"

She reached a hand out to her, but again, Patra moved away.

"You ole pregnant fool, come back here," she called, running after Patra when the horse took off.

Chevalier was glad he was a long ways off in the barn. He was laughing.

Emily got just a few feet from Patra and was able to grab the bridle finally. Patra nipped at the brim of her hat. "Stop that," she told her, and started to walk.

She landed on her butt on the hard ground when Patra set her feet and wouldn't move. Emily stood up and pulled harder at the reins, but Patra only looked down at her. She finally walked over to the horse. "What is your problem today?"

Emily pulled hard against the reins, and Patra took one step and then stopped and whinnied.

"Come on!"

She leaned back, her entire body pulling against the stubborn mare. "Fine... be that way."

Emily left Patra out and headed back for the barn. "Stay out here all night. See if I care," she called back, but the mare was already pulling at the grass.

When Emily got into the barn, she took off her hat and slammed it into the ground, growling. The tiniest noise escaped Chevalier as he laughed from his perch above her. She spun toward the back of the barn but didn't see anyone. Giving up, she kicked her hat at the wall and stormed off to the house.

Emily opened Kyle's door and peeked inside. She saw he was awake, and he smiled at her from the bed.

"How are you?" she asked, stepping inside and shutting the door.

"Never better," he replied as he repositioned and grimaced.

"I thought heku didn't get hurt," she said, and sat down on a chair by the bed.

"Well… mortals can't hurt us, but we're pretty good at injuring one another." He watched her.

"Good to know, I guess. I owe you another thank you it seems." She leaned toward him.

"I couldn't just let you leave that mad, Em. I'm glad I was there though. So enough about me… how are you?" He watched her intently.

"I wasn't hurt at all. I'm good." Her eyes told a different story.

"I'm not talking about what happened on the mainland, and you know it. Are you talking to him yet?"

She shrugged.

"I'll take that as a no. I've been thinking about that quite a bit this morning, and I'm not sure it's as bad as I first thought."

"Are you kidding me? Kyle, I drank blood!" She wrinkled her nose, fighting back a gag.

"Is that the real problem?" He raised his eyebrows.

"Well no… he lied to me, and I trusted him," she said sourly.

Kyle nodded. "If he'd told you, would you have done it?"

Emily shook her head.

"Are you sure about that? You are as in love with him as he is you. I have a feeling you would have done it anyway."

She looked at the ground. "At least if I had, it would have been my choice."

"Fair enough… but didn't he spare you the agony of having to decide?"

"You're on his side now then? Is that it?" she asked, getting mad.

"I didn't say that." His voice was almost pleading, "I just said that he's good for you. I can see that, and I wish you would too. I wouldn't punish him for too long for one bad judgment."

"He lied to me!" Her voice faltered.

"He loves you… he lied to protect you. I'm not saying it wasn't wrong, but look at it from his side. Would you lie to him if it would save him the pain of making an impossible decision?"

Chevalier stood outside the door and listened. He'd planned on going in to talk to them both, but Kyle's words hit him, and now he just stood by the door, awestruck.

Emily didn't answer.

"Just give him a break, okay? I've known him for almost 950 years, and I've never seen him like this, the way you make him. I hate to use the word happy, but it's close. I've no doubt he doesn't want anyone to know you two are bonded. It would show he has a weakness… a very human emotion."

"That or he's embarrassed to be married to a mortal." Chevalier could feel some of the self-loathing creep back into her, and he cringed.

"You know that's not it. If he were embarrassed, he wouldn't have paraded you back through the island. He would have stayed in Colorado. It wouldn't have been the first time he disappeared for a few years."

Emily's voice was much softer and Chevalier could feel her emotions changing, "I still don't know, Kyle."

Kyle laughed. "Well do me a favor, and next time you decide to take off... don't."

"We'll see."

There were a few minutes of silence before Kyle spoke again. "That ring suits you."

Emily looked down at the large glittering ring on her finger. "Yeah... well, for some reason, I can't get it off."

Chevalier winced.

Kyle laughed, "Did he not explain anything to you? You can't get it off... not until the bond is broken."

"Do what?" she gasped.

"It's an essence ring. In the bonding, it's the symbol that you are tied to the giver. It won't come off until the bond is broken."

"Nice... and how does one break the bond?" she asked, still tugging at the ring.

Kyle's voice became nervous, "I'm not going to tell you that. That's between you and Chevalier."

Chevalier was thankful for that and stepped away, leaving them alone. He walked slowly to the solitude of his office. He shut his eyes and focused on her again, moments before the phone rang and broke his concentration. He cursed under his breath and answered it.

"What?" he snarled into the phone.

He straightened up when the nasally voice spoke, "I have called to inform you that the Elders will be making a formal visit to your coven in three days. Please be prepared to discuss..." He heard papers shuffling. "Past Encala attacks, and they also request the presence of one of your coven by the name of Emily Russo."

He cringed. "She's not in my coven."

"She is still required to be in attendance."

"Fine, we'll be ready." No one refused the Elders, not even a member of their Council.

Chevalier slammed down the phone and yelled for Storm. When she knocked on his office door, he stepped out.

"Yes, sir?"

"The Elders are coming in three days. We need this place ready. Set up the conference room to accommodate six."

"Yes, sir." She sounded panicked and immediately sped off, barking orders at heku as she passed them, ordering to clean faster.

Chevalier knocked softly on Kyle's door, and the two inside became quiet.

"Who is it?" Kyle called.

He sighed, "Me."

"No," Emily whispered.

"I can't deny the Chief Enforcer," Kyle whispered back.

"Then I'll go out the window." Chevalier heard her chair scoot a bit as she stood up.

"We're on the third floor, Emily, just sit down," Kyle whispered, and then turned toward the door. "Come in."

When Chevalier entered, he saw Kyle sitting up in bed and Emily looking out the window. He saw how her fingers tensed around the window frame and could feel unease coming from her.

"How are you feeling?" Chevalier asked, sitting in the chair by the bed.

"Fine, sir, thank you."

"Kyle, I owe you a great debt of gratitude… again." Chevalier couldn't tell him how much he owed, it was more than words could describe.

"It's my duty." His voice was professional, but Chevalier understood it was more than a duty.

"I need a favor," he sighed, and looked toward Emily. "From both of you."

Emily turned to look at him.

"I have no right to ask. I know that, but there's no time to make things right before." He watched Emily.

"Before what, sir?" Kyle asked.

Chevalier reached out with his senses and caught nervousness from Emily.

"The Elders are coming… in three days." As Chevalier spoke, Kyle sat up farther in bed.

"Here?" he asked, shocked.

"Yes, to discuss their recent meeting with the other Elders."

"That sounds easy enough, but why do you need Emily? I can make a full report of what I saw here that day." Kyle was watching Emily also.

"They have requested an audience with her." He saw her shoulders tighten.

"What? Why?" Kyle was frantic.

"I don't know, but there's one tiny problem." He glanced at her hand.

Kyle sighed, "The ring."

Chevalier nodded. "She's obviously bonded to a heku and... well... it can't be me."

Kyle nodded. "I see."

"I don't see," Emily said, turning to face them finally.

Chevalier hesitated, so Kyle spoke up, "The ring is an essence ring. It puts off certain... shall we call it... vibes... that tie you to a heku. It pretty much lets others know you are taken."

He hesitated also when he saw her wince.

"The Elders will want to know who you have bonded to, and as we've mentioned, for Chevalier to remain in his position, he can't have fallen in love." Kyle sighed, "So for this meeting, I will be your mate."

Emily frowned. "That's absurd." She tugged at the ring.

"Love to a mortal is a weakness, at least as seen by most heku. The Chief Enforcer can't show any weakness. The Elders are going to want to know why you've bonded and to who. I'll be there too to make it official." He saw the need for this and couldn't understand how to make her see it.

Emily just shook her head. "Whatever, I haven't agreed to stay."

Both Kyle and Chevalier inhaled sharply.

"What?" she demanded.

"The Elders can't be denied, Emily. If they show up and have requested an audience with you, and you aren't here... they will find you, and you would be punished for being disloyal," Kyle explained.

"I'm not loyal to them," she hissed.

"It doesn't matter... you 'belong' to a heku from the Equites, so in their eyes, you belong to them, too."

Chevalier finally spoke up. "It's formal too, and I'll have Margaret get on it right away. You two are going to have to work out how to be convincingly in love." He froze for a split second when he felt an odd emotion coming from Emily. She was uncomfortable acting in love with Kyle.

As Chevalier watched Kyle, his mind reached out to Emily, and he was relieved to find she was looking at him differently. The anger wasn't gone, but it was being masked by her deeper feelings for him. He finally understood that things would be alright.

***

"Emily, we're going to be late," Kyle said from her bedroom.

"They don't like waiting," Chevalier called to her.

She stood, horrified, in front of the mirror. She had given Margaret strict orders that the formal dress she was making was to be modest, and now she wondered if Margaret needed to re-learn the word. She liked the material, the way the long layers of soft fabric flowed when she moved. The top wasn't too bad. A circle of pearls wrapped around her neck, and the upside-down V of fabric draped from it did cover her, mostly. One problem was that it left her shoulders bare and the sleeves, if that's what you could call them, were split open all the way down and hung from her arms by small beads of pearls. The color was alright also. The top was dark blue, and it faded as it went to the floor, ending in white with what seemed to be runes stitched in contrasting blue thread.

She turned to the side though and gasped.

"I'm coming to get you in 30 seconds," Chevalier called out to her.

She stepped out into her room and blushed. Suddenly, she wasn't sure she liked her hair piled elegantly on her head with draped ringlets. She figured her hair would have hidden her body nicely. She felt uncomfortable as both Chevalier and Kyle looked at her and smiled.

"See, that's not so bad," Chevalier said, motioning for the door.

Emily sighed and stepped toward the door, spinning when the two heku started to laugh.

"I'm warning you." She eyed them.

"I'm sorry. It just took us by surprise," Chevalier said. He couldn't tell from the front, but the top of the dress in its flattering inverted V shape left her back and sides completely uncovered. The back dropped dangerously low and accentuated her small waist, exposing down to just above her hips.

He fought the desire to reach out and run his fingers along her delicate spine. He had to stay away from her tonight though. He couldn't let the Elders be suspicious.

Kyle glanced away nervously as he noticed that the revealing top also left the smallest portion of the outside of her breasts uncovered. He walked up beside her and held out his arm, which she took timidly and smiled at him. Chevalier repressed the desire to remove Kyle's arm.

They descended the steps and met the Elders at the bottom. The two male elders gasped at the sight of Emily. They hadn't imagined she would be so beautiful. They stepped aside, so Emily and Kyle could lead the way to the conference room. Kyle grinned as Emily blushed. She knew how revealing the back of the dress was, and she could feel their eyes on her.

Kyle opened the door for her and barely touched the soft skin on her back as she walked past him. He could feel Chevalier tense up, but he had his orders. He had to act like they were together. Touching was a vital part of that and one which he was enjoying too much.

He kept his hand on her back as she walked to her seat. Her seat was obvious as there was a glass and pitcher of water in front of it. The other seats faced an empty portion of the table. Kyle pulled out her chair and scooted her in as she sat. He reached down and kissed her lightly on the shoulder before sitting down beside her.

Emily watched Chevalier, and his face was unnaturally still. She felt Kyle's lips against her skin and stiffened, ready for Chevalier's rage, but it didn't come. She sat back in the chair and waited for everyone to be seated.

The female Elder, Selest, spoke first. "Thank you for allowing us this meeting, Chief Enforcer, and you, Lady Emily, for gracing us with your presence."

Emily just smiled politely, feeling uncomfortable as all eyes turned back to her. Kyle squeezed her hand gently.

"You know you are welcome here any time," Chevalier said. Emily was proud of him. He was acting perfectly normal, though she knew his jealousy had to be raging.

A young servant entered and placed a glass of red wine in front of Emily, then bowed and walked out. Again, all eyes turned to her, and she could feel her face flush.

"We have spent the last week in the company of the Valle and Encala Elders," Selest began. "I can't say as though any progress was made, but we did ascertain that, for now, there will be no further attacks." She emphasized, "For now."

The Elder to her right began. "We do believe we have found that the attacks on the Encala's coven were from the government of Greenland, not from one of the other factions. They do send their apologies for the unwarranted attack on this island."

Chevalier growled.

"We understand the frustrations, but things are explosive. We had to come to a mutual peace understanding, or we fear these attacks would continue and grow."

"So what happens now?" Chevalier asked. "My way of life was attacked. The people I protect were put in danger, and that's unacceptable."

"We all understand this. The Encala Elders were most upset by the attacks and have punished those involved. We have received…" He glanced at Emily. "Proof of their punishment and have accepted it."

Chevalier scowled.

The Elder to the female's left then spoke, "We will leave the proof with you to do with as you wish."

This seemed to calm Chevalier some, but Emily wasn't sure what they were talking about.

The female Elder smiled. "Now on to more joyous things, Emily?"

Emily jumped at her name and stammered out, "Yes?"

"You were of some contention in the meeting, child."

Emily frowned, but Kyle spoke, "What kind of conflict could my wife bring?"

"The Valle are trying to seek a claim to her."

Emily gasped, and she saw a twitch in Chevalier's face. Kyle wrapped an arm around her waist. "They have no such claim."

The Elder smiled. "It is true, more so now with the bonding, and we will tell them about that when we return."

Emily's body was tense, and she found little comfort in Kyle's arm.

"We didn't realize though, how very young Emily is. How old are you, child?" the female Elder asked her.

She looked at Kyle and he nodded and smiled. "I'm 24."

"Ahhh, so young, we had no idea."

Emily couldn't help it. "I'm not a child. 24 is an adult."

The oldest Elder laughed. "Still a child, dear."

Emily scowled and felt Kyle rub her back.

"And beautiful, the Valle failed to mention how stunning you are."

Emily blushed.

"We look forward to seeing the children this union produces. To think a Winchester heir could be in our ranks." He smiled reassuringly, but Emily froze.

"I... I... I can't have children," she finally managed to say.

"Why is that, dear?" the Elder asked, sounding honestly concerned.

Emily shook her head. "I just can't. The doctors told me that a long time ago."

The Elder turned to Kyle. "And you knew of this?"

Kyle didn't miss a beat. "Of course I did. I didn't marry Emily for the sole purpose of reproducing. I love her."

"Kind, very kind of you, dear. It's just so rare that we as the immortal get a chance to procreate that we thought it might be part of your plan," he said, not sounding at all like he meant to pry.

Emily looked at Kyle questioningly.

"Immortal women cannot bear children," he whispered in her ear. Her head suddenly filled with questions.

Emily grabbed the goblet and took a sip of the wine. It gave her a moment to think, and the alcohol cleared her head. She set it down and noticed everyone watching her again.

She looked nervously at Chevalier. "Why don't we let Emily go then. We have more to discuss that doesn't involve her," he said to the Elders.

The Elders stood as Emily did, and one reached out for her hand. She hesitated and placed her hand in his and tried not to grimace when he kissed it softly, then held it as he addressed her. "It was good to meet you, child." His eyes glanced down to her exposed waist. "Very nice indeed."

She pulled her hand away and left the room, ignoring the feel of eyes on her bare back. Once she heard the door shut behind her, she slipped off her heels and ran to the kitchen, then flung open the door and began to go through a nearby cupboard.

"Can we help you, child?" one of the young chefs asked from behind her. She dropped her hands. She could only imagine what skin was exposed with her hands extended.

"First, stop calling me child… second, I want more of that wine I just had." She was looking around the kitchen when the chef appeared ahead of her with the bottle.

"Thanks," she said, heading back out to her room.

She couldn't get out of her dress fast enough, and piled it onto the floor. She then slipped on one of Keith's old t-shirts and sat in a chair with the bottle of wine between her knees. She pulled and tugged on the cork, but it wouldn't come loose.

Frustrated, she stepped out into the hallway, held it out, and said, "It's stuck."

Within less than a second, a strange heku appeared and pulled the cork out, and then vanished.

"Thank you!" she called after him.

She had the bottle to her lips before she got to the chair, and she drank deeply. The alcohol burned her throat, and she sat down, gasping for breath. She noticed a glass sitting on the table but ignored it as she put the bottle to her mouth and drank. Emily smiled as she felt the effects from the wine start to warm and relax her. She slumped down in the chair and drank more.

As the world began to spin, she slid down to the floor, holding the bottle in front of her. She couldn't seem to drink enough to take the memory away.

"Keith?" She walked up to him while he was shoeing a horse.

"What? I'm busy," he snapped at her.

She paused, took a deep breath, and then continued, "I just got back from seeing Dr. Meacham."

"Yeah? So?" He didn't look up at her.

"He said I'm pregnant." She took a step back as he stood up and walked toward her.

"Oh yeah? Who's the Dad? Huh, Emi?" His fierce eyes raged.

She took another step back. "Don't act like that, Keith. You're the only one..." Before she could finish, he punched her hard, and she fell to the floor of the barn as blood seeped from the corner of her mouth.

"I am, eh? Not the entire male population of Cascade? I'm not going to spend my hard-earned money taking care of you and some asshole's little brat." He finished by kicking her in the side.

The doctor looked down at her from the table. "I'm so sorry Emily. The baby's gone."

Emily was numb, and she just nodded her head.

"I'm afraid there's more." The doctor put a warm hand on her arm. "The horse did more damage than we'd first thought."

She looked up at him.

"You can't have any more children. I'm so sorry." The doctor had tears in his eyes that Emily didn't. She felt relief at not bringing a baby to become part of Keith's fury.

Emily took another long drink. The warmth spread through her faster, and her mind finally began to block it all out.

She leaned back onto the floor and looked up at the ceiling tiles as they danced and moved above her. She smiled as she watched them. Suddenly, a face blocked her view of the swirling tiles, and she frowned.

"She's drunk," Chevalier said from above her.

"Yeah... I see that," Kyle said from somewhere in the room.

The dancing ceiling stopped as Chevalier picked her up off of the floor. She could still feel the bottle in her hand, and she brought it to her lips just as Kyle pulled it away.

"I think you've had enough," he said softly.

"Give it back." Her demand was slurred.

She reached out and tried to hit him but missed. She fumed when Kyle left the room with her bottle.

"Go get it back," she told Chevalier unevenly as he laid her on the bed.

"And risk you getting too drunk to talk? I don't think so." He was covering her with a blanket.

"I don't wanna talk." Her words were slow and hard to understand.

Chevalier sat down beside her on the bed and watched her for a moment as she marveled at the ceiling again.

"Emily?"

She didn't look away from the tiles. "Huh?"

"Do you want to talk about this?" he asked, partially amused.

"Talk about what?" She was reaching out to touch the ceiling.

"About why you are drinking. It's not like you."

"What makes you think I was drinking?" It made perfect sense to her. Deny it, that's what Keith always did.

Chevalier chuckled, "Oh, I have my suspicions."

"Gah, it's not true," she said as her fingers danced with the movement of the ceiling above her.

He watched her hands for a moment. "I keep going over it in my head, and I'm not sure which part would upset you... is it because of the baby comment?"

He knew he'd struck a nerve when her dancing hands stopped, and she glared at the ceiling.

"Emily, I didn't marry you to have children. I wish you would have told me, but that wouldn't have changed anything." He stroked her cheek softly.

He was actually relieved that she'd told the Elders. They would tell the Valle, and Ulrich could stop worrying about him fathering a Winchester child.

"I was once," she said in a daze.

"Was what, Em?" Chevalier kissed her lightly.

"Pregnant," she said as she covered her face with her hands and started to cry.

Chevalier tensed. He didn't know that. The crying didn't last long. The alcohol in her system kept the memories from surfacing all the way.

"Keith wasn't very happy," she said, reaching for the ceiling again.

"I see," was all Chevalier could say.

"Does the ceiling dance in your room?" she asked, her words more slurred, and she suddenly became tired.

Chevalier didn't answer, but watched as her eyes slowly shut, and she relaxed.

He held her all night as she lie motionless. He wished he could kill Keith again, this time more painfully. What right did a man have to do this to a woman who loved him? How could a man manipulate and control someone so completely? His anger ebbed as dawn approached. He had rid the world of Keith, and he took some comfort in that.

Emily groaned as the light erupted into her room. She grabbed her head and buried her face in the pillow.

Chevalier touched her hair lightly and spoke softly, so as not to make her headache worse, "There's coffee here, Em."

"Kill me," she said into the pillow.

He smiled. "Not today. Here... drink some."

He held the coffee cup up for her.

She sat up, wincing at the light, and took the coffee from him. She also noticed aspirin on the table and swallowed four of them.

Chevalier sighed, "You should have told me. It would have helped last night if I had known."

She winced, "Yeah, well, I guess we both kept some things private." Her head hurt too badly for her to notice how he grimaced.

"Truce then?" he offered.

She nodded, then groaned and went back to her coffee.

Emily laid back down until the aspirin worked and she could sit up without getting sick.

He smiled. "Feel better?"

"Mostly... I don't drink wine." She gave him a half-smile.

He grinned. "I noticed."

She leaned toward him and curled into his chest as he wrapped his strong arms around her.

"Time for some questions then?" she asked.

"Ask away," he told her, knowing it was coming.

"If heku don't... erm... can't have a baby... how do baby heku happen?" She knew it must have sounded insane when she heard him chuckle.

"When's the last time you saw a baby heku?" he mused.

She frowned and thought about that. She was sure she'd never even seen a child heku before. "Never, I guess."

"It's extremely rare for an immortal man to fall for a mortal woman. That's the only way a heku can procreate. That's also where the incubus comes in."

"Who?"

"An incubus is a male heku that seduces mortal women in their sleep for the sole purpose of reproducing."

"That works?"

Chevalier nodded. "Yes, but it's a mortal baby that is produced."

She looked up at him. "Really?"

He smiled. "Sure."

"So how are heku made then?" She curled back against his chest.

"It's a long process that involves draining the mortal's blood and replacing it with that of a heku along with some ancient magic." He said too much and refused to go further.

Emily frowned. "Magic?"

"Yes"

"Like what?"

"Nothing you need to concern yourself with. We don't turn mortals into heku haphazardly. It's only done with great care and only to individuals who could further the power of the coven." He pulled her tighter to him.

She thought for a moment. "How can a bond be broken?"

He stiffened, not sure exactly where this was going. "Were you going to give it a go?"

She laughed. "No, just curious."

For a few seconds, he debated. He felt she had the right to know, but also feared an irrational bout of emotions might drive her to it. "Why?"

"Curiosity sake is all." She kissed his neck lightly.

"You aren't playing fair," he said, grinning. "Fine… the bond is automatically broken when one of the two of them die. It's also broken after any infidelity or harsh betrayal."

She frowned. "So when I die, you're free to marry again?"

He fought to keep his composure. He had thought about that a lot lately, and he wasn't sure he could stay awake if she were gone. He was planning an eternity of stasis when she died. "If I would choose to."

"Hmmm"

He wished she'd say more than that, but her thoughts changed pattern. "You aren't upset that I can't have children?"

He felt her stiffen slightly beneath his arms. "Not at all. I wouldn't have gotten mad had it happened, but I've never seen myself as a father. It's so rare for a heku to do it that it's ludicrous to consider it."

"Still, when we got married, it had to have crossed your mind."

"Maybe… but we hadn't discussed it. I wasn't sure if you even wanted children." He kissed the top of her head.

She looked up at him and grinned.

"What?" He smiled back.

"Want to practice though?" She was on her back before she could laugh.

Coming Out

"Keep the blindfold on, Em," Kyle said. He was leading her carefully down a hallway.

"It's hard to walk... are we close?" she asked, with her hands outstretched.

"Yes... very."

She felt his hands leave her arm and heard a door open. He led her inside, and the warm mugginess of the room seemed odd.

"Ready?" Kyle asked.

"Sure," she said as he lifted the blindfold.

"Ooh... Kyle!" she gasped as she looked out over the swimming pool. It was full of sparkling blue water, and the hot tub bubbled in the corner.

She threw her arms around him. "Thank you!"

"Margaret put a swimming suit in the dressing room. I'll be outside this door if you need me. Just enjoy your swim and don't drown, or Chevalier will kill me." He shut the door with a grin.

Emily ran to the dressing room and undressed. She didn't even complain as she put on the tiny sheer swimsuit and hurried out to the pool, dipped in one toe, and then dove in when she felt how warm it was. The water felt incredible against her skin. She'd always felt comfort from water, and the room was so warm that everything was perfect. For over an hour she swam, from one end to the next, feeling the way her muscles strained against the water as she swam laps.

Out of breath, she floated on the water a bit and then eyed the hot tub with its inviting steam. She climbed out of the pool and shook her head as she passed the mirror. "Only Margaret would put me in a see-through swimming suit." She laughed to herself and crawled into the bubbly water.

The warm jets pounded against her skin, and she relaxed, laying her head back against the side of the tub. She breathed deeply, taking in the scent of chlorine and the muggy feel of the air.

Emily raised her head and glanced around, checking to make sure no one was watching. She reached around and untied her top and pulled it off, tossing it to the side. Laying back down, she shut her eyes and relaxed.

She yelped when hands gently caressed her exposed breasts, and then she grinned when she saw Chevalier had joined her.

"You really shouldn't sneak up on me," she reminded him as he pressed against her.

"You really should keep your clothes on." He grinned and began kissing her neck.

"I thought I was alone," she said as she shivered, his hands tracing soft patterns in her skin.

He didn't answer. His mouth was pressed firmly to hers.

***

Scooping up her swimsuit, she handed it to Chevalier and tightened the towel around her. "Take that back and tell her I would prefer a one-piece that you can't see through."

Chevalier smiled. "No way. I liked that one."

She smiled and walked toward the door, then felt a hand on her shoulder. "Kyle's out there."

Emily turned around and looked down at herself. "I'm covered."

Chevalier stepped back and eyed the towel. "Yes you are, but poor Kyle. You're going to drive him mad."

"How so?"

"We're men, Emily. It's obvious you are only wearing a towel."

"He'll live... I'm more covered in this towel than in that so-called swimsuit," she said, pushing on the door. She'd forgotten how heavy the door was when it opened for her.

Kyle gasped and looked away as she emerged and headed for her room. He followed behind her, keeping his eyes on the wall.

"*Good Man,*" Chevalier thought to himself.

Emily changed quickly back into her jeans and t-shirt and found Chevalier waiting in her room when she emerged.

"Dang," he said with a laugh.

"What?" She eyed him suspiciously.

"I'd hoped to give that blue dress another go." He chuckled and stood up.

"No chance!" She slapped his arm playfully. "Unless you were the one wearing it."

"Uh hu." He grinned and kissed her.

Emily pulled away from him and set out for the door.

"Where are you going now?" he asked. He planned on staying in this evening.

"I have to go feed the cows," she said, and turned to look at him.

He was instantly in front of her and began kissing her ear, flicking her earlobe with his tongue. She shivered.

"I can have someone do that for you," he hinted.

She hesitated and pulled away. "Nope, my cows, remember?"

He sighed, "Yes, I do."

"Besides, I'm pretty sure I know what you had in mind, and it can wait." She turned and headed out the door.

Emily first headed into Patra's stall, not bothering to wonder who had put her in. She pet the mare and rubbed Patra's expanding middle. "How ya feeling, Patra?"

Kyle smiled. He found it fascinating how she talked to her horse.

"So when is the big event?" he asked, leaning back against the wall.

"Hmm." She did the math in her head. "Seven more months." She started pouring fresh grain in the trough for the mare.

"So I heard something interesting today…," he began.

She didn't turn to him but started to brush Patra.

"Rumor has it, in the castle, that you were married before and that Chevalier killed him."

She turned with a frown. "You knew that already."

"Yes, but the interesting part is that somehow, so does everyone else now."

She cringed, "Seriously? Everyone?" She ducked out of the stall and pulled the door shut.

He nodded. "I'm going to talk to Chevalier about it. I don't like people talking about you and especially that. They shouldn't judge."

Her body suddenly tensed. "What all do they know?"

He shrugged. "I'm not sure."

"Do they know he... well…" She waited for him.

"I don't think so. No one mentioned it."

She relaxed some and loaded a bale of hay onto a small four wheeler.

Kyle cringed. "I wish you'd let me at least load the hay for you. It's heavy."

She smiled and climbed onto the ATV. "Then it would be your cows and not mine."

He followed behind her as she drove the ATV out to where the cows were grazing, then grabbed her pitchfork and went to work. Kyle's mind began to run through training scenarios for the guards. It didn't do for him to watch her work if he valued his life. His thoughts turned to her too often, and as much as he tried to control it, he couldn't.

"Emily, I'm going to go talk to Chevalier. You're safe out here," he reassured her needlessly. She felt safer out here than anywhere else on the island.

Kyle disappeared into the house, and Emily went back to work. She hummed to herself as she fed the cows and looked back proudly as they all ate. She checked their water and poured it out for fresh, then took the ATV back into the barn.

As she put away her tools, a sound in the barn scared her, and she turned toward it. She was relieved when she saw a barn cat looking at her. "Well, hello."

She walked over to it and sat down on the clean straw to pet it. It purred loudly and wound itself around her hand. "Keeping the mice away I hope?"

Emily continued to pet the cat as she watched him, "You need a name though... let's see...."

Emily thought for a moment and then smiled. "I'll call you Peanut."

The cat meowed and went back to rubbing against her arm. Peanut climbed up and leaned against her chest, his soft head at the nape of her neck. "You're a friendly thing aren't you?"

She stood up. "I'll be back tomorrow. You watch over things."

The sun was setting, and the full moon was already starting to creep into the sky. She stepped in through the back doors and frowned. Everything seemed too quiet. Even though she rarely saw heku servants, she could often hear them and could always feel their presence. Tonight, the castle seemed empty and cold.

Emily slowly wandered through the kitchen, into the foyer, and even peeked into the library, but still heard nothing. She made her way back into her bedroom and changed into an oversized t-shirt. When the silence had gone on too long, she left and went down to the TV room. It didn't take long to thumb through the movies and find a good romantic comedy. Emily put it in the DVD player and turned the sound up, curling up on a beanbag with a light blanket around her.

The movie ended, and the silence in the castle became irritating. She vowed to find where everyone had gone. Getting up, she headed out into the silence. Starting on the ground floor, she went room to room and listened at the doors. She frowned when, after an hour, she still hadn't found anyone. Suddenly, she had a thought and tried to remember where the court room was located.

It wasn't long before Emily found the spiral staircase that led down into darkness. She walked slowly, feeling her way along the wall. As she got closer, she heard voices, angry, shouting voices. She felt the door and stopped to listen.

"You can't do that!" a high, squeaky voice exclaimed.

"I can and I will. Now sit down!" Chevalier was angry, she could tell by his voice.

"I said nothing about the girl," another strange voice croaked.

"You deny spreading rumors about Lady Emily?" Kyle yelled. He was calmer than Chevalier, but still mad.

Emily frowned. This entire thing was about her again. Did she truly care that the staff spread rumors about her? Not rumors, she corrected, they told the truth... gossip then.

"The court has made its decision, and if no one objects, then we talk punishment," Chevalier growled.

Emily knew this was going to get her into trouble, but she did it anyway. She slammed open the doors. "I object."

All eyes turned toward her, including those in the topmost section of the room, Chevalier, Kyle, Storm, and the pier guard, Travis. She suddenly felt underdressed in just the oversized t-shirt that barely touched the top of her knees and had 'John Deere' written across it in green writing.

Kyle was by her side in an instant and whispered to her, "You can't object."

He tried to lead her out of the room, but she spun away from him.

"I object. You said that unless someone objected, they would be punished." She was making her way through the chairs toward the frightened heku along the front row. Kyle followed behind her but hesitated to grab her arm forcefully enough to drag her from the room.

Chevalier glanced down at Emily, and his eyes lit with rage. "Step back, Emily."

"No! It sounds to me like these proceedings are about me, and as such I have every right to defend whoever I wish." She nodded and sat down between two of the accused.

She smiled at one of them, and they looked up at her, terrified.

Kyle shrugged at Chevalier, who motioned him back to the chair. Storm stood up. "What is your defense then? State your case."

Emily stood up again, glancing down at her t-shirt. "Well, I don't feel that spreading gossip is grounds for punishment. At least not the punishment that you all hand out."

Mumbles ran through the court room.

"Quiet!" Storm bellowed, and the entire room fell silent.

"It's not a matter of gossip. It's a matter of breaking rules set forth by the Chief Enforcer and Lord of this coven," Storm explained.

"Oh... well... let me see then." Emily looked at one of the accused, and he stared at her with wide eyes. "What was the proposed punishment?"

Storm turned to Chevalier and he looked down at Emily. "Come here."

"Hmmm," she said, shifting slightly. She turned and put a reassuring hand on the shoulder of one of the accused and then walked up onto the top platform.

Chevalier, Kyle, and Travis turned their chairs to face away from the crowd while Storm watched over them.

"What are you doing here?" Chevalier asked her, irritated.

"Apparently defending the wrongly accused," she said matter-of-factly.

Kyle frowned at her. "You shouldn't be here."

She glared at him. "No one told me not to come down here, so I did, and what I heard was insane! You can't punish someone for gossip unless it's going a day without wages or..."

Chevalier stopped her. "That's enough! You will go back up to your room and wait for me."

She put her hands on her hips. "No."

Travis gasped. He'd not been around Emily enough to know that she didn't follow Chevalier's orders.

Chevalier nodded and growled, "Now."

Emily leaned down toward him. "I'm not one of your minions to be commanded. If you want me gone, you're going to have to remove me."

She turned and walked back down toward the accused and was almost to them when she was swept off of her feet and rushed out of the room.

"Kyle, put me down!" she yelled, kicking furiously.

He didn't answer, but ascended the steps quickly, and she was back in her room a few seconds later. He set her down on her feet and winced as she slapped him across his face.

"How dare you." Her gaze was fierce.

"You shouldn't be down there. It's none of your concern."

"It is so!" She headed back for the door, but Kyle blocked her.

"You aren't leaving." She'd never seen him this angry.

Emily took a step toward him, and though he towered above her, she met his gaze. "Let me through," she hissed at him.

"No," he said, not moving.

Emily swung at him, but he dodged and grabbed her hand, then wrapped it around to her back gently. "Stop before you hurt yourself."

Kyle slipped his free hand around her waist and picked her up, carrying her back to the chairs. "Sit."

He let her go and she immediately ran for the door. He quickly overtook her and hauled her back to the chair.

"I said sit!" he growled at her, and shoved her into the chair harder than he intended. The chair buckled under the force of the throw.

Emily landed on her back with the shattered chair underneath her, and she kicked hard, her foot connecting directly with Kyle's groin. He recoiled a bit and then grabbed her foot as she crawled away.

After picking her up, Kyle sat in the one remaining chair and pulled her onto his lap. He trapped her legs with his and wrapped his arms securely around hers, pinning them to her side. She screamed and thrashed to be let go.

"You have no right to hold me!" she yelled at him.

Kyle opted not to speak and just held her tightly.

Emily leaned her head forward and slammed it back into his nose, breaking it. He winced but held tightly, knowing the pain would clear in a few seconds.

"Let me go!" she screamed again.

"No, you don't know what you are doing, and until you see how things work around here, you need to keep out of it." His voice was calm. He worried about the reaction Chevalier would have when the bruises from the chair appeared on Emily's back.

She fought harder. "It's my decision! They were talking about me."

"That's not the issue. They disobeyed a direct order. Covens are made up of violent creatures. Laws and orders have to be obeyed to prevent anarchy." He thought he'd made an impact.

"Fine, but you're hurting me. Let me go." Her voice was calm, so he let her up.

She stood and faced him, rubbing the bruises on her wrist. He stood up. "Are you ready to stay up here? "

"Sure," she said, stepping toward the chair. He moved away so she could sit down but unexpectedly felt the chair slam against his back. The impact shocked him but didn't hurt him badly, and he ran after Emily as she reached the door.

"No more," he said sternly, and threw her across his shoulder, then hauled her back into the room. "Sit!"

He sat her hard on the bed, and she glared up at him, angry at not gaining any ground. Kyle stood up and stretched his back. She could hear bones moving back into place. She shuddered at the sound and reeled as he grabbed her and held her in the same position he had on the chair. She growled, frustrated.

Kyle held Emily for over an hour as she attempted occasionally to get free. Chevalier joined them finally and looked around the room with a frown, then walked over to where Kyle was restraining her.

"What happened to the chairs?" he asked Kyle.

Emily strained against Kyle's arms, no longer seeing reason. She was beyond mad and her scream echoed off the walls. "Let me go!"

Chevalier stared at her, open mouthed with his eyes wide. He'd never seen her this angry, and some of the damage in the room was making sense. He also noticed Kyle's nose looked different and realized it had been broken.

He knelt down in front of her as Kyle held her tightly. "Emily?"

He tried to look into her eyes, but she was straining too hard to get away.

She finally turned her hostile glare to Chevalier. "What did you do to them?"

"They were dealt with. I don't want you interfering with my job," he said, trying to stay calm.

Emily relaxed and nodded.

"Let her go Kyle. It's okay," Chevalier said.

Kyle shook his head. "That's when she broke a chair over my back, after she'd done that to me."

Emily screamed at him and came close to slipping her legs out from under Kyle's.

"She broke a chair over your back?" Chevalier asked Kyle, slightly impressed.

"Oh yes, and broke my nose, and kicked me in the groin. She's full of that Irish blood, isn't she?" He was almost laughing, which infuriated Emily more.

Chevalier leaned his head back and laughed. "Way to go, Em. That's my girl."

He stopped laughing when he looked at her.

"Find that funny? Wanna go a round with me?" she hissed at him, her jaw tightly clenched.

"It's too late. The punishment has already been given. There's nothing you could have done. You have to understand that these things are mine to deal with," he tried to reason with her.

"What did you do to them?" she asked. Her eyes turned from hatred to hurt.

He emphasized, "It's none of your concern."

He waited for her to respond, and when she didn't, he nodded for Kyle to let her go. When he did, she slumped onto the floor, her eyes down.

Chevalier grabbed her hand and flipped it over, looking at the dark bruises forming on her wrist.

"I'm sorry, sir," Kyle said, wincing.

Chevalier shook his head. "I don't think you had a choice."

"Did you kill them?" Emily's voice was a soft whisper.

Chevalier tilted her chin up with his hand so she was looking at him. "Stop, Em."

There was a gruesome cracking sound as Kyle re-set his nose. Emily shuddered at the sound, and Chevalier grinned up at Kyle.

"Anything else injured?" he asked.

"Nope, that's about it." Kyle smiled at Emily. "I'd watch her, though. We had a few tangles, and I was as careful as I could be but sent her through a chair at one point." His mouth twitched.

Chevalier laughed, "I didn't know she had that in her. Thank you, Kyle, you may go and take the night off, go feed."

Kyle nodded and left the room.

"I'm glad you find that amusing," she grumbled at him.

"Not funny, necessarily... impressive maybe." He guided her back up, so she was sitting on the bed instead of the floor.

"What?" She looked up at him.

"You would have put a mortal man in the hospital," he told her, and then grinned. His mind suddenly wondered why she never fought Keith back like that, but then remembered the control Keith had over her.

"Where else are you hurt?" he asked, looking over her arms and legs.

"Nowhere," she hissed at him.

"Then why do I smell blood?"

She shrugged, but winced slightly.

Chevalier walked around to her back and lifted her shirt. He inhaled sharply as he saw the deep cuts and bruises on her back. "Must have been the chair," he murmured to himself.

"I suppose you'll punish Kyle for that too," she said sarcastically.

"Nope... he deserves a raise for putting up with that kind of fight and holding on." Chevalier again sounded pleased.

He sat down beside her. "Listen to me carefully, Emily. Covens don't operate like mortal society. When you get a group of a thousand natural-born killers together, things have to be tightly controlled, or they get out of hand. Not one small infraction can go unpunished, or we risk mass murders and heku running around breaking rules. It is my job in this coven to do the punishments and to enforce and create the laws. I can't help it if you don't like it, but that's how it is and that's how it will be."

Emily watched his eyes.

"I don't like it any more than you do, but I've seen covens that have no enforcer, no laws, and it's chaotic. Innocent people die. I won't let that happen here. We have too much of a good thing going and, for the most part, my laws are obeyed. I can't let even the smallest infraction go by without notice." He kissed her bruised wrist lightly.

"What about me then?" she asked.

"They know you are an exception. No one's asked why, and no one dares to question that. They know you are bonded now, but they have wrongly assumed it's to Kyle. I won't lie if they dare ask me, but they won't. They are happier seeing it the way they want to." He gently kissed her other wrist.

"I'm causing too many problems here."

"No, this happens even without you here. Someone always has to try to break the rules, to see how far they can go. As long as I keep control, things will go smoothly," he assured her.

"I'm sorry about court then," she whispered.

Chevalier started to laugh, "I've never seen a more shocked group of heku. When you came in with only a t-shirt on and sat down by the accused, I thought the entire room was going to twitch to death. Had you been immortal, they would have kicked you out themselves, but by my orders, they were afraid to even look at you, though who could help it."

Emily watched as he laughed and kind of had to smile at the mental image.

"You really are too attractive to be living. It should be a crime against humanity to have you near men." He laughed harder when the blush rose to her cheeks.

Once he'd calmed down, he brushed his lips lightly across hers and kissed the nape of her neck. "Why don't you get some sleep now. It's late."

She nodded and laid down. He crawled in next to her, and she curled against his chest, falling asleep quickly.

Alone

Chevalier came back from a long day out in his study and found Emily's bed empty. He glanced at the clock and saw that it was only 3am. Kyle was away on a two-week long mission, and Emily hadn't let Chevalier replace him, so her antechamber was also empty. He caught her emotions and she was upset and worried, which made the need to find her more pressing. He smelled for her, but her scent was faint. She hadn't been in the antechamber in hours.

"Find Emily," he ordered into the air, and the sound of scrambling feet echoed through the castle.

It was only five minutes before he heard a voice on the wind whisper, "Barn."

He appeared in the barn seconds later and walked around to Patra's stall. Patra was lying on the clean straw, panting, and Emily was at her side rubbing the mare's tummy. He suddenly understood.

"How is she doing?" he asked from outside the stall.

Emily looked up at him with tired eyes. "It's taking a long time."

"Is there anything I can do?"

She shook her head and went back to rubbing the mare's belly. Chevalier appeared at her back and began to rub her tight, knotted shoulders.

"Mmmm," she moaned, and leaned her head forward.

He smiled and continued to rub the knots out of her shoulders, "Kyle will be sad he missed this. He's been waiting to see her foal for 11 months."

Emily just nodded. She was clearly worried about the time it was taking Patra to deliver.

Patra raised her head and whinnied loudly as her stomach contracted violently. "Come on girl, push," Emily encouraged.

After a few minutes, the mare laid her head back on the straw, panting heavily, and Emily sighed.

The hours passed slowly, and the more Emily worried about Patra, the more Chevalier worried about Emily. Her shoulders grew into hard knots, and he knew her head was aching from the stress.

The light of dawn filled the barn, and the mare had just begun to push again when Emily stood up, walked to the rear of the horse, and sunk her arm, shoulder deep, into the mare.

Chevalier watched, shocked, not exactly sure what Emily was doing until she was using her entire body to pull. She groaned, her teeth grinding as she tried to pull the foal free. She panted and again pulled with all of her strength when she suddenly flew back and landed hard against the ground.

"Gah, slippery bugger!" she screamed, and sunk her hand back into the mare.

Emily was sweating now. Her shirt was stained, and her hair was plastered to her head. She pulled again and again, and Chevalier considered putting an end to it but wasn't ready to face her wrath. Emily gave one last scream and pulled two long, thin legs out just as Patra gave what Chevalier could only describe as a bellow. A loud, sloshing sound accompanied the rest of the foal emerging, and Emily quickly began to clear its mouth.

Patra raised her head and craned her neck to begin licking the foal, which was already fighting to stand. The colt stood up on shaky legs and nuzzled toward his mother and began to nurse. Emily laid back on the straw, trying to catch her breath. She was soaked with sweat and covered in blood, but she was smiling.

Chevalier stood and walked over to her, then looked down and smiled. "It's a boy."

Emily nodded, completely exhausted.

He reached a hand out to her. "Come on, get some sleep."

She shook her head. "I can't. I need to keep an eye on him for a while," she said, and then sat up with considerable effort.

"Can't I get someone to do that?" he asked, even though he already knew the answer.

"No, he's my responsibility." She sat back against the wall of the stall and watched the colt eat.

He sighed, "I have a meeting."

"I'm okay, go. When I get done here, I'm just going to shower and go to bed." She looked down at her clothes.

Chevalier nodded. "Good, you stink."

She threw a handful of straw at him, and he left.

Emily shut her eyes for a moment and relaxed as the colt nursed. She opened them to yell at Chevalier but noticed the noise had come from Peanut. "Heya, Nut."

Peanut crawled onto her lap and began to purr as she pet him, "Look what we did… we made a colt." She was smiling.

It was only a few hours later that Emily was finally convinced the horses would be okay. The colt was up walking around on unsteady legs, and Patra was standing up eating. She kissed the top of Peanut's head and went inside to take a shower.

She heard odd hisses as she walked past the heku servants, and she looked down at her bloodstained shirt. She couldn't blame them for being antsy.

The shower felt incredible, and she let it run longer than usual. When she was too tired to stand any longer, she pulled on a t-shirt and laid down on top of the covers on the bed, and she fell fast asleep.

Emily was only partially aware when Chevalier came in and moved her under the covers. The warmth was perfect, and she snuggled deeper into the bed and fell back asleep as Chevalier joined her under the covers and wrapped his arms around her.

Emily stirred and saw the sun was rising. She jumped up and hurried to put on her jeans.

"Slow down... where are you going?" Chevalier asked, wrapping his arms around her waist.

"I need to go check on the colt," she said, buttoning her pants and looking around for a clean shirt.

"He'll be okay, Em." He smelled her neck and gently ran his tongue along the throbbing vein. Emily shivered but pulled away from him.

"Stop, Chev, I need to go check." She found the shirt she was looking for and pulled off the t-shirt she'd slept in, but before she could replace it, Chevalier was holding her closely.

He began kissing her neck again.

She pulled away yet again and shook her head.

Emily put on the other shirt and headed out the door to check on the colt. The barn was awake and hungry as she entered and walked past the other horses and into Patra's stall. She let the mare and her colt out into the corral and watched as the foal played in the grass, running and bucking. Leaning against the fence watching them was electric, this new life now able to think and feel and play. She smiled as she watched them, and Peanut wound himself around her legs.

When the colt began to nurse again, Emily let the buckskin mare and Chevalier's crabby Arabian out into the corral too, where they grazed happily.

Sighing, Emily went back into the barn and loaded a bale of hay onto the back of the ATV and set out. She wanted to get in a decent nap when she was done. She still felt tired from the previous night. The hay seemed heavier today, and the nap looked better and better. She finished later than usual and headed back into the castle.

Emily heard hisses in the hallway again as she passed. By the third hiss, she spun in the direction of it. "Excuse me?" she snapped at the shadows.

The noise stopped, but it still made her uncomfortable. Her bed was inviting as she stripped and pulled on a nightgown, then fell into the soft bed.

She woke slowly and rolled over, looking at the clock. It was only 5pm, but she was starving. Emily made her way down to the kitchen and again heard a hiss from the shadows. She ignored it and opened up the kitchen door. Gordon looked up at her and smiled.

"I wondered when you would eat today, child. What would you like?" He started grabbing some pots and pans.

"Do you have any pork chops?"

His face lit up. "Of course, coming up."

Emily watched Gordon cook. She was astonished at the speed in which he prepared food and the joy he got from it. He was proud when he set down a plate with pork chops and steaming au gratin potatoes.

She smiled and dug in. The flavors were amazing, and she finished it, which pleased Gordon immensely.

"Can I ask you something privately?" she asked Gordon as he cleaned up the kitchen.

"Sure, child." He didn't even look at her.

She thought carefully before asking. "Is there something weird going on around the castle today? I mean... some reason I would keep getting hissed at?"

She smiled as he handed her a glass of cold milk, but then he turned and looked at her.

"Hissing? Someone was hissing at you?" he asked, shocked.

"It's nothing big, and remember, this is just between us... but yeah, I seem to be getting hissed at a lot today." She sipped the cold milk.

"No reason I can think of. You should tell the Chief Enforcer. He wouldn't stand for that." Gordon turned away from her and started cleaning again.

"That's exactly why I don't tell him, Gordon." She saw him tense up. "Oh, no you don't. You said this was private!"

"I'm required to tell him," Gordon said softly, still wiping down the already clean stove top.

"Please, Gordon, I'm begging you." Her voice was pleading.

His hands shook on the counter as he cleaned, "It's not that easy."

"He'll find out you didn't tell him, won't he?" She watched him.

Gordon nodded, his hands still shaking as he wiped down the counter.

"I guess it's not so bad. I won't tell him where I was when it happened, and you don't know, so there's not a lot he can do about it." She watched as he relaxed. When Gordon didn't turn back around to visit, she left and headed out to let the horses back into the barn.

Chevalier met her up in her room, and she could see the anger in his eyes.

"The colt is doing great. He's going to look like a paint," she said, slipping off her jacket.

"Where were you, Emily?" She knew from his tone that he wasn't curious about her previous location. He wanted to know more about the hisses.

She turned to look at him. "Around."

"Hissing is a sign of aggression with heku, a sign they are about to attack," he snapped. "Where were you?"

She sighed, "It was just a hiss, Chev, and once I yelled at them, they stopped." She added a mental, *mostly.*

Chevalier stood up and took her shoulders in his hands. "Tell me… now!"

She tried to pull away, but he held tightly, "No."

"I told you to stop messing with my affairs, and this is definitely my area," he growled.

"No, I'm not going to be a part of this." She again tried to pull away, but his grip tightened and her shoulders began to hurt. "Let go. You're hurting me."

He shook her twice and pulled her off the ground. "Tell me, now!" he yelled at her again, his face inches from hers.

"Chev, please, it hurts," she whispered.

Chevalier dropped her the few inches to the ground and stepped away from her, his eyes still angry. "I'll find out my own way then."

His senses reached out to her, and his heart fell. She truly feared him at that moment. He growled and disappeared from the room. Chevalier quickly headed to the mainland to feed. That would help calm his mind.

Emily sat down on the bed. Her shoulders ached, and she had a headache from when he shook her. She'd done it again, fell in love with someone who hurt her. She didn't count them as exactly the same, though. Keith hit her for fun. Chevalier was truly angry, but Emily wasn't sure that mattered.

"Emily," the voice was soft beside her.

Emily looked up at Anna. She couldn't even talk.

"Are you hurt, child?" Anna touched her arm lightly.

Emily shook her head and moved over as Anna sat down beside her on the bed. "If you don't mind, I want to talk to you."

Emily just watched the heku beside her, her head pounding.

"I'm sure the Chief Enforcer would be mad, because this is none of my concern, but I feel someone needs to try to smooth things over." Anna handed Emily a few aspirins.

She chewed the aspirin, grimacing at the taste, and then leaned back against the headboard.

"Let him protect you, child." Anna's voice was sincere.

Emily looked away from her, her eyes again filling with tears.

"It's in his nature to protect those he loves. He's good at what he does, and when you fight against his natural instincts, it's hard for him." Anna smiled softly at Emily. "He loves you, child. We all know that. We can see it in his eyes. I've known Chevalier for almost 200 years, and this is the first time I've seen him truly happy. Until tonight, that is."

When Emily didn't respond, Anna continued, "He was right about the hissing from the shadows, so we, as a part of this coven, have taken care of it to stop the tension between you two."

Emily gasped, "What did you do?"

"We handled it." Anna smiled. "We also feel protective of you. We all care about you and have grown to love you in our own way. Our people... the heku... we don't take kindly to one of our own being targeted."

Emily realized that Chevalier had been wrong. His staff knew she was bonded to him and not to Kyle.

"Let him be himself around you. Let him protect you. It's what makes him happy." Anna smiled again and touched Emily's arm. "You can't fight nature, and if you are to stay among the immortal, it's time you realize that we are natural fighters, born predators, and it's not within us to watch our loved ones be hurt."

Anna stood up. "I'll have Gordon bring something up for you."

Before Emily could respond, Anna was gone, and she was alone again in the dark room. A few minutes later, Gordon appeared with a mug of warm milk. It tasted funny, but he encouraged her to finish it and left only after it was gone. Warmth spread through her and she was soon fast asleep.

***

Chevalier growled when the knock on his door sounded so soon after returning from feeding. "Come!"

Anna entered the office, her face warm and comforting to him. "I'm stepping out of line. I will warn you, sir."

He glared at her, waiting.

"I've spoken to Lady Emily about things, and I hope it will help." She watched for a reaction.

"You were just with her?" he asked.

Anna nodded. "Yes… and she isn't hurt, sir, not physically."

Chevalier sighed.

"Well we…" She paused. "We took care of Benjamin, sir."

"Benjamin?"

"Yes, he followed the child through the hallways, hissing. He was ready to attack, and we couldn't have that." She waited for her punishment.

"You… you took care of him?" He was stunned.

"A group of us, yes. I do hope it will help." She looked into his eyes and relaxed when she didn't see anger.

He nodded toward her, unable to speak.

"Don't worry about Emily. Gordon brought her some… shall we call it, 'special' milk, and she is already asleep." Anna bowed and left the room.

Chevalier reached out to Emily and found her peaceful and relaxed. His thoughts returned to the feeling of fear she held for him, and he hated himself for it. He'd never been adept at controlling his temper, but for thousands of years, he hadn't needed to. Emily was fragile, unlike members of his coven, and he tried to wrap his mind around a way to keep her safe from his temper.

He soon gave up and joined her in bed. She didn't stir when he walked into the room, and her blood smelled of medicine. He wrapped his arms around her and held her close to him.

***

Emily flipped to her back and floated on the still water. Her muscles ached from more than an hour of laps, but it felt good to her. She steadied her breathing and just floated, hearing nothing but the sound of the filters running. She could feel her hair flowing gently around her, and she sighed.

"Happy anniversary."

The voice came out of nowhere, and she sunk quickly, gasping in a lung full of water. Swift hands pulled her to the surface and held her while she coughed.

"Sorry, Em," Chevalier said, amused.

She slapped him on the shoulder. "Are you trying to kill me?"

"Oh, I can think of much better ways of killing you," he said as he gently ran his teeth along her neck, and then laughed when she shivered.

"Happy anniversary to you, too," Emily said as she brushed her lips softly against his.

Chevalier chuckled. "Don't even get me started. I came to take you away." He carried her out of the water and set her down by the towels.

She looked at him. "Where are we going?"

"Absolutely nowhere." He grinned and watched her dry her hair. "Hrm, I don't like that swimsuit."

Emily looked down and laughed, "It took hours to convince Margaret that a one-piece was the way to go."

He patiently watched her dry off.

"So what does one pack for going nowhere?" she asked, wrapping the towel around her.

"Silly mortal, you don't pack to go nowhere." He quickly re-dressed and then pulled out a black scarf and smiled. "Turn around."

Emily frowned. "What if I don't trust you?"

"Never trust a heku," he told her, and then winked at her.

She smiled but turned around anyway.

Chevalier tied the black scarf tightly over her eyes. "No peeking."

He picked her up, cradled her gently in his arms, and walked. She could feel a change in the atmosphere when they left the castle, and she shivered slightly as the cool air hit her wet swimsuit. She felt him chuckle.

"Ready?" he asked at long last.

"I'm guessing I don't have a choice," Emily said as he set her down and her toes dug into the sand.

Chevalier removed the blindfold, and as Emily's eyes adjusted to the bright sun, a glimmering boat came into view. The majestic ship was flawless as it bobbed with the waves. It was white with pink and magenta stripes, and emblazoned on the side in curly letters was the name of the ship, '*Emily.*'

Emily turned to smile at him. "You bought a boat?"

"No," he said, and faked a frown. "I bought you a yacht."

She turned back to the ship and marveled at how sleek and shiny it was. She headed up the plank to board it, followed by Chevalier. The front deck was lined with cushioned deck chairs, and a hot tub was set into the floor. Emily went room to room looking at the designs and decorations of her new boat. The engine room was set high above the rest of the rooms, and she ran her hand along the shiny helm and slipped on the Captain's hat, which was too big and fell down to cover her eyes.

Chevalier pulled the hat off of her head, laughing, and placed it on his own head. "That's mine."

"I thought the boat was mine."

"It is… but I'm your Captain, so I get the hat." She tried to take it from him, but he caught both of her wrists in one of his hands and turned on the engine.

She turned to look at the sea as he pulled out of port. "Wait! We're leaving now?"

He nodded. "Did you have other plans?"

"I haven't packed anything." She noticed he wasn't slowing down.

"Which way are we going, Em?" he asked her.

She turned to him. "I don't know. You're driving."

"Point… we'll go whichever way you point." He slipped on some sunglasses.

Emily turned and looked at the vast ocean and pointed randomly, watching as the boat turned in the direction and sped off.

"So how many servants are on this thing?" she wondered, looking around.

"It's just us."

"Seriously? Just us two… not even one other heku?" She was surprised. Chevalier seemed to like his servants.

He grinned. "Just us, unless you want me to go back and get some."

"No way, this is great!" She wrapped her arms around him from behind and kissed his back.

"Go relax out on the deck. I'm going to get us far from land, and then I'll join you." She watched as he adjusted some knobs and returned to the helm. Emily was impressed that he knew how to sail.

The sun was even brighter out on the water. She could feel the warmth on her skin, so she slipped off her towel and fell onto one of the deck chairs. It was soft and reclined, and she saw a table beside it with a bowl full of fruit, a pair of sunglasses, and some sunscreen. Emily figured she might as well be good, so she slathered on the sunscreen, and then grabbed the sunglasses before lying back against the white cushions.

Emily was asleep when she felt hands gently run across her stomach. She smiled and shivered as she broke out in goose bumps.

"This is officially nowhere," Chevalier said, and then smiled.

She nodded and patted the chair beside her. "Lie down. Soak up some vitamin D."

Chevalier laughed. "I don't think I'm able to do that... besides... the sun and I don't get along very well."

She looked up at him and noticed he was in a jacket, and between the Captain's hat and sunglasses, his face was completely shaded.

"Mmmmm, your loss. It really feels good."

"I... well I had other motives for being out here." His voice was soft.

She laughed, "I'm sure you have many motives for being out here."

"Mmhmmm, that too." He gently ran his fingers along her inner thigh. "Later, though, come in out of the sun."

Emily sighed and sat up. She grabbed the bowl of fruit and left her sunglasses on the table, then followed Chevalier down the stairs to the living quarters. They were spacious, actually bigger than her entire ranch house, and decorated in dark reds and blacks. The kitchen was small but had what she needed, and the end of the living space held a large wooden framed bed. Chevalier sat on the couch and patted beside him.

Emily ignored his hint and set the bowl of fruit where he'd patted and then sat on his lap, curling up against his chest. She felt his arms wrap around her as he chuckled and kissed the top of her head.

"I love you, Em," he said softly.

She looked up and kissed him gently. "I know."

"So it's time to get it all out in the open. We've noticed in the last year that neither of us has been completely honest with the other, so I figured some time away might help." She kissed along his neck and nodded.

"It'll be nice to get away from life on the island." He groaned as she lightly bit his neck.

"Eeeh… what the hell." Was all she heard before she felt the soft bed at her back.

***

"That wasn't fair," he said as she curled her naked body up against his.

"Oh, were we playing fair?" Emily asked.

Chevalier laughed. "Apparently not. Damn, you bite hard."

Emily glanced at his shoulder and could see the faint outline of her teeth fading. "Sorry about that."

"I didn't say I didn't like it." He ran his fingers through her hair.

"You wanted to talk?" She pulled away from him and propped herself up on her elbow.

"Yes I did, before I was seduced." He kissed her lightly.

Emily laughed, "It was pretty hard to do, too."

Chevalier smiled. "Yeah well…"

"So… what about?"

"Everything we probably should have talked about before the bonding." His eyes were serious.

"Like what?" She gasped, "Are you upset about the baby thing?"

He smiled. "No, that's not important to me, though I wish you had told me, just so we didn't have secrets."

Her eyes fell to his chest as her fingers outlined his chiseled muscles. "I'm sorry."

Chevalier took her hand in his. "You're distracting me, again," he said, kissing her fingers.

"Hmm, you're easily distracted." She smiled up at him.

"Yes... well..."

"Okay so what else?" She was afraid to go further but knew there was no way around it.

"First, I'll start... there were some unexpected byproducts of the bonding that I want you to know about. I honestly didn't know about them. This is the first I've known of a mortal and an immortal going through the ceremony." He was looking deep into her green eyes.

"Ugh, do I want to know?"

Chevalier smiled. "They aren't bad... just... well... intrusive."

"What? How?" Her eyes narrowed.

"I can feel your emotions from a distance. The stronger the emotions, the stronger I can feel them. Regular, normal emotions, I have to concentrate on... but I'm able to pick them up easier and easier it seems."

She frowned. "Okay."

"Lately... and it's only been the last few days... I'm starting to see images of what you are thinking."

She gasped, "You can see what I'm thinking?"

He shrugged. "Not always. It's more like images pop into my head, and I can't figure out how they got there, and then I realized that you were thinking them."

"That's not fair! I'm not getting any of that." She frowned.

Chevalier kissed her nose. "I'm not trying to be intrusive. It's all just sort of happening."

"So nothing's private for me anymore?" She didn't like that, and he noticed how she set her jaw.

"I'm finding I can tune it out to an extent, but there are times when you are practically screaming at me... like just now on the couch." He smiled at the thought.

"This is awful!" She pulled the blankets up to cover herself.

"I'm not doing it on purpose. I'm going to see if I can find someone in our situation and see if it can be controlled."

Suddenly, Emily was feeling exposed.

"I'd like it if I could control it enough to block your thoughts out when I don't need to know them, and to reach out for you when I do... I'd also like to see if there's a way you can use it to your advantage."

"Like how?"

"Like calling for me if you are in trouble."

"Anything else?" Her voice was irritated.

"I'm sorry about the ring, too. That I did know about, and I should have told you."

"Yes, you should have." She glanced down at the beautiful diamond and platinum ring. "Keep going."

"That's all for now, the big stuff." He ran his hand under the blanket along her waist. "Now it's your turn."

She frowned. "What is it you want to know?"

"It's time you told me about your nightmares." He wasn't surprised when her body tensed.

"They are just nightmares." She avoided looking into his eyes.

"They are more than that. Nightmares don't cause people to scream night after night," he said softly. "Please, tell me."

She watched him but didn't answer.

"I'll make it easier. Let's start with the dreams about Keith." He pulled her close to him as she squeezed her eyes shut.

She whispered against his chest, "He's not dead."

Chevalier kissed the top of her head. "He's after you?"

She nodded.

"He's after me too?" He guessed, and she nodded.

"When you scream for him to shut up... what is he saying?" Chevalier prompted.

"Warnings"

"About what?"

"You"

"That I'll kill you?" he asked softly.

She shook her head. "No, that you'll leave me when..."

"What, Em?"

"When you see me as he did."

"I'm not sure that's possible. He was more of a monster than I could ever be." His voice was soft and reassuring.

"He made me... do things." She hid her face against his chest.

"Yes, I would imagine he did. Can I tell you something about Keith?"

She nodded.

"He was controlling your every move. The more he could knock you down, the more control he had."

She didn't move in his arms.

"You've come a long way out of that control since he died, and... he is dead. He wasn't sure enough of himself to know you would stay with him, unless he made you feel undesirable."

Emily relaxed against him.

"As for coming after me... I wish he were alive and did come after me," he said, and then grinned maliciously.

She frowned up at him. "Why?"

"I'd like to kill him again, slower this time. He got off easily because I was angry, and he didn't feel enough pain." She felt the strain in his voice, and his arms tightened.

Emily actually laughed a little, and Chevalier kissed her forehead.

"Enough about Keith... the other dreams where you scream for me to run?" He watched her, but she didn't tense up this time.

"It's dark in those ones, and there are trees." She frowned. "There are voices, and they are going to get you. I can't catch up to you to make you run."

Chevalier smiled softly. "Why are you always trying to protect me in your dreams? I thought I was supposed to be protecting you."

She shrugged, not finding it as funny as he did.

"Maybe." He thought for a moment. "Getting the dreams out in the open will make them go away."

Emily shrugged again.

Chevalier brushed his lips across hers. "We'll talk more later. We have plenty of time. There's something out in the water you'll want to see. I'll stay here."

Emily hesitated and then stood up and pulled on a soft robe that hung by the bed. She shielded her eyes against the glare of the sun on the water and peered over the side of the boat. She smiled widely when she saw humpback whales less than 10 feet away.

She leaned on the railing and watched until they disappeared into the horizon. The water was so blue that she could see fish below the boat also, and it wasn't until dusk that she moved back below. Chevalier was just pulling open a cupboard to reveal a large TV, DVD player, and a few hundred movies.

"I thought we'd watch a movie, if you'd like," he said, smiling up at her.

"Sounds great! Let's see what we have." She sat down and started thumbing through the movies.

Emily giggled and held up *Interview with a Vampire* for Chevalier.

"Gah, we aren't watching that are we?" he asked.

"No, I've already made Kyle sit through it, and he was thoroughly offended. I assure you." She slipped the movie back into the slot.

"I bet he was... I'm starting to think Kyle really does need a raise." He watched Emily on the floor. He couldn't get enough of her, how she moved, how she talked, and the way she flinched in her sleep.

"Oooh, can we watch a horror movie?" She sounded excited.

Chevalier laughed, "Isn't your life a horror movie? You live on an island full of history's vampires."

Emily pulled out the movie and put it into the DVD player, and then disappeared into the bathroom. She emerged, blushing, wearing a sheer black babydoll nightgown. "Margaret strikes again."

Chevalier's eyes took her in as she came to sit by him. "I think she is reliving her youth through you... with my approval, of course."

Emily pulled a blanket over her shoulders and curled up against Chevalier's side to watch the movie. He thought it was utterly stupid. How could people be so afraid of a clown? He did like the way Emily pulled closer to him when the clown appeared, so he didn't complain.

Chevalier wasn't sure exactly when she fell asleep, he just noticed she suddenly quit jumping when things on the TV got tense. He gently carried her to bed and curled up next to her, watching the movement of her face as she slept.

Emily woke to the smell of bacon, and she smiled. "Smells good."

"I hope so."

He loaded up a plate and set the tray on her lap when she sat up.

"Oooh, breakfast in bed even." She smiled and started to eat. "Wow, this is really good."

"One of my many talents."

Emily thought for a second, and then decided to ask, "When do you eat?"

"When I'm thirsty."

"That sounds like avoidance. I thought we were being open." She stabbed an egg and ate it.

"True… I eat about once every two or three weeks is all. We don't need to eat as often as you do." He pulled her foot out from under the covers and began to massage it.

"What do you eat?"

He raised an eyebrow. "What?"

She smiled. "I mean… who? Where do you get the blood?"

"I have voluntary donors."

"Women?" She took a bite of bacon and avoided his eyes.

"Mostly, yes." He knew where this was going.

"Do you sleep with them?"

"Not anymore."

She stared down at her plate, no longer hungry.

"Emily?" He wanted to see her eyes.

Emily shrugged and pushed the food around the plate with her fork.

"I'm not going to lie and say I never used to sleep with the women I fed from, but I promise you, I haven't since we went to Colorado."

"It still seems so… intimate." She didn't look up.

"It can be, but not anymore. Now they are simply nourishment."

She grimaced.

Chevalier sighed. There really was no way to lessen the blow for this. "When I used to find a donor attractive, I always went for the neck, so I could be closer to her."

She inhaled sharply and turned away from him.

"Now though, I only use their wrists. You are the only one I want, Em, the only one I can see anymore." He took her hand and kissed it softly.

She swallowed dryly. "Did you ever turn one... one that you liked?"

He shook his head. "No, I haven't turned anyone in decades for myself, and then it was only if I saw something in them that would benefit the coven. It's not something we as heku take lightly."

"Just feed from me then. You won't have to have donors." He saw the brief wince before she looked over at him.

"No, I won't regularly feed from you."

"Why?"

"For one, I love you too much." He stroked her cheek lightly. "For the other, it's too dangerous. Your blood is so amazingly succulent that I find it harder and harder to stop. I won't risk draining you."

She grimaced visibly at that.

"Don't worry about my feeding, Em. I wouldn't do anything to hurt you." He reached down and kissed her. "It's just part of who I am."

Though not hungry, Emily finished her breakfast in silence. When she was done, she got up and cleaned the kitchen while Chevalier watched her.

***

The following week was a lot less stressful. They spent their days talking about nothing important and their nights together. Emily's nightmares seemed less frequent out on the water, and she felt better than she had in a long time, well rested and content. Chevalier was also pleased that Emily was becoming more comfortable around him and wasn't hiding her body as much as before.

From his perch at the helm, Chevalier could see Emily down on the deck. She was lying face down on a deck chair, topless, and her skin was bronzing with all of the time in the sun. He slipped on his sunglasses and jacket and went down to join her.

Her skin tingled as he ran his fingers lightly down her spine.

She turned her face to him. "Done playing Captain?"

He nodded. "For now. Are you about ready to go back?"

Emily sighed, "Do we have to?"

Chevalier laughed, "No."

"Yeah... I guess it is time to head back. I'm sure Kyle will appreciate help with my animals."

"It'll take us a few days to get back, no rush," Chevalier said, and inhaled deeply.

She glanced up at him. "Are you smelling me again? It's making me self-conscious."

"It's so incredible, Em. I think the time on the boat has made it stronger, and lately, there's a change. Maybe all of that vitamin D."

Emily stifled a giggle.

"What?" He couldn't help but smile at her.

"Nothing"

"Tell me what's so funny."

This time, Emily laughed for a bit before she was able to talk. "I was thinking that you have about as much control as that moody Arabian when my poor Patra is in heat."

Chevalier grinned. "You're comparing me to a horse?"

"Yes, I am. He doesn't even notice her, and then he'll start sniffing around, and the next thing I know, he's fighting to get out of his stall."

"Well if she smells this good, I can't blame him," Chevalier said as he flipped Emily over in her deck chair and kissed her passionately.

Returning

Chevalier pulled the yacht up to the pier, and the guards immediately tied the boat to the dock.

"Welcome back, sir," Travis said as he slid the plank up, so they could get off.

"Good to be back, Travis. Head in with us, will you? I'd like a full report." Chevalier stepped off first and extended a hand to help Emily off.

Travis jerked as she passed him, and he turned his face away from her. Chevalier glared at him, and he faced forward again. He made a mental note to demand an explanation from Travis when they were alone.

Emily crawled into the Bugatti and watched the houses fly past. "I think maybe Travis isn't feeling well."

"Oh? What makes you say that?" Chevalier knew why but wondered if she had noticed.

"He was just acting weird is all."

They pulled up to the castle, and the two guards moved to greet them. As one of them opened Emily's door for her, he winced and stood up quickly. His eyes glanced toward the Chief Enforcer. Chevalier was glad that Emily didn't notice the reaction, and she headed inside when it began to rain.

"I'll deal with you later," Chevalier growled at the guard, and then followed her inside.

As Emily walked into the foyer, Kyle appeared from the opposite end of the room. He ran at her and picked her up in a hug. "Welcome back!"

Chevalier felt his anger rising when he saw Kyle inhale deeply and set her back down a little roughly. He then took a step back, his eyes wide.

"I... will... be... well... I'll get your things," Kyle stammered, and then stepped into the fresh night air.

Emily shrugged, smiled at Chevalier, and then headed up the stairs, "I know you have a meeting. I'm just going to take a shower and go to the barn."

He nodded at her and stepped outside, shutting the door behind him. Less than a second later, he had the guard pinned against the stone walls of the castle, his hand around his neck. "Explain yourself."

The guard choked and fought to breathe, his words coming out in a whisper, "I apologize, sir. It won't happen again."

Chevalier let go of his neck and glared down at him, "It better not."

He then spun on Kyle. "You of all people know better," he hissed.

"It just caught me off guard. I think I may need to go feed tonight." Kyle took a step away from Chevalier's icy glare.

"I'll expect you to keep well fed in the future if you are going to keep your position." His words were fierce.

"Yes, sir," Kyle said, looking down at the rocky ground.

"Now come inside. I need a full report," he said to both Kyle and Travis as Travis walked up.

When they sat down in the conference room, the three guards sat as far away from Chevalier as they could. He had a command-presence about him that left no doubt who was in charge.

"Travis," he said.

Travis began, "Nothing new on the pier, sir. It's been a very quiet week. I had one group of tourists stop to use the bathroom, but when I mentioned the quarantine, they left quickly."

"Mason"

The door guard looked up nervously. "Nothing to report, sir."

"Kyle?" His voice sounded angrier.

Kyle sighed, "There's been some speculation that there may be a Valle among us."

Chevalier's jaw tightened, "Speculation?"

"Yes, one of our informants from the Valle said that a small group of their reconnaissance team has gone missing, and as he's on the Encala Enforcement team, he suspects they've come to our side."

"And they think they are actually here in this coven?" Chevalier leaned forward toward Kyle.

"Yes, sir. One of the Valle's speedboats is missing, and because we're the only coven on an island…"

Chevalier growled, "Any idea who it is?"

"Not yet, sir, but we're keeping our eyes and ears open. We have three open positions here in the castle we've not filled because we don't know who we can trust."

Chevalier nodded in agreement. "Keep them empty. I'm not going to risk a Valle informant in this castle."

Kyle knew only too well that the Valle would love to get their hands on Emily, and just the thought made him hiss slightly.

"Put a task force together and get me those Valle," he demanded.

"Already started, sir." Kyle nodded at him.

Chevalier stood up and left for his office. He needed some time to think. If the Valle were in his coven, they might already know too much about Emily. He wondered if he should take her back out on the ocean again but wasn't sure how to do it without making her suspicious. Finally, he decided to keep things as they were but to keep a strict eye on her.

There was a stack of papers from Storm on his desk, and he let his mind pull into work mode as he went through them.

Chevalier lost track of time when suddenly he felt excited and realized that it must have been from Emily. It was 5am. He smiled, knowing that she was up early to go check on her livestock. He shut his eyes and focused on her. He loved to feel her emotions when she was out in the barn. He could hear her talking, but it wasn't clear enough to understand what she was saying.

He fought to see through her eyes, but the picture was gray and blurry. Soon, he thought, he would be able to clear up that image.

A scream suddenly echoed through his head, sending every fiber of his being into action. He was immediately out the door, flying toward the barn, and he could feel Kyle close behind him. Even his heku speed wasn't fast enough, and he growled when the screaming stopped. As he ran into the barn, his mind whirled with the image.

Emily was lying on the straw, and a heku was at her neck. A stream of blood was pouring out of the puncture wounds as the heku drank deeply. Patra was kicking at the stall angrily. With one swift movement, Chevalier grabbed the strange heku off of Emily and used every ounce of restraint to stop from tearing his head off. He threw the heku back to Kyle, who restrained him and growled angrily.

Chevalier knelt down beside Emily as she fought to get to her feet. Her hand covered her neck as blood seeped through her fingers.

"Lay down, Em."

He forced her back down and could see from her eyes that she was dazed. Chevalier glanced over her quickly. Her skin was clammy and her face was colorless. The heku had overfed. She shouldn't have been that pale after a feeding.

Two more guards arrived and took the strange heku from the barn, one of them hissing at him as he struggled.

Kyle knelt down and slipped off his shirt. He held it over the gaping wound on Emily's neck to try to stop the bleeding. She struggled to get up, her eyes still glazed over.

Chevalier picked her up and cradled her in his arms while Kyle held pressure over her neck. "Look at me, Em."

She looked toward him, but her eyes were unfocused.

"It's okay. We're here now." He kissed her forehead and grimaced at the clamminess of it.

"Let's get her inside," Kyle said. He knew that Emily was dazed, but he wasn't sure Chevalier was thinking straight either. When Chevalier didn't move, Kyle guided him forward with his free hand.

As they stepped into the castle, Kyle pulled his blood-soaked shirt away from Emily and ordered a towel from the shadows. He pressed the new cloth hard against her neck, and she groaned weakly.

"Get her upstairs, Chevalier," Kyle demanded, and within a few seconds, he was laying Emily down on her bed. Anna, Gordon, and Travis had joined them at her bed.

Kyle took a fast look beneath the towel. "It's clotting."

Emily tried to open her eyes, but they were heavy. "Stop," she whispered weakly. She tried to get up, but a gentle hand stopped her.

"It's over. You're safe," Chevalier said. Some of the control had come back into his voice.

He turned to Kyle. "Where is he?"

"He's down in the holding area. I have him well guarded with strict instructions that he's not to be harmed."

Chevalier nodded. "Get some B12 and folic acid up here with some orange juice."

He sat down on the bed beside Emily and took the bloody rag from Kyle. He held it in place with one hand and gently pushed her hair away from her face with the other.

Emily tried to get up and was again pushed down by soft and gentle hands.

"Get him," she whispered.

Chevalier locked eyes with her, but they weren't focused. She was still too dazed. Gordon appeared with orange juice, and when Chevalier pulled the rag away, the flow of blood had stopped. He slid an arm under her shoulders and lifted her up, so she could get a drink. She turned her head away.

"No," she whispered, and her hands pushed weakly against his arm.

"Em, drink this," he said, trying again, but she wouldn't drink.

He set her gently back on the bed and pushed her head to the side to see her neck. There were multiple sets of puncture wounds plus one gash left from when the careless heku had gotten greedy and took a bite out of her. It was clotted now, and the skin around the area was red and swollen. Anna handed him a roll of gauze, and he bandaged around her neck.

Kyle came back with two bottles of pills and handed two of each to Chevalier.

"Em… Emily… take these." She squeezed her lips shut tightly.

Kyle leaned down, glanced once at Chevalier, and then spoke angrily, "Emily, you take these right now!"

She hesitated, but then took the pills and swallowed them dry. Chevalier held her up again, and she didn't fight when he brought the orange juice to her lips. She took a sip and then grabbed the cup in her hands and began to drink deeply.

As he laid her back on the bed, she pulled at the bandage on her neck. "Get it off," she whispered.

Her eyes were on Chevalier, and they were starting to focus.

He grabbed her hands and held them in his. "No."

"Kyle, Travis, go find out what you can from that heku, but don't kill him," he said through gritted teeth.

They both nodded and left as Anna sat on the bed beside Emily and adjusted the bandage. She took the empty glass and disappeared.

Chevalier sat in silence and watched Emily. She was restless as she started to come out of the daze. Her pale complexion was unsettling and in contrast to her vibrant green eyes. He held her hands as she tried to free them to pull at the bandages. He knew the wound on her neck had to be painful.

Emily tried to clear her head. She had to warn them that there was a heku with her in the barn. She had to tell Chevalier, but the pain in her neck wouldn't allow her to talk. Her mind was telling her to get out, to get way, but something was holding her back.

Her hands were tied. She could feel them restrained, and she didn't seem to be able to break the bonds. She had to get loose. Her mind fought to pull away from its fog and to call for help.

"Help," she mumbled, trying to pull her hands free from Chevalier's grasp.

"You're safe. I'm here." He worried about how restless she was.

"My neck." She flung her head to the side, trying to relieve the burning sting.

"I know," he whispered back to her, and noticed that there was some blood on the gauze, but not a lot.

She groaned.

He held her hands all night and watched her. Her color didn't improve, but she finally settled down into a peaceful sleep. Once in a while, she would try to pull the bandages off of her neck, but his voice would settle her back down. It wasn't until dawn that he heard a knock on the door.

"Enter," he whispered, and watched as Kyle came into the room. He looked exhausted and worried about Emily.

"How is she?" he asked, looking down at her.

"A little better. What did you find?" He was anxious to know.

"He's a Valle, sir."

Chevalier's eyes narrowed.

"There are more here. I haven't gotten the names out of him yet, but I will." His voice was icy, "He was told to find Emily only but said her scent was too strong, and it called to him."

"As soon as I can leave her... I'll go talk to him," he said ominously.

Kyle nodded and left the room. Chevalier could only imagine what tortures Kyle and Travis were putting the Valle through, and he hoped it was horrific. His eyes turned back to Emily as she gasped.

"Get it off!" she yelled, trying to pull her hands free.

Chevalier held them gently and met her eyes. "Leave it on, Emily."

"It burns, Chev, help me." Her eyes were pleading.

"It's not the bandages." He winced as her back arched, and she screamed. "Look at me."

Her eyes met his, and her accusing gaze was angry.

"You've been badly bitten. We have who did it, but your neck is pretty torn up, and you've lost a lot of blood." He hoped it was getting through to her.

"It burns." Her voice was strained.

He nodded, unable to speak for a moment.

She moaned loudly and squeezed her eyes shut.

"Emily, you need to take these." He held her hands together with one of his and helped her sit up with the other. He gave her two pills from each bottle and held the cup while she drank them down.

When she was comfortably lying down again, he let her hands go but kept his close. She raised one hand to her neck but didn't try to pull down the bandage. She inhaled sharply when her hand touched the wound.

Her eyes met his and they were filling with tears. "Why?"

Chevalier shook his head. "I'll know soon enough."

"I'm so tired." She shut her eyes.

"Sleep then, you'll feel better when your body replenishes the blood supply." He wasn't sure she heard, as she was fast asleep.

Emily heard the voices as if in a dream.

"You know her scent has been stronger… more appealing," Kyle said.

"Yes, I noticed."

"It's hard to resist, not as an excuse for that lowlife, but just as an observation."

"I suspect it was the sun, Vitamin D as she put it," Chevalier was whispering.

"The Valle has given us two names, Emanuel and Paul. We've managed to track down Paul, but as of yet can't seem to find anyone in the coven named Emanuel." Kyle sounded tired.

"Where are they now?"

"Both Paul and Ian are in the prison, though Ian won't be talking any time soon." He sounded proud, "I will call for some antibiotics. Her wound doesn't smell right."

"Good idea, it wouldn't hurt to get some peroxide either, to clean it."

The voices faded and were forgotten by her.

***

"Take more of these," Chevalier said, handing her four pills.

She took them with a glass of orange juice and crossed her legs, sitting up in the bed.

"Okay, now let me see." He started to un-wrap her neck. She winced as the fibers from the gauze clung to the large scabs.

"Hmmmm," he said, looking at the wound.

"Any better?" she asked, looking out the window.

"Well, it's hard to tell, but I'd say the infection is down." He pulled out fresh gauze and began to re-wrap it.

"Maybe it's you that needs a raise and not Kyle," she said with a half-smile.

"Why's that?" He was concentrating to put the bandage so it was covering all of the wounds.

"Compensation for added stress." She tried to laugh, but her neck burned with the movement, and she winced.

He grinned. "Stop laughing. You'll break it open again... and I do consider myself fully compensated."

"Gah." She winced again. "How long is it going to burn?"

"I'm afraid for a while. He got you pretty good." He sat back and looked at her. She had some color to her lips finally but was overall still pale.

"Did you send Kyle away to get some rest?" She insisted Kyle go rest when she'd seen him. His clothes were torn, and he was exhausted. Chevalier knew he'd been putting in extra time with the Valle and didn't envy the enemy at all.

"Yes, he left this morning for the mainland," Chevalier said, and saw that Emily looked relieved.

She sighed, "Just go, Chev. I'm okay here."

He blinked at her. "What?"

"I know you're itching to go talk to the Valle. Just go." She smiled at him and grabbed her book from the table.

"Are you sure?" he asked, already standing up.

She nodded and motioned him away with her hand, her eyes already on the book.

Chevalier grinned to himself as he left the room. He'd been waiting six long days to talk to the Valle heku personally, and his excitement carried him faster. He found himself down in the cell dungeon within a few seconds. Travis looked up at him and motioned for the guard beside him to move back.

"Out," Chevalier told the guards, and they bowed and left the cell area.

The shrieks echoed through the castle. Emily flinched but tried to focus on her book and ignore the sound of blood-curdling screaming. It continued ceaselessly for hours. The heku servants looked wide-eyed at one another, and a visitor to the castle turned and ran away from the front doors. Just when the screams ebbed, they began again but were even louder.

Emily laid down and pulled pillows over her head to try to mute out the noise. Heku in the castle stopped working and stepped out into the hallway to look at one another. The two guards by the cell entry door fidgeted nervously. They wanted to go in and help, and to see exactly what happened when the Chief Enforcer hit his limit.

Travis stood silently in the kitchen. He had been talking to Gordon when the screaming began, but Gordon left early on, mumbling about heading home. Travis was grinning, though he, like the guards below, wanted to go and join his commanding officer.

When Chevalier walked out of the door, the two guards grinned at him. His shirt was caked in blood, but his face was exuberant. He had a malicious presence as he walked up the stairs.

The two guards went back into the cell and gasped. Blood covered every inch of the cell space. One heku sat trembling in the corner, but the other was nowhere to be seen. They escorted Paul back to his cell as he rambled about bunnies. He'd gone insane.

Chevalier went to his room first to shower and change. He knew he looked grotesque and figured Emily didn't need to see him like that. He felt so alive. His senses were more acute, and he could hear the sound as a heku sighed across the castle from him. He let the hot water of the shower pour over him, and he concentrated on Emily and the rhythmic sound of her heartbeat in the next room. He smiled and threw on a robe, then crawled into bed with her and pulled her close to him, tossing his robe to the side.

She stirred slightly when he pulled the pillows off of her head and set them by the side of the bed. Chevalier inhaled deeply while he held her. Her scent was back to normal and was growing stronger every day as her body produced more blood. He kissed her lightly on the forehead and grinned when she frowned slightly in her sleep.

Just after dawn, Emily jerked awake suddenly and sat up. Strong hands wrapped around her and pulled her back down into bed.

Chevalier kissed her softly. "Nightmare?"

Emily just snuggled closer to him.

He ran his fingers through her hair.

"So am I released today?" she asked, yawning.

He smiled. "We'll have to see how your neck is doing before I answer that."

Emily laughed slightly, "Doesn't matter. I can't stay here another day."

Chevalier kissed the top of her head. "Oh, you think you can leave if I say no?"

She nodded up at him. "Yes, I do."

"I just had those chairs replaced. Please try to refrain from attempting to maim someone with them this time, okay?" He didn't let her answer as he pressed his lips to hers.

Chevalier shut his eyes and reached his senses out to her. He reveled at her emotions and the passionate way she went about everything. For now, she felt relaxed and content, and he smiled.

When Emily sat up, it broke his concentration.

He raised an eyebrow and looked at her.

"Let's get it over with. I want to get out to Patra," she said, unwinding the gauze from her neck.

The sight of the wounds on her neck never failed to bring his temper forward, and he fought back a growl and looked carefully, "Okay, I'll admit, the swelling's down, and it's looking a little better. I guess you can go."

She kissed him lightly. "Good choice."

She scooted out of bed and went to the bathroom to get ready. Anna had already laid out fresh gauze, so she wrapped it quickly around her neck. She knew the scent of blood made the heku nervous. She made sure she had it as covered as possible before she pulled on her jeans and t-shirt, and went back out into the bedroom.

Gordon had left a tray full of pancakes and sausage, but the smell made her nauseous, so she ignored it and headed out to the barn.

***

Kyle was wandering out to check on Emily when he saw her standing in the backyard, staring at the barn. "Morning, Em."

She didn't respond.

He frowned and walked closer to her, noticing her eyes were locked on the barn.

Kyle followed her gaze and looked into the empty barn. "Emily?"

When she didn't answer, he looked closer at her. Her body was rigid, and she was breathing quickly. He walked into the barn and looked around, then used his senses to look for anything out of the ordinary but found nothing.

He walked back out to her and took one of her fists in his hand, smoothing her hand in his. "It's okay. There's nothing in there."

Kyle pulled lightly on her hand, leading her toward the barn, but her feet were planted firmly, and she didn't move.

"Come on. It's okay." He pulled harder, and she took a hesitant step forward.

He pulled her hand again, forcing her to take another step.

"Kyle, stop," she whispered.

"I'm here, come on." He pulled her another step, ignoring the panic in her eyes.

She dug at his hand that was holding her other one, trying to pry it loose as she was forced to take another step. "Let me go."

"Nope," he said, forcing her to take another step. "We're going to the barn."

Chevalier appeared at her side in an instant. His fierce eyes flashed to Kyle pulling on her arm. "What's going on here?"

"We're going to the barn," Kyle said, pulling her another step forward as her nails dug into his hand.

Emily ignored Chevalier. Her panicked eyes were fixed on the barn, "No."

"Let her go," Chevalier said.

"With all due respect, sir… no." Kyle forced her another step.

"She's not ready," Chevalier said, placing his hand on Kyle's shoulder.

"Yes, she is," he said, pulling her another step. Blood appeared on his hand where Emily dug with her nails to make him let go.

Chevalier hesitated and then walked to the barn door. He knew, deep down, that Kyle was right. The longer it took Emily to return to her animals, the harder it would be.

"I'm in here, Em. Come to me," he said as Kyle pulled her even closer.

"No!" she screamed, and Travis appeared at her side. He looked oddly at Kyle and Chevalier, and then fell back to stand by the door.

"Come on, it's okay. We're both here," Kyle said, pulling her another step.

Chevalier appeared in the door with Patra, who stomped angrily at him, and he grinned. For some reason, the mare hated him.

"Stop," Emily begged as she got within a few feet of the barn.

Kyle let up the pressure on her arm and let her calm down for a few minutes. "Just a few more steps."

He let go of her hand and wrapped an arm around her waist before she could run, and then he flexed his injured hand. The blood flow had already stopped, and the skin was healing. "Come on. Chevalier is in there and Patra's wanting to get away from him."

Emily took a timid step as her eyes fixed on her mare. Patra pulled at her reins, trying to get closer to her, but Chevalier took her a few steps farther into the barn.

Emily could feel her heart pounding hard in her chest as she neared the barn. A sweat broke out on her forehead, and she could feel that her breathing was out of control. Emily thought about fighting Kyle. She figured she could break away from him but was sure he'd catch her easily.

She took another step forward, but the smell of the barn, once a smell she actually loved, filled her body with panic, and the wound on her neck began to throb.

Kyle was relentless, and she was soon in the barn. When she was a few steps in the door, her eyes fell on the straw where she had been attacked the previous week. The straw was clean and fresh, and she realized that Kyle had changed it out. She pulled forward, away from Kyle, and walked up to Patra, burying her face in the horse's neck.

Kyle and Chevalier stepped back to the walls of the barn and watched.

Emily wrapped her hands around the mare's neck. "Good morning, girl," she whispered. Patra bit at Emily's long red hair, and she laughed.

After a few minutes, Kyle and Chevalier left the barn and met Travis at the door.

"Stay by the door. Don't go into the barn, unless there's trouble," Chevalier told Travis.

Travis nodded and turned back to watch the barn.

It wasn't long before Emily felt the old exhilaration that working with the animals brought her. She let the horses out into the corral and watched the colt play for a while before going in to grab some hay for the cows. She felt her neck wound pull painfully as she lifted the bale of hay and cursed when she felt the bandages. Blood was soaking through them. She decided to deal with that later and loaded a new salt lick by the hay. The ATV ride was always fun, and she enjoyed it today, as well. She inhaled deeply and smiled.

Training

Chevalier came out of his office and looked around the castle. Things were going smoothly. Nothing had happened to cause concern in over two months. He headed up to Emily's room to see if she was there. He had trained his senses enough not to feel the common emotions she experienced, which lately, was constantly. He was also able to hear voices from her dreams, though, and he found it fascinating.

She wasn't in her room, but the heavy curtains were tied to the side, and bright sunlight filtered in from the balcony door. He stepped onto the balcony and looked out over the grass, then froze as his eyes fell onto the three figures on the lawn.

Emily was lying down on her back on the thick green grass. Travis was on top of her. His teeth were at her neck while Kyle stood aside and watched. Fury raged through him as he jumped from the second-story balcony and landed on the ground, denting the soft grass as he landed. He blurred to them and ripped Travis off of her, throwing him far enough that he landed against the side of the castle, and the rocks crumbled beneath him.

Kyle was at Chevalier before he could get to Emily. "Chevalier! It's not what you think," he said, but was pushed aside.

Emily was on her feet quickly and had her hands on Chevalier's face. "Stop, Chev, stop... it's okay."

She locked gaze with him, and her green eyes calmed him. He was able to repress the rage long enough to see that she wasn't injured. He quickly scanned her body. Her neck was fine, so he ran his eyes past her sports bra and down to the muscles in her tight abdomen along the curve of her delicate waist, no injuries. Her cut off shorts were sitting low on her hips as his eyes traveled down and noticed no injuries along her legs.

He stepped back and frowned at her, confused.

She touched his face softly. "It's okay, Chev, honest."

Travis returned as he tweaked his back into place and kept well away from Chevalier.

"Chevalier, it's not what you think. We're teaching Emily some self-defense is all," Kyle said, stepping over next to Travis.

Chevalier shook his head. "You're doing what?"

"Self-defense, that's all," Emily said, stepping back from him, smiling.

"But… he was biting you…" His mind swam.

"I was not!" Travis said, offended. "We were trying out a different position. It's no good teaching her to fight a heku if it's not as close to real as possible."

"Watch, Chev!" Emily said proudly. "Come on Travis. Let's show him what we just went over."

Travis hesitated and gave Chevalier a wide berth as he approached Emily. His eyes were weary as he grabbed her from behind, one arm around her stomach and the other high on her chest. He kept a close watch on Chevalier as he brought his teeth to rest against Emily's neck. He noticed Chevalier tensed and crouched slightly, but he didn't attack.

Rapidly, Emily kicked back and her foot connected with Travis' knee, knocking it out of place as she dropped her body weight and rolled away from him while he fell to the grass. Travis groaned and grasped his dislocated kneecap as he pushed it back into position with a grinding pop. He winced and slowly got to his feet. Emily stood up and smiled at Chevalier.

"See!" she said proudly.

Chevalier was shocked, "Why didn't I think of this?"

"We aren't guaranteeing it'll work against a real attacker, but Travis said it's quite painful and would make him think twice," Kyle said.

"Yeah... it hurts pretty badly for a few seconds. We figure if she can just buy a little time until help arrives." He was now standing straight, and his knee was entirely healed.

"Okay, back how you were," Kyle said.

Travis hesitated and then climbed on top of Emily as she laid on the ground. He watched Chevalier cautiously before again bringing his teeth to her neck.

Kyle studied them and sighed, "I'm thinking... there has to be a way. Emily, can you even get your foot up to his knee?"

She brought her knee up but wasn't able to position her foot by his kneecap. "Don't think so."

Chevalier growled, "Let me do it, Travis."

Travis scrambled quickly to his feet, and Chevalier took his place, his jealousy finally subsiding. As he placed his teeth at her neck, he grinned and kissed her neck instead.

Emily slapped his arm. "Behave."

Travis knelt down beside them, studying the location of arms and knees.

"I can knee him," Emily said, bringing her knee up slightly.

"That won't stop a hungry heku," Kyle said, bending down.

Travis moved closer. "Can you get your hands on his head?"

Emily reached up and put a hand on each side of his head.

"That's it, Travis, good idea!" Kyle said. "It's the element of surprise that'll make this work. If he knew it was coming, he'd be able to stop it, but I doubt anyone will think of this."

"What?" Emily asked, thwapping Chevalier's head as he kissed her neck again.

Emily focused on Kyle, who was demonstrating the move behind Chevalier's back, and she winced, "Seriously?"

"This whole training will only work if we know it's possible for you to do," Travis said, standing up.

Chevalier felt Emily's body tense moments before his head was wrenched to the side, and the crack of his vertebrae echoed through the lawn. He growled and rolled off of her, readjusting his head and cracking his neck back into place.

"Are you okay?" She was crouched by his side.

"I'm okay. Just give me a minute." The pain was lessening quickly, and he could feel the bones reforming correctly in his neck. "Damn, Em."

"I'm so sorry." She stood up and glared at Kyle and Travis, who were laughing.

"No, no, it's okay." Chevalier stood up and chuckled, "Just wasn't expecting that."

"Let's consider that exercise a pass then. The trick is that the heku won't know it's coming," Kyle said finally. "Maybe we should try a wrist attack?"

"No one's going to go for her wrist… male at least," Travis said, and then his body tensed as he turned to watch Chevalier.

Emily blushed when she remembered Chevalier saying he'd always go for the neck if he found his donor attractive.

"I guess you're right," Kyle said, thinking. "Besides, you can't control her body if you only have focus on her wrist. By taking her neck, you have your entire body against hers."

Chevalier growled low in his chest, but Kyle ignored it.

"Femoral?" Travis asked.

"Usually only works consensually. I can't imagine going for the thigh while trying to control a hostile victim." Kyle was deep in thought.

Chevalier tried to remember they weren't talking directly about his wife, but he found it hard, and he was getting antsy. He was also overtly aware of the visible skin Emily was currently showing.

"Let's try a non-feeding attack," Kyle finally said.

"True... good idea," Travis said.

"What? Why?" Emily asked.

"Just a precaution, Em," Kyle said, and turned to nod at Chevalier.

"She'd be running more than likely, right?" Travis said, focused on Emily.

"Yeah probably... run, Em, and Chevalier, you restrain her and let us have a look," Kyle said, moving into position.

Emily gasped at the look in Chevalier's eyes, and she turned to run. She wasn't more than 2 feet away when he grabbed her from behind and pulled her off her feet with his hands around her waist.

"Perfect, now freeze," Kyle said, and walked up to them and studied their position.

Emily took the opportunity to kick at his knee, but she couldn't reach it and her hands were pinned at her side by his arms. She struggled and could feel him chuckle.

Travis came up from behind and considered options.

"Easy enough, I held you similar to this once," Kyle said, nodding at Emily.

On cue, she brought her head forward and slammed it back into Chevalier's nose. Travis winced when he heard the loud crack. Chevalier let go of Emily suddenly, and she fell to the ground, landing hard on her butt as she looked up at him.

"Argh!" Chevalier yelled, and readjusted his nose. Emily wasn't sure, but it sounded like he might have been cursing in another language.

"Sorry, hun," she said, getting to her feet.

"It's fine... that one stung a bit," he said, smiling at her, and his nose was completely healed.

"Would it make you drop her, though, if you really wanted to hold on?" Kyle asked. "When she did that to me, the only reason I kept a hold of her is that I think she was more shocked than I was and she froze."

Travis tried to suppress a grin.

"No doubt if it's mortal, she'll win... immortal, though, if I had to keep a hold on her, I think I would have." Chevalier looked over at her.

"Why even worry about fighting off a mortal?" Emily asked.

She noticed that the three heku glanced at each other quickly.

"What aren't you telling me?" She put her hands on her hips.

"Paul mentioned that there are donors out working for the Valle. We have to be prepared for anything," Chevalier explained, moving closer to her.

"Paul?"

"One of the Valle we have down in our cell," Kyle answered her.

"Still? He's still down there?" Emily frowned.

"What are we supposed to do with him? We can't let him go," Travis piped in.

"Next," Kyle said, changing the subject.

Chevalier grabbed Emily without warning and threw her over his shoulder, nipping at her side playfully.

"I hate this one!" she said, feeling like a child.

She looked up at Kyle and glared when he laughed.

"This one's harder to get out of. There're no vital parts left exposed," Kyle said, studying the newest restraint.

"Okay... put me down," Emily said, but Chevalier didn't let go. She bent into him and bit his back.

"Ouch! Damnit, Em, stop it," he said, grinning.

"Biting an immortal won't work," Travis said seriously, and then looked up when Chevalier chuckled.

"I don't think that was for training purposes," Chevalier explained, smiling.

"Oh!" Travis grinned and looked away quickly.

"Emily, how far back can you throw yourself?" Kyle asked, ignoring the other two.

Emily's body tensed, and Chevalier could feel the strength in her abdomen as she brought her upper body up off of his shoulder and flung herself backwards. Chevalier wasn't prepared for the sudden shift in weight and almost dropped her when she fell back and slammed into his thighs.

"Ouch!" Emily cried, and Chevalier lowered her gently to the ground. She grabbed her knee. "That hurt."

"Sorry, Em." Chevalier knelt to massage her knee, "The sudden weight difference threw me forward, but I wouldn't have let go, and it didn't hurt me at all."

"Hmm, was just a thought," Kyle said, watching them, his mind deep in thought.

"Let me see. Travis, grab Kyle," Chevalier said. Both Travis and Kyle looked to see if he was serious and followed his order when they saw that he was.

Travis easily swung Kyle over his shoulder, though they were the same height.

"Let's just get this over with," Kyle said, irritated.

Emily lost control and giggled from the ground.

"Don't worry, your butt isn't nearly as attractive in the air as her's. I'll hurry," Chevalier said.

Emily blushed but laughed again at the odd expression on Travis's face. He was humiliated.

"Kyle, do what Emily did but hook your arm around his head on your way," Chevalier said, standing back.

"What if I take his head off?" Kyle asked.

"Oh true... Emily, trade places with Kyle," Chevalier said.

"What if I take his head off?" Emily asked sarcastically.

Chevalier laughed, "Just do it."

She sighed and stood up as Kyle fell nimbly to his feet. Travis gently lifted her up and slung her over his shoulder. He looked straight forward as he felt the soft skin from her waist on his neck.

"Okay, Em, hook his head on the way," Chevalier said, no longer jealous as he was focused on how her movement affected Travis.

Emily groaned as she came up straight, hooked her elbow around Travis's head, and flung herself backwards. Travis lost his balance and fell forward, landing hard on top of her and knocking the wind out of her. He quickly scrambled to his knees by her side.

"Breathe, Emily," he said, helping her sit up. Kyle and Chevalier knelt at her side also.

She waved them off as she gasped for breath, "I'm okay," she was able to say at long last.

"Well... that won't work," Chevalier said, and sighed, then helped Emily to her feet.

"Let's take a break before Em gets hurt," Kyle suggested. "Let me see if I can find a way out of that hold."

"Yeah... sounds good," Emily said, stiffly walking inside. Every muscle in her body ached from that last fall.

Chevalier turned to Travis and Kyle. "Thank you."

They both bowed and headed out as he ran to catch Emily. He picked her up gently and carried her up the stairs. "You okay?" he whispered.

She nodded.

As he walked into the bedroom, he heard the doors lock behind him and shifted her around so his hands were around her waist, her feet off the floor. "How good are you?"

She smiled and wrapped her legs around him and her arms around his neck. Emily pressed her lips against his.

Chevalier spun and pressed her back against the wall, returning her kiss.

***

Emily stepped into the jetted tub and winced as the hot water burned her skin, but continued to sink into the bubbly water. She sighed and leaned back against the tub, relaxed.

"Well that's a first. You broke my house," Chevalier said, sitting beside her as he started to massage her neck.

Emily smiled broadly. "Who needed that lamp on the wall anyway?"

"Are you okay? Really? Travis hit you pretty hard."

"Yeah I'm okay, but I think you owe me an explanation," she said, her eyes still shut.

"Oh?"

"Are you expecting more trouble?"

"Nothing we know about, but we didn't know about Ian's attack until it was too late either," he said softly.

Emily just nodded. When she got hot, the scars on her neck seemed to stand out more against her skin. They had faded a lot over the last couple of months and were almost invisible most of the time.

"It was smart of them to teach you some self-defense, though," he said matter-of-factly.

"Yeah it was. I just think maybe they need to figure out how to do it without me."

Chevalier chuckled. "It doesn't work that way."

She glanced over at him. "I'm okay, Chev, really. I know you have work to do. I'm going to get out of here eventually and maybe take Patra for a ride."

He thought about it for a moment. "Take Kyle with you though, okay?"

She nodded, and he stepped out of the room.

Once her muscles relaxed, Emily got out of the jetted tub and dressed quickly, knowing full well that she wasn't headed to the barn. She was glad that her antechamber was empty as she slipped out into the hallway and down the stairs, unnoticed. She held her breath and ran quickly to get to the dark hallway that led down to the prison. She'd followed a young heku down there when he was first assigned to guard duty, so she knew the way by heart.

She pushed open the heavy wooden doors and smiled as two strange heku turned to her, their eyes wide.

"Lady Emily?" one of them said nervously.

"Good afternoon, gentlemen." She smiled sweetly at them. As much as she hated to admit it, she found she could get her way a lot with that smile.

"You shouldn't be down here, child," the other guard stammered out, unsure if he was allowed to say that to her.

"It's okay. I have permission," she said, flashing her green eyes up at him.

He nodded, still unsure, and watched as she walked over to the holding cells.

"Hrm." She looked through the cells. "Which one of you is Paul?"

"He's not all the way with it, Lady Emily," one of the guards said to her.

She turned to face him. "What's wrong with him?"

The guard looked at the other guard and back to Emily. "He umm… well… he went insane I guess, sort of. He mumbles a lot to himself."

Emily frowned and turned to the heku that was sitting in his cell on the floor, talking to a board.

"Let me in," she said to the closest guard.

He gasped, eyes open wide, "Lady Emily, I can't let you in there!"

"Why not?" she asked sweetly.

"He's dangerous… what if he…" The guard shuddered.

She sighed and slid down to the floor, sitting cross-legged in front of the cell.

"Paul?" she asked softly.

He looked up at her and grinned evilly. "Emily."

She fought the urge to run. His eyes were pure evil, and his grin sent shivers down her spine.

"Will you talk to me?" she asked after she'd regained her nerve.

He crawled over to her and inhaled at the bars. "Emily," he said again. His eyes shut as he savored her scent, then he ran his tongue over his teeth and sighed.

"Will you talk to me?" she asked, again.

"Yes," he hissed, looking at her eyes. Paul sat against the bars, pushing into them to be as close to her as possible.

She leaned a little closer to him and whispered, "Do you know who I am?"

He nodded and watched her neck.

"Who am I?" she asked.

"Lady Emily, a Winchester, and granddaughter to..." He inhaled deeply, and when he opened his eyes again, they were full of hunger. "My master."

"Ulrich is your master?"

He nodded, his eyes falling to the rise and fall of her chest as she breathed.

"Did he send you to watch me or to bring me back?" She tried to ignore the feel of his eyes on her.

"Mmmm, Emily." His tongue reached out and touched the air. He could almost taste her.

"Answer me or I leave." She decided to try that approach.

"To bring you back," he said, now watching the throb of the small vein in her wrist.

"Did he say why?"

"Mmmm, let me taste you, child." He reached out for her, but she pulled away.

"Answer me."

"You are his. You belong to my master, and he wants what is his," he hissed.

"Now that you failed, will he try again?" She shivered at the way he looked at her, and her mouth went dry.

"Mmmm... yes, he'll try." He inhaled again and his body shook. "I bring you to him. He will let me taste, I think."

There was a loud crack as one of the guards hit the bars of Paul's cell with a metal pipe. "You won't talk to her like that, or I'll kill you myself, fiend."

"Master will get you for keeping her to yourself," Paul said to him, and then turned back to Emily. His tongue flicked out toward her again, savoring the air around her. "They feed off her. They should share," he said as he scanned her face with a cruel grin.

"They most certainly do not, and if you ever see Ulrich again, you can tell him from me that it'll be a cold day in hell before I come to him," she said sternly.

"Bonded, though." His eyes glanced at her ring. "Bonded to an immortal. Master knows this."

"Good, then he knows I'm not leaving." She forced herself to meet his eyes, though the sight of them turned her stomach into knots.

"Break it, he will... Mmmm, break it with Paul maybe." His dark eyes were pleased, and his tongue ran along his parched lips.

"What in the hell!?" Travis yelled, pulling Emily to her feet by her arm. "What are you doing down here?"

"I just wanted to talk to him." She pulled her arm, but Travis didn't let go.

"Perry, come with me," Travis ordered one of the guards as he angrily hauled Emily back up the stairs.

She stopped fighting when they stopped at the door to Chevalier's office and knocked. Emily looked over at Perry, and his eyes were terrified.

"Come," she heard Chevalier order.

Travis opened the door and pushed Emily in hard enough that she slammed into the desk. Chevalier was on his feet in an instant, glaring at

Travis as he stepped in, followed by Perry. The hostile look on Travis' face was directed in Emily's direction.

"What is going on here?" Chevalier growled.

"You want to tell him where I found you?" Travis hissed at her.

Chevalier turned to look at Emily and sighed, "Where, Em?"

"I just wanted to talk to him," she whispered.

"Who?"

Emily shrugged.

"She was sitting cross-legged in front of Paul's cell while he..." Travis paused and took a deep breath.

Chevalier growled, "What?"

Travis turned to Perry. "Word for word," he ordered.

Perry, his eyes staring down, started when Emily entered the cell area, and with picture-perfect memory, went over exactly what was said and what the heku had done in Emily's presence. Emily winced. It sounded worse when he said it out loud.

"Get out," Chevalier yelled, his eyes on Emily.

Travis and Perry left the room quickly.

"What were you thinking?" Chevalier asked, leaning back on his desk.

"I had some questions."

"You think we haven't asked them already?"

"I have no doubt, but I wanted to hear them for myself." She looked at the ground.

"You sat close and let him savor you, Em." His voice was shaky.

"Do what?"

"It's uncivilized, so you won't see it often. When a predator stalks their prey, they use all of their senses to enjoy the kill longer. What he did was rude and insulting."

"I got what I needed. I don't care if he wanted a sniff." She set her jaw and met his eyes.

"It's your lack of self-preservation that scares me," he growled, frustrated.

"I wasn't in danger! I asked questions and got answers. That's it."

"You can't let heku treat you like that. Ever!" he yelled.

"It wasn't a random heku on the street. He is in a cell, and he couldn't get to me."

"That's not the point! What he did to you was disgusting, and you let him." He took a step toward her, his eyes fierce.

"Let him? You act like I let him grab my ass, Chev. All I did was talk to him." Her Irish blood began to boil.

"Get out." He could feel himself losing control, and he refused to hurt her again.

She stormed out of his office and slammed the door. Emily immediately turned to the outside doors and ran off to the barn.

"We riding?" Kyle asked as he caught up to her.

She turned on him, and he took a step back when her angry green eyes glared at him.

"Whoa... what's up?" he asked wearily.

"You want to have a go at me too?" she growled, taking a step toward him.

Kyle stepped back. "No? What's wrong?"

"Apparently I was savored by Paul." She took a menacing step toward him. "Are you going to make a big deal out of it?"

Kyle's eyes flared. "How did he get out of his cell?"

"I went to him, and I dare you to tell me I shouldn't have... come on... I dare you." She stepped toward him again, her hands balled into tight fists.

Kyle growled and disappeared.

Emily went into the barn and threw a saddle on Patra, then tied the colt to a tether that she wrapped around the horn. She swung up onto the saddle and headed out into the hot afternoon sun.

Kyle went down into the cell area and walked silently over to stand by Chevalier at Paul's cell. Paul was rambling on about the 'tasty girl' and Chevalier's eyes were livid.

"She'll be mad if you do it... let me," Kyle said, stepping up to the cell door.

Chevalier didn't respond. Emily was too far away from the castle to hear the screams.

***

Emily led Patra and the colt back into the barn, and after unsaddling them and giving them food, she sat down on the straw. The ride was invigorating and calmed her mind. Peanut appeared and started to curl up in her lap.

"Hi, boy," she said, rubbing his back.

"Can you believe them? All I did was talk to that heku and they all freaked out over him smelling me," she sighed, then smiled as Peanut looked up at her.

"Rude of him, they said. I'll tell you what's rude, Nut. Treating me like an idiot." She nodded and rubbed Peanut's ears.

"He couldn't get to me through the bars. What do I care if he wants to smell and say disgusting things to me? I got what I wanted out of him." She sighed and stood up.

"Time to face the music?" she asked Peanut, but he was already wandering off. "Wimp."

She walked into the castle slowly.

"Hello," she said as she walked into her bedroom and saw Chevalier sitting in the chair by the fire.

He watched her but didn't talk.

"On a scale of one to ten, how mad are you?" She sat down in the chair beside him and pulled off her boots. The warm fire felt good against her cold feet.

When he didn't answer, she kept talking, "Fine then... one a scale from one to ten, I'd say I was about an 8, but after the ride, I'm maybe a 3 or so, so you will probably survive the night."

"Emily." His voice was soft, "I'm not so much mad as... well... disappointed."

She frowned at him. "Disappointed?"

"Yes, I had hoped your time here was teaching you how dangerous heku are and how you can't take anything they do for granted."

"Oh... I don't. He was behind bars. There was no way he could get to me."

"That isn't exactly the point. What he did was intimate and intrusive." He took her hand and kissed it lightly, then frowned slightly and turned her hand over, smelling her wrist.

She shrugged and jerked her hand away from him. "You mean like what you just did?"

"I'm allowed," he said seriously, and then leaned forward and inhaled against her neck.

"Stop it. I'm serious," she said, and leaned away from him.

"So am I, Emily." He leaned back and his eyes narrowed. "You smell different again."

"So stop smelling me and let's get to the point. You don't believe I'm smart enough to stay safe around a heku in a prison cell," she grumbled.

"Yes, I do. What I don't understand is how you could let him treat you like that, how you let him talk to you as if you were his for the taking." He leaned back in his chair again.

"I didn't care. I got what I wanted to know," she said, her voice flaring up again.

"Like what? What did he tell you that you just had to know?"

"That Ulrich sent him here."

"We knew that."

"I didn't. Then he said that he was here to take me, not just to check up on me."

"We knew that."

"Nice to know. It's also good for me to know that Ulrich plans on breaking our bond when he takes me."

Chevalier tensed. That, he didn't know. "He won't get that chance."

"No he won't, not if I can help it." She watched as Gordon brought a tray up for her and then left quickly.

Emily picked up the lid and grabbed some cheese toast off the tray, then returned the lid. She sat back and took an uninterested bite.

"Were you out in the sun a lot today?" he asked finally, allowing her to eat some.

"Of course, I was out on Patra."

He nodded.

"So are you mad or not?" she asked finally.

"I'm not mad. I just wonder where this stuff comes from. What would possess you to all of a sudden decide to talk to a prisoner?"

"Curiosity"

"That's it?"

"Yes," she said, shrugging.

Suddenly, he was down on his knees in front of her, kissing her neck. "That scent is toxic."

"Good to know." She flinched away from him.

"You're still mad," he said, rocking back on his knees.

"Hurt, not mad," she told him, and then got up and went into the bathroom.

Chevalier thought for a moment and whispered Kyle's name so Emily wouldn't hear. Within a few moments, Kyle appeared at his side.

"Well?" he whispered to Kyle.

Kyle's eyes filled with panic as he fought the desire to inhale deeply. "It's... again."

Chevalier nodded. "I wanted to know if you caught it, too. It's almost irresistible."

Kyle was afraid to answer but finally nodded once.

"You may go. I just wanted to know for certain." He sat back on the chair.

"What causes it?" Kyle asked.

Chevalier shrugged. "I haven't figured that out yet."

Emily came out of the bathroom in her nightgown shortly after Kyle left, and she headed to bed. She crawled under the covers and rolled onto her side, obviously wanting to be alone.

Chevalier walked to her side and kissed her forehead, and then left, heading into his study.

She was still irritated in the morning and ate her breakfast in a hurry so she could go out to the barn quickly. Chevalier stopped her in the hallway and wrapped his arms around her.

"I need to go away for a few days," he said, softly kissing the top of her head.

She immediately lost the irritation. "Why?"

"I need to go see the Elders about the Valle, and I need Kyle to go with me." He tightened his grip on her when she tensed.

"You are both going?"

"Yes, we both have to go."

"For how long?" she asked, laying her head on his chest.

"A week, no longer," he promised.

She nodded.

"We have someone here to watch over you. He's new, but right now, he's all that's available." She could tell by the tone of his voice that he didn't like doing this.

"A week... I think I can stay good for a week."

Chevalier reached down and kissed her on the tip of her nose.

Emily was disappointed to learn that they had to leave immediately, and she drove with them to the ferry and waved as they set off. As she walked back to the castle, she stopped to visit with a few members of the coven along the way. They were always pleasant to her, and she appreciated the welcome.

The castle seemed quiet and cold without Kyle and Chevalier there. She shivered and went to the TV room, deciding a movie would help pass the time.

Potential

"This attack was bad," Chevalier said angrily. "The Council has to intervene and put a stop to it."

"This Council is aware of its responsibilities but doesn't feel that it can take further action because of an attack on a mortal," Selest said stiffly.

"Not just a mortal, my wife!" Kyle growled.

"Bond or no she is a lower life-form, a mortal. Starting a war with the Valle over an attack on her would be premature."

"Mortal or not, she is in my coven, and that makes her an Equites, which also makes her your responsibility." Chevalier was glaring at the Elders.

"We take no serious stand on protecting the mortals that our covens decide to harbor."

"A Winchester," Kyle hissed.

"Yes, a Winchester, but one with no significant powers. If it were up to us, we would send her to the Valle to live with her family. As it were, the affairs of this coven we leave up to the Chief Enforcer."

Chevalier growled.

"She has shown potential for powers, though. Given more time they may surface," Kyle said, just as they had planned.

"What kind of potential?" one of the Elders asked.

"There are times when her scent is strong enough to bring down the most controlled of us. We suspect this is the start of her coming to her own, so to say. It's long rumored that the Winchesters had blood strong enough to drive any heku insane." Kyle's lines were well rehearsed, but sounded natural.

"At what times does this scent happen?"

"We haven't narrowed it down yet, but we will. If we can find out the cause, we may be able to see if we can provoke powers from her during that time," Chevalier said confidently.

"The scent is simply stronger?"

"Yes it is stronger, but it is also different," Kyle added.

"If it is in any way tied to the destruction of the immortal, we will need to know immediately," Selest said, watching them intently.

"Of course," Chevalier told her strongly.

The Elders turned and talked among themselves while Kyle and Chevalier waited impatiently.

When they turned back around, Elder Leonid stood. "We deem this needs further attention and have agreed that we will inform the Valle that Emily Russo is now under the protection of the Council but will remain housed in your coven for now."

"For now?" Kyle asked, seething.

"For now, yes," the Elder confirmed.

"She is my wife!" Kyle shouted.

"That is all," Selest said, and the Council filed out of the room.

It wasn't until they were back on the ferry that they spoke again.

"A week of questions and all they can tell us is that 'for now' we keep her?" Chevalier grumbled.

"I'd like to see them try to take her." Kyle glared out the front window.

"I won't let them. That's true."

"It's been a long week, and I'll feel better when we get back."

Chevalier nodded. He was always nervous when he left Emily, but in this instance, he was afraid if they had taken her and the Elders had smelled her new enticing scent, that she wouldn't have been free to leave. He knew Kyle feared the same.

The Island came into view, and the moonlight glittered off of the white sand. Once at the pier, Chevalier sped his Bugatti toward the castle. The guard opened the door for him, and he stepped out.

"Any news?" Chevalier asked.

"Nothing from us, sir," he stated.

"What does that mean?" Kyle turned on the guard, irritated.

"There was one... incident, but it didn't involve us."

"What incident?" Chevalier asked, taking a step toward the guard.

"Lady Emily, she... we... she disappeared for two days." The guard winced as Chevalier hissed.

"What do you mean disappeared?" Kyle growled.

"We couldn't find her. She somehow slipped onto the ferry and visited the mainland for two days and then returned," the guard said, fearing for his life.

Chevalier disappeared angrily and blurred up the stairs, stopping in her antechamber. He spun to the corner and took a chilling step toward the young guard.

"You lost her for two days?" he growled.

"Y... Yes, sir." The guard recoiled.

"How can you lose a mortal for two days?" He closed the gap quickly and pinned the guard to the wall, his hand around the guard's neck.

The guard tried to speak, but no words came out.

"You had one task... one simple task, and you failed me," Chevalier hissed irately.

"Sh... she climbed out the balcony."

Chevalier threw the guard at the door and whispered, "Get out."

The guard disappeared quickly, rubbing his neck.

Chevalier turned angrily to the bedroom and stepped inside. Suddenly, his senses were assaulted and the predator surfaced quickly. He fell into a crouch, his mouth salivating at the incredible scent in the room. A hiss escaped his lips as he stepped toward the bed, the smell coming at him faster. The sight of her wrenched Chevalier to his senses and he cringed at how close he came to attacking her.

The desire for her blood was staggering. The strong smell in the room was more intoxicating than ever before, and he felt the burn in the back of his throat grow stronger, the longer he was in her presence. Fighting against his natural instincts, he backed out of the room and shut the door, blocking most of the painful scent. Chevalier fell to his knees and panted, fighting every intrinsic need he had to feed. After a few minutes, he was able to stand again.

"It gets worse when she sleeps," the soft voice said, and he spun around, crouched to attack. Anna held a hand up to him. "I'm not after her."

Chevalier winced and stood up. "What's happening?"

"I don't know, sir. The... shall we say... aroma, grows stronger when she sleeps. I had to ban anyone from entering her room at night, as soon as I noticed it was apparent to all of us."

He was slowly regaining his control. "I take it that's when she snuck out on the balcony?"

"That was my fault then, if a fault needs to be blamed. I couldn't risk harm to the child, but the pull of her blood is too strong..."

"It's okay, Anna. I don't blame you," he said, sitting down in a chair by the fire.

Anna sat down beside him. "It's not as bad during the day, but it is still strong, and I've had to let two house servants go."

"What happened?" He had a hard time getting angry. How could he when he had almost attacked her himself?

"Just a hiss, sir, but I couldn't have that. Most of us are able to turn away from her and are able to control ourselves. You have very loyal followers, sir," Anna tried to reassure him.

"Does she know?"

"No, sir, she spends enough time outdoors that we were able to handle things ourselves in here, and my orders to stay away from her room weren't hard for anyone to obey. They would rather avoid her, than hurt her."

"I need to find a way to be with her at night, or she'll know something is wrong," he spoke mostly to himself.

Anna watched him in the firelight.

"What did she do on the mainland? I'm surprised she wasn't attacked."

"No one dared to ask her. It's none of our business," Anna explained, and he knew she was right. Chevalier could understand why her absence was never questioned.

He shut his eyes and reached out to her. He could feel she was having a restless night. She felt uncomfortable and alone.

He sighed, "I need to be in there."

Anna nodded and stood up. "Follow me, sir."

Chevalier didn't hesitate. He followed Anna from the antechamber and down the hallway, never once questioning where he was going. She led him to the servant quarter's area and into a tiny room. The room was painted orange, and the small bed was pushed off to the side. There was still barely enough room for the little chairs that sat around a round table.

A mortal sat on the bed as they stepped inside. "Feed first, sir, which may help."

She motioned to the young man on the bed, and he held his wrist up to Chevalier.

In an instant, Chevalier had a vice grip on the donor's hand, and his teeth were sunk deeply into the flesh of his wrist. He hated the taste of mortal men's blood, but the strong desire to feed was left over from his brief period in her room. He pulled away when his instincts told him he'd had enough, and he gasped. His mind was honed in on the beast, and it was firmly locked away. Chevalier was ready to try again.

Anna waited in the antechamber. "I can't come in there if you fail, sir."

Chevalier nodded. He knew what she meant by fail, and his insides twisted at the thought. He also knew that no heku could help him if the predator won out over his control.

Bracing himself, he stepped into her bedroom and the door shut quickly behind him. The abrupt assault came again as soon as he was in the room, and he turned away from her, hoping to lessen the desires, but her scent was coming from all around him. He squeezed his eyes shut tightly as he fought to gain control of the natural predator that threatened to strike. Chevalier exhaled and opened his eyes, then turned to look at her.

She was lying half in and half out of the covers. Her thin nightgown wasn't enough to keep her warm in the chilly night air, yet she was covered in sweat. Her supple lips were moving slightly. She was whispering in her sleep, but her words made no sense to him. Chevalier took a chance and moved a step closer to her. The smell became stronger. He fought the need to inhale deeply and took short panting breaths through his mouth, but even the taste of the air was exquisite to him.

Chevalier forced himself to sit on the edge of her bed, keeping a close eye on the predator inside of him. He seemed to have regained control.

Emily stirred when he sat down, and her eyes slowly opened. She smiled and threw herself onto his lap with her arms around his neck. His teeth began to ache for blood as her exposed neck came dangerously close to his mouth. He pulled from millennia of experience to control himself, and when his mind overpowered his body, he held her tightly.

"I missed you," he whispered into her ear.

"I'm so glad you're back." He felt his shoulder become wet with her tears.

"Emily, what's wrong?" He pulled her face back with his hands and looked as her green eyes swam.

She shook her head and laid her forehead on his chest. "I'm afraid."

Chevalier wondered if Emily noticed more than Anna had been aware of, but he couldn't be sure. "Of what?"

She pulled closer to him and cried softly, suddenly falling still as she fell asleep against his chest.

He found it easier to be near her, now that he'd become accustomed to the strong scent, and he held her. As she slept, he watched her face and again marveled at her intense beauty. Emily wasn't restless in his arms.

She didn't start to wake up until almost noon. She gripped him tighter as she became aware of how he still held her. "I thought I'd dreamed you came home."

Chevalier smiled. "I'm here now."

"It's been a long week," she whispered.

"Are you going to tell me what you were afraid of last night?"

"No," she said, nestling her head in the crook of his neck.

He laughed, "Alright, then do you want to tell me what you were doing on the mainland for two days by yourself?"

"You know about that, huh?"

"Not a lot happens around here that I don't know, and I can't believe you climbed out of a second-story balcony." He kissed the top of her head.

"It wasn't that hard. I knotted sheets. Besides, I get the impression that I'm being avoided around here for some reason. Gordon's even started leaving my trays out in the antechamber," she sighed.

"Yes, well, I'll explain that once I know the reason. So what did you do on the mainland?" he asked again.

"I went to visit someone."

"Oh? I didn't know you knew anyone close enough to visit and get back in two days." He felt she was leaving something out.

"I do," she whispered.

Chevalier lifted her chin with his hand, so she was looking into his eyes. He hated how her eyes were fearful. "Tell me."

She swallowed hard.

"Did someone do something to you that you aren't telling me?"

Emily squeezed her eyes shut and whispered, "I'm pregnant."

Chevalier's mouth fell open, his eyes wide. "What?"

She didn't answer him, but turned her eyes down toward the floor.

"Are you sure?" He was stunned.

She nodded.

"But... but the doctors…" He didn't know what to say.

"Were wrong," she said softly, still looking at the wood-grain pattern in the floor.

Chevalier placed a hand on each side of her head and forced her to look at him. When their eyes met, he pressed his lips against hers and then hugged her tightly. She melted into his arms and kissed him deeply, tears still streaming down her face.

He pulled his face away from hers and looked into her eyes. "This is what you were afraid of telling me?"

She nodded.

He grinned. "I'm going to be a father."

Emily nodded again and gasped when he kissed her fiercely, and suddenly, she felt things were right.

Books in The Heku Series

Book 1 : Heku

Book 2 : Valle

Book 3 : Encala

Book 4 : Equites

Book 5 : Proditor

Book 6 : Ferus

Book 7 : Eternity of Vengeance

Book 8 : Ancients and Old Ones

Book 9 : Banishment

1501630R00180

Made in the USA
San Bernardino, CA
21 December 2012

1501630R00180

Made in the USA
San Bernardino, CA
21 December 2012